ALSO BY OLIVIA WILDENSTEIN

THE KINGDOM OF CROWS

House of Beating Wings
House of Pounding Hearts
House of Striking Oaths

HOUSE
OF
BEATING
WINGS

HOUSE
OF
BEATING
WINGS

OLIVIA WILDENSTEIN

sourcebooks
casablanca

Published by Sourcebooks Casablanca, an imprint of Sourcebooks
P.O. Box 4410, Naperville, Illinois 60567-4410
(630) 961-3900
sourcebooks.com

Originally self-published in 2022 by Olivia Wildenstein.

Cataloging-in-Publication Data is on file with the Library of Congress.

Printed and bound in the United States of America.
LSC 10 9 8 7 6 5 4 3 2 1

To all those who never quite fit in.

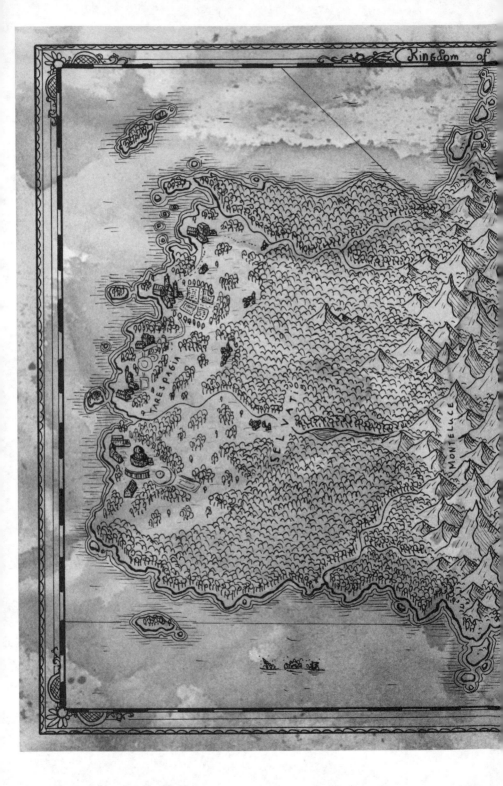

Lucin Glossary

Altezza—Your Highness
bibbina mia—my baby
buondia—good day/good morning
buonotte—good night
buonsera—good evening
Caldrone—Cauldron
castagnole—fried dough rolled in sugar
corvo—crow
cuggo—cousin
cuori—heart
dolcca—honey
dolto/a—fool
furia—fury
generali—general
Goccolina—Raindrop
grazi—thank you
-ina/o—affectionate ending to first names
Maezza—Your Majesty
mamma—mom

mare—sea
mareserpens—sea serpent
merda—shit
micaro/a—my dear
mi cuori—my heart
nonna—grandma
nonno—grandpa
pappa—dad
pefavare—please
piccolino/a—little one
piccolo/a—little
princci—prince
santo/a—holy
scazzo/a—street urchin
scusa—sorry
serpens—serpent
soldato—soldier
tare—land
tiuamo—I love you
tiudevo—I owe you
zia—aunt

CROW GLOSSARY

adh (aw)—sky
ah'khar (uh-kawr)—beloved
álo—hello
behach (bey-ock)—little
beinnfrhal (ben-frol)—
    mountain berry
bilbh (beehlb)—dumb
chréach (kre-hawk)—crow
cúoco (coo-wock-o)—coconut
éan (een)—bird
focá—fuck
ha—I
Ionnh (yon)—Miss
khrá (kraw)—love
mo—my
Mórrgaht (morr-got)—Your
    Majesty

o ach thati—Oh but you do
rahnach (raw-nock)—kingdom
rí—king
rih bi'adh (ree-byaw)—king of
    the sky
siorkahd (shuhr-kaw)—circle
tà (taw)—yes
tach (tock)—the
Tach ahd a'feithahm thu, mo
    Chréach (tok add a fay-
    tham thoo, mo kre-hawk)—
    The sky awaits you, my
    Crows
thu (too)—you
thu leámsa (too leh-awm-sa)—
    you are mine

HISTORICAL TIMELINE

MAGNABELLUM
Great War waged 522 years ago between the Kingdom of Luce and the Queendom of Shabbe. Costa Regio won the war and became the first Fae king of Luce.

BATTLE OF PRIMANIVI
Battle waged 22 years ago between a Lucin mountain tribe and the Fae. Costa's son, Andrea, who had ruled over Luce for the last century, was killed. His son Marco Regio took over, won the battle, and was crowned king of Luce.

PROLOGUE

T he canals are narrow, yet sometimes, they feel like glass walls, unbreakable and insurmountable, dividing two worlds: the land of the pure-blooded Fae and the land of the half-blooded ones. Even the water that flows around our twenty-five islands marks our differences—a warm, jeweled turquoise in Tarecuori and a chilly, muddy sapphire in Tarelexo.

I was born on the wrong side of the canal—the dark side, the home of the half-bloods, or halflings as we are sometimes called. Cauldron forbid, not to our faces. The high-society Fae pride themselves on being too genteel for such vilifications, but I hear them talk, because although the canals are a rift, they aren't walls.

The voices of merchants carry over the liquid arteries of Luce, skating across the glass bridges garlanded in flowers before swirling through the teeming Harbor Market.

"We will take one kilo of your golden plums." Nonna nods to a wooden crate filled with yellow fruit no larger than marbles. "The smallest ones." Her basket overflows with imported produce that she plans on pickling to last us a fortnight. Unlike purebloods, we don't have enough coin to shop in the Tarecuorin market twice a week.

"Mamma prefers the green ones, Nonna." Although I want

to set down my heavy basket, sprites are renowned thieves, small and quick as they are. I've chased my fair share of them across the islands and bridges, but they have an unfair advantage—wings. Although they cannot fly high, they can fly, and I cannot.

"But you prefer the small ones, Goccolina, and this way, we have no need for sugar."

I tilt my gaze toward my grandmother, whose face is as unlined as my mother's. "No need or no coin?"

Nonna's moss-colored eyes close for a heartbeat, then open and lower to my violet ones. "No need, Goccolina."

Although I've no salt to slip on her tongue to compel her to speak the truth, I know she's lying. Nonna may be a full-blooded Fae, but her magic cannot cloak the distinctive tells that pucker her face when she's trying to protect me from some harsh truth.

A lady swishes past us, her emerald skirt catching on the homespun cotton of my dress, pulling at a thread and snapping it. I balance my basket to thumb the snagged fabric until it lies flat against my bony thigh again. If only I could stretch the fabric, extend it down to my ankles, but cotton holds no elasticity.

I may be slight as a droplet, but the summer has lengthened my limbs and grown my fiery brown locks. The skirt now hits my knees, which is unbecoming of a twelve-year-old, something my peers never cease to remark on. Although Headmistress Alice punishes the girls who titter and the boys who ogle, she convened Nonna last week to discuss the dress code.

To think my attendance in the private Tarecuorin institution hinges on the length of my skirt.

I've begged Nonna to transfer me to the school on Tarelexo, but she says it's a great privilege to attend the same school as the royal family. I think she hopes proximity to purebloods will rub off on my family's ruined reputation, even though she insists my presence in Scola Cuori has nothing to do with reputation and everything to do with legacy; every Rossi before me has attended that school.

What she leaves out is that every Rossi before me was born with pointed ears and magic.

A blade skims my cheek, just over my rounded ears. Nonna gasps and sends her basket crashing to the cobbles to wind her arms around my shoulders and pull me into her tall, lithe form.

"Since when do guards raise their swords on children?" Her voice is full of venom.

The white-uniformed male sheaths his sword in his leather baldric, his amber eyes skimming over the sharp points of Nonna's ears. "Ceres Rossi, your granddaughter needs a haircut."

"Were you planning on giving her one with your sword, Commander?"

The guard lifts his chin to make himself look more frightening. "I'm sure you'd prefer I didn't. I'm not known for my hairdressing skills."

"Are you known for any skill?" Her stern whisper flutters the hair that frames my face. The hair that is apparently too long.

"What was that, Ceres?" His eyes narrow because he has, in fact, heard her.

Nonna doesn't tremble, so I don't either, but I do swallow repeatedly. Especially when two more patrolling Fae sidle up to Commander Dargento's sides. "Her hair will be cut tonight."

Silvius Dargento's triangular jaw ticks, clicks. "I should measure it."

Nonna's callused hand sails through my thick tresses. "But you won't."

Their eyes lock, joust.

Although saddled with a witless daughter and a half-human granddaughter, my grandmother's scrutiny is as sharp as the jewels that adorn the lengthy shells of Tarecuorin ears.

Flickering wings catch my attention. Two sprites have

descended on our spilled loot. I break away from Nonna and fall to my knees, hurrying to salvage the food she cannot grow on Tarelexo. The sprites hook a bushel of rowan branches, and together they heft it away.

"Oh no, you don't!" I scramble to my feet. Rowan infusions are the only thing that calm Mamma when she becomes restless.

"Fallon, no!" Nonna yells my name instead of the nickname she baptized me with when I was born and Mamma, in a rare moment of lucidity, touched my forehead and whispered, "Raindrop."

I zigzag through the throngs of Fae, tossing apologies as I jostle arms laden with exotic wares. The thieves book a right, and I zip after them, across a glass bridge. They pivot, and so do I.

One of them bangs his head on the awning of a floral candy shop. Muttering, the winged pest dips, dragging his companion along.

I lunge toward them, and my fingers close around the fragrant sprigs that cost us a full copper. "Gotcha!" My victorious grin flashes off my face as my slippered feet catch on a mooring post and I list sideways into the canal, thumping my shoulder against a passing gondola.

The Fae inside shriek as I jostle their boat.

"Merda." My curse word gets lost in the grand splash my body makes in the blue, blue water.

Fear hits me at the same time as my feet hit the sandy bottom of the shallow canal. For a moment, I'm paralyzed, hair fanned out around my face like the spokes of a wheel. My lips part, and water sneaks in. I slam my mouth shut, lungs hugging the air inside.

Although I've never swum—no one in their right mind does, not with carnivorous creatures slithering around the kingdom—my water-Fae heritage kicks in, and I flutter my legs. I hook the side of the gondola and heave myself up. I'm about to kick my leg over the side when an oar whacks my hands.

"Scazza, let go before you upturn our boat!"

4

I blink at the Fae who just called me a street urchin and hit me. Blood beads from my knuckles, dribbling around my fingers.

When he raises his oar, I spring my fingers open and sink back into the water. I reel my hands into my pumping chest, shocked by the man's cruelty, shocked that he made me bleed.

The current shifts, stealing my attention off the blurred shape of the gondolier overhead. My eyes burn from the heavy glint of sunshine and copious amount of salt, but I keep them open and set on the pink scales glimmering on one of the malevolent beasts that inhabit our canals.

I kick my feet and glide my arms up and out, pulling myself through the water toward the embankment. My fingertips meet the wall just as the serpent strikes, snagging my ankle and towing me under.

All the faces of the people I love, which aren't all that numerous, flash behind my prickling lids—Nonna, Mamma, Sybille, Phoebus, and Dante.

I fling my arms out and pump them through the water, kicking to dislodge the shackle of pink scales. The creature's grip turns viselike, and I think it might just snap my foot clean off my leg.

Heart in my throat, I twist, hinge at the waist, and punch the head slithering up my body. With a whimper that sounds all too human, the beast releases my ankle.

Although the serpent is twice my size, the width of its body is no larger than my thigh, and the ivory horn atop its head is a mere nub. A juvenile, like me.

Please be kind. Please spare me.

I tip my head toward the faces dappling the clear surface, finding the green gleam of Nonna's eyes and the black curtain of hair she keeps trimmed as short as mine, even though she's allowed to grow it however long she wants.

Her mouth opens around shouts muffled by the water pressing in around my body. The serpent darts its equine muzzle in front of my face, obsidian eyes leveled on my violet ones. Like Dante taught me, I hover my fists around my jaw to protect the tenderest parts of my body.

The creature swipes its forked black tongue through the crimson ribbon pluming off my knuckles, slitted nostrils flaring, head tilting.

Mareserpens have little love for our kind who hunt them relentlessly, snaring them with metal nets, burning them with Faefire, and skewering them with spears. Although no part of them is wasted—their meat roasted, their skins sewed into accessories for the wealthy, and their horns ground into elixirs or displayed as art—their barbaric killings have always enraged me. All animals' deaths, be they big or small, dangerous or tame, incense me.

If only the young serpent could sense that I mean it no harm. Perhaps I could show him. Or her. I relax my fists, spreading my palms wide to show the creature I'm unarmed. Mareserpens may not have empathy, but they're unarguably smart.

The water vibrates with noise, shrill yells and raised voices. Although purebloods bleed, they can't die, yet none have jumped in to succor me. Why would they? Bastard children are the lowest of all the lows, one notch over humans. I bet some of the onlookers are hoping the serpent will lasso me down to Filiaserpens, its lair thousands of meters beneath sea level.

When its tongue darts past its lipless mouth, a full body shiver rakes through me, doing away with my residual oxygen. I propel myself upward, and my head breaks the surface.

"Fallon! Fallon!" my grandmother cries.

Although two guards are restraining her, she shrugs them off and falls to her knees, her arms shooting out and down, palms extending toward mine. "Goccolina, my hand. Take my hand!"

But the pink serpent loiters between us, preventing me from getting close.

The white-haired guard who was holding Nonna stares with

wide eyes between me and the pink-scaled body. He's probably wondering how I'm still alive.

I wonder the same.

"Cato, do something!" Nonna screams at him.

He unsheathes his sword and lifts it. The serpent latches on to my middle and drags me backward, to the heart of the canal, then lifts its head and hisses at Cato.

"Fallon," Nonna weeps.

The serpent laces its body around mine, and although my heart palpitates, I don't dare move. Barely dare breathe.

"What the Cauldron is it doing?" a male Fae on the glass bridge above me exclaims.

A Tarecuorin lady ensconced in red and gold brocade shades her eyes to better watch the spectacle. "Playing with its food."

Tentatively, I try to squirm away, but the creature's head swivels. I freeze. Although it doesn't hiss at me, its tongue darts out and swipes the underside of my jaw.

Did it just—did it just...*lick me?*

I frown, raising a hand to snare its neck and wrangle it back, but it does it again, its velvet tongue lashing up my throat to the underside of my jaw. When my palm connects with its scales, the creature stills, stares at me, then laps the broken flesh of my knuckles. My skin prickles and, before my very stunned eyes, begins to knit.

The creature pushes its stubby horn against my palm as it continues to lavish my skin.

"Tasting its supper," the lady garbed in a curtain answers.

But I don't think that's what it's doing.

I think the serpent is healing me.

Instead of pinching its neck, I let my fingers drift down its retracted dorsal fins. The animal's eyes drift closed, and its long body rattles, the vibrations breaching my skin and rattling me in turn.

"You healed me," I murmur in awe.

Its black eyes open.

"Why would you do that? I'm the enemy."

"Is she talking to the beast?" Curtain woman asks.

"In what tongue?" her neighbor remarks.

As they gossip, I caress the serpent's scales, and the creature vibrates.

Mareserpens don't have hearts, Fallon. They're animals. Dangerous and insensitive. Our flora and fauna professor, Signora Decima, has boxed my ears with these decrees.

But this one must feel.

Flames spark in my peripheral vision. "Move your face to the right," the commander shouts, "or I will burn you *and* it."

"No!" My voice is hoarse yet carries to the fire-Fae on the bridge with the extended palms.

The serpent's body hardens.

I stroke my hand down its neck and whisper, "Go."

It doesn't.

I push it away and repeat the word. Still, it doesn't move, but then suddenly its coiled body falls away from my legs, and it whimpers.

"What have you…" My words turn to breath as I spot Nonna wriggling her fingers as though wielding puppet strings.

She's growing the floral vines wrapped around the bridge, transforming them into ropes. They scurry around the harmless dragon and snare it. The serpent whines as my grandmother hauls its body out of the water.

"Nonna, no!"

My grandmother's complexion is pale as frost. "Get out of the water now, Fallon!"

"It wasn't—"

"Out!" Her voice bursts with nerves that strum my already frantic pulse.

I swim to the embankment. The onlookers are still, as though someone has cast a spell over the kingdom and turned everyone to stone.

I grab the slick cobbles and heave my wet body out, flopping onto my back to catch my breath. "I'm safe. Now let it go, Nonna. Please."

Blood has begun to dribble from where the vines dig into its scales.

I roll up to sitting. "Nonna, please!"

She snaps out of her daze, and the vines release the serpent, who plummets with a soft whine.

Veins of fire coat the commander's palm. "What magic does your granddaughter wield, Ceres?"

"Kindness. That is Fallon's only magic." Nonna kneels beside me and cups my cheeks, and although no tears glisten on her long lashes, her eyes shine with fear. "You almost stopped my immortal heart, Goccolina. And over what? Rowan branches?"

Branches I failed to retrieve.

I look toward the canal for my bushel and then keep looking because the serpent rests listlessly on the sandy bottom, inky blood blooming from its body like dye.

Nonna grips my chin and redirects my eyes onto hers. "Never again."

Does she mean chase after sprites, dive into a canal, or pet a serpent? Probably all three.

The commander snaps his fingers closed. "You will be fined for the use of magic, Ceres."

Nonna doesn't respond. Doesn't even look his way. "Home. Now." There is no pliancy to her tone, her fingers, or the arm she winds around my waist after I've regained my footing.

In silence, she tugs me back across the market, toward our baskets that are near empty, plundered by hungry half-bloods or more sprites. After stacking them, she hooks them onto her forearm. Even though I try to help, a pointed glare stops me from insisting.

When we reach our two-storied house on one of the farthest islands, Nonna slams the piled baskets down onto the kitchen table and braces her palms on the thick slab of wood. Her spine is hunched, her torso rising and falling.

I step toward her and press my hand against her curved spine. A sob splinters the air, lodges itself inside my small, beating heart.

"I'm safe, Nonna. Please don't cry. I'm safe."

"You're anything but safe," she snaps, glaring up at the ceiling toward the room Mamma never leaves.

"It didn't harm me. It healed me. Look." I wiggle my fingers in front of her eyes.

She presses them away. "I'm not talking about the serpent. I'm talking about the commander." Her rushed words float like specks of dust. "He will come and take you away."

"For having survived a swim in the canal?"

"No, Goccolina. For having charmed a beast."

"Charmed? I merely petted it, Nonna."

"Have you ever heard of Fae petting serpents?"

No. I haven't. "I'm a water-Fae. Maybe my magic is finally manifesting."

"Water-Fae can control water, but they cannot charm beasts." She heaves in a deep breath. "When the royal guards knock, you will insist on being given salt—"

"I could just lick my lips." I start to smile. "I'm covered—"

"You will *insist* on being given a crystal, and once it dissolves, you will tell them you were terrified." She grips my face, her long thumbs digging into my cheekbones. "Understood?"

I bite my lip, tasting the brine of the canal and the fear of my grandmother on the pillowy flesh, and then I give the woman who raised me what she wants.

I promise that I will lie, because unlike the Fae, I can.

1

Ten years later

Mamma's hair is a thing of beauty, red as the setting sun that burnishes Monteluce, the mountains she spends her days gazing at from the armchair she only leaves for her bed.

No Fae inhabit the rocky peaks forever swathed in clouds, but the purebloods thrive on the other side of the treacherous range, in the lush wilds that sprawl toward the ocean, renowned for idyllic coves, lush jungle, and pearlescent sand.

I've never traveled to Tarespagia, but my aunt Domitina lives there with my great-grandmother Xema. Together, they run a luxurious seaside ranch that attracts wealthy Fae from all over the three kingdoms.

Although the distance between us is a half-day sea voyage, Domitina and Xema have never stopped by Tarelexo. Not even during their trips to Isolacuori to visit my grandfather, Justus Rossi, the leader of the king's guard.

Domitina, like Xema, like Justus, is ashamed of me.

I run the brush once more through Mamma's shoulder-length tresses, careful not to graze the tops of her ears. Although my grandfather rounded them with a steel blade the day her pregnancy was discovered, twenty-two years later she still winces whenever they're touched. From pain or shame, I'm not quite certain. Since she's hardly ever lucid, I fear I'll never get an answer.

Briny gusts lift off the brackish canal and brush over the crowns of the tall conifers abutting the mountain range. Unlike the rest of the kingdom, that wooded area has no official name. It's only known for what it holds: swamps, or racocci in the Lucin tongue. Colloquially, it's come to be known as Rax. It's a place we Fae are warned against visiting, filled with humans, poverty, and corruption.

"Have you ever set foot in Racocci, Mamma?"

My mother, as always, doesn't reply, simply stares at the thin island with its army barracks and checkpoints and the mainland beyond. Lights flicker amongst the gray-green foliage and reverberate against the brown water. From a distance, the torches and candles give the forest an enchanted quality, but I've heard from the guards patrolling the swamps that there's nothing enchanting about the mortal lands.

I set the hairbrush down on the small vanity table beside a teapot of freshly brewed rowan tea. "Do you think it's truly as awful as everyone claims?"

A gondola of soldiers passes under her window, pointed ears gleaming with gold darts. Where Tarecuorin citizens favor cut stones, soldiers prefer to match their jewelry to the pommels of their swords.

I smile down at the males; they don't smile back. High-ranking military Fae are forever grim-faced, as though about to charge into battle. As far as I know, and I do know quite a lot from working with Sybille at Bottom of the Jug, our people haven't been at war for over two decades, so their ominousness is unwarranted.

Mamma murmurs something I don't catch, because another gondola has slipped behind the military one, and it's filled with Fae who, from the pitch of their voices and rowdy laughter, have been indulging in faerie wine. One of them, a male with black waist-length hair, gives me a saucy wink.

I shake my head before turning back to my mother. "What is it you said, Mamma?"

"It's time."

I frown. "For what?"

Mamma's lashes reel up so high they skim her auburn eyebrows. "Bronwen watches."

Goose bumps scamper over my skin. "Bronwen?"

My mother's blue irises, four shades lighter than my violet, bob in a sea of white. "Bronwen watches." She starts rocking back and forth, those two words unceasingly dropping from her shivering lips.

I clasp her shoulders and crouch before her. "Mamma, who is this Bronwen?"

Her reply is those same two words.

I release her and pour her a cup of tea, then bring it to her lips, hoping it'll calm her sudden agitation. Perhaps Nonna will know whom Mamma speaks of.

As though she sensed me thinking about her, my grandmother trundles into Mamma's bedroom with a stack of sheets. "Everything all right?"

I force more tea down my mother's throat, and as always, the infusion works its magic on her, and she calms. Once she's stopped rocking in her chair, I set the cup down and sidestep the armchair to help Nonna stretch the cotton that smells like wisteria and sunshine.

"Mamma was saying that a woman named Bronwen was watching. Do you know her, Nonna?"

The sheet slips out of my grandmother's grasp and rolls across the mattress toward my side.

"I've not the faintest idea." Her stiff fingers and throbbing pupils tell another story. Without looking up at me, she retrieves the fitted sheet and stretches it, this time hooking it beneath the mattress with a snap.

I glance toward the window, at the curls of lavender smoke rising over the swamplands as humans light bonfires to heat the night. "You think it's an inhabitant of Rax?"

"For all we know, it's someone who lives in Agrippina's head."

My heart smarts for the seated woman whose excised ears made her lose her grip on reality.

I hate King Marco for having forced my grandfather to punish his daughter, but I hate my grandfather more for not resisting and protecting his flesh and blood.

"True, but for once, the words made sense." I wonder if Bronwen is from Luce or from a neighboring kingdom. "She also mentioned something about it being time."

Nonna feeds the feathery duvet, which has yellowed and thinned with age, into a cream cover, mended in so many places it resembles a topographical map.

"Fallon Rossi!" My name thunders through the gaping window of Mamma's room, shaking the wisteria vine that's taken over three of our walls.

I sprint to the window, a smile already blooming over my lips, because I know that voice, even though I haven't heard it speak my name in over four years.

I lay my forearms on the sill and grin at the upturned face of my visitor, at the blue eyes that glitter like morning dew. "You've returned!"

I sound breathless and giddy, which makes smirks rise across the faces of the prince's entourage, but I don't much care what his friends think of me. All I care about is what Dante thinks of me.

Growing up, I kept expecting him to cast me aside, but he never did.

"You're even more beautiful than I remember."

I laugh as the air-Fae gondolier struggles to keep the boat from rocking, what with two grown men shifting around in their velvet

14

seats and one standing. "Are you home for good or for your broth-er's betrothal?"

"For good."

Four years look delicious on him. His shoulders have filled out, his face has been whittled into a sharper landscape, and his mass of brown braids has grown longer. It now skims the jeweled handle of the sword strapped into his ornate leather baldric. Only his blue eyes and brown skin have remained the same.

He hooks his thumb over his shoulder. "My barrack is right across from your house, Signorina Rossi."

"How convenient."

I feel a presence at my back. Since Mamma cannot stand, I know it's my grandmother.

Dante bows. "Signora Rossi, looking otherworldly as always."

I snort at his endearment.

"Welcome home, Altezza. I hope your trip up north has been most auspicious."

"It has, thank you. If war ever comes, we have great allies to count on."

"War will come." Mamma's voice is low, yet it must reach the prince's ears, because a dent mars the smooth span of his forehead.

Purebloods have unparalleled hearing.

My cheeks flame from the shame of my mother's proclama-tion. I hope Dante missed the ominous whisper, but in case he didn't, I change the subject. "I'd love to hear of your adventures, Dante."

Nonna tsks.

"Princci Dante." I roll the r and my eyes, because before being the prince of Luce, Dante is my friend.

The boy who convinced his brother not to have me carted off to the castle for further assessment the day I bonded with a serpent.

The man who gave me my first kiss in a thin alleyway the evening before he set sail toward the Kingdom of Glace.

A swath of white illuminates Dante's face. "I'd love to regale you, dearest Fallon."

"Come find me when you have time then."

"Where?" He grips the varnished wooden bulwark, the boat rocking from how treacherously far he leans out.

"Ask around. All of Luce knows where the notorious beast charmer toils." I close Mamma's window as the air-Fae steers the boat away from the embankment.

One of Dante's friends must inform him where I work, because the prince's smile vanishes. They probably forgot to clarify that I cater to the patrons' stomachs and livers and not to their nether regions.

"He will never marry you, Fallon." Nonna's voice snips my smile.

"I'm not looking to marry."

"Are you looking to be his harlot?"

My head rears back, and my mouth twists in disgust. I've got nothing against women who sell their bodies—I consider many my friends—but I could never...*would* never do that. Purebloods deem the profession shameful, and I've brought enough shame to my family by simply being born.

"He isn't king." I fuss with the wool coverlet I've draped over Mamma's emaciated thighs.

"Perhaps, but a prince cannot marry a commoner. Not if he cares to preserve his title."

I feel Nonna looking at me but don't meet her stare. I'm too flustered and annoyed and—

"Fallon, set your heart on another man."

"My heart is set on no one, Nonna."

She expels a sigh laced with so many words. I'm certain most of them are wise, but I'm in no mood for wisdom.

"I'm going to be late for work." I kiss Mamma's cheek but not Nonna's, then slip past her, down the spiral staircase, and into the shadows of Tarelexo.

Nonna claims shadows will keep me safe, and perhaps she's right, but they also keep me invisible, and I want Dante to see me.

2

Being a water-Fae with not an ounce of magic is a depressing fate when living on islands pocked with puddles of filth. Especially on market days.

The western wharf is busy with sailors offloading the last of the produce that didn't sell in the royal harbor. The fruits are bruised, the vegetables speckled with rot, the milk sour, the fish cloudy-eyed, and the bags of grain infested with insects, yet half-bloods and humans will snatch up everything before twilight sets in. Growling stomachs aren't picky.

I sidestep a foul-smelling spill, tugging up my long skirt to avoid it dragging in anything that will oblige me to wash it. Since I have no magic and own only two other dresses, I avoid stains like humans avoid falling into Mareluce.

Laundry is on my list of loathed chores alongside changing sheets at Bottom of the Jug when the human maid, Flora, stays home to tend to one of her twelve children.

Sybille's parents, who own the popular tavern frequented by the entire Lucin military and many a genteel Tarecuorin, have considered hiring a second maid, but humans are prone to lying and stealing, and Fae, even halflings, have trust issues.

I pass by three sailors stacking empty crates in a vessel that has none of the grace of the gondolas and all the sturdiness of a fishing boat.

One of them whistles, which makes the other two turn. "How much longer will you keep my poor heart waiting, Fallon Rossi?"

I shake my head at Antoni's antics but smile because the male is relentless. "Have Beryl and Sybille turned you down again?"

Antoni chases anything with a skirt. I've heard the male has slept with half of Luce, be they human or Fae, and is a very attentive lover, but the romantic I am would prefer that my first lover be my last, and I doubt I'd be Antoni's last.

"I haven't asked either of them to marry."

Right. Because they didn't object to sleeping with him.

He trots up to me, then turns and walks backward as I make my way down the busy wharf toward the brightly lit tavern. "I've almost enough coin to buy an apartment."

"Congratulations."

He stops walking, forcing me to stop in turn, and cants his head toward me, eyes shimmering like the stars above. "I'm not jesting, Fallon."

"And I wasn't either. I'm genuinely thrilled for you."

"I meant about my marriage proposal." The scent of brine and fish scales lifts from the triangle of bronzed skin peeking out from his shirt's open collar.

"You only want to marry me because I refuse your advances."

He spears one hand through the thick honeyed locks dusted in sea salt that curl around his rounded ears. "I want to marry you because you're by far the prettiest and kindest girl in all of Luce."

My fingers tighten in the heavy folds of my maroon dress. "Flattery won't get me to say yes, Antoni."

"What will then? Pearls? I'll brave the serpents in Mareluce to bring you jewels if that's what it takes."

The corners of my mouth dip because he sounds serious. "I'd prefer you don't end up trapped in their lair."

Although I haven't swum since the fateful day in the Harbor Market, when no one watches, I comb my fingers through the canal's brisk waters and murmur the name I gave the pink serpent Nonna scarred.

Unfailingly, he comes.

Yes. *He.* Males are larger than females, and Minimus is huge, which is unfortunate considering the moniker I chose for him.

"A new dress then? I'll commission the merchant who sells the finest silks in Tarecuori."

"My love cannot be bought, Antoni. It must be won."

"And how does one go about winning your love, Fallon?"

A military gondola accosts the wharf. I cannot help myself from checking for Dante, but he isn't amongst the six men who disembark. The strings of faerie lights illuminating the docks reflect on the gold buttons of their uniforms and the earrings lining their peaked ears. My gaze locks on one familiar face—Cato.

The white-haired Fae often comes by our house. I think he comes for Nonna, whom he trails with his eyes every chance he gets, but she insists he only drops by to spy for my grandfather. Justus Rossi may not want anything to do with us, but he keeps tabs nonetheless.

Antoni makes a sound low in his throat. "A uniform? Should've guessed."

I return my attention to the fisherman. "What about uniforms?"

"Nothing." He backs up, lips tight on his handsome, sun-bronzed face. "Have a pleasant evening, Fallon." And then he's jogging back toward his friends.

I frown at his retreating figure. What did he mean about uniforms? Does he think I long to marry a soldier? Because I don't. I don't yearn to marry anyone.

Even as I think it, I taste the lie, because there is one man I'd say yes to in a heartbeat: Dante.

I gaze out at the pitched tents that I hear are sturdier and more luxurious than the rainbow-hued houses on Tarelexo. Although I've received my fair share of advances since starting at Bottom of the Jug, soldiers aren't allowed to bring civilians to their barracks. Sybille's convinced it's because there are military secrets they want to hide from us, but Sybille loves conspiracy theories almost as much as she loves teasing Phoebus about his squishy heart.

As I start back toward the tavern, shouts and hollers pin my slippered feet to the salt-crusted cobbles. A turquoise serpent jumps out of the canal and upturns a bucket of fish. My heart holds still as tendrils of magic appear in men's palms, as well as swords. The boisterous crowd stands ready to slice and burn the scaled raider.

I gasp a raucous *no* that gets lost in the evening din and lunge toward the edge of the pier but stop after two hurried steps. Nonna's warning about keeping my affection for animals a secret presses against my lungs as tightly as the boning in my corset.

I set my palm on my collarbone, attempting to confine my scattering heartbeats before they draw anyone's attention. The back of my neck prickles, signaling I've garnered a small audience. Hopefully, it's very small.

I swivel around to find Antoni staring as well as two women stuffing vegetables into burlap satchels. Their lips shape my nickname—Beast Charmer. If I weren't so worried it would earn me a visit to their den, I'd emblazon it on my skin.

I wonder what people would think if they found out serpents weren't the only animals that liked me. Every feline and lizard in Luce knows my address. Even the mice, which most Fae and humans sweep out of their houses with brooms or a blast of air magic, find their way to me. Although I don't toss them out, I do carry them away before Nonna catches me feeding them crumbs or petting them.

Humans have pets, but rare are the Fae who keep domesti- cated animals. This is why I sometimes believe Rax mustn't be so terrible.

A splash makes me whirl back toward the canal. Just a man emptying a bucket.

As I lift my gaze, I catch movement on the Racoccin shore beyond the military barracks. A lone figure stands on the black sand, a skirt snapping around her legs. She lifts a hand to her turban as though to keep the wind from unraveling it.

Even though the distance is great, I don't miss the odd sheen of her skin and eyes. For a full minute, I scrutinize her, and not once does she blink. Is she blind? I hear humans often suffer from such afflictions, since their bodies are frailer than ours, but it's unsettling nonetheless.

Bronwen watches.

Mamma's whisper brushes the rounded shells of my ears as though she stands right beside me. I jump and glance over my shoulder to make sure she doesn't.

I find only darkened air.

When I look back toward the shore, the woman is gone.

3

I fill a jug of sparkling faerie wine to the brim for Commander Dargento, the male I hate as much as doing laundry.

No. That's untrue. I loathe him far more.

Giana, Sybille's older sister, slides her platter onto the wooden bar. "I can take it to him after I check on room vacancy."

Like Sybille, Giana has the palest silver eyes, made even paler set against her deep-brown skin. Although six decades apart, the sisters have the same parents, a rare occurrence in Luce where fidelity isn't required. Especially considering purebloods live six to seven centuries and half-bloods half as long. If I were alive that long, I'd probably tire of my partner.

I stare across the tavern at the seated commander. "I can contain my repugnance long enough to drop the jug on his table instead of on his lap."

Sybille trundles out of the kitchen carrying a big pot that spits out thyme-scented steam. "Whose lap do you want to soak with wine?"

"Silvius's," I murmur without moving my lips.

Sybille snorts. "Imagine how rich you'd be if you charged him a copper for every time he touched you."

Giana glares at the round table where the commander,

Cato, and three other high-ranking officials are destroying the slabs of boar meat she just placed between them. "Does he still do that?"

I seize the jug by its handle. "If I started charging your patrons for touching me, I'd be off buying a manor in Tarecuori."

Sybille snickers but Giana doesn't. She's still glowering at the commander, who's wiping grease off his pointed chin.

"It's fine, Gia."

"It's absolutely *not* fine." Her gaze snaps to mine. "Caldrone, how I hate this place."

"No, you just hate its patrons," Sybille says before zigzagging around the rowdy diners.

Giana scrubs down her platter. "Our patrons are animals."

"Animals are kind."

She peers up at me, and I want to pinch myself. Although Giana has never judged me, the only way halflings like their animals is roasted and slathered in sauce.

"You're right," she says. "Our patrons are worse."

"Don't lob us all in, Gia. Some of us are remarkable specimens." Phoebus props his forearms on the bar.

I smile at my favorite blond Fae. "Haven't seen you all week, Pheebs."

He links his fingers together and places them on the back of his head to stretch. He's probably just rolled out of bed. My friend lives for the night. "Been busy with my family."

I frown because Phoebus detests his family. He moved out of Tarecuori into Tarelexo the minute we graduated school. "Why?" I wrap my fingers around the jug and heft it.

"Flavia just got betrothed."

"Your sister got betrothed? To whom?"

"To another pureling."

"Which one?" Not that I know *everyone* in Luce, but the pointy-eared people represent twenty percent of our population, and having attended the one and only school in Tarecuori, I'm familiar with most family names.

"Victorius Surro."

Phoebus pronounces the name with such disgust, I cannot help but smile. Although pointy-eared himself, Phoebus acts as though the appendages framing his face are round. Sometimes, I fear his act will earn him the iron culling my mother underwent, but he'd have to commit a grave sin, and for all his brazenness, Phoebus is pure of heart and spirit.

I nod to the ceiling. "Your future brother-in-law's currently occupying the room right above us."

Phoebus tracks my gaze, his green eyes dimming. "Cauldron rust."

I grin at the tame insult before skirting the bar to carry the wine to the commander's table. I make sure to stay beside Cato, whom I trust with my body if not with my secrets. "Will you men be needing anything else?"

The commander slides his amber eyes over me. I itch to jump into the canal to wash his leering gaze away but square my shoulders and plant a smile on my face.

He leans back in his chair, making the wooden rungs creak under his broad, muscled frame. If he weren't a currish ear licker, I may admire the lines of his body, but character matters more to me than physique, and the commander's character is as rotten as the fruit peddled on the wharf.

"Are you aware that Justus believes you do more than serve wine around here, Signorina Rossi?"

Cato flinches.

I don't.

"My grandfather believes many terrible things about me. I think it's my ears." I fling a smile Silvius's way because there's nothing more disarming than a smile. Males aren't sure what to do with a smile but have plenty of ideas what to do with a blush.

25

"I hope you've set him straight that the only thighs I rub are the boars you so savor, Commander."

Even though I'm not trying to be funny, amusement touches the corners of Silvius's mouth. "You must rub them well because they're incredibly tender."

I walked right into that one. "If that'll be all—"

"Does Ceres approve of you working in this establishment?" He cants his head to the side as though trying to see past me, except his eyes are locked on mine, so perhaps what he's trying to do is see into me.

"Why wouldn't she? Marcello and Defne treat me like their own daughter. Besides, my grandmother encourages financial independence."

One of his tablemates snorts. For all our forward thinkers, females are second-class citizens in Luce.

"And have you achieved it?" Silvius's lips glisten with swine fat.

I've yet to bond with a boar, since they only thrive in the wilds of Tarespagia and the only ones I've met were quartered and preserved in salt, but I'm certain I'd enjoy their company more than this male's.

"So, Signorina Rossi?" Silvius gives his mouth a slow lick. "Are you financially independent?"

Since he knows I'm not, I don't bother answering.

"Anything else?" My voice is no longer sweet as honey but tart as golden plums.

"No. Thank you, Fallon." Cato, ever polite, nods to me.

A gust of wind brushes my skin, announcing the arrival of a new customer. The first indication that it must be someone of great import hits me when the doxies, perched on the knees of potential customers, stop whispering sweet nothings into pointed ears.

"Luce's beloved prince has returned." Silvius is still leaning back, but his eyes are thankfully no longer on me.

I spin around to find Dante darkening the tavern entrance, the gold embellishments, hooked here and there in the thick mass of his braids, glimmering as brightly as the studs running up the sides of his long ears.

"Please." He sweeps a hand through the air. "Don't stop merrymaking on my account."

The noise level rises like my pulse when his eyes find mine, and he smiles. I make my way toward him, heart flapping as swiftly as sprite wings. I'm about to say, "You found me," but what if his tavern visit has nothing to do with me? The thought is sobering.

"Welcome to Bottom of the Jug, Altezza."

His friends—spiteful, redheaded Tavo and even-tempered, blond Gabriele—funnel in behind, gazes combing the crowd, the former on the lookout for fun, the latter for trouble.

Like every night, I've pinned up my hair to keep it out of my eyes and off my neck, but as I stand in front of Dante, as his gaze traces my features, I regret the hairstyle because it makes the shape of my ears all the more apparent.

I wrangle back my unease. Since when do I care? I don't. The same way Dante doesn't, or he wouldn't have paid me a visit earlier.

"Just the three of you?"

"Yes."

Tearing my eyes from the object of my obsession, I lead them to the table beside the commander's in the back of the tavern, the area reserved for the most esteemed guests, which can be shielded off with a heavy velvet curtain if the patrons so desire.

"When did you start working here, Fal?"

The heat of Dante's body sinks into my bare skin.

"After graduation." I keep my attention on the floor to avoid tripping over any outstretched legs or wandering harlots.

The men at the commander's table stand, even Silvius, and they all bow.

"At ease." Dante must be standing right behind me, because

27

his warm breath teases my neck as he murmurs, "I hope you will be the one tending to us tonight, Fallon."

I turn to face him. "Well, that is my job."

"Your only job?" His raised eyebrow conveys his meaning.

"Yes, Dante. My *only* job. I leave charming men to the professionals."

"Good." His answer is as soft as the smile that precedes it.

As we stand there together, as his eyes hold mine, the crowd blurs into a fragmented kaleidoscope. He dampens his full lower lip with his tongue, and it tosses me back to that dark alleyway where one of my childhood dreams was granted.

A thin arm hooks my waist. "Looking awfully glittery, Dante." Sybille's voice drags me brutally back into the balmy tavern. "I'm surprised your ears haven't begun drooping under the weight of so much gold."

Dante releases my eyes to ferry a smile over at Sybille. "And I'm surprised your tongue hasn't forked under the weight of so much jesting."

She tosses her head back and laughs, while I'm still too prince-struck to so much as chuckle.

"What's on the menu tonight, Syb?"

"For mains, roasted boar with quince, stewed turbot, or lin-guine in Mamma's kingdom-renowned eggplant cream sauce."

He looks back at his friends, who've both settled into their seats, thighs spread and backs reclined. "We'll take one of each. Make the servings plentiful. Our trip home was grueling."

Tavo lets out a wolf whistle as Beryl, one of the favorite half-ling doxies at Bottom of the Jug, passes by the table. He hooks her waist and drags her onto his lap, her ample breasts bouncing as she falls. Where I would've bitten him had he tried that move on me, sweet Beryl titters, and she keeps laughing as his hand vanishes beneath the skirt she keeps shirred in the front to reveal her shapely legs.

"We'll get that to you in a bit." Sybille physically tugs me back, but I plant my feet when the pungent aroma of roses drifts into my nostrils.

Like a serpent scenting blood, Catriona glides toward the prince. Unlike the other professionals, she's a courtesan. In other words, instead of coppers, she charges silvers, and instead of parading around half-naked, she doesn't exhibit her wares until paid.

Her bejeweled nails scrape over the white uniform that hugs Dante's muscled chest, over the gold trim of his standing collar. "Welcome home, Altezza."

Although I admire Catriona for having made her own way, at the present moment, I want to tighten the lace choker she's matched to her burgundy gown.

Sybille's fingers dig into my waist in warning. Good thing I have no magic, or my mind would've carried a pitcher of water and upturned it over the courtesan's glossy blond locks.

Dante plucks Catriona's roaming hand and tows it off. "Catriona."

My anger cools.

Although she's been with most of Luce, I know for a fact that she hasn't been with the prince because her mouth is as loose as an inebriated sprite's. Sometimes, I'm surprised men and women still want to bed her considering her propensity for gossip, but she's considered the very best in Luce, and purebloods deem they deserve only the best.

I slide my teeth together as she whispers something into Dante's ear that commandeers his full attention and carries his gaze to their clasped hands. He may not have wanted to be petted, but apparently, he doesn't mind touching her.

Jealousy throttles my chest anew.

"Fallon," Sybille snaps under her breath. "Kitchen. Now."

This time, when she yanks me back, there's no give to her arm.

4

F allon! He made it! He actually made it!" Phoebus stumbles into my house on the heels of his loud yells.

I look up from the turnip peels littering the kitchen table. "Who's made what?"

"Dante. He's crossed the channel!"

My heart journeys into my throat, because the channel between Isolacuori and Tarecuori rests over Filiaserpens, the underwater trench inside which dissenters are tossed. Without fault, the sea serpents snag the dissidents and drag them away.

Since Fae can only die from tremendously old age or by decapitation with a steel blade, I imagine many lie in the fault line, unconscious but alive, their flesh being picked off before regenerating to be eaten anew. It's a merciless form of torture, one the king threatened Nonna with when she chose my mother over my grandfather.

To this day, she hasn't told me how she escaped. Occasionally, I'll bring it up, but it darkens her mood, so I don't push.

"Dolto." Nonna's censure flutters her lips as she scrapes her knife more forcefully over the scrawny, wrinkled carrots.

I want to tell her that Dante isn't a fool, but isn't he? He risked his life for a throne his brother inherited after the Battle of

Primanivi two decades ago, a throne Marco waited a century to sit on. I don't see him conceding it during his lifetime.

"It's a rite of passage for kings, Ceres," Phoebus reminds my grandmother, although I doubt she's forgotten. "Now, Dante can lawfully sit on the throne." His green eyes whip toward the open doorway to check for eavesdroppers, since wishing misfortune on the king is treasonous and could land him in the channel.

Since our cerulean house abuts the southwestern end of Tarelexo, we only have two neighbors, and both are presently at work or in school.

"If anything ever happened to his brother, that is," Phoebus adds. "Cauldron forbid."

I've sworn a salt oath to Phoebus and Sybille that if either of them were ever tossed into Filiaserpens, I'd jump in with them, because that's what friends do, especially beast-charming ones.

Phoebus drums his fingers against our doorframe. "Well, are you coming or what?"

I stand up so suddenly my knees knock into the table. I take a step toward him but then glance at Nonna. "Are you coming, Nonna?"

"And witness a prideful boy become a hubristic man? I'll pass." My grandmother's eyes are locked on the rust-colored peels that curl as they fall onto our pockmarked table.

"Oh, Nonna. Dante's nothing like his brother. Marco doesn't befriend halflings. Dante—"

"Once upon a time, King Marco had many halfling acquaintances. Power changes people. Don't ever forget that, Fallon. You too, Phoebus."

"Yes, ma'am."

I can't imagine the severe and ruthless Fae king ever befriending curved ears, but Nonna has been around for three centuries and King Marco only one and a half. She knew him long before the crown of golden sunrays graced his head.

31

"Fal-lon." Phoebus decomposes my name and taps his brown boot. He has many virtues, but patience isn't one of them.

"Coming!" I slip my feet into my shoes, then race out after him.

We run down narrow cobbled streets and across the wooden bridges of Tarelexo toward the wider, sun-drenched roads and glass bridges of the Tarecuorin isles where the flowers are brighter and the air purer.

Twenty minutes later, we erupt onto the eastern harbor and elbow our way through the throng of people who've come to applaud the prince's courage. The air teems with excitement and sprites. Some hover over their masters' heads, dressed in matching silks and leather; others, the unpledged ones, buzz excitedly over the frolicking turquoise surface of Mareluce, remaining high enough to avoid becoming a serpent's snack.

The stench of warm blood and fish guts tangles with the floral and citrus perfumes lifting from the pureblood quarter. Unlike our shoddy wharf, the cobbles here are scrubbed until they glisten silver, and since today isn't a market day, I'm perplexed by the stomach-churning odor.

"Look at the size, Mamma." A human child holds out a thick white steak that spans his two palms and glistens like his shaved head.

His mother touches her mouth. "Gods bless Princci Dante."

My palm grazes my mouth too, but not in gratitude. In horror. Because the white flesh is ensconced in pink scales.

I step back, forgetting I'm surrounded, and end up squashing someone's toes. They mutter and shove me.

"Fallon?" Phoebus's brows are drawn. He backtracks toward me and steals one of the hands strangling the scratchy fabric of my skirt. "What's come over you?"

I swallow, but my saliva cannot slide past the ball of grief swelling in my throat. Phoebus doesn't know about my friendship with Minimus. No one knows I meet the serpent nightly to feed him scraps and caress his scales and beautiful horn.

No one can know.

And now, no one will ever know because...

My lower lip begins to wobble. I snag it with my top teeth.

I hear my name fall from Phoebus's mouth again but cannot answer him. My anguish is too thick, too terrible.

"Fallon, what—"

"Who? Who killed him?" I murmur.

"Him?"

"If you've gotten your serpent meat, please move to the back to allow those who have not to receive the royal offering," a guard bellows from the center of the crowd.

As people shift, I catch the glint of gold against brown braids, the swing of a honed arm cloaked in flesh that glimmers bronze from sweat and seawater, the gleam of a wide silver machete as it comes down on what remains of the beast's trunk.

I want to run away.

I want to cry.

Instead, I lower my hand from my trembling mouth, snatch my fingers from Phoebus's, and push through the Fae and half-lings standing before me.

Over the years, I've mapped out every white scar on Minimus's body. He has five—four from Nonna's vines and one from the horn of a fellow serpent.

I know them by heart because I stroke the scaleless, rubbery flesh every single time we meet, wishing I had the power to heal him like, once upon a time, he healed me.

Cato stands in front of the prince, keeping the crowd at bay. When he catches me approaching, he gives the smallest shake of his head. Does he think I'll harm Dante for having murdered an animal? For all my despair and disgust, I could no more harm a man than a beast.

Phoebus palms the small of my back and dips his mouth to my ear. "Let's go."

Although I'm grateful for his support, I cannot leave.

Not before I see.

My eyes trace over the coiled remains of the dead serpent, hunting for discrepancies amidst the pink, but see none. I make another sweep of the tubular body, just in case. Although this serpent is as long and thick as Minimus, it's not Minimus. Tears of relief and of shame for being relieved trickle down my cheeks.

I scrape them away, praying no one saw them, but Dante's eyes are on me.

Blinking back my emotion, I start to turn when a gondola docks next to the prince, and the royal Fae healer, a giant of a man dressed in his customary black robes, steps off the boat.

Dante hands the meat cleaver to one of his many guards, then goes to the healer, who stands so close to me I can count the number of gold hoops speared through the tall shell of his ear—thirty. Each one is adorned with a healing crystal, which he fingers to extract its essence when he works on his patients.

Dante watches me, a dent cutting into his forehead. Like Phoebus, he must sense my anguish since he knows I cannot stomach animal cruelty. Slowly he pivots, exposing his back to the healer. Blood weeps from a deep gouge beneath his shoulder blade and dribbles down his spine.

"The beast attacked me first." Dante doesn't say my name, but I know his words are for me.

Although my eyes sting, I keep them open and on his wound.

Dante was hurt first.

He was hurt first, I repeat.

When I look back at the lifeless serpent, my heart aches less. In truth, my heart ached less since the moment I realized it wasn't Minimus.

Selfish.

I'm so selfish.

The healer clasps a fire-red crystal and hovers his palm over Dante's back until the dark-bronze skin of my prince begins to steam and seal. Once healed, the enormous male bows to Dante. On his way back to his vessel, his gaze strays to me, lingers.

Is he looking for fodder to hand Justus Rossi? Something that may incriminate me?

I tear my eyes away from his before he can spot anything and stare at the jewel of Luce—the Regios' glass and marble castle ringed by limpid canals and golden bridges that sits on its own island. *Isolacuori*. The beating heart of our kingdom.

"Phoebus." Dante nods to my friend, bloodstained fingers curling into his palms. "Take Fal away from here."

Phoebus's arm glides around my waist. "It was my intent." As we make our way back through the famished mob, Phoebus sighs long and deep before kissing the crown of my head. "Your heart is going to get us into so much trouble someday."

"Us?" I raise my prickling eyes.

"Yes. *Us*. You, me, and Syb. For better or for worse. For the rest of our very long lives. Remember? We took an oath and swapped blood."

Gods, I love this boy. I wind my arm around his waist and squeeze him. Once we've broken free of the crowd, I say, "Nonna was wrong."

"About?"

"About the channel-crossing changing Dante. It didn't render him boastful. If anything, he seemed repentant, which cements my belief that power doesn't alter *all* men."

5

The days pass with no more serpent killings. With no more Dante either. Hopefully, it's Marco's looming betrothal and other stately duties that are keeping my prince away and not amorous trysts.

The memory of Catriona's fingers running over his dark skin plays on a depressing loop inside my mind whenever I'm not busy enough, which prompts me to keep very busy. When not working or helping Nonna accomplish tasks around the house, I lose myself in books.

Reading was one of my mother's favorite pastimes, and perhaps because of this, it's become one of mine. But instead of reading stories to myself, I read them out loud to my mother.

"And they lived together, happy, wild, and free." I close the leather-bound tale of the two Fae from warring kingdoms who overcame their differences and set aside their beliefs to be together.

The pages are worn thin from how often I've thumbed through them, the silk thread binding the pages of the cover unraveling at the bottom. According to Nonna, *A Tale of Two Kingdoms* was Mamma's most cherished book. I don't know if that's true because she never shows emotion, but it's definitely become mine.

"This one again?" Nonna always scoffs when she walks into the bedroom during story time. "Of course it'd also be your favorite."

Nonna says I'm a dreamer, but if I don't dream, then what am I left with? A mother who gave her body to an unworthy man and a grandmother who gave her heart to a punitive one? Reality is too heartbreaking. At least I have Sybille's parents. Their love is a thing of beauty.

Sybille gives me such grief for my romantic obsession and claims I have unrealistic expectations. Ironic coming from a girl whose family life is a dream come true, but those who have it all are often oblivious to their luck.

"Bronwen watches." The whisper leaves Mamma's lips just as I slot the book on her little shelf beside a smooth rock with a carving of a V.

"Who's Bronwen, Mamma?"

Running my thumb over the grooves in the rock, I approach the window and stare out over the brown canal that glitters gold in the setting sun. My thumb freezes because someone stands in our line of sight, beneath the weeping branches of a cypress—a woman with a turban and a dress as black as the shadows engulfing her.

Could it be the same lady I spotted from the wharf a few nights ago?

Her build is the same. Her clothes too. I squint to make out her features in the darkness, but a gondola glides beneath my window, arresting my attention. I feel the eyes of the men on the boat swivel up to my face, hear one ask if I'll be at the Bottom of the Jug tonight because he apparently will.

I want to blow their boat away.

By the time they're out of sight, so is the woman.

I squeeze the little rock I'm still clutching. "Was that lady on the shore Bronwen, Mamma?"

Silence.

"Mamma?" I fan my hand in front of her face, but she's retreated into her scarred mind.

Sighing, I return to the shelf and place the rock beside the book. For several minutes, I stare at the engraving, wondering what the V could stand for, or rather who. I unearthed it from one of her dresses' pockets when my body finally filled out and I inherited her wardrobe. I told Nonna it was mine so that she wouldn't throw it away.

It isn't that my grandmother lacks empathy, because she doesn't; she merely believes the past will harm Mamma further, so she endeavors to keep it from her.

The little rock blurs as I picture the turbaned woman from Rax. Should I go to her? The idea of traveling to the mortal lands is as terrifying as it is tempting. Nonna would never let me go, but I'm twenty-two. I don't need her permission. What I need is coin and a pass to board the ferry that travels between the wharf and the swamps.

Coin I have, but a pass will be difficult to come by. After all, I'd need a valid reason to visit Rax, and it isn't as though I can tell the Fae guards in charge of delivering the passes that I'm looking for a stranger by the name of Bronwen. They'd report my request to my grandfather, who'd not only object but also inform Nonna to rein in her granddaughter.

I catch the splash of a yellow serpent tail, and my pulse foams like the water it's disturbed.

I could call to Minimus and grip his horn so that he swims me across. But what if he carries me into his lair instead? I could, I suppose, paddle beside him. He'd surely stick to my side. What if he didn't, though? What if he abandoned me midway? Would one of his fellow serpents snatch me?

A better idea forms, one that calms my pulse. I'll write a letter, which I'll ask Flora to deliver to Bronwen.

After inking a small note card asking how she knows my

mother and what she wants from me, I kiss Mamma's chilled cheek, pull a wool blanket over her freckled shoulders, and leave her to her sunset gazing.

I get to work early and offer to help Flora prepare the upstairs bedrooms. My suggestion earns me a frown, but the mother of twelve doesn't turn me down. After all, she'll get home earlier, and even though I've heard her tell Sybille's parents how glad she is to get away from her brood, I can't imagine she prefers working over mothering.

I wait until we've finished with the third bedroom before I ask, "Flora, do you know a woman named Bronwen?"

She hisses as though I've just splashed hot oil over her skin.

"You do know her."

Her brown gaze shoots to the open doorway. "Nay."

"Then why did you hiss?"

Flora concentrates on fluffing the down-filled pillows.

I slip my hand into my pocket for the note but extract a copper instead. "I just want to know who she is. That's all."

Flora glances at my offering, then away, her overworked fingers bundling the soiled linens.

"Anything said in here will remain between these walls. I swear it on my mortal life."

She looks at my coin again. I retrieve a second copper. Her eyes gleam hungrily, and she nods to her skirt. My heart pounds as I drop both into her pocket.

"I'll daineye spehking 'bout 'er if I'm quaistioned, 'ear me, 'alfling?"

"I hear you."

She looks at the open door, then back at me. "Like I sayed before, I dain't know 'er meeself." Between her low volume and strong Racoccin accent, I have to concentrate on her shifting lips to parse out her words. "But I know of 'er. It is sayed she's a dayviner."

"A diviner? She can tell the future?"

"Shh." Flora's usual ruddy complexion is as pale as the sheets she holds against her ample bosom.

"Sorry," I murmur.

"'Er blindness giv'er the saight."

So I wasn't just imagining the odd sheen to her eyes. "She's made predictions that came true?"

What little color remains in Flora's cheeks leaches out. "She predicted my cousin's wee li'l one would drown on Yuletide. We all took turns watching 'im, 'fraid 'e'd fall through the ice in the canal. Two minutes to midnight, we were celebrating 'er mistakenness when we found 'im floatin' face first in the bath 'is seeblings forgaht to drayn."

"Oh gods, I'm so sorry, Flora."

"If yee aysk me, she's wicked." Her face grooves with bitterness. "So sty ahwhy from 'er, Fayllon."

Flora lumbers out before I can hand her my note. As I make my way back down into the dining room, I turn all I've learned over and over.

My foot catches at the same time as a thought. I clasp the handrail tight, my heart beating out of rhythm. How can Bronwen watch if she is blind?

Is it my future she's watching? Is that what Mamma means? And if it is what she means, then the woman who gave birth to me is aware of Bronwen's clairvoyance. How?

My mood sours at being left with more questions than answers.

6

I sneak yet another glance out the small tavern window at the human marshes beyond. Although the panes could do with some scrubbing and the moon is veiled, I can make out the Racoccin shore.

The *deserted* shore.

Chair legs screech across wood, and a hiss rises from the Fae I'm serving wine to—or rather on.

"Oh gods. I'm so sorry, Signore Romano."

The elderly Fae is kind enough not to yell at me or demand a free jug of wine for my incompetence. Then again, he's been coming to the tavern since it opened two centuries ago and shows up every evening without fail, so he knows I'm not always this clumsy.

"It's all right, Fallon. No harm done." As I sponge away the mess, he smiles. "I'd be distracted too if I were in your shoes."

My spine straightens until I'm as stiff as the weathered boards beneath my feet. "You…would?"

Did he hear Flora and me talking? He is Fae after all, and he was already seated when I came down the stairs.

A smile tinges his warm amber eyes. "I've no doubt you'll be receiving a ribbon."

I blink. "A...ribbon?"

His wrinkled brow ruffles like the water in a ship's wake.

"Oh. Right. The ribbons." I slap my forehead, pretending I've just remembered what he's referring to, even though I haven't the faintest clue why I'd be preoccupied over bits of silk.

My act must be convincing because he winks conspiratorially at me.

I scurry back to the bar and sidle in close to Sybille as I rinse the wine-soiled rag. "Syb, do you know anything about ribbons?"

She stops filling a row of carafes with water to cock an eyebrow so high it almost touches her hairline. "How do *you* not know about them?"

"Um..." I shrug. "My mind's been on other things lately."

"You don't say." A smirk clings to her mouth because she assumes my other things are Dante and more Dante.

She leans her hip against the wooden counter she keeps immaculate even though it's out of sight from patrons. Like her father, Sybille is obsessive about neatness. Phoebus often jokes it's an affliction, but I think he's secretly jealous, what with him being the biggest slob. Wherever things land, they stay. His apartment on the next island over is absolute chaos.

"The royal family is ferrying gold ribbons by way of written invitations for the king's betrothal revel. Dante's idea apparently. All of Luce is waiting with bated breath for one, but not all of Luce will get one."

Will I? The prospect of attending a royal ball blows away the sullenness, which has clung to me like cobwebs.

"Apparently, his guards are going door-to-door tonight."

The realization that Nonna would likely forbid me from attending a party on Isolacuori deflates my mood.

"What's with the pout? I'd have imagined you'd be vibrating with excitement about attending a ball with your favorite prince."

"Do you really see Nonna letting me go?"

"I love your grandmother dearly, Fallon, but you're an adult now. You're in charge of your comings and goings."

Sybille's right, yet deep down, I know I would never defy my grandmother, because that woman gave up everything for me. It's only fair I give up certain things for her.

Catriona bustles over in a swish of topaz silk and slides onto one of the high chairs propped beneath the bar, cheeks shimmery with powder, eyes black with kohl. "Evening, girls." Her long fingers play with her gold choker.

Sybille's large gray eyes begin twinkling like silver coins. "Is that what I think it is?"

Catriona raises a vainglorious smile. "The prince gave it to me last night."

My chest feels tight. She saw Dante last night? He wasn't at the tavern, which begs the question of where? Did she visit the palace? Courtesans are often convened there for private parties with the high-ranking officials of Luce.

Catriona flicks the end of the bow. "Have you two gotten ribbons?"

Sybille sighs. "We'd be wearing them if we had."

Giana twirls out of the kitchen with a platter of cheese.

I move aside to let her pass and feign ignorance when I ask, "Dante was here last night, Catriona?"

"No. Our paths crossed in Signore Lavano's house where I was hired to entertain."

"If you three are done gossiping, Mother needs help boning the fish, and I could use a hand in the dining room." Giana's brown corkscrew curls halo her angular face. Unlike Sybille, who's been straightening her hair since she learned how to, Giana never lengthens her tight spirals.

"I'll go." Sybille pushes into the kitchen, gusting herbal steam and sizzling butter our way.

Giana nods to the stairs. "The commander's ready for you in the burgundy room, Catriona."

"Ah, Silvius." Catriona motions to the amphora filled with the golden liquid Marcello brews from fermented honey and clover. "Pour me a drink, will you, micara?"

Since I'm the only one Catriona calls *darling*, I know she's addressing me and not Giana.

"I'm going to need it with that man," she says.

I thumb the cork from the glass bottle and drizzle the syrupy liquid into a thimble-sized glass.

She upends it as soon as I slide it over, then taps the rim for a refill. "You know, you should join us. Silvius speaks of you all the time."

Giana recoils as though Catriona had invited *her* upstairs.

"I'd sooner swim across the channel than join that male in bed." I punch the cork back into the amphora with a satisfying whack.

"*That male* pays generously. I've no doubt I could get him to offer you a gold coin, what with you being—"

"I don't need money."

"Are you certain about that, micara?" Her gaze skims over the mended fabric of my dress, rendering me self-conscious.

You don't care about such things, Fallon. The same way you don't care about jewels or praise.

"Fallon's much too sweet for your profession." Giana piles copper mugs onto a platter, then tenders her hand for a jug of water, which I deliver.

"Once upon a time, I too was sweet." Catriona lifts the mead to her lips and shoots it down. "It wears off fast, whether you take off your clothes for one man or for many."

"Let it go, Catriona." Giana narrows her eyes on the courtesan before turning and carrying her platter away.

"I see the way you look at the prince," Catriona says.

The copper mug I'm washing clinks against the basin and gets lost beneath the suds.

"I see the way he looks at you," she continues.

I peek at Catriona past my lashes.

"I could help you get him. And not just for one night."

My heart palpitates so fast it vibrates my tongue. "I'm a halfling."

Her eyebrows, so much darker than the golden hair curled around her neck, writhe. "So am I."

Heat stains my cheeks as I realize she wasn't referring to marriage.

"Luce may not allow us to rise above the curve of our ears, but marriage isn't everything, Fallon."

"How would someone like you know?" My tone is brusque.

Catriona doesn't flinch, inured to people's opinions, but her expression sharpens. "I've seen many things during my century of life, but never a loving marriage amongst the nobility. If you want loyalty and affection, then avoid purebloods."

I've no illusions that winning Dante's heart will be a feat, but if I go into this battle already defeated, then what chance do I have of winning?

7

The stars are already fading when I return home, and the house is so quiet I can hear our fishmonger neighbors brewing tea next door, readying to trawl the placid sea before the wind awakens.

After a fruitless search of my kitchen for a golden ribbon or a letter with an official seal, I tiptoe up the twisted staircase, wincing at every squeak. What little hope I harbor of unearthing an invitation shrivels at the sight of my bare bed and empty desk.

Both Sybille and Giana received a ribbon earlier, as did their parents and, of course, Phoebus. He may reside in Tarelexo and trim his golden hair in solidarity, but as long as his family hasn't disowned him, he will remain a Tarecuorin, and all Tarecuorins, from what I heard in the tavern, have been invited.

I fall into bed fully dressed and curl onto my side. Although I refuse to shed tears, they rise and spill onto my pillowcase. I'm angry at my mother. So angry. All this is her fault.

I have no prospects because of her, only an abysmal reputation.

It's a wonder we haven't been transferred to Rax with the heathens.

"You're home late." Nonna stands in my doorway, a shawl covering her black nightgown. "Or rather early."

"It was a big night, what with all the excitement surrounding the ribbons." I keep my back to her and my eyes on the window overlooking the pearlescent sky. "Have we received any?"

Silence settles so thickly in the room that I think Nonna has gone back to bed, but her lemon and wisteria scent wafts toward me, spiraling around my rib cage like vines.

"No."

"Of course not." If there's a list of halflings forbidden to set foot on Isolacuori, the Rossi women are on it.

"Royal revels are overrated, Goccolina."

A shard of sorrow sharpens inside my throat. "Guess I'll never find out."

"Mi cuori…"

I don't feel like being her heart tonight, or her raindrop. I don't even feel like being Fallon Rossi. "Good night, Nonna."

She pads over to my bed and sits, and then her palm lands on my hair, brushes it off the damp tracks on my cheeks.

"I said good night." I shift so that her hand slips off.

She lingers a moment, whispers, "I love you."

She waits for me to say it back, thin frame denting my mattress, floral fragrance assaulting my senses. Realizing she won't get tender words from me, she stands and pads out.

The rusted hinges creak as she pulls the door to my small bedroom closed. It's only when I hear the click of wood settling into the frame that I press my mouth into the pillow and release my bone-jarring sob.

⟲

The tavern, like most shops and businesses, closes the day of the revel.

Gondola after gondola draped in white blooms and bolts of sparkly organza traverse the canals, carrying partygoers to

Isolacuori. Each time one passes under Mamma's bedroom window, my heart cramps.

I watch the lucky few carve across the canal in their glamorous silks and glittery jewels, pitches high and bright. Some even sing bawdy tunes, commencing the party in their boat.

As though the lizards that roam the wisteria vines of our house sense my sadness, four dart over the windowsill, golden scales refracting the sun's rays, and scurry up the walls, putting on a show for Mamma and me. One even swings itself onto Mamma's lap and crawls onto her clasped hands until it's found the ideal indent for its miniature body. The corners of Mamma's mouth twitch, and it blows away some of my sadness.

The reptile's lids shut as I read words that glance across my mind like a tossed pebble. Hopefully, they penetrate my mother's. Once she falls asleep, I carry her new friend back to the sill and shut the window, then head outside for a walk. It's a terrible idea, because the streets are empty and quiet.

Sybille and Phoebus aren't aware I haven't been invited, and I haven't dared confess it for fear it'll alter their plans, or worse, that it won't. As the sun bastes the sky in oranges and pinks, I end up at the wharf where I find Giana locking the tavern door. I try to turn down an alley before she spots me, but I'm not quick enough.

"Syb left with Mother and Father over an hour ago." She scans my attire. "Why aren't you dressed?"

I look down, petting my simple frock. Instead of wallowing in more self-pity, I widen my eyes in mock horror and whisper, "Have I worn my invisible dress again?"

Giana has the decency to chuckle at my paltry joke.

I nod my chin at her simple attire. "What of *your* gown?"

"Gods, you thought I'd attend an Isolacuorin revel? Not in this lifetime."

Since we don't have more than one lifetime, I take it she never plans on attending one. "Where are you headed?"

"To Rax. Humans are throwing a party of their own since ribbons never made their way across the canal."

Unsurprising. Humans aren't even allowed to navigate the waters surrounding the royal isle.

"How are you getting to Rax?"

She slides her lips together. Once. Twice. Finally, she sighs. "On Antoni's boat. He and his friends didn't make the list."

"I didn't either."

She lifts a single eyebrow. "That's hard to believe."

"Believe it." I lick my lips. "Can I come with you?"

The setting sun outlines Giana in gold, darkening her brown skin until it appears pitch-black. "Your grandmother—"

"Doesn't need to know."

"Fallon..."

"Please, Gia. I beg you." I walk over to her, palms joined in prayer. "I'll do anything. Anything at all."

A deep breath gusts out of her. "Just save me from becoming a serpent's meal when your grandmother tosses me into the canal, all right?"

"Yes!" I all but shout before lowering my voice and adding, "But she won't toss you in. I swear it on all our faerie gods."

Giana smiles and shakes her head but then points to the wharf where Antoni stands, his gaze riveted to us.

The anticipation of heading to Rax has plugged in all the little holes inside my chest. Not only do I want to let loose and shed my melancholy, but I also want to meet Bronwen.

Antoni watches me through low-slung eyebrows. "You're not at the revel, Fallon?"

"I'm a Rossi, remember?" I bite the inside of my cheek, not hard enough to draw blood but hard enough for it to sting so it distracts me from the pain prickling my chest anew. "Our status is rather dismal these days."

He still doesn't shift aside to let me onto his boat.

"I'll pay." I plunge a hand into the pocket of my skirt.

"Fallon, please." He clasps my forearm. "Your money's no good on my boat."

I suck in a breath and take a step back. "I understand. I—"

"You've understood something but clearly not what I was saying." He holds out his palm.

I frown at it, then at him.

"I'd never take money from you, Fallon." He says this so gently that his tone alone calms my stuttering heart. "Rossi women are always welcome aboard my boat."

Swallowing, I place my hand atop his and allow him to lower me inside. As I settle by the bow, he unwinds the lines, and I catch hints of flexing biceps beneath a loose navy shirt that's fresh off a laundry rack.

Although I don't think he'd mind my perusal, I cast my gaze on the soldier barracks that are quiet tonight, most military personnel having been summoned to the palace to assist the royal guard. Still, a few uniformed men prowl the slender isle that fences off Rax from Tarelexo.

I'm glad for the darkness but do ponder how we'll pass through the checkpoint. "I don't have a pass."

Antoni hops in beside me, leaving his friends to row.

"You don't need one on my vessel."

"How come?"

"I don't only peddle fish." I'm not sure what he means by this, and it must show on my face because he adds, "Secrets, Fallon." He winks while I wonder what sort of secrets he keeps and trades. "They make for wonderful currency."

"So they won't even stop us?"

"No." Wisps of briny air quarrel with his locks. He presses them away, a smile growing on his chiseled face, deepening the cleft in his square chin. "I can't believe Fallon Rossi is standing on my boat, headed into the swamplands."

I return his grin, harnessing the strands of my own hair back.

"And eager about it. Did a sprite tinkle in your coffee this morning?"

I wrinkle my nose. "Yuck. Why would you even say that?"

"Their urine's reputed to make Fae behave...*wildly*."

"First off, that's disgusting." Albeit informative. How has Phoebus, who grew up with sprites waiting on him, not informed me of this? "Second, I brewed my own pot and own no sprite."

A blue serpent emerges from underneath the boat, its ivory horn slicked in moonlight. It pays us no mind, merely swims away, causing Giana to release a muted shriek and wavelets to crash against the side of the boat. My footing falters.

Antoni snaps his arm around my waist as I slam into his side. "Let's keep the swimming for the after-party."

I crane my neck to look up into his face. "Swimming? You swim?"

"My element *is* water."

"True, but no one's element is mareserpens."

His gaze is so heavy on my face that my cheeks smolder. "Save you."

"I've only ever met one." I lower my eyes to the canal, wondering if Minimus is somewhere beneath the moonlit water. "Maybe the others would hate me."

"I don't think any being could hate you, Fallon."

I inhale a deep breath, filling my lungs with salt and wind and starlight. "My grandfather does."

"Your grandfather's a fool."

I gasp because we're a boat length away from the checkpoint, and two Fae soldiers are standing by the floating gate. "Don't say such things." Antoni's brow creases, and I realize he must think I'm defending the man. "His influence is too great and his ears too sharp. And even though you swim, I don't want you ending up in the channel."

Slowly, the furrows smooth and his easy smile returns.

I expect the guards to stop the boat, but at the tick of Antoni's head, they slide the gate open. I sense one staring at me and turn my face into Antoni's neck to shield it from the man's attention. "They won't tell anyone they saw me on your boat?"

Antoni's fingers tighten around my waist. "Not if they care to keep their secrets a secret."

Wood and metal creak as the gate is drawn closed behind us, and I release the breath stuck in my lungs.

"Those secrets you peddle must be quite terrible."

"Quite."

Although I think I should put space between our bodies, I feel indebted to Antoni, and it'd be a lie to claim I'm not enjoying his firm grip. The only other hands I've had on me were Dante's, and that was so long ago, I've forgotten how they felt.

The bow of the boat carves through detritus—broken planks, bobbing bottles, bloated fish, chunks of feces—sending up a stink that makes me inhale solely through my mouth. No wonder the canal in these parts is so murky.

"Why don't fire-Fae clean up the water?" My voice comes out a little nasal from how hard I'm trying not to pull in air.

"Because the king believes that humans must live in their filth and has made it illegal to use magic to improve life in Rax."

My fists clench at my sides in shock and in anger. "That's… that's…heartless. If Dante were king—"

"He'd keep the ban alive."

"He wouldn't."

Antoni's arm turns rigid, then slips off in time with his smile. "I forget he's your friend."

"He cares about all his people—purebloods, halflings, *and* humans."

"Yet you're here with me instead of at the palace with him, so he mustn't care enough."

My chest stings. "It's the king's revel, not the prince's."

Antoni has the good sense not to press the issue, yet as we near the gnarled roots of the cypresses lining the shore, our argument festers between us like the refuse atop the water.

8

ere." Giana presses a lumpy, earthenware mug into my
hands as she sits on a rusted barrel that's been flattened
to look like a bench. "You seem like you could use this."

I sniff the fizzing liquid, and the smell alone makes my eyes
water. "What's in this thing?"

"Alcohol."

"I got that. I meant what type?"

"Home-brewed ale. It tastes better than it smells."

I take a tentative sip and all but cough up a lung at the bitter
tang.

Giana's wide mouth splits into a grin. "It's an acquired taste."

"How long did it take you to acquire it?"

She laughs. "A while."

So this isn't her first time in Rax...

"Antoni's in a positively foul mood. What in Luce happened
on the boat?"

I glance over the crackling bonfire at where Antoni and one
of his friends have taken residence on a felled tree trunk. "We
discussed politics."

"And he and you don't share the same views?" She lifts her
mug and takes a sip.

I attempt another swallow. This time, it goes down without maiming my lungs. It's still revolting. "He doesn't think Dante would be any better a ruler than Marco."

"Ah." A simple sound that carries a complicated weight.

"What's *ah* supposed to mean?"

She lowers her mug to her lap and encircles it with both hands. "It means that once you've been around as long as both Antoni and I have, your views may change."

"You *know* Dante, Gia."

"And I *knew* Marco. I may not have gone to school with him, but he used to frequent the tavern. It would be a stretch to claim we were friends, but we were most definitely friendly."

The idea of Marco sitting at a table in Bottom of the Jug is so jarring that I don't say anything for a long minute, but then curiosity gets the better of me. "Did you and he...?"

"Cauldron, no. Even when I was still debating whether I preferred males or females, I never preferred *him*. His ego was as large as all of Tarelexo. All of Tarecuori too, for that matter." The flames of the fire dance in the pale gray irises she shares with her entire air-Fae family. Even though she looks no older than a human in her early thirties, Giana is almost a century old. Those eyes have seen things. "And it only got worse after Primanivi. He returned from that battle acting like a god."

I observe the huddles of bald and turbaned humans tittering and dancing as though they haven't a care in the world, as though the five half-Fae who crashed their party didn't share blood with the man who'd crushed their uprising two decades ago. "How come the humans allowed us to partake in their revel?"

She stares around her, meeting a few sets of guarded eyes and a few sets of inquisitive ones. The same feeling I had when we arrived at this party comes over me again—that my fellow Lucin outcasts are more familiar with these humans than they let on.

"Because they need coin." She pushes back a springy curl,

letting her index finger linger on the curved shell of her ear. "And because of these."

I sigh.

Because of *these*, I'm sitting here instead of on a tufted chair in Isolacuori. I brush away the morose contemplation before it can take root and further ruin my evening. "Coin?"

"What?"

"You said humans need coin. I take it someone paid for us to be here. Which one of you paid, and how much do I owe?"

"Fallon—"

"You know me. I don't like debts."

"Antoni took care of it. He took care of all of us, so there's no need to feel indebted." Giana touches my wrist. "As for our earlier discussion... I know you care for Dante, and frankly, I'd like to think that if he were in a position of power, he'd change things, but I've learned that if Fae have nothing to gain, then they have nothing to fight for."

"Except he'd have so much to gain!" I toss my hands in the air, sloshing ale from my mug and garnering the attention of the humans closest to us. I dry my wrist on my skirt and press my lips together, regretting having drawn attention.

"Name one thing the royals would gain from helping lesser Fae and humans out?"

"Our loyalty."

"They already own us." Giana dips her lips into her ale, gaze on the flickering flames.

"Taking something and being given something is not even close to the same."

She looks at me. "I'm not the one who needs convincing."

"Aren't you? You sound resigned."

Her eyes skim back to the fire, the silver hardening like cooling metal. "I'm anything but, dolcca."

Giana hasn't called me honey since I was a child and I'd stop by the tavern for the sweets she'd buy Sybille and me every Friday. I'd trace the chips in the candied petals with my stubby fingers, wondering out loud why the flower heads weren't as pretty as the ones in the window display. Giana explained that imperfections lessened the value of things. The following Friday, she'd presented me with both a perfect and imperfect sprig of lavender and had lain both in front of me. *"Tell me, dolcca, does the pretty one taste sweeter than the damaged one?"*

They'd tasted the same. Her lesson had upset me so deeply, so fundamentally, that I hadn't returned to the tavern for days, and when I did return, I turned down her offerings, claiming I was too old for sweets.

I watch bubbles pop atop the surface of my ale. "You're the one who taught me that value is measured by appearance." When a V forms between her eyebrows, I add, "The day you bought me the candied lavender."

Her forehead smooths.

"I was furious that day. Not at you but at the injustice of it all."

"I always wondered what had happened."

"You know what I did? I dragged Dante to the candy shop with me and made him buy a reject and a perfect candy. Mind you, the saleslady refused to sell the prince a reject, just gave it to him. You know what he said? He said he couldn't tell what the difference between them was, neither in appearance nor in taste. That's the sort of man he is, Gia—fair and aware."

"I admire him all the more for it, but those traits won't upend the hierarchy. Not without a fight. And that fight will cost people their lives if they're not prepared. Who do you think will die, Fallon? Whose blood will baste the cobbled streets? You really think Dante would kill his own brother to make things right? To make things better?"

Her words are hushed yet sound yelled, not at the world but at me. I feel knee-high to a sprite and no older than the babe one human is carrying in a sling against her chest. "I know you think me naive, but—"

"Idealistic, not naive. Gods, Fallon, I wish *I* could still dream wide awake." She squeezes my wrist before letting go and standing. "I'm going to get myself some more ale and make the most of being here." She starts to walk away but then turns. "And I apologize."

"For what?"

"To have caused you such anguish so young."

"I don't regret it."

"It doesn't change the fact that *I* do." She smiles, but it's a soft, almost imperceptible curve. "Now, go have some fun." She flicks her eyes over the crowd. I don't think she means to single out Antoni, but her gaze lands on the grumpy halfling, who's staring at the fire as though it's the vilest element of them all.

I bite my lip, slide it between my teeth. I'm still mad that he thinks poorly of Dante, but I reason he doesn't know him like I do. I drink my ale, every last, bitter drop of it, and then I stand.

His eyes are on me, and although his attention doesn't ignite my pulse like Dante's does, it does warm my blood.

I walk over to where he now sits alone, Riccio and Mattia having evidently found companions. "Can I sit with you?"

His blue eyes smolder in the firelight, but the rest of him is so cold, I think he's going to refuse, especially when he lowers his gaze to his mug of ale. But he proves me wrong by nodding.

I sit, placing my empty mug beside my mud-caked shoe. "Did it also take you time to get used to the flavor, or did you always enjoy it?"

He peers back at me with a deep frown.

I crank my chin toward his mug, which is made of metal and not fired clay.

"I've always enjoyed it, but I'm not a very difficult person to please."

The words *unlike you* stain the air. "Gia said you paid for me."

"Did she really?"

"Don't be mad at her." I lay my hand on his knee. "I *made* her tell me."

"I wasn't aware you could compel people." The edge in his voice is so sharp it cleaves my hand from his leg.

"I have *no* power, Antoni." I bury my fingers in the folds of my dress, peeved by his pettiness. "None. Not even the measly amount you and the others of our kind possess."

I should've stayed on my bench. I start to rise when fingers curl around my hand. Antoni's callused thumb dips into my palm, forcing my fingers to bend over his, even though I'm not sure I want to hold his hand.

"Forgive me?" The bite to his tone is gone.

"For what? Reminding me how useless I am?"

"For acting like a sprite-ass. And you're not useless."

I glare at the squelchy mud that's stained the hem of my dress. If I had any power, I could make clothes spin inside the sudsy basin we use for washing. Instead, I have to scrub each piece of fabric until my nails ache.

"Maybe I can help you figure out how to move water."

"I'm twenty-two, Antoni. I should've been able to move water a decade ago."

"Maybe you're a late bloomer."

"Or perhaps I won't bloom at all."

The pads of his fingers are rough, but so are mine, and although he doesn't seem to care, I do. I tug my hand away, but he holds on. And then his thumb begins to move over the line that, according to Sybille, measures how long I'll live, which I hope is all myth and legend, since it breaks close to where it starts.

"You've bloomed in all the important ways, Fallon."

I snort. I cannot help it.

"Not to mention you survived an encounter with a mareserpens.

Perhaps you cannot move water, but you can apparently move the hearts of the creatures who thrive within it, serpents and water-Fae alike."

I shake my head, but his words crack my bad mood. "You have such a honeyed tongue."

"I'm usually told this *after* my tongue has ventured on a woman's body, not before."

I side-eye him, my stomach swirling from the ale, from his touch, from the idea of his tongue on my skin. He tugs on my hand gently, as though to test for resistance. When he encounters none, the pressure grows until he's pulled me onto his lap.

"I know I wear no uniform, and I know you can do far better than a fisherman, but before you cast me and my heart aside, give me a chance, Fallon Rossi." He raises our hands to his mouth and kisses my knuckles before sliding my hand to the nape of his neck. Once he feels secure I won't shift it away, he wraps his fingers around the indent at my waist, sharpened by my corset.

Guilt, gratitude, and ale churn within me. Even though I don't want to marry Antoni, I realize that I wouldn't mind kissing him.

I must say it out loud because a nerve feathers his jaw. "I want to kiss you too, Fallon. As for marriage...put it out of your mind."

I skip my fingers over the knobs of his spine, breathing in the sun-warmed brine flavor of his skin. "I've only ever kissed one other person, and you've kissed thousands." I'm not sure why I confess this. I'd blame the ale, but it's probably some deep-rooted insecurity.

"Your experience is of no importance to me. As for the thousands I've kissed before, none of them made me feel the way you do, Fallon."

"Insecure?"

"Mad with desire," he rasps before pressing his lips to mine. Lips that have belonged to so many but that tonight belong to only me.

The kiss is slow and languorous, nothing like the heated one I shared with Dante. There's no urgency to it, no accompanying tears or heartache. Neither of us is going anywhere. Even though it feels wrong, I imagine I'm sitting on Dante's lap, kissing Dante's mouth. I picture Dante's hard length digging into my thigh.

I part my mouth, deepening the kiss. Antoni sweeps in gently, as though fearing that if he goes any faster, he'll scare me. Or maybe he's gentle because that's his technique. I try to remember what Sybille said, but the thought that my best friend has been where I am now makes my gut churn.

No thinking of Sybille.

Or Dante.

No thinking, period.

I force myself to concentrate on the feel of Antoni, the pliancy of his tongue, so at odds with the rest of his body. I tangle my fingers in his loose hair and press his head closer to mine until the kiss is no longer sweet.

I don't want sweet tonight. I want the sort of kiss that obliterates minds and hearts. That lights up storm clouds and heats winter nights. The sort of kiss I've read about in Mamma's books.

Antoni pulls away and pants my name. I try to kiss him again, but he skates his mouth off mine. I stiffen in his arms. He's still hard, so I assume he still wants me, even though he apparently no longer wants to kiss me.

"They rent rooms here."

I'm not ready for more, but Catriona's hands on Dante fill my mind. Although the prince didn't slide her onto his lap or follow her upstairs, he allowed her hands to knead his shoulders and neck. Is he letting others caress him tonight? So many desire him, and although I thought he desired me most, I'm sitting on another man's lap in Rax, so he mustn't desire me enough.

"But we don't have to—I shouldn't have—" Antoni moves a lock of hair off my face. "I'm content just kissing you, Fallon."

I eye the wooden tavern with windows so tiny I imagine darkness reigns there day and night, then eye the poverty around us. The bed linens mustn't be changed very often. Perhaps this makes me snobbish, but I don't want to lie with a man in a cheap and dirty bed.

Especially not for my first time.

"Not here." My answer makes his hand still, and I realize he'd been expecting me to refuse taking our tryst any further.

"Let me get the others and—"

I press my fingertips to his flushed mouth. I'm not ready to go home. "Let the others have their fun. The night's still young, Antoni."

I replace my fingers with my mouth to reassure him of my interest so he doesn't rush us out of Rax before I can find Bronwen.

9

As I kiss Antoni, my head spins and my bladder aches. The latter is a by-product of the ale, but is the former too? Or do my thoughts twirl from the heat Antoni has coaxed inside my veins?

Whatever the reason, I need to relieve myself. I tow my lips from his, my breathing as rushed as it was the day I met Minimus in the Harbor Market. "Tell me humans have bathrooms."

His eyes carry the same glaze as his swollen lips. "They have boarded-up sewage holes."

I wrinkle my nose.

"You cannot hold?"

I shake my head no, then shake my head again when Antoni insists on escorting me to the outhouse behind the tavern. There are places a girl needs to go alone. His eyes trail me as I walk toward the small wooden structure that exudes an odor far worse than the Racoccin canal.

The urge to keep my legs crossed until we return to our more civilized neck of the kingdom is strong, but the desire to ease my cramping abdomen wins out. I pull open a rickety wooden door, getting another face full of pungent fumes. My stomach heaves, and I jerk my hand up to pinch my nose, then fumble in the darkness for a latch, which I never find.

Keeping one hand on the door handle, I release my nose to raise my skirt and lower my drawers, then squat over the barrel, holding my breath.

If only Nonna could see me. *Oh gods, Nonna!* She must be worried stiff. I hope she assumes I went to the tavern. What if she does, though? She'll find it locked and then assume something even worse...that I squirreled away on a gondola headed to Isolacuori.

I pray she doesn't go looking for me. She rarely leaves Mamma alone after night falls. Please let tonight be no different.

My bladder feels better, but my head keeps whooshing as I stumble out of the rank-smelling booth. I lean against the wall of the tavern and close my eyes.

The aroma of broiling grease wafts through the open window beside my head, and although a moment ago my stomach was revolted, now it growls. I'm about to return to the party and ask Antoni if we can purchase food when an unfamiliar voice calls out my name, stopping me in my tracks and casting goose bumps over my skin.

I look for the speaker, but the darkness from where the voice emanates is so thick, I can barely decipher the wall of cypresses girdling the area. "Bronwen?"

The shadows shift. "You know my name."

It's not a question, yet I answer, "My mother mentioned you were watching me. And then I saw you..."

"Has your mother shared anything else?"

"Nothing. She can barely speak, let alone string sensical words together." I hunt the darkness for Bronwen but still cannot see her. "How do you know her? How does she know you?"

"It matters not."

"It matters to me."

"We don't have much time, Fallon."

My goose bumps prickle as though a new wave has splashed my skin.

A gust of wind combs through the branches over our heads, allowing moonlight to squeeze through the canopy of leaves. I make out the folds of a turban, crumpled skin that resembles melted wax, and milky eyes that gleam white.

I take a step back, my heart palpitating inside my throat. Flora warned me Bronwen was blind but failed to mention she was disfigured. What happened to her?

"Free the five iron crows, and you will be queen."

I freeze. What the what? Iron crows? Queen? Marco's blasé mien flashes behind my lids, eliciting a shudder. "Not only is the king betrothed—and clearly not to me—but also, I've no love for the male."

"I'm aware the Regio male you love is another."

This time, the goose bumps sink beneath my skin and bob along my chilled blood. "How?"

"Because I see, child."

A shiver runs down my spine, because if she does, it's not with her scarred eyes. "Are you saying that if I find five metal...*statues*, Dante will become king and choose me as his bride?"

"I am saying Luce will, one day soon, belong to you, Fallon Báeinach."

"Bannock?" I repeat the foreign word she tagged to my name. "Why did you call me Fallon Bannock? What does it mean?"

She backs up. "Free the crows, Fallon."

"Free them? These objects are trapped?"

"Yes."

"Where?"

"They're hidden across the kingdom."

I toss my hands up in frustration. "Then how in the gods' names am I supposed to locate them?"

Bronwen stops withdrawing. "The first will lead you to the others."

"Great. And where is the first?"

She pauses for so long that I blow a breath out the corner of my mouth.

"Do keep up the suspense. It's so *very* enjoyable."

"I see one in the palace."

"Well, that's unfortunate, since I'm neither allowed nor welcomed onto the royal isle." Under my breath, I add, "Trust me, if I were, I'd be *there* tonight."

"You're here because it was time." She folds herself into the darkness as though her body lacks substance. "Speak of me and your undertakings with no one, or you'll damn us all."

"Damn us all?" I mutter under my breath. "Who's *all*?"

Silence.

"Who are you? And why me?"

More silence.

"And how does my mother know you?"

A cool drift flutters my hair and relays another haunting whisper. "He waits for you, Fallon."

"Who? Dante? Antoni?" My exasperation resonates against the cypresses' trunks, against their gnarled roots and the inky sky itself.

I want to growl and claw through the darkness until I reach the infuriating woman who speaks in riddles.

"Are you all right?" Antoni's voice makes me spin around.

I exhale raucously, my fingers jerking to my hair and sailing through the thick locks. "Yes," I lie.

"Who were you speaking with?"

"Some human woman." Although, *is* Bronwen human? The notion that she may be something else raises the fine hairs along my arms.

Antoni sidesteps me, hollering for the woman to show herself. Unsurprisingly, Bronwen doesn't.

As he delves deeper into the shadows, I realize I got what I came to Rax seeking, yet I am so *utterly* confused that I want to grip my hair and tug at the roots. Instead, I ball my fingers at my sides and focus on Antoni's broad figure cutting through the abounding blackness back toward me.

"I shouldn't have let you come out here alone," he mutters.

I grip his biceps to calm him. "I'm fine, Antoni."

His teeth grind. "What did she tell you? What did she want?"

"Money." *Lie.*

"Did you give her any?"

"One copper. So she could feed her child." I'm just bursting with falsehoods tonight.

His arms twitch and then metal jangles. "Here." Even though my fingers still cinch his upper arms, Antoni's managed to produce a coin from the leather purse hooked onto his belt.

I shake my head. "I already owe you for tonight."

"Fallon—"

I release his arms to fold his fingers back over the proffered coin. "Please, Antoni. I may not be rolling in Tarecuorin gold, but I'm not destitute either."

In the end, he relents and stashes it back inside his drawstring purse. "We should go home."

This time, I readily agree. And not because I intend to crash the royal revel to find a statue but because I need distance from this place...from the blind woman who just informed me I could be queen if I located and freed five metal crows.

Why would anyone trap a statue? Several at that? Because they're made of iron? And why in the world would a blacksmith model them after the pet birds of the mountain tribe that attacked us two decades ago?

10

I'm so lost in thought that I barely register we've crossed the canal until I'm standing on the wharf and Giana's hand clasps my upper arm, pulling me away from the three men who are tying up the boat.

"What's going on with you?"

How I wish I could tell her, but I'd apparently be damning a bunch of strangers.

I stop nibbling the life out of my lip. "Just wondering about... things."

"*Things* being Antoni?"

Her eyes are alight with something. I cannot tell if it's worry or amusement, which, I'm aware, are vastly different sentiments, but my mind is currently not at its most discerning.

"If you don't care to take things any further, tell him. He's one of the few who'll listen."

My tryst with Antoni is the furthest thing from my mind, but now that she's brought him up, our kiss comes back front and center and, on its heels, what he may expect. Over Giana's shoulder, I watch him emerge from his boat with the seasoned grace of a male used to existing between land and sea. He catches my eye but doesn't smile. Like me, he's been on edge since we left Rax.

I return my attention to Giana. "I'm uncertain as to what I want." Well, besides rewinding this entire evening. This entire week.

I wish Mamma had never mentioned Bronwen and that I never went looking for her, because the blind woman's managed to both befuddle and unsettle me. Could I, a halfling, lawfully become Dante's bride thanks to a treasure hunt?

Bronwen asked me not to speak of my quest or of her, but she didn't specifically tell me I couldn't ask about bird statues.

I lift my eyes to the twinkling sky. "Gia, do any blacksmiths in the kingdom work with iron?"

She tucks her chin into her neck. "Only the one in Isolacuori, who supplies steel blades to the military."

My pulse skips. Bronwen said the iron bird was in Isolacuori. Could it be in that man's forge?

"Why?"

I frown as an inconsistency hits me. Only pure-blooded Fae can live on Isolacuori, but Fae can't handle iron. "The blacksmith is Fae?"

"No. He's human. Fae can't touch iron."

"A human lives on Isolacuori?"

"Like a king. Generation after generation." Her eyes narrow. "Why the sudden interest in blacksmiths?"

A skein of teal-feathered ducks takes off behind her, water collapsing like dropped diamonds from their wings, spattering the serpent that disturbed their rest.

"Maybe I want a weapon? A girl should have one on her person, shouldn't she?"

Giana's voice drops to a hard whisper. "Did Dargento hurt you?"

I startle that she drew that conclusion. "No. I promise he didn't."

"What's going on over here?" Antoni sidles in beside us.

69

"Nothing," I mumble at the same time Giana says, "Fallon wants a weapon. An *iron* weapon."

I snag the inside of my cheek with my teeth. Why did she have to go and tell him? Instead of making a big deal of it, I say, "Fine. Yes. I'd feel safer."

Antoni looks at Giana. After a pregnant pause, his gaze returns to me. "The possession of anything made of iron is an instant death sentence. And considering your history with serpents, they wouldn't make you walk the plank."

"I'm aware. It was a stupid idea." One that led me nowhere. Or rather to Isolacuori, where I need to go anyway. "Can you both please forget it?"

They exchange another lengthy stare that makes me arch a brow because it feels laced with more than just concern; it feels laced with connivance and secrets.

Riccio and Mattia amble over to us, chattering boisterously about their human conquests. Riccio slugs freckle-faced Mattia on the back. He must be teasing his cousin because Mattia's forever sunburnt face appears ruddier than usual.

"How about we go inside for a nightcap?" Giana hooks the golden chain around her neck, lifting the tavern key tucked inside the bodice of her dress.

Riccio and Mattia readily agree and follow her.

Antoni cants his head to the side. "What would you like to do, Fallon?"

If I go home now, I'll run into Nonna, who'll sense my turmoil and confront me, and that woman knows me inside out. If I loiter about another hour or two, the odds of her being asleep will be higher.

Wait... Antoni wasn't suggesting walking me home, was he?

I smooth my clammy palms down my skirt. "I'm not ready to go home." Neither to his nor to mine.

He nods to the tavern. "After you then."

I stride ahead of him, the mud on the hem of my dress weighing down the fabric.

"Lock the door," Giana says as Riccio, the only fire-Fae in the group, takes care of igniting the wicks on a few oil lamps.

Tarelexo is so empty and quiet, it feels as though the five of us are the only Fae alive in the entire kingdom. Even the sprites, usually buzzing about the wharf, are absent.

Because everyone's at the palace.

The palace that could be mine.

Me, a queen...

It's so completely absurd.

Yet I can picture myself at Dante's side, and I don't hate the daydream.

My reverie takes epic proportions as I help Giana lug five glasses to a round table in the back of the tavern, behind the curtain that shields us from the windows and the rest of the room. I take the seat between Antoni and Riccio.

Although he weaved more than walked back to the boat, the black-haired Fae drags a glass of faerie wine toward him and chugs it down.

"Your manners are appalling, Riccio." Antoni hooks the stem of the next full glass and places it in front of me. "Ladies always come first."

"And he wonders why you get all the action and he so little." Mattia's innuendo isn't lost on me, but my mind is too full of metal birds and Dante for it to warm my cheeks.

Iron crows. Iron crows. Iron—

Something clicks. "You all fought in the Battle of Primanivi, correct?"

My question rids my tablemates of both breath and smile. They glance around at each other, lips bloodless, necks stiff, spines straight.

"I didn't." Giana is the first to twitch back to life, leaning over the table to splash wine into three more stemmed cups. "Women aren't allowed to become soldiers, remember? Our sex is too feeble."

Neither her sarcasm nor her social commentary is lost on me. The inequality between genders is as ridiculous as the inequality between races. However much I'd enjoy discussing both at length, I have a more pressing concern. "But you were around, right, Giana?"

Her eyes are as guarded as her voice. "Yes."

"In school, we learned that the tribesmen equipped their birds with iron talons and beaks to turn them into weapons."

No one speaks.

"Were any of their birds equipped with full iron suits?"

Antoni's brow furrows with the same frown that touches his mouth. "Suits?"

"Armor." I gesture to my torso. "Full body armor?"

"Armor for birds?" Mattia leans forearms covered in blond fur on the round wooden table. I swear, the man is part boar.

Riccio smirks. "Here I thought all you'd consumed in Rax was Antoni's spit."

My cheeks prickle.

"Leave her alone, Riccio. And no." Antoni tips his head from side to side, eliciting a series of little pops and cracks as though his body were full of tension. "Only their beaks and talons were made of iron."

Could Bronwen have referred to them as iron crows because of their metal appendages, or am I supposed to find statues fashioned after lethal birds? "Did any of them survive?"

"The ones who lived flocked to Shabbe," Riccio says.

I startle. "Shabbe?"

"You know…that tiny isle in the south our dear and equitable king would do just about anything to conquer?"

I take it Riccio really doesn't like Marco.

"I know all about the queendom."

Riccio hooks an arm on the back of his chair and pivots to face me. "Do you really?"

"Yes. I really do. I know they're savages who detest the Fae and use humans as slaves, which incited King Costa to erect wards around their island to keep them out of Luce." Those wards had marked the triumphant end of the Magnabellum, the Great War between Luce and Shabbe waged five centuries ago. "I know they practice blood magic, which tints their eyes pink. I also know that only the women have powers." I dip my fingertip into my wine and glide it over the rim. "I admit I didn't know the crows had flocked to their shores." A soft hum lifts from the glass and winds itself through the ominous silence. "I understand that staying in Luce wasn't an option, but why not migrate east to Nebba? I hear they have incredible forests and mountains."

"The crows went to Shabbe because the Shabbins venerate animals." Giana's gray eyes gleam silver in the light of the oil lamp.

My finger freezes midcircle. Her revelation doesn't abruptly make me feel a kinship to them, but it does make me question their barbarity.

Riccio's chair creaks as he reclines into it. He twirls his glass of wine, making the bubbles lacing the sweet liquor fizz. "Why such interest in crows?"

I pull my fingertip away from the rim of my glass and dry it on my lap. "Because it was my first time in Rax, and since some humans aided the mountain tribe that attacked us"—I keep my eyes on his to cement my lie—"it got me thinking about Primanivi."

Riccio nods slowly. "All the ones who aided the tribesmen, Fallon...they went down with the tribesmen. *Literally*."

"Meaning?"

Mattia taps his knuckles against the scratched tabletop. "After Primanivi, Marco trapped the dissenters on a galleon, which he sank off the southern coast of Luce in the graveyard of boats."

My heart clocks each bone in my corset. "The graveyard of boats?"

Riccio watches Giana refill his glass, yet he seems kilometers away, adrift on Mareluce. "Seas and currents are so wild, they'll shatter any ship that wanders through those waters."

"Marco fed them to the serpents?" I gasp in horror.

"Why so surprised?" He snaps out of his daze. "The Regios have always disposed of their enemies in that way."

There are no windows in this part of the tavern, yet Mattia glances toward the wall that gives onto the wharf. I think he's worried someone may be eavesdropping until he says, "I wonder if serpents would drag you into their den, Fallon."

Giana hisses. "Don't say such things, Mattia. Don't even think them." She swipes her thumb through a puddle of spilled wine, then stamps his lips with the ruby droplet, a Fae tradition to prevent spoken words from occurring.

"I know everyone thinks I can charm beasts, but it's not true." As always, I perpetuate Nonna's lie. "That day in the canal, the serpent attacked me."

He gestures to where I sit. "Yet you still breathe."

"Because it was a juvenile. That's the only reason I still breathe."

Antoni reaches under the table and clasps my bouncing knee. "No more talking of serpents, crows, or wars, all right?"

"Aye, aye." Mattia raises his glass.

Antoni's hand remains on my leg, and although it doesn't calm me, it seems to calm him, so I let his palm linger.

As the cousins alternate between debates on fishing spots and women, Giana disappears into the kitchen to fetch some food.

Although I try to pay attention, my mind keeps returning to Bronwen's prophecy. Why *five* crows? Could five of them have been trapped in Luce?

It's been over two decades, though. How long do crows live? Cauldron, I hope I'm not looking for corpses.

I long for pen and paper to jot down everything I learned, but a written trace is surely a terrible idea. So I run everything on a loop inside my mind instead. Sometime during the twelfth loop, I'm struck with a thought.

The crows that lived flocked to Shabbe.

The Shabbins like animals.

My knee bangs against the underside of the table. What if these relics have a link to Shabbe? What if Bronwen is Shabbin?

Antoni leans over and murmurs in my ear. "Am I moving too fast?"

I turn toward him, glad he assumes my judder has to do with him stroking my thigh.

Glad he's not trying to read my thoughts.

Glad he can't.

I paste on a timid smile. "A little."

He kisses the corner of my mouth and returns his hand to my knee where it stays until Marcello and Defne return from Isolacuori with stars in their eyes.

Their effusive description of the revel flushes away my buzz.

Sobered, I stand and whisper good nights.

Antoni rises in turn and insists on walking me home. Since it's still dark out, I don't put up much of a fight. In truth, I'm happy for the company. Antoni may not be Dante, but I trust him.

As we amble along the canal, I ask something that's been niggling at my mind for the past hour. "I know the wards around Shabbe keep the Shabbins from trespassing into our waters, but what if a Shabbin were already here?"

My question pins his boots to the cobbles and makes his fingers stiffen against the small of my back. "The wards would've dragged them out. The magic used magnetizes their blood and forcibly pulls their bodies back to their island."

There goes my theory about Bronwen being Shabbin.

As we start up again, I say, "Marco should've sent Dante to Shabbe instead of Glace."

Antoni grunts. "If he'd wanted his brother dead."

I suck in a breath. "Why would you say that?"

"Because Costa killed the queen's daughter and used her blood to create the magical barrier between their island and the rest of the world."

My jaw has grown so slack that my chin will no doubt touch my collarbone soon.

"The Shabbins loathe the Regios as deeply as the Regios loathe the Shabbins."

Then the Shabbins won't help Dante win the throne.

I'm back to square one. The only silver lining is that I'm armed with more information than I was the last time I stood on the first puzzle piece. Not that any of it is helping me make more sense of how five birds will lead Dante to the throne.

Antoni squeezes my waist. "One day soon, there'll be peace."

I frown because I hadn't realized we were at war.

11

Antoni has been the perfect gentleman all evening, so why do I feel like I'm cheating on the prince with this handsome fisherman? Because Bronwen planted the seed in my head that Dante and I are destined to marry?

The stars are so bright tonight that the flowering vines climbing up the sides of my blue house resemble the tinsel that's draped over Luce at first snow and left up until first bloom. Yuletide is one of the seasons I love the most, and not because I was born on the shortest day of the year but because a festive spirit envelops all the Lucins, and everything shines, even the murkiest canal.

When we reach my front door, Antoni, whose hand has been on the small of my back since the tavern, glides it up my spine. He grips my nape gently and tips my face back. For the hundredth time, I push Dante out of my thoughts, because Dante isn't the one who made tonight special.

I breathe in and out slowly, waiting for Antoni's mouth to descend upon mine, but he doesn't kiss me, simply keeps staring with an intensity that heats my flesh.

I try to read his expression, but he's so intent, so very serious, I cannot fathom what's going on inside his mind. In the end, I cave and murmur, "What is it?"

"I'm still trying to come to terms with the fact that Fallon Rossi's lips were on mine tonight, and not in a dream but in reality."

My heartbeats hasten. "You dream about me, Antoni?"

"Every night since I spilled a pallet of fish over you."

Ah, our meet-cute was light on the cute and heavy on the pungency. I'd barely stepped past Bottom of the Jug's threshold when Sybille had wrinkled her nose and pointed to her apartment at the very top of the tavern, requesting I visit her bathing room and closet.

"That was three years ago. Surely I don't plague *all* your nights."

"You don't plague them. You enchant them."

He must be exaggerating, since he and Sybille slept together last year. Not to mention all the other women I've spotted him with. He can't possibly be thinking of me while lying next to them. Even in slumber.

"No need for winsome lies, Antoni. You've already captured my attention."

His crooked smile falters. "They're not lies."

It's because I've refused him. Challenges spur obsession. I'm well placed to know this. Except now, according to a crazy lady in Rax, I *can* have Dante.

I mentally pull apart the letters in the prince's name and toss them to the warm summer breeze, then latch on to the collar of Antoni's shirt and tug him close. He backs me into my front door, pressing all the hard bulges of his body into all the soft valleys of mine.

"Gods, the things I want to do to you, Fallon Rossi." He knuckles the slope of my neck to the ridge of my collarbone, then glides his loosely balled fist back up the length of my throat and the underside of my chin, tipping my head to align our lips.

My blood steams at his words. I want to know what things.

I want to experience *the things*, but I cannot possibly bring him upstairs, not with both my mother and grandmother at home. Our walls are too thin and Antoni too large to pass undetected.

I may be twenty-two, yet bringing a boy home still seems terribly illicit. I wonder if I'll ever feel differently. Perhaps once my age is in the triple digits…

He presses his palm into the wood beside my head and rests his forehead against mine. A hard shuddering breath later, our lips connect, and oh, the sounds he coaxes from my throat with that skilled tongue of his. His hips grind against me in a slow, sultry dance that makes warmth converge behind my ribs and between my thighs.

Tonight feels surreal. A delicate dream that will evaporate like morning dew at first light.

Antoni's teeth scrape against my lower lip, teasing the flushed skin, nibbling it, as though to remind me that he's real. That this is really happening. That *we* are really happening.

After another lustful minute, I skate my mouth off his. "Antoni, we have to—"

The door at my back gives way, and we're falling. By some miracle, that miracle being Antoni's palm, we don't crash onto the honeycomb tiles.

"Buonsera, Signora Rossi." Red creeps up Antoni's throat and bathes his jaw.

Nonna narrows her green eyes on his face and then on the arm wrapped around my waist, which he retracts like a child caught stealing sweets from a jar. "Good evening, Signor Greco."

He scrapes one palm down his face as though to mitigate his blush.

"Antoni was just walking me home, Nonna." Perhaps because it's my grandmother, or perhaps because Antoni's skin is as blotchy as Mattia's, I cannot help but smile. "No need to give him the third degree."

"Walking you home, you say?" Her gaze doesn't soften on poor Antoni. "Were you two having trouble locating the doorknob?"

My smile intensifies. "We hadn't gotten to looking for it."

She sends Antoni a glower as strong as the tea she brews morning and night.

I'm no longer smiling. "Stop it, Nonna. Antoni did nothing wrong."

My grandmother's attention finally shifts off the poor man and onto me. "Where were you all night, Fallon?" Her irises are as dark as the forest on the mainland, and the skin beneath her lash line is a darker lavender than usual.

I turn to Antoni and whisper a quick, "Go."

He doesn't. Not immediately anyway. But he must realize leaving is the best option—the only one—because he finally spins on his mucked boots.

He lingers by the door. "Thank you for tonight." He's no longer blushing. If anything, he appears exceedingly sober and exceedingly worried about letting me deal with my grandmother on my own.

"I'll see you tomorrow."

Another heartbeat of resounding silence.

Two.

And then the door settles with a muted clack into its frame.

"Where were you?" Nonna pulls her shawl tighter around her shoulders to ward off the chill that curls off the canal at night.

"I was with Antoni."

"Where?"

"I'm not thirteen anymore, Nonna."

"Where?"

"The tavern."

Her eyes drop to my skirt. "I wasn't aware the tavern was so muddy."

My lungs tighten as I attempt to come up with a lie she'll

believe. "Antoni took me on his boat, and fishing boats aren't particularly clean."

"I didn't know he fished for mud."

I bristle. My grandmother has always been protective of me, but this is taking it too far. "I wasn't in Isolacuori, if that's what you're worried about."

"They don't have mud in Isolacuori, so no, that wasn't what I was worried about. The only place there's mud around these parts is in Rax."

The silence that echoes between us is so loud it presses against my eardrums.

"Tell me you didn't go there."

I could keep lying, since no amount of salt on my wicked tongue would betray my deceit, but I choose not to. "I did. I went *there*. And it was eye-opening. You know what else I did tonight? I kissed Antoni. And since you want to know all about my business, after we returned from the mortal lands, I went to the tavern for a drink with Giana and Antoni's crew before he walked me home and kissed me again."

Nonna's mouth twists as I spill my evening beat by beat.

"There. You're up to date on all things Fallon-related. Now, can I go to bed, or do you require more details?" My heart is battering my ribs, and although part of me is aware I'm being disrespectful, another part reminds me I'm allowed some privacy.

"Have you slept with him?" Although my grandmother has very few wrinkles, her forehead is so puckered she suddenly looks all three hundred and forty-seven years of her age.

"Not that that's any of your business, Nonna, but no."

"That man has a reputation."

Up till that moment, I only teetered on the edge of insolence. Now, I dive right in. "And so do Rossi women. I guess Antoni and I are perfect for each other. Especially since he's no prince. At least now I'm not overreaching, right?"

I watch each word settle on my grandmother's face before stomping up the stairs and slamming my door shut, not caring if my outburst has hurt her or woken my mother.

If only I had the means to move out so I could live my life the way I please and not the way that pleases everyone else.

I think of Antoni and his suggestion to marry and then of Bronwen and her prophecy. Although both options would allow me to escape my grandmother's yoke, both would also keep me chained.

I hate how limited our choices are as women. Maybe I should brave the southern seas and escape to the Queendom of Shabbe.

I envision myself carving through the wards and docking on the island of pink sand.

Until I recall the reason for the color...

According to the sailors who frequent Bottom of the Jug, it's a ruinous land where the white beaches have turned pink from centuries of spilled faerie and human blood, where people live in dirt huts and men are castrated for the measliest of offenses.

The image turns my stomach and nulls my desire to escape. Luce may be far from perfect, but it's my home.

Filled with *my* people. My friends. My serpent.

And maybe, just maybe, my throne.

12

The drapery pins of my curtain jangle, jolting me out of my fitful sleep. My first thought is that it's Nonna, come to discuss our quarreling, but I get an eyeful of pink frills, gold sequins, and ebony skin.

"You better have a *really* good reason for ditching Phoebus and me last night."

"Go away, Syb," I mumble as shards of sunlight slash my clamped lids. "Too early."

"Not happening."

"Why do you never listen to me?"

"I listened to you last night—about meeting on the gondola—and guess what? You. Weren't. On it."

Groaning, I open my eyes. "I'm aware."

Bright light outlines Sybille's crossed arms, pouty mouth, and puffy dress.

"Did you just get back?"

"No, I spruced up my nightgown collection," she deadpans. "Why in the three kingdoms didn't you come?"

My brain, like my lids, prickles. "Because I wasn't invited, that's why."

"What do you mean, you weren't invited? Of course you were invited."

I fluff up my two reedy pillows and prop myself higher, wondering if she swallowed a trumpet before leaving the castle, because her voice is especially shrill. "Must you shout?"

"I'm not shouting," she yells.

I knead my temples. "I must've drunk too much ale."

"You went out *drinking*? Where? But wait, we're veering off topic." Staying up all night has always made Sybille extra energetic. Until she lays her head on a pillow. Then she drops into slumber like a stone. "You were definitely invited, Fal. I asked Dante, and he said he had a ribbon sprite-delivered to your house."

"Well, his sprite must've had the wrong address."

She shoots me a droll look. "*Everyone* knows where the Rossi household is, and since disrespecting a royal order costs sprites their wings, that ribbon was delivered."

"I looked." My heart is wide awake now. "I looked everywhere, Syb. Don't you think I wanted to go?"

Sybille is finally quiet, but I can tell her head is full of thoughts, and from the direction of her gaze, all of them are about the women sharing this roof. Or rather *one* woman, since the other has a limited grasp on reality.

"Why would she sabotage your evening?" Sybille's voice thumps no louder than my pulse.

"To protect me."

"From what?"

From yearning for a man so far above my station.

I substitute another truth, one that will paint Nonna as a caring grandmother instead of a meddling one. "You know how she feels about the general of the king's army."

"What does your grandfather have to do with you attending a revel?"

I was angry with Nonna last night, but now, I'm hurt. Not

84

so much because she ruined my chances of attending a ball but because she made me feel like a societal reject. And still, I defend her because even though her method was awry, her intent wasn't malicious. Besides, that *I* hold her in contempt is one thing; that anyone else does…that's not something I tolerate.

I rub the sleep from my eyes, even though it feels like I'm scouring my puffed lids with salt. "Nonna worries he may say or do something cruel to me."

"Has he ever?"

I frown. "No. At least not to my face." Although I have no doubt he knows what I look like, since I know how he looks, I've never actually met my grandfather face-to-face.

Sybille's query makes me wonder if Nonna's lies extend to my grandfather's character. What if he isn't as unpleasant as she's made him out to be? What if he doesn't hate me? What if the only reason he's never visited is because she keeps him away?

I squash all those questions beneath a single hard fact: if he had any love for me, he'd have sought me out. After all, what sort of general leads an army into battle but fears entering his former spouse's home?

I loose another sigh and push myself up to sitting. "Tell me how it was?"

Sybille strides over to my small bed and sinks onto the rumpled sheets. "Magical. Regal." Her wide gray stare glitters as though some of the sequins adorning the peaks of her high cheekbones had caught onto her lashes. A second later, she changes her tune. "Horrid. Absolutely horrid."

I flick her because I know she's lying to make me feel better. That's what friends do. "I'm not jealous. I had a pretty enjoyable night myself."

"Drinking ale?"

"Drinking ale."

"Not alone, right?"

"Not alone. Don't you remember the salt oath we made? Not to drink alone until we're at least two hundred and rumpled from forehead to toe?"

She rolls her eyes. "We were nine."

"Still, I swear I wasn't alone. Gia was with me."

"And? I mean, I love my sister, but she's rather staid."

"Gia's not staid."

Sybille cocks an eyebrow. "Um, all my sister does is work, work, work. What she *doesn't* do is social anythings, especially if it involves drinking."

"Well, she was with me, and we drank."

"Ale? You really drank ale?" Sybille wrinkles her nose because it's the cheapest type of liquor that exists in Luce and therefore frowned on by anyone with an ounce of Fae blood.

"Ale is hardly the worst thing I've put in my mouth. Remember those squishy mollusks Phoebus dared us to eat?"

She gags. "Oh gods, don't remind me. Why did we go along with his dare again?"

"So he'd stop mooning over Plimeo and ask him out."

"Oh right. You and I…always so selfless."

I laugh, still remembering the crimson stains on fifteen-year-old Phoebus's cheeks as he walked toward the object of his obsession and asked if he wanted to stargaze on his parents' obscenely spacious rooftop.

"Who else was at this ale fest besides my sister?"

My expression turns cautious. Although I know Sybille is not in love with Antoni, never has been, guilt worms itself through my thin nightshirt and penetrates my breastbone. "Antoni, Mattia, and Riccio."

Her lashes sweep high. "Aha. Now we're getting places." She tips her head to the side and squints at me as though trying to solve a puzzle. "I'm going to go with Mattia."

"You're going to go with Mattia *what*?"

"My guess as to who put that flush in your cheeks and that hickey on your neck."

I palm the patch of skin she's directing an eloquent smile at. "Not Mattia."

The corners of her mouth waver. "Riccio?"

My headshake wilts her smile.

"I'm hoping it's Giana."

"Why?"

"Because Antoni is a total playfae."

"*You* slept with him."

"My point exactly. Half of Luce has slept with him, and that's only because the other half are males, and Antoni doesn't swing that way." After a pause, she adds, "To Phoebus's massive regret."

"I still don't see why my liking him is wrong. Unless you're jealous? In which case, I'll back off."

"Honey, I'm totally not jealous." She pats my leg. "Hand over some salt so I can prove it."

"I believe you." I bend my knees and gather my legs into my chest, rankled that, like Nonna, my best friend isn't being supportive. "I'm aware Antoni has a reputation, but I still don't see what's wrong with me taking advantage of his skills."

Sybille sighs. "Because you, my dearest Fallon, get attached, and I know he's offered you marriage, but he'll never deliver on his promise."

"I don't want to marry him."

"Are you telling me you'd be fine with becoming one more notch on that man's bedpost?"

"Yes," I growl, annoyed. And tired. But mostly annoyed.

After a beat of silence, she breathes out, "Okay."

"Okay what?"

"Okay, I'll support your decision."

"You're my best friend. You're obliged to support all my decisions, even the dreadful ones."

Sybille flops onto her back, arches her spine, and stretches her arms over her head. "Yes, yes."

I finally toss my legs off the side of the bed and get up. "Now regale me with every last detail of the revel."

Sybille leaves nothing out, and by the end of her account, I feel as though I attended the great ball, sandwiched between her and Phoebus and thousands of other glamorous Fae.

Keeping my gaze on the mirror over my dresser, I ask, "You didn't happen to see any bird statues around the palace, did you?"

"Bird statues?"

Although my wavy hair is already soft and glossy, I keep running my boar-bristled brush through it. "Someone mentioned a pretty statue, and since you know how much I love animals…"

"Didn't see any. Then again, we were corralled in the garden piazza, and there were literally hundreds of Fae by square centimeter and just as many sprites, so it was crowded. I could've missed it."

Sybille rarely misses anything. At least not before her third glass of faerie wine. What her answer reveals is that the crow statue I'm looking for isn't displayed in the gardens, which leaves…oh, the entire castle.

I think of the people who might know.

My grandmother?

Can't exactly ask her.

Cato?

My curiosity would get back to someone at court, be it my grandfather, the sovereign, or worse, Nonna.

I lower my brush, my mind latching on to someone who's been inside the king's private quarters. "Catriona…"

"You heard? So tacky."

"Heard what?"

"That she was all over Marco." She wrinkles her nose.

I frown, because Sybille's never judged the courtesan before. "That's her job."

Sybille flops onto her stomach and hoists herself up on her forearms. "Yes, but it was his betrothal ceremony. His poor bride-to-be was so crestfallen, I sort of wanted to hug her, and you know how much I abhor hugging strangers."

"I didn't mean last night, but agreed, that's rather tasteless." I suppose Marco's intended needs to get used to it. In passing, I wonder if Dante would ever cheat on his betrothed, but that sours my stomach, so I push the contemplation away.

"I have to give it to Eponine. She stayed stoic the entire time." Sybille sighs, gaze riveted to the cloudless blue sky. "To think women dream of marrying kings. What a miserable life that would be."

"Not if it's a marriage of love."

She side-eyes me. "Since when do monarchs marry for love?"

They don't, but that'll change.

Maybe.

I square my shoulders.

No maybes. It *will* change when I become Dante's queen.

She rolls her eyes. "You read too many books."

"And you read too few."

A hummingbird zips in front of my window to quench its thirst on our wisteria, wings pumping so fast its body appears suspended. It reminds me of my life-changing iron crows.

"I *live*. You dream."

Because dreams are safe, and life...well, life isn't. And it's about to become a whole lot less safe if I have to gather relics that have the power to dethrone a king.

"Syb, if someone gave you a key to open a door you've always fantasized about opening, would you open it?"

A small vertical groove appears between her thin black eyebrows. "I'd knock first."

"It's a hypothetical door."

"Then I'd hypothetically knock."

I'm uncertain how to apply her advice.

Find out more about the iron crows?

The only way to access the Great Library on Tarecuori is by pricking your finger on the spindle at the entrance and pressing your finger into a ledger to leave a record of your passage.

I may be angry with Nonna but not to the point of breaking my promise to her about leaving traces of my strange blood.

13

I'm drying glasses when Catriona waltzes into Bottom of the Jug, garbed in a new ocean-hued dress with cap sleeves that drape off her shoulders. When she notices me gaping, she does a slow twirl.

"Courtesy of His Majesty. Along with these beauties." She pushes her blond hair to the side to reveal ear cuffs pavéd in sapphires. Her new jewels taper to a point over the rounded shell of her ear, giving the illusion of peaks.

I don't ask what she did to deserve such gifts, since I already know, but she tells me anyway, without leaving out a single detail. A fly on Marco's wall wouldn't be as well-informed about the king's anatomy and kinks.

Speaking of walls... "I've always wondered, what does a monarch's bedroom look like?"

Her eyes sparkle as vividly as her earrings. "Oh, it's a thing of beauty. His ceiling has a glass dome that gives onto the sky, and his walls are covered in mirrored tiles, which makes you feel suspended in the sky. And his bathing room. Gods, I'm in love with his bathing room. He has running water that comes out of pipes."

I almost make a quip about Catriona being familiar with all

Marco's pipes but decide to stay the course. "Does he possess art? Or statues?"

"A map of the kingdom. The amount of land he rules is impressive. Did you know that Tarespagia is four times the size of Tarelexo and Tarecuori put together?"

"I didn't. But now I do. Anything else?" I've been wiping down the same glass since she burst in, but Catriona's too deep in her reverie to notice.

"Not that I remember."

So the crow isn't in the king's private chambers. One more area to check off my treasure map.

She blinks out of her trance. "Why didn't you come?"

"I misplaced my ribbon."

"You—" A gurgle of laughter drifts from her mouth. When she realizes I'm not laughing, she sobers. "I'm sorry. Truly a shame."

I grind my teeth, my anger at Nonna swelling anew. She wasn't home when I left with Sybille, but I have every intention of confronting her about it after my shift.

Catriona fingers the spiky tips of her earrings. "So you stayed home alone?"

"No. I went out with friends who didn't receive invitations."

"How positively compassionate of you." She yawns, revealing what she thinks of my compassion.

Unless she's tired.

I prefer to think she's tired.

I keep my gaze on the glass I'm drying. "Did you see Dante last night?"

"I did. He was on his best behavior. Then again, the princess of Glace was in attendance."

I jerk my gaze to her face. "What does the Glacin princess have to do with his behavior?"

"He's courting her, silly. She's quite frigid. And pale. Ghoulishly so. You'd think the sun doesn't shine in the north."

Before I can peel my jaw off the countertop, the door of the tavern swings open, and Antoni strides in, balancing a pallet stacked high with fish and ice. The second his eyes alight on me, a smile commandeers his mouth, and he swaggers over with his fish.

"Fallon. Catriona." He says both our names but only looks at me.

He circles the bar and walks into the kitchen to deliver his loot to Sybille's mother, who was elbow deep in onions and garlic last time I was in there.

Catriona watches the swing door that has yet to settle. "Your flame is burning hot, micara."

"What?"

"Antoni almost walked into the wall instead of the door. Marco asked me tons of questions about you. And Silv—" Her eyes open wide. "Your maidenhead's intact, correct?"

Heat swarms me even though I'm still stuck on the king inquiring about me. He's never even met me.

"How would you like to earn a gold piece?"

My heart kicks at the boning in my corset. A gold coin would cover my rent on an apartment for at least a year.

"Make that three if a king is in the mix," Catriona muses aloud.

I set down the glass but don't pick up another. "How?"

"By doing what I did eighty-two years ago."

My pulse sprints because I think I know what she's getting at. "What did you do?"

"I auctioned off my maidenhead."

"You—" I wrinkle my nose and shake my head. "No. I could never."

Antoni steps out of the kitchen, filling the air with the brine of pearlescent scales and the pungency of chopped bulbs. He sidles up to me, and I think he's about to grip my waist, but his destination is the sink.

He dips his hand in the basin full of sudsy water, then takes the bar of soap and rubs it between his palms. "What are you up to, Craftiona?"

Her index and middle fingers shoot up, wedged tight, a vulgar gesture popular amongst halflings and humans. "None of your business, Antoni."

"If it has to do with Fallon, I will make it my business."

My spine stiffens, because a kiss doesn't make me his business.

He eases the kitchen rag from my white-knuckled grip to dry his hands. "I'm serious, Catriona. Don't corrupt her."

She snorts. "That's fresh coming from someone who's slept with more people than I have yet whose business is...*fishing*." She plucks a rosemary-roasted walnut from the bowl I've just replenished and pops it into her mouth. After thoroughly chewing it, she adds, "And not for bedmates."

Antoni and Catriona glower at each other, and I briefly wonder if they ever slept together but stop because I prefer not knowing.

The cacophony from the wharf leaks into the tavern and slices through the wall of tension that's gone up in lieu of the wooden bar.

"There you are!" Phoebus pushes a hand through his blond locks, eyebrows slung low over his glittery emerald gaze.

Best timing ever. "Here I am."

He sets a forearm on the bar and grabs a handful of walnuts. "Syb and I spent all night searching for..." His voice puffs away as Antoni spears his fingers through mine.

I don't close my hand around his but I also don't pull away.

"We'll pick up where we left off when the tavern isn't as crowded." Catriona swipes another walnut, then twirls in a whoosh of cobalt silk and climbs the wooden stairs I mopped earlier because one of Flora's children is ill—*again*—and Sybille turned in for a nap. To be honest, I didn't hate the mindless task.

Antoni tucks a lock of hair behind my ear. "What time do you get off?"

"I'm not sure."

Phoebus tosses nuts into his mouth, observing our interaction with fascination.

"No matter. I told Mattia and Riccio to meet me here after we're done with our deliveries."

I detach my gaze from my simpering friend and rest it on Antoni, who takes it as an invitation to lean over and kiss me. His mouth tastes of salt and sun and sinful promises. I'm so nervous, my lips stay stiff, and so does my body. Even my heart feels as stiff as my bones.

I press my palms into his chest, promptly unfastening my mouth from his. "Not here."

"Sorry." He sketches the shape of my angular jaw with his callused thumb before backing up. "I'll catch you later, Signorina Rossi."

Phoebus turns in time with Antoni and watches the male leave, a grin tickling the edge of his mouth. "And the mystery of why Fallon abandoned us is solved. Spill. E-v-e-r-y-t-h-i-n-g." He manages to decompose the word into more syllables than it contains.

"That's not why I didn't come." Heat prods my face. "He's not why."

"Uh-huh."

"I swear. I thought I didn't get a ribbon, so I wandered."

"Into Antoni's bed?"

I grab a walnut and toss it at his smirking face. "Shut up."

Once he's done chuckling at my expense, he says, very seriously this time, "Why would you think you didn't get a ribbon? You're one of Dante's favorite people."

I shrug. "Rossi reputation and all that."

"Let me tell you, Dante was *very* distraught." Phoebus glances over his shoulder at the windows giving onto the wharf, his features uncharacteristically tense. "And will surely be even more so once he learns how you spent your night." The points of his ears stick out through his sleek shoulder-length bob. "I'm all for cock-fights, but I'm not sure how I feel about the one you're stirring up, Piccolina."

I roll my eyes at his favorite endearment. "Have you again forgotten we're the same age, Pheebs?"

"I call you that because you're tiny."

"I'm not tiny. You're just freakishly tall."

We smile at each other for a moment, but then what he said settles back over us like the clouds forever swamping our mountains. "There's no reason for them to fight over me."

"Isn't there?"

"Antoni and I...it's not serious. All we did was kiss. And Dante... Well, I heard he has his sights set on a princess."

Phoebus snorts. "For duty's sake. Trust me. There was zero attraction between the two of them. Not like there is between the two of you." He chews down another mouthful. "I should ask you for pointers, since I've yet to snag a man's heart with my kisses."

"Perhaps because you kiss them below the belt, and hearts are higher up."

Phoebus grins. "Did my favorite maiden just make a dirty joke?"

"Can you all stop mentioning my maiden-ness?"

"That's not a word. And who's *all*?"

"Catriona suggested I auction it off."

He hovers a walnut in front of his pretty face, mouth agape.

"She says I could get a couple gold coins for it." I slide my lower lip between my teeth as I picture how much easier life would be with that much money.

"No."

"No what? I'm not worth that much?"

"You're worth so much more, but that's beside the point. You'd regret it." After a beat, he adds, "If you need money, my purse is your purse."

"Your parents cut you off."

"But they didn't change the locks to their doors or to their safe. You should see all the gold they stockpile inside. And not just in the form of coin."

"Pheebs, I could never take your parents' money." I reach over and squeeze his hand. "But thank you."

I steer the conversation off my virginity and finances and onto his current flame, a Tarecuorin Fae by the name of Mercutio who isn't well-endowed but makes up for it with a mouth and fingers Phoebus describes as godly. Between him, Sybille, and Catriona and their love for oversharing, when the time comes, I feel confident I'll know exactly what goes where.

"What is given isn't considered taken," Phoebus tosses out before leaving the tavern. "Just saying."

It takes my mind a moment to understand that he isn't speaking of sexual acts.

I hate to admit that I'm tempted to borrow money from him, but thankfully, he leaves before I can give in to the temptation.

But gods, it lopes around my mind without pause, growing louder than the din of the tavern. Growing so loud that I volunteer to head to the cellar, a place I usually try to avoid, not a fan of dank, cramped spaces.

I press my palms against my temples to stifle Phoebus's offer. Once I feel like I've stomped out my weakness, I grab the wine cask.

"Are you hiding from me, Signorina Rossi?"

My heart jerks in time with my body, and the wine cask slips from my hands and hits the floor with a worrying thump. By some miracle, the cork stays put and the thick glass intact. I cannot say as much about my newfangled calm.

I crouch to retrieve the cask. "Why would I hide from one of my closest and oldest friends?"

14

Your *friend*? Is that all I am to you?" Dante stands in the entrance of the tavern's underground wine cellar, arms crossed in front of his white military uniform, gilt collar loosened, and long braids draped over one shoulder. The gold beads speared throughout the dark mass refract the glow emanating from the single oil lamp.

He drinks me in with those liquid blue eyes that have enchanted me since the day a group of Tarecuorin girls jostled me in our classroom, sending me sprawling onto my knees. Not only did he help me gather my books, he also offered me his hand and protection that day. No one ever shoved me again, which wasn't to say I wasn't bullied in other ways.

"I waited for you all night on my lonely, diminutive throne."

"With a princess at your side. I'd hardly call you lonely."

"Alyona is just a friend. Marco desires an alliance with the north, and since Eponine is from Nebba and he can only marry one woman, he wants me to court the other. That is all."

As I pick up the cask, I say, "What about what you want?"

"I'm the prince, Fal. My desires come second to my responsibilities."

Except I don't want to come second to another woman.

"But nothing happened between us last night."

My thundering heart shakes the wine inside the cask. "What about before last night?"

"I was gone four years." His Adam's apple slides up and down his throat, and then he's pushing off the doorframe and heaving the cask out of my arms. Where I needed all ten of my fingers, he hooks the recipient with two. "Which you cannot hold against me. Especially considering you work in a brothel."

"It's a tavern, Dante."

"It's also a brothel." He sighs. "You've had your adventures; I've had mine. Let's leave the past in the past."

I focus on the stubble darkening his jaw so he doesn't spot the hurt in my eyes. I can count my adventures on the fingers of one hand—on one finger—whereas he surely needs more than his two hands.

"Look, I didn't come down here to fight. I came down here because I missed you last night and I was worried something had happened. Why didn't you come?"

"I misplaced the ribbon."

If he believes I'm lying, he doesn't call me on it. "Did you at least like the gown?"

My attention climbs to his. "You—" I lick my lips to sweep away the astonishment that was about to trip out. I'm about to lie again, because what choice do I have? If I admit I didn't receive his gift, I'll either get Nonna in trouble or his winged messenger.

"You didn't get it?"

"No, I…I did. It's gorgeous."

"Violet, like your eyes."

"The exact shade. It's as though you know their hue by heart."

"I do know their hue by heart, but the dress wasn't purple; it was gold. How about you start telling me the truth without me needing to invoke a salt oath?"

I wrinkle my nose, feeling a lot like a spider caught in a web of her own making. "I never received either."

"Why did you lie?"

"Because I think my grandmother may have hidden both from me."

Bronwen's words clang against the walls of my skull: *You're here because it was time.*

Could *she* have done away with my dress and ribbon? I hadn't even contemplated this possibility. Rage blisters my chest. If the blind woman's behind this, then damn her and her stupid treasure hunt. She can go hunt down her own damn crows.

But then the reminder that these birds are my ticket to becoming Dante's queen stifles my resentment. Perhaps she isn't working against me. If only she'd picked a better evening to intercede in my life.

Dante observes the play of emotion that ripples across my face. "Any chance I could participate in that conversation you're having with yourself?"

"I was contemplating the possibility that my grandmother is for naught in this whole story."

His mouth twists. "I will have my sprite's wings cleaved if he forgot—"

"Please. No. No punishing anyone. It's in the past." I lay my hand on his shoulder, which is corded with so much muscle it feels like wisteria vines. "Besides, it was only one night. Now that you're home, we can have another. Many even."

My promise softens his mood but abrades my own. Prophecy or not, if Dante learns I was out kissing another man last night, he'll regret having sent me a dress. It's on the tip of my tongue to confess, but before I manage to push the dreaded words out, the hand not holding the cask sets on my spine, and Dante's mouth lands on mine.

The musty cellar fades, and I'm tossed four years in the past, in the shadows of Tarelexo where this same man, only a boy at the time, put his mouth where no other had ever rested.

This kiss feels familiar and different, like a first and yet a second. It pins my heart to my breast and funnels its beats into my nipples. The pink beads of flesh are so stiff, I fear they'll poke right through the sturdy fabric of my dress and tear up Dante's silken uniform.

I raise my hands to his neck, palm the hot skin and the muscles twitching beneath. Dante's tongue pushes into my mouth, lashes against my own, demanding and harsh, commandeering every dark corner, as though the man is reminding me that he is my prince and everything in Luce is his to take, including my body.

"Oh. I—" Giana's voice hurls me back to the low-ceilinged, dank cellar.

Even though I'm hidden from her line of sight by Dante's breadth and height, I don't dare move. I thank all our gods for his size, even though it's probably his parents I should thank. But I don't much appreciate his mother, who believes round ears deserve no regard, so thanking our divinities feels more fitting.

"Apologies for interrupting, Altezza. I needed some wine."

My cheeks flame. Dante smiles, amused to have been discovered, or perhaps he smiles because he's proud to have caused my body to react so brightly. I'm still hoping Giana will assume Dante was kissing some other woman, but then he shifts sideways to extend the cask he took from me earlier, and I don't have time to dash behind the wooden shelving.

Giana's gray eyes land on mine, eddying with so much reproach that my insides squirm. I want to tell her I didn't initiate this rendezvous *or* the kiss, but she's already heading upstairs with the wine. I cover my face and hang my head.

"Hey." Dante slides his hand beneath my wrist to cup my cheek. "I know you're at work, but I'm the prince. You can't get in trouble for kissing a prince."

I'm so absorbed by my roiling guilt that I cannot get myself to open my eyes and look at him.

"If she gives you any grief"—he rests his thumb on the sharp bone in my cheek—"I'll sever her tongue."

That makes my lids fly up and air rush down my throat. "Dante," I hiss. "No." I shake my head, shaking his palm off at the same time.

"I won't tolerate anyone hurting you, Fal. With words or with actions."

"Giana would never hurt me."

"I saw the look she gave you."

"She's like a sister, Dante. A caring and concerned one."

He watches me through lowered lashes, his irises more spilled ink than midday sky. "Well, her concern is misplaced, because I would never do you harm."

"You're a prince. *The* prince. And I'm...I'm the girl from the wrong side of the canal with the curved ears. That's what she sees. That's what the world sees."

He dips his chin nearer his neck. "You're the girl I want to spend my nights with, Fallon."

A new rush of heartbeats batters my ribs and whisks away my guilt and nerves. What if Bronwen didn't *foresee* I'd marry him but is somehow compelling him to desire me? "You mentioned nights. What about my days? Don't you want to spend those with me?"

He moves into my space again and spears his long fingers through my hair. "I didn't mention daytime because it's filled with work."

"So not because your brother and my grandfather wouldn't approve?" *Or because of your princess?*

"I don't much care for their approval, Serpent-charmer." He brushes a lock of hair off my cheek, then kisses me once more. "I'm needed in the palace again tonight and for the week to come, but as soon as I'm discharged of my princely duties, I'm taking you out." He steps back. "And I want you to wear your new dress."

I wonder if Antoni is upstairs and, if he is, whether Gia has spoken to him.

"Fallon?"

I suppress my guilt under a bright smile, because I'm destined for a throne, not a fishing boat, and Dante is destined for me, not a foreign princess. "Just tell me where and when, and I'll be ready."

Dante's mouth curls. "I'll be counting down the hours until we meet again. The minutes. The seconds."

My heart pelts my chest as he backs up with a wink, leaving me feeling so very wicked. I replay all that happened and what's left to be done: have a dreaded conversation with Antoni. I decide to be blunt and honest. He can't possibly hold my feelings for Dante against me.

Besides, I never made him any promises.

As possible openings lope through my mind, I finally head back to the dining room.

It was time.

Bronwen's words clang yet again inside my head, heightening my already frenzied pulse.

If he takes me to the castle for our date, and I locate the bird statue…

The idea of someone steering my destiny is more frightening than comforting. Especially since forecasting the future isn't a Fae power, and humans are powerless.

What the underworld is Bronwen?

15

ad a nice evening last night, Beryl?" The lord whose plate I'm clearing palms Beryl's bouncy behind, guiding her toward his lap.

"Didn't everyone, Signore Aristide?" She's so accustomed to flirting that her bright smile looks genuine.

The man has a foul reputation, but he pays handsomely, so no one complains.

"You aren't going to follow in Catriona's footsteps and inflate your prices now that you've bagged a royal, will you?"

I stack the soiled ceramic dishes slowly. Before I can think better of revealing my eavesdropping, I blurt out, "You tended to King Marco also?"

Aristide tips his gaze to me. "This beauty slipped off with the prince."

The handful of cutlery I'm gathering clatters against the plate. Dante mentioned he was worried about me, but when exactly did he worry? While sleeping with Beryl or while entertaining his princess?

The lord smirks. "Methinks the serving girl is jealous, Beryl."

I picture stabbing him. With a fork. In the cheek.

She bops the tip of his long nose. "Leave her alone, Aristide."

As he buries his face in her cleavage, eliciting a titter from her dark pink lips, she glances at me and mouths, *Sorry*.

For what? Having slept with Dante or Aristide's bawdiness?

"Enjoying the show, Signorina Rossi?" The lord's voice is muffled by her oiled skin.

I shake myself out of my stupor and leave before he can smash my pride to more smithereens. Sullenness swallows me whole, and my eyes sting so hard that I keep them trained on the floor. So focused am I on harnessing back my tears that I almost plow into the customer entering the tavern.

Of course, it has to be Antoni.

He steadies me with such gentleness that I want to latch on to his hand and tug him out of the tavern. I want to shut out the world and lose myself in him. A fresh wave of guilt washes over me because using him in that way would make me no better than everyone else in this room.

Mattia and Riccio step in after Antoni and drop greetings I'm too tense to return. After a deep swallow, I point them toward three empty spots at the bar and wind my way back to the kitchen to drop my stack of dirty plates.

Instead of heading back out immediately, I stay in the kitchen. I need a minute.

Or ten.

I need to gather my emotions and sort through my thoughts.

Sybille's parents are working in tandem, plating dishes and stirring pots. They dance around each other in perfect synchronicity, two centuries of matrimonial life having made them perfectly attuned to each other.

The show is mesmerizing, and before I know it, the knots in my stomach have loosened.

Marcello cocks a thick eyebrow. "Everything all right out there, Fallon?" Although he can grow his hair to his shoulders, I've never seen him sporting it any other way than sheared close to his scalp. Unlike Defne, who is constantly toying with her hair's length and look.

"Great. Can I be of any help in here?"

Marcello and Defne exchange a look because I usually steer clear of the kitchen, not really liking the sight of feathers being plucked from pigeons or animal flesh being pounded. Just the smell of blood causes my insides to squirm.

"No need, sweetheart. We've got it all handled." Defne smiles at me, her teeth a blast of white against her brown skin that's several shades darker than her husband's.

I'm about to pick up a spatula and poke it into the cauldron simmering by the fire to show them how useful I can be when Giana bustles in with an empty casserole dish. She drops it into the basin of sudsy water and rolls up her sleeves, but I bump her away and stick my hands into the water before she can.

"I'll do the dishes," I all but exclaim.

Her lips press into a line, and a muscle feathers her slim jaw. She relents, but before leaving, she murmurs, "You can't hide in here all night."

"I'm not hiding."

"Fallon…"

My nape prickles from her parents' stares, our quiet exchange obviously not going unnoticed.

"When you're done *not hiding*, go on break. You haven't taken one since you arrived this afternoon."

"No need for breaks." My soles are screaming that there's a definitive need for one, but I don't think I could sit still if I tried, and if I went out on the pier for a breather, Antoni would join me, and I'm not sure about him or anything anymore.

Giana shakes her head before leaving the muggy wood and slate kitchen with a platter of soft cheese, grapes, and a steaming sourdough loaf.

I scrub until my skin prunes and my fingers ache and there's nothing left to scour because the fire beneath the stoves has been snuffed out.

"Want to talk about it?" Defne asks, taking a clean dishrag from a shelf to help me dry all the clean dishes I slotted onto the dripping tray.

I bite the inside of my cheek. "How did you know Marcello was the one?"

Her gray eyes comb over my profile, which is still angled toward the sink I'm draining into buckets that Marcello will carry outside and dump into the used-water trough of the island so that the fire-Fae on waste duty can purify it. "Our dreams aligned. And he made me laugh. Still does every chance he gets."

My teeth are still poking a hole inside my cheek.

"*And* he tells me I'm the most beautiful woman in the kingdom. Silly, I know, but his daily reminders make me feel special."

"It's not silly. It's admirable." Dante makes me feel beautiful. And he makes me smile. And our dreams definitely align, since he crossed the channel to merit the throne, and I've sort of agreed to collect iron relics to be at his side.

"More importantly, though, Fallonina, Marcello and I keep no secrets from each other."

I really need to learn to school my features so they stop parading all my thoughts.

"Now, get yourself home. I prepared a dish with some leftovers for your mother and Ceres. Send them both my love, and tell Ceres to come by some day. It's been *ages* since I've seen her."

"I will." Reluctantly, I fold my damp rag and set it on the wooden island, grab the lidded dish, and push my hip into the swing door.

The dining area is quieter but far from quiet, the diners having given way to the drinkers. Card games are being waged at the far end of the tavern, while a steady flow of patrons trundles up and down the stairs, hand in hand with their favorite doxies.

I finally look toward the bar for Antoni but find only Mattia and Riccio upending shots with a chattering Sybille. My stomach writhes with more nerves. Has he left the tavern or only the dining room? I stare at the ceiling. If he went upstairs with a girl, then at least it'd take the decision as to what to do away from me.

"He's on the dock, tossing stones into the canal." Giana breezes past me with a tray of empty drinks. "You're the first girl he's truly taken an interest in."

"Please don't, Gia. I already feel awful."

"I don't mean to make you feel worse, Fallon. I'm just sad for him."

Grimacing, I murmur, "I should never have kissed him."

"Which *him* are we speaking of?"

Frankly, I'm not quite certain.

Our muted discussion catches Sybille's eye, and she marches over. "What did I miss?"

"Nothing," I mutter.

Sybille rolls her eyes. "Clearly."

"Thanks for the invitation to stay the night, but I'm going to head home."

Sybille bats her curly black lashes at me. "*Home*, huh?"

Her innuendo tightens Giana's expression. She grabs a filled jug and heads off to deliver it.

"What's eating Gia?"

"You know how you and I feel about Phoebus? That's how she feels about Antoni."

Sybille frowns.

I nod to one of the thick wooden beams that hold the tavern as upright as structurally possible on an island eroded by strong tides and stronger winds. "Dante kissed me."

"Four years ag—"

"Today. He surprised me in the cellar earlier and kissed me, and then he asked me out on a date."

Her lashes smack her brow bone. "What? Why am I hearing about this only now? Oh..." Her mouth rounds. "So *that's* why Antoni was in a mood."

"I don't think he knows."

"Well then...merda."

Yes, *shit* seems appropriate. "Any words of wisdom?"

"I got nothing for you, babe, but I can hold your hand while you decide which man you like best."

And she would.

I give her a one-armed hug good night, square my shoulders, and step out into the starlit darkness, reminding myself that it's not cheating when no promises were made and no oaths struck.

So truly, I have no reason to feel angry at Dante or fraudulent about my hookup with Antoni.

16

Antoni sits in his boat's berth, boots propped on the stern. His spine straightens as I near. How he senses my approach is a mystery, because my slippered feet shuffle over the pier noiselessly.

"Done hiding from me, Fallon?"

His comment jars me back to the cellar where Dante asked me the same question. Except from him, I wasn't hiding. "Yes."

Antoni glances over his shoulder, eyebrows raised. I take it he wasn't expecting candor. I set my dish down and take a seat beside him.

My disappearing act has blunted his eyes' perennial sparkle. "Why?"

I watch an enormous yellow serpent undulate beneath the tightly packed boats, scaring away a raft of ducks that quack and honk as they spring off the blue-black sea. "Dante came to see me earlier." I glide my lower lip between my teeth. "He kissed me and then he asked me out."

I'm done with secrets. Antoni may not be the love of my life, but perhaps Dante won't be either.

Prophecy, schmophecy.

Out of the corner of my eye, I catch a dark emotion rippling across Antoni's face. "He didn't even invite you to the revel."

I finally look his way. "He did, but my grandmother hid the ribbon so I wouldn't attend." I'm still not certain whether it was her, but since I cannot tell Antoni about Bronwen, I perpetuate my first theory. "I told him yes."

Antoni's pupils shrink to dots. "Did you also tell him about us?"

"I didn't. He didn't ask."

"And if he had?"

"I would've told him. I have nothing to be ashamed of. Especially considering...considering..." My voice turns to a pained wheeze.

"All we did was kiss?"

"No. I mean yes. But that's not where my mind went."

Antoni glides his arm around my waist and tucks me against his side. I rest my cheek on his shoulder that feels so warm and solid, so comforting and safe.

"Considering he slept with Beryl?" His whisper is as soft as the wind that buffets the rolled sails of the rocking boats.

I lift my head off his shoulder. "You heard?"

"Not many secrets stay secret at Bottom of the Jug."

"Gods, Antoni, I'm so fucking naive," I croak.

"I don't think I've ever heard you swear." He runs the callused pad of his thumb down my bare arm to the bend at my elbow, then back up. "You're not naive, Fallon. You're young and idealistic."

Resolve solidifies within me. I wanted to move out of my house to prove to Nonna I was a grown woman, but a grown woman is worldly. She has experience. What do I have besides sappy dreams and unrealistic expectations? "Rid me of it."

He stops stroking my arm. "Excuse me?"

"Rid me of my naivete." At his frown, I add, "Sleep with me, Antoni. Show me what I've been missing out on. Teach me how not to expect love from sex."

His hand drops away from my arm as his head rears back, freeing honeyed-brown tendrils from his man bun and sending them frolicking around his square jaw. "I'm not some heartless gigolo, Fallon. I have feelings."

"That's not what I meant. All I meant was that you've done it a million times, and you've never gotten attached."

"Maybe I have."

"Have you?"

His mouth thins, giving me the answer he seems reticent to admit. Suddenly, he springs to his feet, apparently done with this conversation.

Done with me.

It stings, even though I deserve it.

His jaw flexes, his knuckles too. "You want to know how it feels to fuck, then let's fuck."

17

I'm tempted. I'll admit that much.

Even spoken so harshly, I'm tempted.

But deep down, I don't want my first time to be prompted by anger and jealousy, and in my heart of hearts, I don't want it to be with Antoni. Dante and I may not be dating, and I may not mean all that much to him, considering the company he keeps, but he means something to me and my silly heart.

Antoni and Dante may be able to dissociate their bodies from their hearts, but I cannot.

"I take that as a no." Frustration beats down the harsh line of Antoni's shoulders as he jumps onto his deck. Before disappearing through the door that leads down to the single cabin, he calls out, "He's going to break your heart."

Maybe. I choose to believe he won't, though. I choose to believe that the only reason he's still entertaining other women is because he doesn't think I can be *it* for him. "What do you care about what happens to my heart, Antoni?"

His fingers are on the handle, the door half-open. His spine stiffens. "You're right. I don't. We established that earlier, didn't we?"

What I hate above his bitterness is that I'm the reason for it.

"All I care about are fish and pussy."

"Don't say that. It's not true. You care, and one day, you'll find someone worthy of all that love you have to give."

His blue eyes sear a path to mine. "I wish you the same."

Although it sounds kind, his parting words are bladed reminders that he doesn't believe Dante a worthy recipient of my love.

He steps into his cabin and shuts the door with such force, it makes his boat rock from side to side. I raise my face to the tapestry of stars shining over Luce, waiting for the burn of my lids and throat to subside.

It was the right decision.

If Dante hadn't come home...if Bronwen hadn't spoken of our tangled future, I may have succumbed to the charming fisherman, but the fact is Dante is home.

Before rising, I lean over and dip my hands into the water. In spite of its murkiness, the desire to glide beneath the surface clangs inside my marrow.

Ripples swell around my hands, and I blink because I think...I think—

A scaled pink muzzle pokes out, followed by a long neck ringed with white.

"What a strange creature you are."

Minimus snuffles my palm, on the lookout for a treat, and I laugh. I scratch under his cheek, then lift the top off my casserole dish and pinch a soft leek. I hold it up to him, and he snatches it from my fingers.

That rattling noise he makes when happy agitates the water, and his dorsal scales fold in on themselves.

Glancing around the pier to make sure no one is watching, I give him one last stroke, then straighten, heft up Defne's pot, and head south to the first of the six bridges I must cross to reach my island.

As I walk along the water, I catch the glimmer of scales. Minimus is following me like he does most nights, as though to keep me safe. And maybe he is. Or maybe he's just strolling the waters for the pleasure of my company.

Whatever his reason for shadowing me, I'm grateful for his presence. Halfway home, I pass a gondola filled with Fae chanting bawdy songs. One of them offers to escort me the rest of the way to my house. I turn him down, knowing gallantry isn't his intent. He asks again, his voice louder. Again, I say no.

My rejection makes him call me something distasteful.

"Gorbellied clotpole," I mutter under my breath, willing the water to churn around his lacquered boat and rock it.

When wavelets form, I stop walking and hold my breath.

"What the bloody underworld?" the man sputters, clutching the sides of the boat along with the rest of his now silent friends. "Did you just use magic, scazza?"

Did I? I stare at my hands. No blue sparks scamper along my palms, but perhaps some appeared earlier?

I uncover the answer a second later when a long pink tail slaps the water beside the boat, propelling it into the embankment.

Oh, Minimus. I smile fondly at my pet serpent. That is until one of the men unsheathes a dagger, and another—the one who offered to take me home—raises fire-coated palms.

Anger surges through me so fast that I contemplate jumping into the canal to spook Minimus, but Nonna's complexion the day I bonded with my beast shoots to the forefront of my mind.

The Lucins may suspect I have an affinity for sea serpents, but they don't know it for a fact. If I jump in now, I'll reveal it, and gods only know where that would lead.

To the palace, a soft voice whispers into my mind.

Santo Caldrone. Is Bronwen stirring up this chaos to keep me on track?

Minimus slaps the boat again, and the wood whimpers. The two weaponless men scrabble up the embankment like spiders while the fire-Fae and the armed one stay behind.

The man with the dagger swings. The clay pot slips from my hands and crashes at my feet.

The noise startles them long enough for me to grab my slipper and lob it at his head. It collides with the fire-Fae's instead, making him shoot flames sideways instead of at Minimus. A stomach-curdling shriek rises from my serpent, hurtling through my ribs and into my heart.

The dagger sticks out of Minimus's cheek like a vicious barnacle, so close to his eye that I roar as though the blade sliced through my own face.

"You crazy giglet!" the fire-Fae yips at me.

I contemplate my cracked pot and using the largest piece to drop his squawking ass into the canal.

"Clyde, get the guards!" he barks at a sprite dressed in the same red silk as he wears.

Another cry, softer this time, curdles my insides.

Even though the water is dark, I spot Minimus writhing, trying to get the knife out of his cheek. Fearing all he'll manage is to drive it in farther, I climb onto the railing and jump.

Nonna will murder me if the king doesn't beat her to it.

My body collides with a wall of cold, my legs sinking like toothpicks while my skirt billows up like a jellyfish. I punch the material until the rest of my body glides beneath. My lids are pried open as I spin on myself, searching for Minimus.

His long body flashes beside me, still spiraling spasmodically. I touch his neck, and he hisses. My heart bolts into my throat. When his eyes lock on mine, he finally stops moving and floats like algae.

Algae that keens.

I grip the dagger with one hand, brace the other on his horn, and yank. As it drops to the silty bottom, more blood clouds the water, followed by a bone-deep cry.

I wish I could suture his wound, but my saliva isn't miraculous like his. Gods know I tried after the market incident. The only thing I achieved was getting Sybille and Phoebus to wonder if I was dropped on my head at birth.

Minimus laces himself around my scissoring legs and abdomen as I stroke his dorsal fins, relieved the dagger didn't blind him.

I'm going to need air soon, but until my lungs shrivel, I hug this strange animal, wishing I could shield him from the cruelty of men and establish peace between our two species.

When the tingle in my lungs turns intolerable, I nod to the surface, and intelligent beast that he is, he swims me back up. But before we break through the agitated surf, I push him away. He doesn't leave. I press him again. He stays.

I shape the word, *Go*, getting a lungful of salt in the process. I seal my lips and shove. His eyes, black from lid to lid, stare steadily into mine. He must sense my anguish because he finally loosens the coils of his body and turns.

Praying he didn't misunderstand my reasons for making him leave, I propel myself to the surface, sputtering when my head emerges. My dress billows around me again, and I push it back down as I kick toward the embankment opposite the Fae swine. I make it to the ladder hooked into the stone wall and, hand over hand, scale it.

When I reach dry land, I spit and hack the salt that clings to my throat and squeeze the water from my hair. When I look over my shoulder, I find a military vessel carving the canal toward us. Cato's hair snaps like a white flag, luminous like his eyes. The sprite springs away from the sergeant and zips back toward his master.

"This girl attacked me!" the fire-Fae proclaims. The man's ears are long and weighed down by rubies as large as my thumbnail. More red stones sparkle in his waist-long brown hair and decorate the vest he wears over an untucked white shirt. He is, without a doubt, a high-ranking member of the nobility.

Cato's boat eases to a stop between us. "Why did she attack you, Marquess Timeus?"

Figures my run-in would be with a marquess. One step beneath duke. Two steps beneath the royal family.

"*Why?*" The marquess's amber eyes bulge. "You do mean *how?*"

"No. I do mean *why*. Why would a girl attack you?"

"Because the pureling called me a whore," I huff.

Cato's head spins toward me, shooting me a look that urges me to buckle my lips.

"You should be beaten for your insolence," the marquess barks.

"And you should be—" Before I can utter the word *neutered*, Cato barks out my name.

He turns back toward the nobleman, whose eyes are slitted in my direction. "How did she attack you, Marquess?"

"With my slipper," I mutter at the same time as Timeus bellows, "With her pet serpent."

Fear claws at my throat. "What? No—I—" If he demands Minimus be put to death, I will find a steel dagger and pierce his black heart. Subduing my temper before it can get me into any more trouble, I say, "I don't have a pet serpent."

"Fallon!" My name uttered by Cato is as sharp as the wind biting into my skin.

"Fallon. Of course..." The marquess's pointy jaw lifts. "The market rat, also known as the Serpent-charmer."

My fingers ball into fists at my sides. "I'm soaked in salt, Timeus." I purposely leave out his title. "I cannot possibly lie." I lick my lips, making a show of consuming more of the truth-telling mineral that's only ever bettered my mendaciousness. "I confess I hit the nobleman with my shoe because he tried to maim an innocent sea creature. Forgive me if I care about beasts more than I care about men."

"Treasonous cunt." The marquess's flush deepens to burgundy.

"Refrain from libels, Marquess!" Cato roars.

"She called me a—"

"Pureling." A nerve feathers Cato's stiff jaw. "That's hardly an insult."

"I demand her crime be reported to the king immediately!"

Cato stays silent, still working through the anger sharpening his features. He's very, *very* mad at me, but it'll pale in comparison to how Nonna will react when she hears about my midnight swim.

"Clyde!"

Timeus's sprite jumps.

"Head to Isolacuori and report—"

Cato spins toward the man. "Your sprite's wings will be cleaved off his back if he penetrates the palace without being granted an audience."

The sprite recoils with a hiss that echoes over the canal like the drone of a bumblebee.

Timeus crosses his arms. "My boat has incurred much damage. My silk pillows are soaked in dank canal water. I expect her to cover *all* expenses."

This time, I'm the one to hiss. "I didn't do anything to your boat."

Timeus narrows his eyes. "Your eyes are blue, girl. Don't pretend you didn't wield your magic to make that snake attack me."

"I have no magic." I push my wet hair out of my face so he can see the shape of my ears. "I'm not a pureblood like you, *sir*."

"Halflings have magic."

"Not all of us."

"Well, you did something. I didn't crash into the embankment by—"

"You're the one who used magic."

"To defend myself! That is allowed. Besides, like you pointed out, I'm a pureblood and a marquess, and we carry permits to use our magic as we so please."

Cato sighs. "Fallon…"

"I swear I didn't use magic."

"Regardless of whether you did or didn't, scazza, I want the king to hear how you chose a pest over your fellow man. *And I demand two gold pieces to replace the upholstery and fix the damaged hull."*

I blanch because I don't have that sort of money. Oh gods, what have I gotten myself into?

I scan the darkened houses and cobbled streets for the burnt face with the milky eyes. *Please, Bronwen, be behind this. Please, help.*

But aside from Cato, who has started to haggle with the nobleman over the price of repairs, dragging the amount down to one gold piece, no blind soothsayer sweeps in to save the night.

After the amount is settled, Cato steers his boat toward me and gestures for me to embark.

"I can walk—"

"Get in *now*, Fallon." His jaw is stone, his tone too.

Timeus watches me, arms folded in front of his expensive clothes that reveal so much of his chest that he looks like a harlot. I'm surprised he's not rubbing his palms together.

The day I'm your queen…

Firing off a look that I hope carries every last ounce of my contempt, I take Cato's proffered hand and hop into his boat. "Where are we going? To the palace or to my home? You know what? Let's head to the palace." I'd much prefer to face the king than my grandmother.

One corner of Cato's mouth tugs up.

"Smile away. I know she terrifies you too," I mutter.

Cato snorts.

Terrifies and fascinates him.

I wonder for a moment what life would be like with a man in the house. Not just a man. Cato.

Nice, I decide.

If only Cato had the courage to ask her out, but between his much younger age and his station, I doubt Nonna would accept his advances.

Biting the inside of my cheek, I start hoping she's fed my gifted gown to the ocean so that I have an ace to play when she blows up at me. Because she *will* blow up. Hopefully, her anger won't make the wisteria vines strangle the walls of our house, because however much I love seeing the sky, I do love having a roof over my head.

Thinking of crumbling houses makes me think of Timeus, which in turn makes me think of Catriona and the going rate of maidenheads.

"Did the marquess specify the amount of time I have to pay my debt?"

"I took the liberty to negotiate monthly payments."

"Of..."

"Of ten silvers."

My eyes bulge. "Ten silvers *per* month? I make *two* at the tavern." And one of those is used for food. The other goes into an emergency pot that covers home repairs, clothes, and shoes.

Speaking of shoes... I stare down at my bare toes, recalling the slippers I regrettably lost tonight were my only pair.

Catriona's words tumble through my mind, both alluring and revolting. In the end, the revulsion of reddening some stranger's sheet wins over the allure. I didn't refuse Antoni to end up spreading my legs for someone who isn't Dante.

What if the highest bidder is Dante, though?

On the heel of that thought comes a sobering one: What if the highest bidder turns out to be the commander? Oh, the joy that man would take in hurting and humiliating me.

I cannot take the risk. Not to mention I cannot bear the idea of Dante paying me for sex. How can I become someone fit to be queen, *his* queen, if I sell my body?

I've never contemplated thieving, but I don't see how I'll come up with ten silvers a month. I suppose I could pick up a second job.

"How much do soldiers make?" I muse aloud.

"Women cannot become soldiers."

"Right. Because we're so governed by our whims."

Cato side-eyes my waterlogged dress.

Fine. "I admit I acted a tad impulsively tonight, but at least I acted. Can you imagine me using that impetuosity and courage in battle?"

Cato fights off a smile. "I'd pity the opposing army."

I grin.

"*And* your fellow battalion."

My lips flex higher but then collapse, because my blue house is within sight, and it isn't dark as it should be this late in the evening.

18

As the gondolier berths the vessel, Nonna, who still wears her day dress beneath her shawl, fills our living room window.

Gods, she was waiting up for me.

Her lips pinch and roll when she spots me, and then her throat follows suit at the sight of the white-haired Fae helping me out of the boat. She shuts the window and turns away, ashamed, disappointed.

She hid your ribbon and dress, I tell myself.

I may have brought her shame, but she brought it on me first.

I pull my shoulders back as I circle my house to reach the front door. Footsteps echo behind me. I stop and stare at Cato. "Are you shadowing because you don't trust me to pass my threshold, or are you worried Nonna will strangle me with her vines?"

"Neither."

"Then—"

"Let's go inside to have this conversation."

I sigh. "Which you intend to be part of."

He nods, and we trudge on silently.

I'm surprised to find the front door gaping and my grandmother standing there, waiting.

Her arms are still crossed, her lips still pursed, but there's a sheen to her eyes that makes my anger deflate. Nonna never cries, so those can't be tears, yet her lashes are clumped together, and her skin is as snowy as Cato's hair.

"I'll make tea." She moves into the kitchen, her back to us. Her spine, always straight as the mast on a boat, is hunched, the line of her shoulders bent. With her back to us, she says, "Please tell me you stumbled into a sewage trough."

I wrinkle my nose. "Do I smell *that* awful?"

Although she's placed the kettle on the stovetop and coaxed the flickering flame into a shallow fire, she keeps her back to us. "How much trouble is my granddaughter in, Cato?"

His sigh is substantial enough to make her turn around. "There was an incident, which hopefully will be resolved with coin."

"Hopefully?" Her voice is uncharacteristically toneless.

"Fallon jumped into the canal because a group of Fae assaulted a serpent."

Nonna closes her eyes. I feel her lips shape my name even though she doesn't sound it out.

"They also called me a whore, Nonna. Which is why Min— the serpent attacked them."

"Min?"

I play dumb and twirl a soaked lock. "Huh?"

"Is this the same serpent you feed and play with when you get home at night?"

My fingers freeze midtwirl, and I gape at Nonna.

"Cato is aware of your...amity."

I gape at him next, then go back to gaping at Nonna. "I wasn't aware *you* were aware of it."

"Goccolina"—she sighs—"I only play dumb to avoid fighting with you."

"Is it just him?" Cato asks. "Or do you have more serpent friends?"

"Just Minimus." I clap my palm in front of my mouth. It's only a name, yet it feels like I've just given Nonna and Cato power over my beast. What if they use it to call to him? What if they—"Please don't hurt him."

The kettle whistles, slicing through the tense atmosphere.

Nonna pours the water over a medley of dried sprigs and yellow petals, then carries the pot to the table and sets down two mugs. Cato's cue to leave? She fills them before pushing one toward the sergeant.

Apparently not.

She keeps the other for herself.

I guess I'm undeserving of tea tonight. I've too much pride to ask for a mug, so I start toward the stairs.

"Sit, Fallon." My grandmother's voice makes my vertebrae tighten.

I gesture to the table. "I assumed I wasn't invited to the tea party."

"You are. Now sit."

Even though it's the last thing I want to do, I yank out a chair and gracelessly flop down onto it.

She sets another mug in front of me. It's filled with water so brown it looks like canal water. I sniff it. Smells like it too.

"Drink this first, then I'll give you something more palatable."

I don't miss the deep frown on Cato's face. It surely mirrors mine.

"Is it noxious?"

"Not to you."

"That's not reassuring."

"Drink." She slides into the seat across from Cato's, her shawl falling down her shoulders. "Which Tarecuorin Fae did you anger?"

"Ptolemy Timeus." Cato wraps his long fingers around the delicate handle of the mug, one of the few items Nonna brought from her previous home.

"Oh, Goccolina…"

I take it he's Luce-renowned. "The man's a pig, Nonna. I take that back. It's unfair to pigs."

Cato snorts.

Nonna doesn't. "He may be despicable, but he's powerful, and we're not." After a beat, she asks, "You mentioned coin. Is he asking to be paid for his silence?"

"No. For boat repairs."

"Boat repairs?" she sputters.

I focus on my rank-smelling drink, which I still haven't brought myself to taste. "Minimus sort of…drove the marquess's boat into the embankment."

Nonna's complexion fills with color. "And we must pay why?"

"Because Minimus has no savings."

She narrows her eyes on me, apparently not finding me funny. "I'm serious, Fallon."

"He claims I *made* Minimus do it."

"And did you?"

"No. Minimus was trying to protect me because he must've sensed Ptolemy Timeus"—I commit his name to memory—"was harassing me."

Nonna stays silent for a full minute. I can tell she's livid, but is it with me, Minimus, or Timeus?

"He can't prove she ordered the serpent to attack him, right?"

"I didn't order—"

The loftiness of her black eyebrows indicates my answer isn't welcome. She wants to hear Cato's piece.

"No, he can't prove it. But he was with three other Fae, and they all saw her throw her slipper at his head."

I roll my eyes. "It was a cloth shoe, not an iron dart." *Unfortunately.*

"You're not allowed to assault citizens, Fallon," he says calmly.

"He assaulted my character with his words."

"Did you miss the shape of his ears and the length of his hair?" Cato drums his fingers against the rough-hewn wood.

"It's completely unfair." I don't usually pout, but tonight I do.

"You want fairness, move to another kingdom." Cato gulps down some of his tea before wiping his mouth on the back of his hand and leaning back into his chair. "I hear they let women into the military in Nebba."

My grandmother's eyebrows writhe. "Do I want to know what that's about?"

"Probably not." I finally pluck my drink up and shoot it down. It tastes as disgusting as it smells, like warm Racoccin water. Just the comparison makes my stomach heave and almost expel it. I press my hand against my mouth to keep it down. "Are you sure you're not trying to poison me?"

Nonna disregards my question. "How much is the marquess demanding?"

"One gold piece," Cato answers while I take inventory of my organs, checking if any are shutting down.

"One gold—" She chokes on the end of her sentence.

Cato peeks at her. "I have savings."

I gape at him.

"I can lend it to—"

"No. We're not taking your money, Cato."

"Why not?" I find myself asking.

"Because—" Her fingers tighten around her mug. "We'll find some other way."

Cato sighs. "Ceres…"

"No."

"How long have we been friends?"

"We're not friends," she snaps.

He flinches.

"Nonna!" I gasp.

"Friends can be trusted." She fusses with her shawl, eyes

127

averted from Cato, who's observing her in stunned silence. "You're in Justus Rossi's employ, Cato."

"Everyone needs to make a living, Ceres." When, after a full minute, nothing more is said, he rises from his seat. "Thank you for the warm beverage."

Nonna doesn't acknowledge his gratitude, the same way she doesn't meet his stare as he retreats.

I smile at him. "Good night, Cato. And thank you."

He gazes at my grandmother one last time before letting himself out.

After the door shuts, I whip back toward Nonna. "That was rude."

"Cato is a boy, Fallon."

"He's a hundred and seven!"

"Like I said, he's a boy. And like I said"—she places her forearms on the table—"he's in your grandfather's employ. Do you want him to get in trouble?"

"You reject him to protect him?" My lashes scrape my brow bone. "So if he wasn't working for—"

"A gold piece." She stares into the glass teapot at the frolicking sprigs and petals that have bloated in the piping hot water.

I lean back and fold my arms. "You could probably get a nice sum for the gown Dante dropped off for me. That is if you haven't asked our fire-Fae neighbors to incinerate it yet."

She swallows.

So my blame wasn't misplaced. "He asked me out on a date, by the way."

That makes her look up from her tea.

"I said yes. Perhaps I can get him to pay Timeus—"

"Never be in a man's debt, Fallon. *Never*. And no, I didn't burn your dress. It's hanging in your mother's closet. I'll take it to the market tomorrow to see how much we can get for it." After a beat, she asks, "What happened with Antoni?"

"We parted ways." I catch her peering into the mug she set in front of me. "So, are you going to finally reveal the secret behind this horrid drink? If it was to punish me for going to Rax—"

"It's a tonic that'll keep your womb empty for a moon cycle."

In spite of my sodden dress, heat creeps up my neck. "Oh."

"Aren't you glad I didn't go into details in front of Cato?" There's a glint to her eyes I haven't seen in forever.

"Well, I had no need for it."

"Perhaps not tonight." She studies my expression. "But I'm certain you'll be glad for it soon."

Color rises into my cheeks, betraying my many fantasies of lying with Dante.

"Make sure whomever you choose is attentive and generous. Generous lovers are much too scarce."

Although I don't want to discuss sex with my grandmother, I use her advice as an opening. "I'm sure Cato—"

"I've had my fun."

"Really? Justus was attentive and generous?"

The glint in her eyes snuffs out.

"I'm sorry, Nonna."

For a long moment, we stay silent, waiting for the storm clouds I carried into our little home to roll away.

"Why did you take my ribbon? Why make me believe I wasn't good enough for Isolacuori?"

Her moss-green eyes sear into me as she reaches over and clasps my hands. "Because I'm scared, Goccolina. I'm scared they'll find out that you're different. I'm scared they'll..." Her voice loses all its power.

"That they'll try and kill me?"

"No. That they'll try and use you, because resisting salt and charming beasts makes you an unparalleled weapon."

I smile because she's forgetting something essential. "Except I'm a person, not a thing, Nonna. I cannot be wielded against my will."

She sets my hands back on the table and leans back in her chair. "Then make sure your will isn't governed by your heart."

"What's wrong with my heart?"

"It beats for the wrong man."

I rear back. It's *my* heart. If I want to give it away to a sprite, then I'll give it away to a damn sprite. Who is she to decide what man is right or wrong for me?

I toss away her comment and stand. "At least my heart beats, Nonna. That's more than I can say about yours some days."

19

I lace up my only remaining pair of shoes—winter boots. The black leather is so at odds with my purple dress that it's bound to raise eyebrows, but no more than walking around Luce barefoot. In truth, my footwear will probably be deemed an eccentricity, and eccentricity beats poverty.

After attempting to run a brush through the voluminous waves I acquired from sleeping on wet hair, I stop by Mamma's room to tell her about my evening. I have no secrets from her, partly because she's a tomb and partly because I want her to know me inside out in case she ever awakens from her stupor.

Her eyes stay fixed on the Racoccin shoreline during my account of the eventful night. "Cold," she murmurs.

The temperature is sweltering, made even hotter by the lack of clouds, but I pick up the folded blanket from the foot of her bed and drape it over her lap.

She shakes her head, which shakes her torso, which in turn makes the thin wool pool around her waist. "Cold."

"That's why I'm putting the blanket over you, Mamma."

She becomes agitated. "Gold. Gold. Gold."

Oh...*gold.*

Sighing, I remove the blanket, cursing myself for worrying her. "I'll find a way to get it."

"Acolti." The warm breeze blowing off the canal amplifies her murmur. "Acolti. Gold."

Shock springs my fingers wide, and the blanket falls at my feet. I've told her a thousand stories about Phoebus, and she's met him several times over the years. Well, *met* may be a stretch. He and Sybille have come over to my house and hung out with me and Mamma, but her eyes always rolled over them as though they were a motif in the cracked fresco the previous owner, an artist fame propelled into Tarecuori, left behind.

I heard he once sold a painting for *four* gold pieces. A single painting. Such a shame my drawing skills are as nonexistent as Ptolemy Timeus's class.

I crouch to pick up the blanket. "Phoebus Acolti cut ties with his family years ago, Mamma."

"Acolti. Gold."

My eyebrows draw together as I drop the blanket on Mamma's bed. Is she telling me to accept his charity? If he's still willing to lend—

My eyes fly to the wardrobe, and then I stride over and yank it open. The cramped space is filled with mismatched sheets, faded towels, and Mamma's simple frocks.

No expensive gown shimmers on the rack. Nonna must've already collected it. My heart plummets that I didn't even get to see it, touch it, smell it. I've never received clothes that haven't swathed another body and absorbed its odor.

Oh gods…my date! With everything going on, I forgot that Dante is expecting me to wear the dress for our date. Not only is that impossible, but I'll also have to wear boots. I grimace. He'll never bring me to the palace if I'm garbed like a pauper.

I toy with the idea of borrowing a dress from Catriona. Although her body's slightly more voluptuous than mine, we're the same height. I hold on to the sliver of hope she'll loan me one when I explain it's for a good cause. Surely, she'll want to support me. She's all about forging important connections.

"Acolti. Gold," Mamma repeats.

"Okay. Okay. I'll ask Phoebus." I press a kiss to her forehead. "Can I get you anything before I leave?"

Her lips shut, leaving my question unanswered, as usual.

I fill a glass of water and tip it to her mouth. Most sloshes down her chin, but her throat bobs so I take it some made it inside. "Tiuamo, Mamma."

I hope that someday, I'll hear her say *I love you* back.

I secure her window with the latch Nonna hammered in herself, afraid Mamma, unsupervised, might get up and climb off the ledge. Although she's a pure-blooded water-Fae, if she fell into the canal, the Cauldron only knows how and where she'd end up—in the serpents' lair or in the open sea?

The walk to Phoebus's apartment takes only fifteen minutes, and although I stick to the shadows to avoid baking in the midday sun, my stockingless feet sweat, and the perspiration makes them chafe against the leather. I can feel blisters forming on the tops of my toes and on my heels. How in the three kingdoms will I get through my shift?

As I cross over the last bridge, I trawl the canal with my eyes, hoping for and fearing a glimpse of pink scales. For all my desire to see Minimus and make sure he's healed, I don't want him anywhere near the surface. Especially in broad daylight.

Although there's movement beneath the blue, it's all clouds of silver minnows and a larger fish here and there. Two elegantly garbed sprites dart in front of me, smacking me in the forehead with a rolled scroll they carry between themselves.

"Watch where you're going, halfling," one of them hisses.

"Hey. *You* ran into *me*."

Without apologizing—sprites never do—they flutter away.

133

"Mites," I mutter under my breath as I turn onto Phoebus's street.

I duck beneath the branch of the squat fig tree covering the right half of the vermilion house and ease past the perpetually unlocked front door. The wooden staircase that leads to his landing is narrow and groans under each footfall, announcing my presence before I've even knocked.

Not that Phoebus swings the door open. Knowing his proclivity for sleeping the day away, he's probably fast asleep. I knuckle the door and wait. After a minute, I knock harder. This time, I hear shuffling and grumbling.

The door creaks open to a squinty-eyed, gnarled-haired Phoebus. He still looks beautiful. Always does. When we were kids, Sybille offered to bear his babies if he desires children someday. Their respective future husbands better be open-minded.

He rubs the sleep from his eyes. "What brings you to my place at the butt crack of dawn, Piccolina?"

I snort. "It's past noon. As for the reason I'm here… Remember how I told you that I'd never accept a loan? Well, I've changed my mind. If your offer still stands, that is."

He lowers his hand to his side, fully alert now. "What happened?"

"It's a long story, and my feet are killing me. Can I come in?"

"Of course. Come." He glances down at my footwear. "Whyever are you wearing winter boots?"

"Because I lost my slippers."

"How does one lose their slippers?" He walks over to the bucket of fresh water he keeps on the wooden countertop of his sprite-size kitchen. Not that Phoebus ever cooks. The only time he lights up his coal oven is in the dead of winter, when the frigid temperatures turn the canals to ice.

The privacy curtain between where he sleeps and the living area stirs, and a man emerges. A fully naked one. Although my first glance lands on his small, rigid manhood, my gaze rapidly scales up to his face. The newcomer reddens and drops his palms to cover himself.

Phoebus gestures between us. "Fallon, Mercutio. Mercutio, Fallon."

So this is Mercutio, the Fae with the... What had Phoebus said again? Godly mouth?

As I take the glass from Phoebus, I bite my lip. "Sorry to have interrupted your slumber."

"I...uh... I should..."

"Go?" Phoebus supplies at the same time as Mercutio mumbles, "Get dressed. And go. Of course."

Although his long brown hair is unbound, I don't miss the deepening flush crawling over his cheeks.

When he's out of sight, I say, "I can come back."

Phoebus shoves away a rumpled shirt and a plate topped with crumbs to make room on the couch for his pant-clad ass. "So can he."

"Not sure he'll want to after the lovely way you asked him to depart."

"Trust me." Phoebus smiles. "He'll want to."

"Careful. Your head may outgrow the rest of your body."

He snickers. "So tell me how you lost your slippers."

By the time Mercutio emerges, combed and dressed, I've filled Phoebus in on my nocturnal dip in the canal.

With an awkward wave and more blushing, Mercutio lets himself out.

Phoebus shoots down his water and puts his glass down on top of a treacherously stacked pile of leather-bound books. "Always up the canal without your oar."

I frown. "What's that supposed to mean?"

"That you have an unprecedented way of getting yourself in messes."

My mouth puckers. "The marquess attacked Minimus."

Phoebus leans over, dropping his forearms onto his spread thighs. "This isn't me judging what you did—I'm your biggest supporter, Fal. It was me pointing out where it landed you."

I twirl my half-full glass, watching the water sparkle in the sunshine carving through the window.

"As for borrowing money, of course I'll help you. Or rather the Acoltis will be honored to aid an underprivileged child."

My eyes flip to his. "I cannot ask your parents, Pheebs."

"Who said anything about asking?" He winks at me as he gets up and vanishes behind his curtained-off sleeping quarters. "Give me ten minutes."

I stare around the chaotic room, feeling an overwhelming urge to clean. "So, that's a first for you."

"What is?" he calls out.

"Sleeping with a pureling." Not even before he cut ties with his family did Phoebus date purebloods.

I start stacking books. Sybille would be proud.

"Mercutio's different." Phoebus emerges, tucking in a green shirt that enhances the hue of his irises. "He's not arrogant like the rest of them."

"He does seem nice."

Phoebus smiles. "You spoke to him for all of thirty seconds."

"I would've spoken to him longer if you hadn't sent him on his merry way."

"My friend needed me. Friends always trump boyfriends."

"Boyfriend, huh?"

He shrugs. "Maybe. We'll see."

"You *really* like him, don't you?"

"I really like his mouth."

"He does have a pretty mouth."

Phoebus grins as he roots through the heap of shoes by the front door until he finds a pair of emerald satin loafers that match his shirt.

As I join him by the front door, I sigh. "I wish we had the same shoe size."

"That would make your feet as long as your calves. Not quite sure any man would find them attractive."

"Your feet *are* clownishly large."

He laughs. "At least Mercutio doesn't find my feet—or any other part of my body—clownishly anything."

I roll my eyes. "You can take the pureling out of Tarecuori, but you can't take Tarecuori out of the pureling."

Another chuckle falls from his mouth as we set off, arm in arm, toward the northeastern tip of Tarecuori.

In the middle of a heated debate on the trustworthiness of sprites—Phoebus believes they can be trusted; I have yet to meet one who can—I confess, "I broke things off with Antoni last night."

Phoebus's blond eyebrows shoot way up. "Damn. I had a bet going with Syb about which man you'd choose."

I look away from the looming checkpoint. "You thought I'd choose Antoni?"

"I actually bet on a ménage."

I choke on my next swallow. "You bet that I'd have a three-some with a prince and a fisherman?"

He grins. "A Fae can dream."

"You dream of me with two men?"

"In my dream, I'm the one standing in your shoes."

"Trust me. You would hate being in my shoes—figuratively and not."

He glances at the leather death traps. "My sister has a large collection. Maybe we can find a pair that fits you."

"I cannot steal Flavia's shoes."

"She wouldn't even notice."

"But I'd know."

"Fine. Then you'll let me buy you a pair."

"Phoebus…"

He pats my hand as we reach the militarized strip of land between Tarelexo and Tarecuori.

A guard steps into our path. "What business brings you to Tarecuori?" His eyes gleam like the polished silver studs adorning his pointed ears.

Phoebus tucks a silken strand of hair back to reveal the shape of his own ears. "The name's Phoebus Acolti. As for my business, which is strictly none of yours, I'm headed to a luncheon at my family estate with my genteel lover."

I pinch his arm, which just makes a grin streak across his face.

"Of course. Pardon me, Signore Acolti." The guard steps aside to let us through.

"Genteel lover?" I whisper. "Really?"

"Would you rather I called you my lusty broodmare?"

I roll my eyes. "Yes, because there are only two ways to describe a woman in Luce."

He snickers before growing contemplative. "I can't believe you ended things with the third sexiest playfae in Luce."

"Third sexiest?"

"Well, there's me, then Catriona, *then* Antoni." He adds a wink to show me he's jesting.

I bite back my smile. "I'm relieved that when you shed all those insecurities, you didn't shed Syb and me in the process."

"I shed my insecurities *thanks* to you and Syb." He covers my arm with his palm and gives it a squeeze.

To think he used to be shorter than me and so gangly that Sybille and I could roll marbles between his ribs.

"Have you told Syb yet?"

"Not yet."

"She's going to rub her victory in my face."

"What did you bet?"

"Swapping lives for a day."

I smile. "No."

"Yes."

My cheeks ache from how wide I grin. "You agreed to wake up before noon, sweep the tavern, and serve obnoxious customers? Oh my gods, Pheebs. You. Will. Die."

"I didn't think I'd lose."

"Clearly." I snort. "Why in the world would your virginal friend not want to lie with two men for her first time?"

"Exactly. Why choose?"

We smile at each other for a little while longer.

"I do think Antoni is the better lover."

I whip my head toward him. I cannot believe he's given this thought. But more importantly... "Why do you say that?"

"He's older, more experienced, *not* a prince."

"What does rank have to do with bedroom skills?"

"Everything. Entitled men feel they're owed everything and they're doing you a favor by sleeping with you."

"Dante isn't entitled."

Phoebus side-eyes me. "He's royalty, sweets."

"So?"

"So lower your expectations, that's all."

"It doesn't matter. Even if he's not as good as Antoni, it doesn't matter."

Phoebus hefts a brow, probably wondering who I'm trying to convince—him or myself.

20

By the time we reach the porticoed entrance of the Acolti manor, I've rearranged my concerns by urgency—debt to Timeus, gathering of crows because I do want to rule Luce (if only to browbeat spiky-eared idiots), Dante's bedroom skills.

I smooth my dress, wishing it were made of silk instead of linen. "Should I tell your parents what happened with Timeus when I ask them for a loan or make up another story?"

Phoebus raises a smile as blinding as the white roses garlanding the columned entrance. "Who said anything about a loan?"

I snap my gaze to Phoebus. "I won't steal from your parents."

"It's not stealing if I bequeath to my best friend a morsel of my inheritance."

My mouth gapes.

He flicks my chin with his finger to close it. "Prepare to be blinded, Piccolina."

As long as I'm blinded by his parent's wealth and not their wrath.

On our way across the grounds, we don't run into any Acoltis. I think it's a miracle until Phoebus explains his family is vacationing at Victorius Surro's beachside manor in Tarespagia, a trip my friend was invited to attend but merrily declined. As per custom, they took all their sprites and a few manservants, leaving behind the gardeners, groundskeeper, private chef, and matronly housekeeper.

I still remember my first visit to the Acolti property. I'd stayed mute for all of it, shocked by the splendor of the estate and the number of staff. Although I'm no longer speechless, I'm still gobsmacked.

As we meander down the manicured pathways hemmed with fat bushes and elegant trees, Phoebus makes small talk with everyone we pass. My friend bursts with natural charm, and none of it is artificial. He genuinely cares about round-eared citizens.

"You'd make such a great king," I say, still clinging to his arm.

"Agreed."

I smack his pec. "Careful. Your pointy ears are showing."

He snorts a chuckle as we skirt a pond covered in lily pads and packed with frogs that would hop over us when we'd lounge on the grass as children.

Every time his parents caught me with one, they'd simper, "Such a vile creature."

To this day, I'm convinced they meant me, even though Phoebus insists they were referencing the amphibians.

Upon entering the house, we remove our shoes, and I sigh in relief when chilled marble and cool air meet my swollen toes.

"Gods, your feet. Whatever you do, hide them from Dante's sight whenever he takes you out on that date."

"Hey. You're supposed to make me feel better about my imperfections, not point them out."

"Blisters aren't flaws."

Footfalls ring on the polished stone. "How may I... Oh, Phoebus!" Gwyneth, the senior housekeeper who's looked after two generations of Acoltis—all still living under this roof—gapes at Phoebus as though she hasn't seen him in decades. "I didn't know you were visiting." She offers me a meager nod. Although a halfling like myself, Gwyneth is so loyal to the Acoltis that any persona non grata to them becomes one to her. "Will you and your friend be staying for lunch?"

Your *friend*? I used to be Fallon. I must've risen on the Acoltis' persona non grata list.

"No lunch. We'll be in and out." Phoebus grips my hand and pulls me up the wide marble staircase. Although his house is two stories high like the rest of Lucin residences, these stories are nothing like the ones in Tarelexo.

"To live here…" My awed whisper ascends to the domed skylight cinched by plaster carvings of grapes and cherubs, skips along the cream stone walls daubed in oil portraits of the family, and bounces against the coat of arms—gold vines twisted into an elegant A.

"Cold and soulless." He drags me down a wide hallway, booking a right at the end of it. "You'd detest it."

"You're projecting."

"No, I'm stating a fact."

I decide to drop it since living here isn't even an option. I peer out the enormous window at the end of the hall at the sprawling gardens that dip right into the turquoise waters of Mareluce. "Will Flavia's nuptials be held here or at Surro's estate?"

"Here."

"When?"

"I've heard talk of Yuletide, but since I'm not planning on attending—"

"What?" Shock stills my feet, which in turn stills his. "You *have* to go. She's your only sister, Phoebus."

"Wrong. I have two more sisters."

"That I don't know about?"

He flicks my temple. "You and Syb, dum-dum. Your midnight swim has made you a little slow on the uptake this morning, huh?"

I smile. "Ass."

Grinning, he pulls me into a room that's so yellow, I feel like I've landed in a honey pot.

"Whose bedroom is this?"

"Flavia's."

"Why are we in your sister's room?" I whisper.

"Because you need shoes. I know I said I'd buy you a pair, and I will, but it'd be criminal of me to allow you to put those boots back on, even if it's only to walk to the cobbler's. I wouldn't want to ruin my chances of obtaining a dukedom."

"Um, what do my boots have to do with you becoming a duke?"

"If you bag a prince, I expect a full ride to Isolacuori."

I smirk. "Naturally."

I trail him into a closet that's as large as my entire house and bursting with multicolored satins and silks. Surrounded by so much luxury, I barely dare breathe, afraid the air in my lungs will wilt Flavia's clothes.

Phoebus leaves my side to go root around her shoe shelves. "Wait till Sybille hears she's going to be a duchess."

I twirl slowly. "How about we postpone telling her until *after* my first date with Dante? Like you said, he may shun me when he sees my feet."

"If he does, it'll be his loss and Antoni's gain."

I shake my head. "Antoni would never take me back."

"The same way I don't believe in choosing, I don't believe in the word *never*."

Except if I'm to be queen, Antoni cannot be my future. How I wish I could confide in Phoebus, but this secret is one I'll have to take to my throne.

"What will you wear?"

"To what?"

"To your coronation," he deadpans.

I blanch. Did I speak out loud?

He rolls his eyes. "To your date, silly."

I twist my lips. "I was thinking of asking Catriona for a gown."

"I have a better idea."

When he starts removing dresses from hangers, I hiss his name and swivel my attention to the entryway, expecting to find a scowling Gwyneth.

"Calm your tits, woman. I'll bring everything back before my family returns from their trip." He tosses a gown that looks woven from sky and clouds—the silk is dawn blue, and the sleeves are white and gauzy.

It's the most beautiful thing I've ever seen. Ever touched.

It's not gold, though. Dante may take offense I'm not wearing his gift.

As I hold it up to my chin in front of a floor-length mirror, I untuck my hair and let myself dream that my ears have points, that my auburn locks fall to my waist, and that this is my closet.

"Earth to Fallon."

I spin away from the mirror to find Phoebus holding out two pairs of shoes—ones with heels and ones without. I nod to the ones without, then hold my breath as I slip my feet into them, praying they'll fit.

The soft leather molds around my swollen toes, and I sigh. "I didn't know shoes could feel this good."

"The trappings of wealth." Phoebus spears his hand through his blond hair. "Once you go rich, that life is near impossible to ditch."

"Yet you ditched it."

"I brought all I could fit into my flat."

"Speaking of... How am I supposed to walk out of here with a dress? I can't exactly bundle it in my arms."

He pinches the handles of a large leather bag propped on a shelf and drops it at my feet.

"That's even worse, Pheebs. Gwyneth will think I've robbed your home."

"Relax. I'll carry it."

I don't relax, but I do fold the dress and settle it inside the bag, then lay the shoes on top. The mere idea of lacing my boots makes my skin break out in hives and my toes in additional blisters. I decide I'll walk barefoot to the portico, then don my borrowed slippers.

"And now, the vault." Phoebus slings the bag over his shoulder and signals for me to follow.

We return into the vaulted belly of the manor, turn down another wing full of closed doors that Phoebus explains leads to his parents' and grandparents' quarters. His great- and great-great-grandparents have made Tarespagia their permanent residence, like most of the older Fae who prefer tropical temperatures year-round.

I have only one great-grandparent left, the three others having perished during the Magnabellum or right after, in Nonna's mother's case. The remaining one resides in Tarespagia with my aunt Domitina, the formidable Xema Rossi whose tongue, according to Nonna, is as sharp as her ears. I've never met the elderly Fae, nor do I particularly care to from Nonna's accounts, but I'm guessing our paths will eventually cross, unless her centuries-old heart stops ticking.

Phoebus pulls me into an oval sitting room decorated in creams and whites with gold wall panels representing flowering vines. It's sumptuous.

"Gaudy, I know."

"Beautiful."

"My great-grandfather had this room built after he visited the castle's trophy room, another oval, gaudy monstrosity."

"I hope I get to visit that monstrosity."

He stops in front of a metal panel, and his fingers scrabble up one vine, down another, up, down.

"Why are you groping the wall?"

"I'm unlocking the vault."

My eyebrows rise. "By fondling the bas-relief?"

He chuckles, but his low laughter is drowned out by the click of a latch and the groan of metal against wood.

He presses his fingertips into the panel, and it swings inward.

I blink, then blink again. Sunlight trickles like raindrops through a latticework of wooden shelves two stories high, barely illuminating the room yet setting it ablaze. Shelves upon shelves shimmer with gold trinkets, trays of precious stones, marble busts of comely Fae polished to a mirror shine, leather-bound books with gilt spines, and weapons encrusted with emeralds. Long spears tipped with ebony points are hooked to the wall, along with strange, black-bladed daggers I've never seen wielded around Luce.

Purely decorative, I assume. Like the silver bird impaled through its wings by two black spikes—a grisly work of art.

As Phoebus wedges the bag to keep the door from sealing us in, a chill tiptoes up my spine.

I'd have called it awe except it tightens my skin and prickles my lungs.

Dread.

I'm in a vault heaped with riches, yet I feel like I've entered a mausoleum full of bones.

21

My gaze slides around the room, on the hunt for the source of my discomfort. The splayed bird is gruesome, but it's more than that. There's this unnerving, eerie hum that agitates my blood and hardens my stomach. "Did someone die in this vault?"

Or does something live in it? Like a ghost. My gaze scrapes over every somber corner for movement.

Phoebus straightens and scrutinizes my face, a corner of his mouth tugging up. "Not yet, but you're looking alarmingly pallid, Fallon. Too much wealth to behold?"

I return my attention to the bird, to the black spikes that protrude from its metal wings—

Santo Caldrone. Is that one of the...one of the...

My hand drifts to Phoebus's arm, grips it for support.

"Are you trying to rip off my limb? Sure, it'll regrow, but I'm quite attached to it."

"Gold. Acolti." My head spins so madly I half expect it to unscrew itself from the rest of my body.

I don't realize I've repeated Mamma's mutterings out loud until Phoebus clucks his tongue. "Yes. Lots of gold. I warned you. Are you about to swoon? You look positively unwell."

Bronwen watches.

Find the five iron crows.

Oh gods, oh gods, oh gods. Mamma sent me to Phoebus not for a coin but for a crow. She knew! *How?* Did Bronwen whisper it into her ear? *Impossible.* Bronwen confessed to knowing the location of just one.

I don't realize I've released Phoebus's arm and strode deeper into the room until I'm standing right beneath the solid metal bird.

"Ah. So that's what got your drawers in a twist." He moves closer to me. "No animal was harmed in the making of this garish statue, Piccolina."

Goose bumps course over my skin at the vivid gleam of the bird's citrine eyes.

"It's so lifelike, isn't it?" Phoebus says, sweeping his gaze down the bird's fanned tail.

I hold my breath. I'm not even certain why. It's not like statues can caw or nip. "Exceedingly," I murmur, transfixed by the definition the artist achieved. It's as though a real bird has been mummified in metal. The mere thought makes bile cloud the back of my throat. "What sort of bird do you suppose it's modeled after?" My tongue palpitates with heartbeats that make my voice palpitate in turn, because I know the answer before Phoebus gives it to me.

"A crow." No hesitation.

I flip my eyes up to his.

"My mother told me. I followed her into the vault when I was a child. I must've been very young because I remember her perching me on her hip so I could get a closer look at the pest. Gods, the stories she recounted about them. It would make even you reconsider your love for animals."

Dante will truly be king, and me his queen. I don't know whether to rejoice or balk that my destiny isn't mine to govern after all.

"I've heard the stories." My timbre is still deformed by my pulse. "I sat next to you in class, remember?"

"Headmistress Alice gave us a watered-down account. Trust me." He points to the curled talons that gleam like thorns, then to the bird's bill. "These birds were trained to kill and had a taste for Fae hearts."

I press my palm against my agitated insides. "Why would anyone create an effigy of this bird?"

"To remind us of what we went through? Of what we survived?" He shrugs as though he's not actually certain. "The appendages were clipped off real birds apparently."

"What sort of twisted person clips bills and claws off an animal?"

Phoebus narrows his eyes on me. "I just told you these predators gobbled down Fae hearts, and you're confounded by the snipping of their extremities?"

I close my eyes a second. Phoebus is right. He is also scrutinizing me. If I'm supposed to walk out of here with this bird, which is most definitely not pocket-size, I need to earn his trust.

My pulse sprints against my throat. Am I really expecting Phoebus to let me take it off the wall? Could I unhook it and slip it inside the bag while his back is turned? What if the spikes are wedged so deep into the stone that I need some tool to cleave them out?

I have two options: either return to get it at a later date alone, if I can get past all the staff and recall the dance of Phoebus's fingers on the latch, or tell him it'll somehow get Dante on the throne. Dante is as much his friend as he is mine. Surely, he'd help me steal a statue. But what of dooming a bunch of people?

Ugh. Ugh. Ugh.

"You look about to toss your cornetto."

"I didn't eat any this morning."

"It's an expression, Fal. Why are you so upset?"

My eyes settle on his concerned green ones. "You know me and animals."

"Right. Well, why don't you step out of the vault?" He grips my shoulder gently, squeezes. "I'll grab a couple coins, and we—"

"This statue isn't part of your inheritance, is it?"

His fingers don't lift from my shoulder, but they stop kneading it. "You couldn't hock it without my parents finding out."

"Oh. That's not—I wouldn't hock it."

The corners of his mouth lift again. "Oh."

My own heart punches me in the ribs. "Oh?"

"I just figured out what you'll do with it."

I highly doubt it but heft a brow to egg him into disclosing his thoughts before mine stomp out of my mouth.

"You're going to toss it into the canal so it's out of sight?"

I swallow. *Tempting.*

"Melt it into a weapon with which to threaten the handsy commander?"

"Hmm." I give this actual thought, with chin stroking and everything, which strengthens the curve of Phoebus's smile.

For all my amusement, what if that's how Dante seizes the throne? By melting it into a king-killing weapon? I really wish Bronwen had been more forthcoming with details. An instruction booklet would've been welcomed.

"So?"

"I wouldn't even know where to go to melt iron." It's not like I can visit the Isolacuorin forge or stick the bird in my stove.

"I'm sure there are plenty of blacksmiths in Rax who'd be more than willing to take it off your hands and pay you handsomely for it." Eyes as shiny as the crow's, Phoebus says, "You know what? Let's do it!"

My next exhale wedges itself inside my throat, and I cough.

"It'll piss off my parents to no end and get rid of the embodiment of my nightmares. Like a cleansing of sorts." His hands rise to the black peg while I blink like I've been slapped in the face by a wave.

He's going to hand me the bird. This is too easy. Nothing good ever comes this easily. Bronwen must be manipulating this prophetic hunt.

I lift my hands to the other black spike but freeze when Phoebus hisses.

"Obsidian. It's toxic to humans."

"Except I'm not human."

"You're half-human, so paws off." Phoebus has one foot flat on the wall, and from the rising color on his forehead, I take it he needs the leverage.

"When's your family returning from Tarespagia?"

"Next month."

Another Cauldronsend. Or Bronwensend…

"Oh, and the crow is entirely made of iron, so whatever you do, don't touch it, or it'll singe off your skin. I wouldn't want your hands to be as ruined as your feet for your upcoming date."

My upcoming date with my future husband. *Unreal.* Yet the iron crow exists.

"How deep does this spike go?" Phoebus mutters, sweat dripping down his forehead.

He probably can't get it out because I'm the designated crow gatherer. I eye the spike, itching to curl my hand around it. But what if…what if it does poison me?

Phoebus grunts and groans.

"You sound like a copulating boar."

He goes so quiet that I check he hasn't fainted from exertion. "Copulating boar," he repeats with a snort.

I smile, and it presses away the shroud of anxiety that fell over me upon entering the vault.

"On the upside, if Gwyneth passes by, she'll assume we're getting it on. The perfect cover."

After another full minute during which I scan the vault for a tool to chop off the spike, Phoebus drones, "Alle-fucking-luia."

He's grown a vine as thick as my forearm, and it's popped the spike out of the wall like a cork.

The bird that miraculously was neither bent nor broken in the process swings toward me, ebony dart speared through its splayed wing.

"Watch out!" Phoebus gasps just as the crow's iron talons collide with my bare forearm and the stake grazes my knuckles.

22

I jump back, but the damage is done, and I'm not speaking of the blood frothing at the surface of my gash.

Phoebus's complexion glows bone-white under his sheen of perspiration. He's gaping at my shredded skin, at the rivulets of blood running down the arm I've raised to stanch the flow.

"Oh my gods. We need to get you to a healer!" His voice is shrill with nerves. "Oh my gods." His eyes shine as brightly as his face now, full of tears, because he believes he's just set my death in motion. "Fallon… Oh my gods." His vine drops to the stone floor like a dead snake before reeling back into his palm, while the iron crow keeps swinging like the pendulum of a clock marking my last hour.

"Phoebus, shh. It's okay."

"It's not okay. It's not…" A sob lurches from him along with a deep croak. "Oh, Piccolina, we'll never get to the healer in time." He shoves a blond lock out of his eyes, then grabs one of the broadswords hooked on the wall.

I take a step back. "What are you doing?"

"I'll cut—I'll cut off your—your arm."

My mouth rounds. "No. No one's cutting off anything." I angle my raised arm out of his reach in case he decides to swing anyway.

"The iron...if it reaches your heart. And the obsidian. Oh my gods, the obsidian!" He sucks in a rattling breath. "It's just an arm, Fal. *Please*. I can't lose you."

I'd forgotten about the obsidian.

I check my knuckles. Although scraped, they don't bleed, and my fingers haven't blackened. This may be a hasty prognosis on my part, but I don't think obsidian affects me.

When my friend's lips begin to wobble, I decide to confess the secret Nonna told me never to reveal to anyone. After all, I have a more terrible one now, and too many secrets will end up poisoning me in a way that iron can't.

"I'm immune." I keep my voice low, yet it feels like I've hollered it across the Lucin rooftops.

"What?" The sword tip clanks into the stone.

"I'm immune to iron."

His blubbering halts. "You're imm—you're—you're—immune? But you're—you're—" His look of utter defeat transforms into one of utter confusion. "How?" His wet eyes grow as round as Minimus's. "*Oh*."

He must be having some off-kilter musings, because neither I nor Nonna have the faintest idea why I'm resistant to the metal that's lethal to Fae, the same way I'm immune to the salt that loosens faerie tongues.

"You're—you're a...a human changeling."

"What?" I snap, because...*what*? "Nonna delivered me herself. She saw me come out of my mother." But now that he's said it... what if...?

No. I look like my mother and grandmother. Sure my coloring is different, my eyes a slightly different shade.

The blood drains from my face, pooling somewhere around my ankles. "Oh my gods, what if I am?" My gaze shoots to my knuckles again. If I'm human, though, why isn't the obsidian affecting me? Or is it?

"It'd explain why you have no magic."

"But my eyes are blue," I murmur.

"Violet. Come to think of it, I've never seen another Fae with that color."

"But I resemble Mamma and Nonna."

"Not all that much."

"A changeling…" I touch the shell of my ear with my upraised hand, the room going in and out of focus.

Human.

That means…that means I'm going to die in seven decades. Or sooner.

"Maybe that's why your mother lost the plot." Phoebus tightens the threads until the canvas of his hypothesis is so compactly woven no holes remain.

Does Nonna know? The fact that I'm even asking myself this question startles me. How am I so easily accepting that I may have been swapped at birth?

His cheek dimples as he nibbles the inside in thought. "Maybe something was supremely wrong with the real Fallon, so your grandmother stole you from Rax."

"Except Nonna was just as shocked as you were when she realized I was immune to iron and salt."

"You're immune to salt? All our oaths…"

"I don't need salt to uphold my promises, Pheebs. Especially not the ones I make to friends." A glacial sensation dribbles down my spine, like an icicle melting. "You're still my friend, right?"

He rolls his eyes, which are pink and puffy. "What sort of inane query is that?"

My heart gives a soft, relieved thump.

"I can't believe you're immune to salt. Gods, Syb is going to— Wait. Does she know?"

I shake my head. "No one besides Nonna knows. Well, except for Mamma, but I'm not certain it's registered with her."

Phoebus stares and stares at my bleeding arm before clicking his mouth and undoing the knot in his scarf collar. He rips off a swath of fabric and wipes down my arm, then coils it tightly to stanch the blood. "Thank the Cauldron I didn't let you touch the obsidian."

"It grazed my knuckles."

What little color he regained seeps out of him anew.

"How fast"—I wet my lips—"does it affect the body?"

"It turns human blood black in minutes." He pivots my arm this way and that. Checks between each one of my fingers. "I—" He swallows. "I don't think…"

"That I'm human?"

"I don't know." His eyes hold mine for several heartbeats. "Unless… Yes, that must be it. It mustn't be obsidian. It must be ebony or marble." He shrugs. "They all look alike."

Do they, though? Isn't there a difference between stone and wood?

As he tends to me, I set my concerns aside and concentrate on how lucky I am to have a friend like Phoebus.

He tucks the end of the fabric through the makeshift bandage, an indent marring the smooth skin between his pale eyebrows. "Maybe we're wrong and you're not human."

"What could I be then?"

He peeks up at me through his long, pale lashes. "The child of a serpent?"

"The child of a—" I scoff. "You think my mother had sexual relations with a freaking animal?"

"Maybe Agrippina was kinky like that." A corner of Phoebus's mouth tugs up.

"Yuck, Pheebs. Yuck." A vile visual of a serpent humping a human illuminates the backs of my lids. I shudder.

Phoebus snickers. "You should see your face."

I scowl. "You just implied my mother coupled with a serpent, you cauldron-headed dullard. How exactly did you think I'd react?"

His head falls back with laughter while I shake mine, desperately trying to unsee the image he's conjured.

In between puffs of hilarity, Phoebus grows a new vine that snakes around the remaining peg. Like last time, he inflates the vine until it discharges the spike. He sobers just enough to say, "An advantage to being half-serpent would be a longer life span."

Before it can bang against the floor, I catch the bird by its wings, careful not to touch the spikes. "I'm not half-serpent."

"It wouldn't be the worst thing in the world."

I lower the crow so my glower better meets its mark. "My mother did *not* mate with an animal."

"Hmm…"

"Stop. Stop picturing it." I lug the heavy relic toward the door. "Don't forget the gold coin," I mutter.

Phoebus strolls over to a shelf, grabs a handful of coins, many gold ones in the mix, and shoves them into his pocket.

"That's too many. Won't they realize?"

He gestures to the shelves. "What do you think, piccolo serpens?"

"What I think is that your new nickname better not stick."

"Or what? You'll whistle for your pappa and ask him to whisk me into the fault?"

Even though I honestly don't think I'm related to a serpent, I raise my chin and deadpan, "I'll whistle for my serpent brother and make him drag your ass away."

He grins, wedging his foot in the door and kicking up the bag. He opens it wide so that I can maneuver the bird in.

"You don't honestly think I'm part serpent, do you?"

"No. I don't."

"So, human?"

He sighs. "Hope not. Life wouldn't be half as exciting without you."

"Because your days of pillaging vaults would come to an end too soon?"

His eyes gleam like the statue I've managed to squeeze into the bag. "Exactly." He shoulders the straps, then presses the door wide and holds it for me. "Larceny is much more enjoyable à deux."

I almost tell him I have four more crows to gather but bite the information off my tongue. I've already involved him, and although his pointed ears confirm he's fully Fae, even purelings can incur bodily harm, and I couldn't live with myself if anything befell him because of my desire to sit on the throne beside Dante.

"I cannot believe you were ready to chop off my arm," I tell him as our footsteps click against the buffed floors of his ridiculous mansion.

"Don't remind me." Aquiline nose wrinkled, he drops an arm around my shoulders and pulls me into his side. "But I would've done it because I care like crazy about you, Fallon Rossi, whatever the underworld you may be."

What the underworld *could* I be?

23

As we approach the checkpoint between Tarecuori and Tarelexo, Phoebus presses his arm more snugly against the bag to shield what lies inside. Although we've arranged the voluminous blue dress over the crow and nestled my boots along its wings to disguise the odd shape, sweat glazes my hairline and dribbles down my nape.

If I'd traversed the bridge alone, weighed down by a bag bursting with pretty fabric, I would've been stopped and searched. Phoebus, on the other hand, will probably glide past the Lucin guards like a fish through water.

Or at least that's what I'm hoping.

He lowers his mouth to my ear. "Fallon, I know I confessed that I wouldn't have thought twice about ripping out your arm had you been contaminated, but I'd be much obliged if you didn't rip off my limb in turn."

"What?"

"Your grip, Piccolina." He nods to the hand crushing the rolled sleeves of his tunic.

I spring my fingers wide. "Sorry."

"I'd *love* to invite another man to share our bed tonight, my sweets. Do you have anyone in mind?"

I blink up at my friend, perplexed, until I catch the twinkle in his eye.

The guard from earlier steps in front of us, gray eyes drawn to the bag. "That was a quick lunch."

Even though my battered arm is twisted around Phoebus's, the bloodied bandage peeks out.

"And a brutal one."

Phoebus shoots the man a tight-lipped smile. "Keeping track now, are we?"

"Part of my job." The guard's eyes rove over the lumpy shape of the leather.

"If you must know everything, it turns out my entire family has left for Tarespagia and forgotten to inform me, so I took my girl shopping instead, and she brushed up against a rusted hook, and—*Hmm.*" Phoebus looks the male from gilt stand-up collar to polished boot. "Might you be interested in joining us tonight? We were looking for an extra cock to spice things up."

The guard's attention jolts off our bulky satchel, and a blush steals across his jaw. "I don't—I—" He shakes his head as though to toss off the heat filling it. "Just cross."

Phoebus chuckles at the man's discomfiture and flings him a wink as he tugs me past him.

I don't think I've breathed since the guard stepped in our path.

Phoebus must've realized it too because he murmurs, "Deep breath, Fal."

My lips part, and I all but gasp.

"No offense, but you make a terrible thief."

I nudge him with my elbow. "My ears aren't pointed."

"True, but your tongue can be. You should use it. And not just to lick up the planes of Dante's chest."

I cannot help the stuttering laughter that erupts from my mouth as the tension finally falls from my shoulders.

We made it across.

We *actually* made it.

⌒

As we climb the stairs to my bedroom, Phoebus offers to assist me in finding us a lift to Rax in order to melt the crow immediately. I shush him with an index finger to my lips and shake my head.

Nonna isn't home, but Mamma is. She's fast asleep in her chair, neck and head cradled by a scraggly pillow that wasn't there when I left. Nonna must've come and gone.

I'm glad for my grandmother's absence. It gives me time to clean my arm and decide how to deal with my loot.

"If you change your mind, you know where to find me." Phoebus tosses me a gold coin that flips head over tails as it arches through the air toward me. I cup my palms, just managing to catch the gold piece. "And no paying me back." He starts for my door, but then his attention drops to my feet. "Merda, we forgot about the cobbler."

"No cobbler. You've gone above and beyond. As for the coin…"

He plugs his ears as I insist on paying him back, then blows me a kiss and leaves.

When the front door shuts, rattling our frescoed walls, I head to the bathing room to wash the dried blood off my arm with clean water from the bucket we replenish every day. I make quick work of redressing the wound with a band of gauze I find in a wicker basket dedicated to ointments and oils made from healing herbs, then scamper back to my bedroom and shut the door.

The bag sits atop my bed, the blue frock spilling out like foamy waves. I creep closer and pluck the dress off the crow that glimmers like a shiny lure in the dark depths. Avoiding its bill and talons, I grip the bird by the wings and fish it out, then set it on my faded floral bedspread and stare down at its thick body and broad wingspan, at its right talon that gleams copper where my blood coats the iron.

"One down. Four to go."

I slide my lip between my teeth as I run my fingertip over the delicate barbs, over its fluffed neck and the perfect sphere of its head. I trace the shape of its eye, noticing the black pinprick the artist added beneath the citrine cabochon to give the illusion of a pupil.

"How does a statue and its duplicates get a prince onto the throne?" I muse aloud, raking my fingertip gently over the bird's bulbous chest.

I freeze as a shallow vibration nips my skin. What in the three kingdoms? I snatch my hand back and step away, heart pinned to my spine, which has become as rigid as the crow's wings.

Was that a pulse?

Impossible.

I snort at my silliness, my mind racing through explanations for the ticking. One takes precedence over the others: something must be locked inside the statue. A weapon or a mechanical clock or something…something magical.

I edge back over to it, seize its wings, and flip it onto its stomach, then scour its back for a paper-thin seam or a minuscule latch. Nothing. I lean over to peer between its legs, and my pulse goes wild when I spot a small depression. I dart my finger against it, then spring backward, expecting the statue to detonate.

I'm almost disappointed when nothing happens. I creep forward again, inspecting the tiny indent. Blood pools into my cheeks as I realize what I must've just touched.

I, Fallon Rossi, have just groped a statue's crotch.

This is a new low, even for me. Thank every Fae god that Phoebus wasn't around to witness my fondling.

Pushing out a deep breath, I decide I must've imagined the ticking. I poke my thumbs into what's left of the black spikes through the bird's wings. The surface is hard and cold, slightly crumbly. One eases free, plopping out onto my bedsheet. The other takes a little more prodding but comes loose as well.

I'm about to turn the crow back over when the large holes in its wings shrink before vanishing entirely.

Holy mother of all Cauldrons… I rub my eyes. When I lower my fists, not only are the hollows gone, but the iron body has also filled with color. The statue is entirely black, except for the shiny silver talons and bill.

A soft rustle whispers across my bedroom as the crow's splayed wings retract like a fan snapped shut.

I stumble backward just as the crow plants its claws into my bed to right itself, then pivots its head and sets its cold gold eyes on me.

Oh…

My…

Gods…

When it flaps its wings, a shriek tears up my throat but collides against my clenched teeth, emerging as air.

Everything I know about crows drums into me, heightening the frantic pounding in my chest. Keeping the creature in my line of sight, I scrabble backward like a bug, my heels catching in my dress, making me topple back onto my stinging ass. I miscalculate the distance and bang the back of my head into the wood.

The crow's wings beat frantically, churning the air in the room, the oxygen in my lungs. After another crazed loop around my small bedroom, it arrows for higher ground and perches on my armoire.

My fingers inch toward the doorknob as the bird glares my way.

I swallow, heaving myself to my feet in slow motion.

The creature tilts its head sideways, observing me as though I'm the oddity. As though *I've* just changed color and come to life.

"What the underworld are you?" I hiss.

Great. Now I'm conversing with this...thing. Sure, I talk to Minimus, but Minimus is real.

The crow doesn't caw. It merely keeps observing me with that unnerving intensity.

I twist the knob and pull, the hinges creaking ominously. Before I can slip out, the bird stretches its wings. I bang the door shut, panicked it'll swoop into Mamma's room, or worse, into Luce.

What have I released?

What have I done?

24

I'm uncertain how long the crow and I stare each other down, but my eyes sting from my lack of blinking, my lungs burn from the shallowness of my breaths, and my pulse gushes like a submarine current.

"So...What the underworld are you?" I hiss through clenched teeth.

The bird does not answer.

Why would it, though? It's a bird.

Or is it?

"Are you going to stab me with your beak or carve my heart out with your talons?"

The creature doesn't roll its eyes, but its lids seem to clamp down around the gold, lending it a very judgy mien.

My fingers tremble as I tuck my hair behind my ear, attempting to make sense of a nonsensical occurrence. "What am I supposed to do with you?"

The crow continues to stare at me as though it's wondering what it's supposed to do with *me*.

"A cage!"

That ruffles the crow's feathers. The bird backs up until its tail brushes the wall, getting as much space between us as physically possible.

Huh. "You understand me?"

Why did I assume it wouldn't? Minimus understands me.

As I think of my serpent friend, my gaze finally wanders off the crow and onto my window, onto the canal below. Has he healed? Has he forgiven me for sending him away so brusquely?

The soft click of talons has my gaze jolting back to the armoire. The crow has turned its body and attention to the waters of Mareluce that flow dark in spite of the bright sunshine. As though it feels me staring, its head swivels back toward me.

"How about we make a pact? I won't lock you up"—it isn't like I have a cage on hand anyway—"as long as you don't attack me or anyone living in this house. My mother and grandmother aren't immune to iron." I nod toward its feet.

The crow peers at its talons. Its neck fluffs up as it lifts the bloodstained one, managing to level it in front of its nose. It sniffs, or I imagine it does. It's not like I can see its nostrils from where I stand.

What I do see is its tongue dart out and taste the iron. The creature freezes, looks at me over the gleaming point of its weaponized nail, then smacks its talon down. Although its body is no longer built from metal, the thwack rattles the wood.

Its reaction reminds me of Minimus the first time we met. I never thought my blood smelled odd, but if animals have such strong reactions to it, then it must. I lift my bandaged arm and take a whiff. Notes of copper and warmth dance off the gauze, no honey or brine or Cauldron only knows what arrests animals so.

"So...do we have a deal?" My brain buzzes from the pressure of my nerves. I want to shut my eyes until the strain subsides but refuse to look away from the thing. "If it's a yes and you understand me, nod your head."

The crow becomes statue still. Of course, I was deluding myself. Just because serpents are smart doesn't mean—

The bird's head dips and rises.

I must gasp because a lock of hair lifts off my face before colliding right back into my elevated lashes. A minute passes. Two. "Gods, you do understand me..." I lick my lips. "Any chance you can talk as well? I'd really appreciate hearing how you'll get Dante on the throne."

The crow doesn't react. Then again, what am I expecting? For the bird to actually answer?

"I have a date with him. I'll try to get him to take me to the palace. This way, I can retrieve your *friend*."

The crow's golden eyes turn slitted. Have I offended him by calling the second statue his friend?

The coin Phoebus tossed me burns a hole in my pocket. "I have an errand to run." I move toward the bag that gapes open on the bed, silken blue peeping from its depth, and pluck out my dress. A few threads have snagged where the spikes rubbed against the fabric, but it's nothing too awful. "I'm going to hang this up." I walk over to my armoire and rest my palm on the handle. I hold my breath, expecting the bird to arrow its body low and dive like the scarlet cranes that fish in the canal. Even immune to the metal, an iron beak through the temple would probably put an end to my life.

I twist the knob and the hinges groan.

The crow doesn't flinch. It doesn't attack either.

I draw the door wide, then grope around for a hanger, gaze fixed to the black bird looming over my head. It's not as small as a duck but it's hardly as large as the beasts Headmistress Alice spoke of, the ones reputed to kidnap entire villages.

After putting away my dress, I nod to the armoire. "I'm going to leave the door open so you can nest inside. My grandmother usually doesn't come into my bedroom if the door's closed, but if she hears noise, she might."

I back up to better see the object of Bronwen's prophecy. If only she'd explained what to do with these crows once collected. Will they all come to life? Will my bedroom turn into an aviary? One crow may be concealable, but five? Nonna will find out for certain.

A military vessel passes beneath my window, and my heart holds very still, because aboard is Commander Silvius Dargento.

I grip my floral curtain that lays wilted alongside my closed pane and tug it. "Whatever you do"—I barely shift my lips—"don't move a feather."

Silvius barks out my name, then barks out an order at the man steering the boat.

Thousands of goose bumps spring across my skin.

He's spotted the bird.

Oh gods, he's spotted the bird.

I should've rammed the curtain shut immediately and quickly. The material may be thin, but it would've hidden us from view.

"Signorina Rossi?" He motions for me to open the window.

My heart ramps up, sending so much blood hurtling through my veins that my cut throbs and my bandage dampens.

Opening my window is a most terrible idea.

"Signorina Rossi? The window!"

"I can hear you just fine, Commander," I thunder back.

Annoyance strengthens the point of his jaw. "I have orders to collect you and take you to the palace." A tad mockingly, he adds, "You have a date with the monarch."

"I...do?" I thought Dante wouldn't be able to see me until next week. Not to mention it's the middle of the afternoon. "Isn't it a little early?"

Silvius's black eyebrows dip. "It's two in the afternoon."

"Isn't Dante busy...*soldiering?*" Or whatever it is he does with his days.

The only thing I know about military life is that the soldiers exercise in the mornings. I've watched them enough times over the years from our windows, admired the sheen of sweat on their skin, the bulge of their muscles, the fluidity of their swordplay.

The boat sidles against the thin strip of land belting our house.

"Soldiering?" Silvius grunts. "More like dallying with a certain foreign princess."

Jealousy ignites my belly.

"Must I come to collect you from your bedroom threshold, or will you come downstairs of your own accord?"

"I'll come! Give me five minutes!" I snap my curtain closed.

I squander one minute trying to steady my breathing, then another searching my room for a way to trap the crow, because I don't quite trust the animal. Could I shove the bird back inside the bag? If I managed, then I could clip the satchel closed and hide it under my bed.

My brain throbs again. I thought I'd have more hours to get acquainted with the crow, possibly figure out a method of communicating. The urge to cancel my date seizes me, but then I remember that one of the relics is *inside* the palace.

This must be Bronwen's doing again. If Dante leads me to the crow, then I'll be one hundred percent certain of her preternatural involvement.

"Okay, Crow, time to get down from there. Either you hide inside the armoire or inside the bag. Your choice."

It doesn't choose.

As I unfasten my dress, I try to calculate how to capture the thing. If it starts flapping around my room, the men on the docked vessel will spot movement through my too-thin curtain.

I step out of my dress, and I swear the crow's gaze drops to my bare ankles and rises slowly up the length of my body. I almost want to hide, but crows are birds, not men. Even males.

Is it a male? Probably not. Nothing protrudes between its legs. Come to think of it, I've never seen anything protrude between the legs of cranes or ducks or any other winged animal. Why am

I contemplating bird genitalia? Oh, right...because this creeper is staring.

Using the crow's distraction against it, I raise my arm along the side of the armoire and snatch it.

The animal freezes beneath my fingers. And then...

And then it dematerializes into black smoke.

25

I snatch my hand back so fast, I smack myself in the boob.

Dark smoke smears my pale ceiling as the *thing* I've freed streaks around my room before perching on my headboard. The fumes condense back into razor-sharp down that gleams an inky blue in the yellowed light filtering through my curtain.

Although the air is balmy, a chill sinks into my pores. I hug my arms around myself. "What the Cauldron are you?" I murmur. "First metal, then feathers, now *smoke*? What's your next party trick, Crow? You'll morph into a man?"

The crow glares at me. I glare right back.

"And for your information, I wasn't trying to hurt you. Just to hide you. That man in the boat below my window, he's the commander of the king's army. If he finds you in here, he'll pin you back up." I gesture to the black spikes on my bed. "May pin me up in turn too."

Not only have I robbed a Tarecuorin household, but I've stolen a mythical, murderous creature. I shudder as the depth of what I've done folds over me like dark water.

Through the thin glass of my window, I catch my name on the lips of one of the soldiers but not what he says about me. I do catch some ensuing laughter, and since I'm not known for my comedic repartee, I fathom it wasn't a compliment.

"Fallon Rossi, I'm a busy man!" The commander's voice snaps me back into action. The man isn't known for his patience. In fact, he detests waiting—for his food, his wine, his men, his courtesans.

To think Catriona suggested I sleep with him. Revulsion creeps over my distress and makes me shudder as I pluck the blue dress back off the hanger and step into the fluid silk.

"Just stay in my bedroom," I whisper, "and if you hear my grandmother, hide, or she'll report you." As I button up the dress, I stare squarely at my new tenant. "Do *not* hurt her, or I won't bring your friends back."

That makes the crow stiffen.

"Understood?"

The lines of its body turn sharper still, and its eyes become a cooler shade of gold that rivals the coin I retrieve from my discarded dress.

The crow dips its head, and my jaw slackens. It truly does understand me.

I'm still patting my blue gown to locate pockets when Silvius bellows, "You don't want me to start charging you for my time, Fallon Rossi. You wouldn't be able to afford me."

I jump, then grumble. "Feces fly."

After another thorough perusal of the soft leaves of silk, I come to the conclusion that my borrowed gown has no pockets, which sheds light on why Tarecuorins tote around little bags and clutches. Pockets are for people who cannot afford extra accoutrements.

I heft up the corner of my mattress, nestle the coin on a wooden slat, then grab the black spikes and toss them back into the bag, which I shove underneath my bed. Bedroom spotless, I stand up and smooth out my dress, which needs no smoothing. The material is too fine to crease.

In the speckled mirror over my desk, I catch sight of my gnarled locks and swipe the brush from my desk. "Please don't steal my coin."

One of the crow's eyes grows squinty as though my suggestion peeves it.

As I force the short bristles through my hair, I turn back toward my reflection. The skin beneath my eyes is painted gray with exhaustion, and my skin is wan from stress. I set down the brush and pinch my cheeks, then glide crimson lipstick over my mouth to distract from my enfeebled appearance.

On my way to my bedroom door, I glance at my newest lodger. I cannot believe I'm about to leave a wild and potentially rabid animal with iron extremities inside my house. *Caldrone, protect Mamma and Nonna. And protect me from Nonna's wrath in case she uncovers what I've freed.*

It's only when I'm rounding the blue walls of my house that something awful dawns on me—the crow can morph into smoke, and smoke can pass beneath doors.

"Finally." Silvius's amber gaze slithers up my body as he holds out his hand. "Planning on reducing your sentence through seduction, I see."

I balk at Silvius. "What sentence?"

"Why…" One of his black eyebrows hooks up. "For the crime you committed."

Ice spills down my torso, into my stomach, but must miss my heart, because that organ doesn't freeze like the rest of me. It heats and beats, a staccato that rattles my teeth and bones.

Silvius isn't here to transport me to Dante but to Marco.

Someone from Phoebus's household must've denounced me.

I whip my attention to the men in the vessel, searching for my friend's pale hair and loud clothes amidst the sea of white uniforms.

"I advise you not to run, Signorina, for I am not the sort of man you want chasing you." Silvius's low menace rattles my insides, shattering the ice.

Truer words have never been spoken. I finally unpin my hand from where it sits rigidly at my side and place it in Silvius's. "I commit so many crimes, Commander. May I know which one has earned me a trip to the palace, escorted by my grandfather's favorite right hand?"

Silvius smiles, oblivious, or more likely impervious to my sarcasm. "Your diabolical choice of friends."

Is he speaking of Phoebus?

"Ptolemy Timeus is positively seething."

I don't even attempt to stifle my exhale. "High Fae have such tender egos."

The corners of Silvius's mouth rise as he leads me to a seat at the heart of the boat. Although I don't want to sit, a stray wave coupled with his proximity forces my knees to bend.

"And low Fae have such wicked tongues." Silvius looms over me, amber gaze sliding across my painted mouth. He better not be picturing it on his body, because if there's one place my wicked tongue will *never* go, it's anywhere near this male's skin. "As you so righteously noted earlier, your grandfather does favor me."

I wait to see where he goes with this.

"My influence is consequential around Isolacuori. One word from me on your character and your sentence would be greatly reduced."

"I thought sentences were delivered after trials?"

Once we turn into the southernmost canal that brackets the twenty-five islands, the water-Fae controlling our speed and trajectory propels the boat faster, generating a deep wake. The wind plays in Silvius's long black hair, flinging the pungent scent of the incense forever burning in the private rooms above the tavern inside my nose. Either he's come straight from some doxy's bed or he hasn't showered this morning.

His eyebrows bend. "Sentences *are* delivered after trials."

"Then aren't you getting ahead of yourself by assuming my sentence will necessitate a reduction?"

Silvius's hand lands on the top of my seat, and he leans over, shoving more of his sickly pungency into my face. "Fallon Rossi, this isn't your first serpent infraction."

I tilt my head back to get my nose away from him. "What other serpent infraction have I committed?"

He presses himself back to his full height. "In the royal harbor. A decade ago. Don't think anyone's forgotten."

"I wasn't aware clumsiness was against Lucin law."

He widens his stance as the boat merges onto open water, arrowing toward the looming island upon which resides the king and, ironically, the second of the five crows I need to collect. "It isn't your clumsiness that worries our king."

"It's my sympathy toward animals?"

"You *are* troublingly humane."

"Perhaps because I'm troublingly *human*."

"Only half so." If Silvius states this with zero hesitation, does it mean Phoebus's theory of my being a changeling is false? "May I impart some wisdom with you, youngling?"

"I'd save your breath, Commander."

His mouth, which was ajar, ready to deliver his wisdom, snaps closed. For a moment, he stares at me, his pupils throbbing in irate astonishment. Then he leans over and clasps the nape of my neck. "You're playing with fire, Fallon."

My skin crawls beneath his tightening grip. "Unlike you, I have no fire to play with, Silvius. Now, unhand me."

"*Commander.*" He gives my neck a harsh squeeze to convey his displeasure before finally removing his hand and straightening. "I'm neither your friend nor your equal."

"Cauldron forbid."

A nerve feathers his temple. He's right. I am playing with fire, *his* fire, and since I've no water to put it out or crown on my brow, it's a perilous game.

A low keening followed by a hearty splash has my head spinning sideways. Parallel to the boat, a large pink body dives in and out of the jeweled sea like a needle gliding through fabric. My heart climbs into my throat, skidding further when I catch white bands of flesh amid the pink.

Minimus. I give my head the minutest of shakes, the word *hide* teetering on the tip of my tongue.

Silvius follows my line of sight to the ivory horn threading in and out of the great blue. "That's right. You only play with serpents." My airway tightens when Silvius turns his simpering gaze back on me and adds, "Scarred, pink ones."

26

As we approach the gilded isle with its metal pontoon and verdant flora, Silvius's threat clangs between my temples. If he so much as lays a finger on Minimus—

"The jewel of Luce." The commander's amber gaze is finally turned away from the ocean that hides my pink beast. "Home to our venerable king and his esteemed general."

My thoughts veer off one loathsome male and onto another. I've never considered myself a particularly resentful person, especially toward strangers, yet I simmer with rage as the man who carved my mother's ears and crushed my grandmother's faith in men comes into focus.

Justus Rossi stands on the lustrous dock, hands linked behind his back, rigid body casting a long shadow over six guards. As I behold the monster garbed in burgundy and gold, I never wished so hard to be a changeling.

Silvius leans over to whisper. "Look who awaits, Fallon."

Without breaking eye contact with my grandfather, I deadpan, "Signorina Rossi. Like you said, Commander, we're neither friends nor equals."

I don't miss his staggered swallow over the wavelets lapping at the hull. "Think of your monster, Fallon. Think of him next time you address me with such impertinence."

I grit my teeth at his threat but don't bite out an answer for Minimus's sake. The day my station is above Silvius's cannot come soon enough. Oh, the vengeance I'll seek. First, I'll strip him naked on the Tarelexian wharf so his body can be stared at like boxed goods and touched inappropriately, and then, once his shame is complete, I'll toss him to Minimus.

The boat slows and pivots, then glides expertly into its berth, the bulwark never making contact with the stone embankment. If only I possessed the ability to control my element... I'd steer the boat away. Perhaps even make it tip.

Justus runs me over from forehead to toe. I do the same.

He's broader and taller than I imagined from the few sightings I've had of him over the years, with frighteningly severe features and hair the color of burnt orange rind, a darker shade than Mamma's, threaded with silver strands that reveal the century of life he has on Nonna. He wears his locks in a strict ponytail, and although he faces me, I've no doubt the ends of it skim the bottommost edge of the gold baldric holding a jeweled sword.

My grandmother isn't a soft person, not in character and not in behavior, but in comparison to this man, who has yet to even speak, she's all petals and syrup.

"Good afternoon, General." Silvius stalks away from me, white slacks barely creasing when he lunges up onto the quay.

Justus doesn't acknowledge him. I own his full attention, even though I'd gladly share it.

Two other soldiers on the vessel step onto the platform, leaving me alone with the faerie driver.

Justus and Silvius watch me, urging me to stand without asking, which is the reason I don't. I may be a bastard mixed breed, but I'm not a spineless subject. If they want me to stand, they must ask. And if I want to stand, then I will.

Our standoff lasts forty-three seconds. I count them.

Silvius breaks first. "Signorina Rossi, please proceed onto the quay."

I glance from my grandfather to the commander, whose posture is as taut as a bow string yet whose face ripples with nerves. Incredible how the presence of a superior can impact even the greatest brute's composure.

"Signorina Rossi, did my command not reach your ears?" Silvius all but growls.

"Hmm. Which one? You give many."

Even though his nostrils are slimmer than my beast's, Silvius pulses air as loudly as Minimus. "The one to disembark."

"Oh. I did hear that one but wasn't certain whether I was, in fact, welcomed onto Isolacuori."

My grandfather's pupils constrict to dots no larger than the gold and ruby studs skimming the shells of his ears.

"Did you expect to be tried on the pontoon?"

"Right. My trial. It slipped my mind there for a moment." *A mighty pleasant one.*

Both men's jaws flex, while the soldiers around them side-eye one another or me. Doing my best to hide my satisfaction at triggering such agitation, I finally stand. The boat captain holds out his arm, but I don't take it, don't even glance at it. Everyone else got off the boat without assistance, and so will I.

I hike up my skirt, glad to have worn something elegant and expensive in spite of the circumstances, and climb onto the golden quay. "General Rossi, I've heard so much about you."

His Adam's apple glides up and down his long throat. "I would've been surprised if you hadn't."

His voice is so...*ordinary*—neither particularly deep nor acutely shrill—that his answer doesn't immediately register. But when it does, I wonder if it was born from conceit or humor. Word on the canal is that he's as arrogant as King Marco.

His gaze lowers to the bandage beneath the gossamer white sleeves on my gown before turning toward Silvius. "Why does her arm bleed?"

Is he expecting Silvius to answer, or does he believe the male mutilated me? What would he do to Silvius if he was to blame? Punish him or congratulate him? I'm tempted to insinuate I was manhandled to see what would befall the callous commander, but I won't risk Minimus's life.

"Clumsiness." I shrug. "A wretched halfling predicament."

He remains perfectly stone-faced. "Fetch Lazarus. I want her wound mended before her audience with the king."

For a moment, I think Justus may care about my well-being if he calls on the healer, but his next words blow the fragile prospect from my mind.

"We wouldn't want her tainted blood to soil Luce's most sacred soil."

Touché, Nonno. Touché. How delusional must I be to believe that a father capable of ear culling could be capable of grandfatherly affection?

The general unbinds his hands from behind his back and rests one on his sword's hilt. "You do not resemble Agrippina."

A simple observation, or is it his way of pointing out my lack of Faeness? "I must take after my father."

The healer arrives, his long black robes snapping in the languid, citrus-scented breeze. It's the same man who healed Dante after his swim across the channel. "You called, General Rossi?"

Justus gestures to me. "Heal the girl's arm."

The...girl?

Even Silvius seems stunned by the way my grandfather has addressed me, but his rounded eyes quickly taper back to their usual thinness.

The Fae healer nods to my arm. "May I?"

Focusing on the row of hoops adorning the man's ears instead of on Justus's glacial blue gaze, I lift my arm and pull my sleeve up. Thankfully, the fresh blood hasn't leached onto the flowy sleeves.

Lazarus's brow furrows as he uncoils the bandage, the grooves deepening once my wound is exposed. "What did you cut yourself on, child?"

I eye the soiled strip, willing the wind to pick up and blow it out of his fingers. "A fishing hook." When one of Lazarus's salt-and-pepper eyebrows rises, I add, "A very large one."

The acrid scent of burning paper tickles my nostrils.

Not paper...*fabric.* Lazarus is burning my bandage? That's... unhoped for.

The healer raises my arm and sniffs, then skims his nose down my wrist and over my knuckles, freezing a beat too long for my comfort.

Can he smell the crow on my fingers? Fae senses are keener than humans, but can purebloods truly distinguish the scent of feathers from a mythical being from that of a duck?

My pulse quickens, vibrating my neckline. Since Fae ears are sharp and not just in appearance, I cloak my trepidation beneath snark. "Will I perish, healer?"

As he straightens, Lazarus's amber irises flick up to my face. "Not today, Signorina."

I can't tell if this is a threat or a plain observation. I'm aware I'm not immortal—no being on this earth is—but will my life run its full course?

He raises his fingers to the uppermost hoop on his right ear and rubs a stone as translucent and yellow as tree sap until his fingertips come away coated with a salve that he presses onto my wound. The contact makes me jerk.

As he heals me, his eyes shut and his chest pumps with breaths as strong as the swells that foam and break against the cliffs bracketing Monteluce. I've never sailed around the continent but have heard tales from fishermen, who keep close to Lucin shores in order to avoid paying the excessive tithe imposed by Glace for sailing through their calmer waters.

Perspiration forms along my upper lip. I lick it away, focusing on everything but the agony thrashing through my veins.

"Almost done." The silver-haired Fae must catch the moisture laminating my skin because his tone is soothing.

I swallow. *Almost* turns out to be another full minute. Did it take him this long to heal Dante, or does my body darn itself slower because I'm only part Fae? Probably the latter.

When Lazarus lowers his hands from my arm, my skin is smooth and unblemished. Only dried blood remains, but he makes it disappear by gloving my entire arm with his Fae-fire.

I jolt anew. "Was it truly necessary to roast my arm?"

His whiskered chin dips. "Yes, child."

My heart, which had settled inside my throat when he ran his nose along my knuckles, squeezes itself between my tongue and palate and palpitates there.

Is it the crow's odor or the iron infusing my blood that he scented?

If he tells my grandfather about the former, he'll be condemning me to death. I'd deny his claim, of course, but what happens once my home is searched? Even if the crow can transform into fumes, they'll catch him. After all, they caught him once with those spikes.

"What was it about her blood that so unsettled you, Lazarus?" My grandfather's voice springs me out of my mind's ramblings.

The healer's gaze roams over me one last time before rising to Justus. "I thought I smelled turmeric and wondered why in Luce she'd treat an open wound with a blood thinner."

"Probably Ceres's doing. She so loves concocting natural remedies."

Although his comment irritates me, Lazarus's lie irks me more, because the healer knows one of my secrets—perhaps both—and like Antoni mentioned, secrets make for dangerous weapons in our world.

What will he do with mine?

27

Bracketed by the general, commander, and six soldiers, I travel down the concentric islands that make up Isolacuori. Unlike in Tarecuori and Tarelexo, the strips of land here are curved.

Every time the narrow road bends, I ready myself for a grand vista, but I'm met with more foliage and more blooms. It's only when we reach the canals between the islands that my scope grows, yet instead of looking forward or around, I survey the limpid water that flows beneath the golden bridges.

Dante once told me grates are welded into the underwater foundations of Isolacuori, effectively keeping out serpents and boats, thus turning the waterways into bathing areas reserved for the royal family and high-ranking members of society. He even told me the water is treated daily with a chemical manufactured in Nebba that thins out the salt density.

If only they could make our canals safer, but gods forbid the high Fae do anything that could benefit the lower echelons of society. Come to think of it, serpents need salt, so it's probably best they don't pour their mysterious Nebban solution on our side of the channel.

Lofty bushes dotted with exotic blooms turn into clipped

hedges, and edifices begin to appear. The first is a giant pillared work of marble—the Holy Fae Temple. Although we have two places of worship on our side of the channel, neither is as immense or as blinding as this one.

Sure, the Tarecuorin temple is splendid and vast, but the stone is veined and dulled from years of exposure to the salted spray. As for ours, it's modest and narrow, constructed from wood painted to resemble stone, with chipped benches and exposed beams.

Even though my entourage doesn't lead me through the temple, I catch a glimpse of its glass roof—a single pane that stretches over the immense expanse, a feat of magical architecture.

Remembering this isn't a social call, I return my attention to the road ahead and to the low whisperings of the guards surrounding me.

"Cato handled the situation," Silvius explains to my grandfather.

The general's mouth thins. I take it he's not a fan of Cato, which increases my fondness for the generous white-haired Fae. "Is he still sniffing around Ceres?"

"I have it on good faith that she hasn't accepted any of his advances."

Goose bumps slosh over my skin like wet paint. Do they realize I can hear all they're saying? Are they speaking freely in the hopes that I can? I cannot imagine the general or commander carrying out conversations meant to be private in public, which tells me they're hoping I'm eavesdropping, but why? To display their reach? With the current state of my luck, they'll find out about my crow before I can unearth the four remaining ones.

"His account paints Ptolemy in a paltry light," my grandfather is saying.

I think Silvius mutters, "Timeus is a contemptible man." The scathing look my grandfather tosses the commander's way tells me I must've heard correctly. "Apologies. My commentary was out of line."

"Make sure not to let your tongue fork again in his presence."

"He'll be in attendance?" Silvius enquires. "I thought Cato had settled the financial aspect of your granddaughter's—"

I lean so far forward that my slipper catches on the seam between the flagstones and another golden bridge. I pinwheel my arms, smacking the back of the guard in front of me. He spins around, ripping a nasty-looking dagger from his baldric.

I spring backward, raising my palms.

A sword whispers through the air. I'm expecting the blade to swing my way, but Justus aims it at the guard. "Put your weapon away before I separate your hand from your arm, soldato."

The admonishment makes the soldier's gray eyes widen, and his Adam's apple jolts over the high collar of his uniform. "Scusa, Generali." He lowers both his blade and eyes.

"It would be in poor form to slice the girl's neck before she can atone for her sins."

That's twice now that I misinterpret condemnation for kindness.

Although the crooked olive trees have done nothing to warrant my anger, I glare at them, at their branches dripping with golden fruit. On our side, olives grow a yellowish green, not a yellowish yellow. I imagine these trees were bred so their fruit matched the bridges and the columns of the estate rising behind the gnarled trunks.

Dante mentioned living in a stone house girdled by gold columns. He even pointed it out once from the rooftop of our school, but the thick vegetation made it difficult to spot. Is this his home?

I must've asked my question out loud because the entire delegation has stopped walking and the two men spearheading it are looking over their shoulder at me.

"Yes. This is Prince Dante's home," Justus says. "Although I hear he much prefers sleeping in the filthy brothel where you toil."

28

I itch to correct Justus Rossi's terminology, tell him that what he calls a brothel is first and foremost a tavern, but I bite back my retort because I don't care what he thinks of me and my job. "You're mistaken. Dante doesn't sleep at Bottom of the Jug."

"Dante?" One of my grandfather's eyebrows crawls up his forehead.

"I did my schooling with him, so I find it difficult to use his title."

"For someone who received the best education our kingdom has to offer, you speak and act like a Tarelexian scazza, my dear."

Oh, this man. I move my grandfather's name to the top of the list of men I will remove from power once I become queen.

Three bridges later, not only have I reached a short list of perfect candidates for his position, but I've also reached the heart of Isolacuori. There are more guards here than on the barrack islands, an entire regiment of men dressed in Lucin whites with golden baldrics slung over squared shoulders, sword hilts glinting even though they're far more modest than Justus's.

The soldiers neither blink nor stare as we pass by them, appearing more like statues than men. I wonder if any would break rank and attack if I stepped out of line or if they're merely decorative.

The clap of a hand against a neck drags my gaze back to my grandfather, who's just splattered an insect instead of allowing it to live out its ephemeral life.

I don't love *all* animals—after all, some sting—yet I cannot help loathing the man a little more for his pitilessness, the same way I cannot help wishing an entire regiment of bees would descend on the man and bloat his lithe figure. He'd surely drown them all before they could embed their stingers, but it would make for quite the spectacle.

At the end of the wall of brawn sit massive golden doors carved with sunrays that match the Lucin crown.

"Open!" Justus yells.

The air-Fae who wanted to prod me with his dagger earlier shoots gusts of wind from his palms that move the thick metal. The doors grind open, revealing an entrance stippled with mosaics depicting the sun surrounded by the embodiment of the four Fae divinities, all of them male.

When I was younger, I asked Nonna why no god was female. She explained it was to cow women into believing they are less and help men feel like they are more. It took me years to grasp what she'd meant.

As I tread inside the throne room, I study the tiled sun before lifting my gaze to the dais and studying its embodiment. King Marco sits on a throne as large and golden as everything else on Isolacuori. In many ways, he resembles the man I love, yet in so many others, he doesn't.

His jaw is squarer, his hair darker, his eyes sharper. As I approach, those eyes rove over the delegation before settling on me. Unlike Dante, whose irises are the blue of summer skies, Marco's are a deep amber that matches the fire crackling in the center of the square room that's as wide as it is tall, a cube of polished gold roofed in glass. Since there's no need for heat, what with the room being bathed in sunlight, I assume it's purely symbolic.

After we circle the hissing bouquet of flames, the commander and general come to stand on either side of me.

I sigh in relief when Justus orders us to stop. Although butter-soft, my slippers chafed my blisters. I don't dare peer down at the damage for fear the azure silk will be spotted crimson. Instead, I keep my attention locked on the king, who tilts his head to see past the marquess.

My persecutor crowds the dais, thighs grazing the raised gold platform.

"*This* is the girl who's caused you so much grief, Ptolemy?" Although deep like Dante's, Marco's timbre rings with a haughty nonchalance absent from his brother's voice.

Ptolemy Timeus spins, his complexion reddening until it's a perfect match to the ribbon braided through his hair. "The Serpent-charmer," he hisses.

Since Dante dubbed me with that nickname a decade ago, I don't hate it, but I do hate the way Timeus articulates it.

Marco tips his head to the side. "Justus, what do you make of the matter?"

"With all due respect, Maezza, the general wasn't present at the scene." Timeus's sprite flits over his master's head, dressed in the same crimson silk as the marquess's shirt.

Marco flutters his fingers. "You've spoken your piece, Ptolemy. And exhaustively at that. Now, I'd like to hear what the girl's grandfather has to say on the matter."

"Gran-grandfather?" The blood drains from Timeus's face.

I'm glad he's unaware of how profoundly Justus Rossi despises me, because the sight of the marquess quaking in his polished boots is fascinating.

"Justus *Rossi*. Fallon *Rossi*." Marco gestures between my grandfather and me. "I'm surprised you didn't make the connec-tion, Ptolemy." After a beat, his gaze slides back over the whiten-ing face of the marquess. "Justus, your opinion?"

"I've personally reviewed the damage the marquess's boat incurred after I was informed of the incident. One gold coin will cover the reparations to the structure and to the garish accoutrements."

Timeus's mouth puckers like Sybille's when she sucks on the candied rowan berries her father makes at the turn of the year, a Lucin tradition to sweeten the bitter moments we lived through and the ones yet to come. "What of the immaterial damage the girl has caused me? We haven't agreed on a price for that."

My eyes widen in time with my mouth. "Immaterial damage?"

"To my person."

I scan his body, seeking injuries. When I find none, I level my gaze back on his face. "Oh…you meant to your ego?"

"Bite your tongue, child," my grandfather growls.

The king draws his index and middle fingers across his mouth, which is tipped into a smirk. "You shook on one gold coin, Ptolemy. Since my general deems the amount fair, I cannot reopen the case. It'll have to suffice for your boat and for your self-worth. You are dismissed."

I would never have thought it possible, but Timeus's complexion burns hotter, as though all his fire magic were converging inside his face. "There's still the matter of the serpent."

"Yes. There is." Marco's amber irises seem to redden like the marquess's face.

"What punishment will you—"

"Can you shape-shift into a serpent, Ptolemy?" the king asks.

"Excuse me, Maezza?"

"Unless you can transform into a scaled beast or are related to Signorina Rossi, then the rest of the girl's hearing doesn't concern you."

The marquess's reedy lips snap shut. "I was there. I can testify—"

"You did that while we waited on the accused. Now, *go*." The word resonates through the throne room, skipping over every golden tile.

Cheeks streaked pink, Timeus whirls, his braid smacking his trusty sprite in the face. The tiny faerie dips, then swoops upward, shaking his head to clear it.

The incensed lord advances toward me, and although I've no illusion of the feelings shared by the two men bracketing me, Silvius takes a step closer to me, while Justus smothers the jewels on the hilt of his sword.

"Expect a visit from my sprite on the first of every month to collect my dues, Fallon Rossi." Timeus rolls the *r* and hisses the *s* in my last name, spittle flying from his mouth. Thankfully, he's not close enough for it to land.

"Noted." Relief that he won't come in person loosens some of the tightness in my bones.

Then again, why would a marquess travel to Tarelexo? Purelings rarely walk the streets of Tarelexo. It's only our canals they traverse, on the hunt for the nocturnal companionship that eludes them in their refined neighborhoods, where women must be courted to be bedded.

Although I'm tempted to raise the reason for our spat, I've already done so, and it resulted in Cato begging me to be quiet. I can't imagine I'll receive any sympathy from the men surrounding me. Besides, I need to expedite this hearing, not drag it out.

A crow awaits me. One I pray Nonna hasn't yet become acquainted with.

Once Timeus steps out of the throne room and the metal doors clank shut, King Marco rises and strides off the dais. Since he's garbed in gold from crown to boot, he sparkles as he walks.

I notch my chin up, in part because the king is tall like his brother and in part because Nonna taught me that boosting one's head boosts one's aplomb, and my aplomb could do with a little boost.

Marco holds out his hand toward my grandfather. My stoicism weakens, and I step back.

Silvius latches onto my arm. "Not scared of serpents—or of marquesses—but scared of a little salt?"

My heart's tempo brakes so suddenly, I feel faint. I thought I was about to be beheaded.

I must sway because Silvius's fingers dig harder into my flesh as Justus thumbs open a gold snuffbox adorned with faceted rubies.

The king pinches out a few coarse white flakes. "Open up, Signorina."

Even though I would much rather serve myself, I oblige the ruler, who flicks salt onto my tongue as though he were seasoning me for a roast.

After my throat dips, he asks, "How is it that our greatest pests have not crushed your bones or dragged you down into their lair, Signorina Rossi?"

I slide my lips together, trying to decide how best to answer. "Perhaps because, unlike certain lords, beasts do not feel threatened by me, Maezza."

Marco snorts. Even though a crown sits on his head and magic lances beneath his skin, the sound reminds me that the monarch's crafted from as much flesh and bone as I am. "I've seen children fall into Mareluce—human and Fae alike—and bleed as they are carried away. I very much doubt the serpents feel threatened by our young." His lids lower over his amber eyes, puddling the orange with shadows.

"Perhaps those children lashed out and scared the serpents. After all, we're taught to hate and fear them before we're taught to walk."

"Yet you don't fear them." Marco binds his hands behind his back, the rich embroideries of his tunic stretching over his chiseled pectorals.

The only serpent I know and trust is Minimus. Perhaps his brethren would drag me under. "I do."

"You fear them, yet you willingly jump into the canal to protect them?" He swings his incendiary gaze toward my grandfather. "Did you hand me sugar instead of salt, Justus?"

"No, Maezza."

"Then how come your granddaughter lies?"

"If I may speak, Your Majesty?" Silvius's tepid breaths bluster through the flyaways framing my face.

"Go on, Commander."

"I've only seen Signorina Rossi interact with *one* serpent. A monstrous pink one with scars along its neck."

My blood becomes an icy current.

"Perhaps she *is* afraid of the others."

Marco steps so close that I must crane my neck. "So you have a pet."

Although murderous daydreams unspool behind my lids, I school my features. "The commander's mistaken. I have no pet."

"Companion. Acquaintance." Silvius tosses a hand in the air. "Call it what you want, Signorina Rossi. It's forever the same beast that lurks beside you. That follows you. That *you* follow."

"I follow no creature." My neck hinges sideways, and before I can think better of making Silvius look like a fool, I snap, "Unlike you, Commander."

Silvius's eyes widen in shock.

I may still be plotting his demise, but now he will be plotting mine too. Yet I dig my grave deeper. "Is the commander watching me so assiduously on your orders, Maezza?"

A groove forms between the king's eyebrows. One that tells me he isn't at the origin of these orders.

"On mine," my grandfather says.

I swivel my neck to look at him. "Why?"

"You were raised by an enemy of the crown."

"I was raised by the mother of your children." I could've said spouse, but I don't want to think of Nonna sharing a house with this man. She already shares his name. "Who, I might add"—I turn my attention to the king—"respects you immensely, Maezza." How fortuitous it is that my tongue's unaffected by salt.

Marco's skin and eyes aren't gilded, yet they glow like the flames swaying beside him. "Although I'm glad to hear your grandmother doesn't harbor ill feelings toward the crown, she isn't on trial at the moment. *You* are. Tell me more about this scaled companion of yours. How do you control it?"

Him, not it. "I don't have a scaled companion."

The king arches a brow at Silvius, who vibrates with barely contained antipathy at my side, because he knows I'm lying.

I make sure to look wide-eyed and forthcoming. "If you doubt my word, by all means, feed me more salt."

The king's eyes drop to my throat. "Why does your heart palpitate so?"

I gulp down the wad of panic building at the back of my throat.

"Because she lies," Silvius murmurs.

"*Because* I'm intimidated," I correct him, attempting to ease both my voice and pulse. "Give me more salt. From another source, since Silvius doesn't trust his general." I toss out that last part, hoping this will make me an ally of the man whose blood flows through my veins.

My quip hits Justus in the ego, the exact spot I was aiming for. "Many men would sacrifice the tips of their ears for your position, Commander Dargento."

"I wasn't…" A blush stains Silvius's sharp jaw. "Your granddaughter put words in my mouth. I would never insinuate such a thing, General."

Justus clicks his little snuffbox back open, then closed, then open. After a protracted look with the king that results in the latter nodding, Justus extends the box toward Silvius. "Put some on your tongue."

Silvius's eyes grow so wide that his irises bob in a pool of white. He darts out his hand and pinches a few flakes, which he quickly ingests.

"Where do your loyalties lie, Silvius?"

"With King Marco and with you, General."

The king studies the commander's fiery face. "Ask your man a question he won't want to answer, Justus."

"I hear you've been thinking of settling down. Which female has caught your eye?"

Perspiration beads across Silvius's hairline and rolls down his temples. "I'd rather not say."

"How come?" Marco seems amused by the commander's unease. "Is she that unappealing?"

"Because...because..." Silvius grits his teeth. "Because she's not a pureblood."

"Ah. One of the ladies from Bottom of the Jug, I presume?" The king smiles darkly. "Their in-house courtesan did mention you spend much time there when she attended to my needs the other night."

I gape at Marco, surprised he's dropped the information of his philandering so freely, before remembering he's marrying out of duty, not out of love. For all I know, his betrothed has a slew of lovers as well.

"The suspense is killing me, Commander. Who is this lucky half-blood you care to marry? Catriona perhaps?"

"No." Silvius casts his gaze on the shiny points of his boots, deeply embarrassed by the turn of conversation.

"Another harlot?" Marco enquires.

Silvius's lips shape what starts off as a *yes* but swiftly becomes a *no*, because unlike me, he's not immune to the truth serum.

I run the list of those who tend to the patrons' livers—the

four members of the Amari family and me. And Flora, but I doubt Silvius would stoop as low as a human. I discard Sybille and Giana's parents, since they're happily married, and myself, since Silvius only wants to desecrate me. Which leaves the sisters. I cannot help wrinkling my nose, because Giana and Sybille would surely rather shave their heads and move to Rax than marry this man.

"Guess it must be salt in my snuffbox after all, Dargento." My grandfather snaps the lid on his little box closed and slips it back into his trousers.

I almost feel pity for the commander, but he's a revolting specimen who's pinched my ass more times than I can count. Serves him right to be knocked down a peg.

As the color recedes from his cheeks, Silvius straightens his head. "Please, Maezza, may we return to the subject of the girl and her serpent?"

With a great sigh, the king relents. "I suppose we should. My bride-to-be awaits me in Tarespagia for another revel. So, Signorina Rossi, tell me...how do you control the beasts?"

"I don't. I swear on the Cauldron and on the Crown that I'm a magicless water-Fae. I have control over neither my element nor the animals who dwell in it."

Silvius inhales a sharp breath. "She's human! Fully human. That's how she lies."

Gods, am I? My worry about being a changeling roars back to life.

"You're certain she's of your bloodline, Justus?" the king asks.

"Yes." There's no hint of hesitation in Justus's voice. "I was present when she spilled out of her mother."

He was? With Nonna? Why didn't she ever tell me? "Why?"

"Originally, I came to end your life."

My eyes bulge.

"But Ceres was adamant you be given a chance."

"So what? You just said...*okay*?"

"No, we struck a bargain. One I've yet to collect." He pats his right biceps. Although the fabric of his jacket is opaque, I picture the glowing band of skin he could call on with a mere stroke of his finger combined with the mention of Nonna's full name.

Twenty-two years, and this is the first I hear of it? How inobservant am I that I never noticed the glowing dot inscribed on Nonna's chest? The one that's said to blister the bargainer's heart from the moment the debt is claimed until its completion. I feel both blindsided and selfish.

"I saw her interact with the beast," Silvius growls, one-track minded. "Throw her into Mareluce! The serpent will come."

The commander's suggestion stills my beating heart, and not because I fear for my life but because I fear for Minimus's. What if he comes?

What will they do to him?

29

I press my palm to my stomach, which feels as though it's bursting with juvenile serpents. "I thought this was a hearing, not an execution."

"An execution?" The king's amber gaze drapes over me. "Didn't you say yourself that serpents were harmless, Signorina Rossi?"

This is my punishment for maligning a man in front of his superiors. "I'm not familiar with every serpent in Mareluce, Maezza."

"So you admit you are familiar with some?"

I've just lunged right into Silvius's sticky web. Damn him.

Damn him to the Queendom of Shabbe and back.

Actually...let him stay there. Castration would be a better vengeance than death.

Since saying no to the king's question is no longer an option, I tread carefully around the truth. "I often see the same serpents roaming the canals of Tarelexo."

"How can you be certain they're the same?" Marco asks.

"By their size, color...the length of their tusk. I work at Bottom of the Jug, so I'm often strolling the wharf."

Marco's thick black eyebrows lift. "You work at the brothel?"

Tavern, not brothel. I avoid correcting the king. "I serve food and drinks there."

A slow smile forms on the king's lips as his gaze slides between Silvius and me. It takes me a moment to realize he may be connecting dots that don't even exist on the same sheet of parchment.

I step closer to my grandfather, who's been exceptionally quiet during this exchange, to the point where I check over my shoulder that he hasn't been called away from the throne room.

The ponytailed general stands beside me, blunt nails tracing the facets of his rubies. If only he'd intervene on my behalf, but the man would probably offer to push me into Mareluce himself.

Since no metal crow adorns the throne room, I imagine I haven't been brought to Isolacuori because of Bronwen's prophecy.

Unless the crow is nailed to the island's submerged foundations...

Oh gods, I'm losing the plot. Completely losing it. Like the king, I'm forming connections that don't exist.

I'm not here because of Bronwen; I'm here because of me. Because I jumped into the canal to protect my beast.

"Come, Fallon Rossi." The king's order, followed by his brusque footfalls, makes me jump.

Oh gods, he's decided to toss me in. A plea scales my throat but stays lodged behind my tongue, which has swollen with dread and sits atop my chattering teeth like a slug, unmoving and useless.

"The king has less patience than I, Fallon." My grandfather's voice stabs my ringing ears. "So you'd best follow him. And promptly at that."

I jerk forward on numbed feet and numbed legs, my knees barely bending. The king strides opposite the entrance toward another set of golden doors, smaller than the ones that lead outside.

"Where..." I swallow, start again. "Where..." I cannot get the end of my question out, the same way I cannot calm the clatter of my heart.

Am I being led into a dungeon?

Toward a blue hole that leads straight into Mareluce?

I clear my throat, part my mouth, try again to ask where I'm going, but my words turn to air when the doors are pitched open by the air-Fae bracketing them like gargoyles. The room beyond is windowless, black as a moonless, starless sky.

I stop moving forward and dig my feet into the floor. Through my leather soles, I can feel the shape of each tile, the burn of each blister.

The king sweeps his hand in an arc, shooting fire from his palm that sparks the wicks of a giant candelabra made of...

Stomach bottoming out, I take in the superimposed wheels of ivory cones banded together by rigid strips of gold and topped with black candles. It rises ten wheels high, the bottom one as wide as the varnished wooden table beneath it. Although the wheels grow smaller, it isn't because fewer serpent horns were used to make them but because the horns are progressively shorter, torn from the skulls of juveniles.

The gruesome light fixture makes bile rise at the back of my throat, and although it isn't serpent blood that drips from wheel to wheel, blunting the ivory, it may as well be.

"Welcome to Isolacuori's trophy room."

Trophy? How dare he call bones trophies!

I knot my arms in front of my chest and cast my stinging gaze to the ground.

How fucking dare he...

"You don't seem a fan of my candelabra, Signorina Rossi." Marco's voice traipses through the air that reeks of must and copper. "My grandfather designed it. He was such a perfectionist that if the horns weren't perfectly matched in length and shape to the ones already in place, he'd discard them and hunt down a new animal. For every piece of ivory up there, I have a chest filled with rejects. I've sold many, mostly to the Kingdom of Glace. The northerners so delight in bangles and home furnishings crafted from ivory."

"No wonder the serpents fear our kind." Although I've steeled my spine, my voice quivers as it springs across the bolt of crimson fabric that adorns the oval room's wall.

Marco plods over the golden mosaic sun whose rays extend to the rounded walls. When his boots darken the tiles in front of me, I finally look up. "They've been our enemies since the dawn of Luce. They steal our fish. Eat our people. They ruin our boats and our embankments. The only thing they haven't caused damage to is you."

I keep my stinging gaze on his cool one, refusing to look at the dripping spoils of an unjust war.

"Unlike my grandfather, I enjoy peace, Signorina Rossi. Peace between man and man but also peace between man and beast."

His declaration drives back the vitriol slickening my tongue. "Then why haven't you dismantled that awful thing?"

"Would dismantling it bring the sacrificed serpents back to life?"

No…it wouldn't. "If you want peace, Maezza, then prohibit serpent slaying."

"And how, do tell, shall I prohibit their species from killing ours?"

"They'd learn. In time, they'd learn." My heart still thuds fast but for an entirely different reason now. After fear and anger, I now feel a glimmer of hope. "It'll take decades, perhaps even a century to reverse the damage, but it can be done."

"Or… Or it could take one willing girl and a little of her time." The crown glints, haloing Marco's head as though he were the sun god himself. "Unless my brother was wrong about you, and you cannot actually charm serpents."

I sip in a brisk breath, surprised by his mention of the decade-old appeal that saved me from standing trial. Dante had claimed that he too was charmed even though he was no serpent. He'd even taken a salt oath to cement his words, which in turn had cemented his place in my heart.

Marco's eyes rake across my features, as serrated as the talons of the crow from the Acolti vault. Every area of skin he grooves with his gaze, I patch up before any stray thought can bleed out.

Does this monarch really desire peace, or is he trying to lure a confession from my lips?

I try to read him like he's reading me, but his features are as impenetrable as the gold walls of his palace. "I want peace too, Maezza."

"Shall we bring it to Luce together?"

The bang of metal tears my gaze from the king's face. I glance over my shoulder, past my grandfather, who's stepped behind me and drawn his sword. His gaze must alight on the new arrival at the same time as mine, because he tucks his sword back into its sheath.

Dante strides forward, white uniform streaked with dirt and brown skin lambent with sweat. "What is the meaning of this hearing?" He sounds positively incensed.

I want to run to him, burrow my face against his chest. I want him to whisk me out of the throne room and off Isolacuori, away from these men who want things from me I don't want to give.

"Good afternoon, Brother." Marco's voice breezes past my rigid neck.

"You've arrested Fallon on what grounds?" Dante's nostrils flare as though he's raced across every bridge in Isolacuori to get to me.

"I haven't arrested anyone."

"That's not the word going around Luce."

"You should know better than to trust the words that circulate around my kingdom."

"I heard them spoken from your personal guards."

"Justus, I thought we employed soldiers, not gossips. Gather their names, and give them leave."

I balk. "It was harmless chatter, Maezza. Hardly worth losing a job over." If anything, I want to thank these men, because they brought Dante to me.

"Is it your army, Signorina?" the king barks.

I pinch my lips shut. *Not yet.*

"If Fallon wasn't arrested, then why is she here?" Dante looms over my grandfather, seemingly as intent on reaching me as Justus seems intent on keeping us apart.

"It's a hearing, Brother. She's being *heard.*"

Dante's jaw clenches. "Heard or interrogated?"

The brothers stare at each other, tension crepitating between them like the fire in the throne room. Unlike Giana and Sybille, who are as thick as thieving sprites, the century of life that separates the two Regio siblings is a rift that neither man seems capable or willing to leap across.

"Have you even provided her with counsel?"

Marco gestures to Justus. "Her grandfather's in attendance, is he not?"

Dante snorts, stealing the very sound from my throat. "Her grandfather works for you, Marco. Duty over blood... That was the first lesson you ever taught me."

Marco's eyes taper closer to his aquiline nose. "Not that this matter concerns you, but I'll indulge you. Your *friend* and I were discussing strategies to bring peace between our people and the serpents. Although she asserts having no control over the beasts, twice she's been seen swimming with a serpent, and *twice* she's survived. Intriguing, wouldn't you say?"

"Twice?"

"Signorina Rossi dove into the canal last night to protect a serpent from Ptolemy Timeus's wrath. I'm surprised news of her midnight dip didn't reach your perky ears."

It is the vitriol with which Marco stamps each one of his words that decides me. Even though I desire nothing more than peace in Luce, I won't help *this* king accomplish it.

"I guess you were too wrapped up in bedsheets to hear much over your whore's moans." Marco wears a cruel smile, as though he senses the blow won't only hurt Dante but also me.

And it does hurt.

Until Dante's eyes fasten to mine, even though it is to his brother that he speaks. "You can send an army of whores my way to keep me distracted from your politics, and I will never touch any."

But Beryl said—

And Lord Aristide—

Marco's smile stutters off his lips. "Don't lie. They all enter and leave your rooms reeking of sex and looking mildly satisfied."

Dante removes a snuffbox from his pants pocket, pinches a few crystals, and lets them melt on his tongue. "The women you send me are harlots, which is why they smell of sex. As for mildly satisfied, I'd say I leave them plenty satisfied, Marco. After all, they all leave with purses bursting with gold coins to perpetuate the rumor that the prince is a drunk and a philanderer."

My heart.

I lift my palm to my breastbone, which palpitates with beats. All of them for this man who has not only proven himself worthy of my love but also of Luce's throne.

30

Dante steps past his brother to reach me, concern etching his brow. "Why would you dive into the canal?"

I take a moment to drink him in, hating that I doubted him, even though my misgivings were of his own making.

"Fallon?" he prompts.

I should've lied while under salt oath. I should've insisted I'd slipped off the bridge. If only I'd played my cards adroitly. Sure, there were *four* eyewitnesses last night, not counting Timeus's sprite, but claiming a mishap may have bought me time.

"Maezza, if we don't depart now, we'll miss the tides and have to pay the tithe to cross through Glace's waters," Justus says.

"The tides?" Marco's tone is as high as the color tinting the walls of his trophy room. "If we aren't traveling with enough water and air-Fae, Justus, then gather some more aboard! Nature doesn't control us; we control it! As for tithes, one of Vladimir's daughters is here. I imagine that should decrease the asking price." His jaw is so tight, he looks about to pull a muscle. "Unless my brother isn't treating her well…"

"I treat all my friends well, Marco."

"Too well, it seems." Marco's pupils tighten before spreading, along with the shape of his mouth, as though an idea has just come over him.

I glance around the room to see if I'm the only one affected by his erratic humor. My grandfather's expression is unreadable, whereas annoyance and confusion are stamped all over Silvius's face, but I think those have more to do with me than with Marco. As for Dante, he's too concentrated on my face to register his brother's.

In a whisper, I finally answer Dante, "I dove into the canal because a dagger was embedded in the serpent's cheek, and you know my tolerance for animal cruelty."

"You could've died, Fal." His answer is just as soft as mine.

"But I didn't."

"Because she can communicate with the damned beasts, that's why," Silvius mutters.

Dante's eyes flick to his while mine roam over the rest of the room, landing everywhere but on the source of the blaze.

I start to turn but freeze when my gaze latches on to the table's centerpiece—a gold and iron bowl. Although the room burns with a thousand candles, its gloom sinks into my bones, because the steel-gray metal is a curved wing.

A wing that leads to a fist-sized head.

So focused was I on the ivory tusk monstrosity, I missed the crow someone bent into a bowl.

My skin breaks out in gooseflesh. I'm not certain how prophecies work—whether Bronwen whispers into men's ears and they obey or whether she tosses strange ingredients into a cauldron and stirs—but my coming to Isolacuori...my discovery of crow number two...*this* cannot be a coincidence.

Or if it is, then bring on more of them.

At the rate of two a day, I'll have won the Lucin crown before Marco even returns from Tarespagia.

Pulse drowning out all ambient noise, I move deeper into the king's oval mausoleum to stand over the crow. His eyes shine as brightly as the first crow's. Correction, one eye shines. The other is obscured by a layer of wax as thick as castagnole dough.

I'm tempted to scrape off the obstruction, glad my nails are short and blunt from hours spent scrubbing saucepots and linens. Even though I'm not entirely certain if the crow feels pain in this form—or in any form—I'd prefer not to scratch out its cornea.

Before my finger can meet metal, Dante yells, "Fallon! Don't!"

I startle and snatch my hand back, burrowing it in the gauzy folds of my dress.

Oh my gods. Had I really been about to touch the iron crow? How could I be so foolish?

"This dish is exquisite. And so lifelike." Do any of them know that there's a real—somewhat real—bird beneath the iron?

"You're not to touch anything in this room without the king's consent." My grandfather's eyes are pools of shiny blue ink.

"Oh no, Justus. Let her." The king flaps a hand, the smile straining over his lips chillingly sunny.

"My sincerest apologies for my terrible manners." Turning back to the crow, I rack my brain for an ingenious way to leave Isolacuori with it, since I cannot exactly stuff it beneath my skirt, however voluminous the fabric.

I suck in a breath as I realize the king wants something from me. Perhaps he'll consider an exchange: the bowl for my serpent charm. I spin around to ask, releasing a muffled shriek when I find myself nose to chest with the man.

I settle my gaze on the Regio brother nearest me. "I really like your bowl."

"Do you now? What is it you like about it?"

Another trap?

Genuine interest?

"Although I'm only part faerie, I'm fully a woman, and you know how much we like shiny trinkets. Not to mention I love animals." The veins in my neck must protrude, but there isn't much I can do to disguise my stampeding pulse. "Did one of your ancestors have it made, or was it given to them by another ruler?"

"*I* had it made after a battle that *I* won."

The only battle Marco won was the Battle of Primanivi, the one that, according to Giana, changed his demeanor and emptied his eyes. His eyes look pretty full to me, though. His irises churn with heated pride while his pupils pulse with dangerous suspicion.

If he had the crow bowl made, then that means he collected the crow himself. I wonder what form the bird was in before it became a bowl. Was it already metallic and rigid or downy and black?

"It's a crow, right?"

Marco acquiesces.

"Headmistress Alice depicted them as giant beasts, but they're rather *small*." I school my features into a mask of perfect innocence.

I feel everyone's gaze slide from me to Marco, then back to me.

"This is merely a miniature made to commemorate the monsters we fought."

"I can't imagine how terrifying they must've been."

He cocks his head to the side. "Can't you? You swim with serpents."

I don't take the bait. "I've never seen such detail."

"Our blacksmith is very talented. I didn't know you had such a vested interest in sculpture, Signorina Rossi."

"You don't know many things about me, Maezza." Although decidedly not the worst words I've spouted today, my needling remark was unnecessary.

"You should really depart now, Marco. You wouldn't want to leave Eponine with our mother for too long. Your poor bride will be eaten alive." Dante winds his warm hand around my elbow. "I'll see to Fallon's safe return."

"I've tasked Commander Dargento—" my grandfather starts, but Dante speaks over him.

"I'm here, Rossi. I'll take her."

Justus's lips fold together, the seam no larger than the space between the golden mosaic tiles. He stares hard at Dante, then flicks his gaze toward the commander, who stands as still as the rest of the guards in the throne room. "Very well, Altezza." Justus's boots squeak as he pivots. "I will see the commander to his boat and ensure yours is ready, Maezza." His eyes snare mine.

I'm expecting a goodbye.

Or a nod.

I get nothing.

Why I still have any expectations when it comes to this man is beyond me.

Without a word, he walks into the brilliant blueness beyond the throne room's outsize golden doors, Silvius on his heels.

Marco lifts a hand and sets it on his brother's shoulder. "Isolacuori is yours while I'm gone." The fabric rumples as he squeezes. "Try not to wreck it."

"I'll do my very best, Marco."

A sharp blade couldn't tear through the wall of tension between the two.

Marco smiles, but it doesn't look like a smile at all. "You seem only too pleased to take up the task."

"If you prefer I stay in the barracks and let your guards safeguard your domain—"

"I trust you." Marco moves his gaze to me, communicating that his trust doesn't extend to me. "Will you be staying on Isolacuori during my absence, Signorina Rossi?"

"I have work and a family to tend to, so no."

His smile grows, slimy as an oil spill. "Such a responsible girl."

"May I ask you something before you depart?"

"You may."

"If I do agree to try to tame the serpents and am somehow successful, would you consider giving me the bird bowl?"

His irises blaze from the reflection of the grotesque chandelier. "Tame the serpents, and then we can discuss your recompense."

Does this mean he'll consider parting with it?

He nods to the entrance of the trophy room. "I wouldn't want you to keep your customers at the brothel waiting, Signorina Rossi."

My spine tenses at his innuendo.

Not to mention I really, *really* hate that he refers to Bottom of the Jug as a brothel when it's a tavern. "Shall I give Giana your regards? I hear the two of you were friends back in the day."

"I'm not certain which Giana you speak of, but do pass on my regards to whomever you wish if it can make their day."

Wow.

"I will see you upon my return next week." He turns in a glinting whirl and marches forward, two armed men preceding him, two tailing him. "Guards, blow out the candles, and lock the doors!"

"Altezza, Signorina." A silver-eyed soldier with a long brown ponytail flourishes his hand, inviting us to exit the room.

I glance at the bowl, itching to reach out and pinch it, but thievery in front of the prince and a regiment of armed Fae is undoubtedly unwise.

Dante gives my elbow a gentle squeeze, and I shuffle forward.

The Fae guard sweeps his hand, snuffing out the king's fire and my prospect of doubling down.

31

Dante and I don't speak during our trek back to the pontoon. It's only after we've boarded the military gondola and drifted a ways from the solid gold dock that he breaks his worrisome silence.

"Why?" He studies the choppy ocean, the darker strait in which dwell the serpents.

"Why what?"

"Why would you risk your life for a serpent? Not only does this make you look unhinged, but it makes me look disloyal."

I lean backward on the varnished bench seat I share with Dante, eyes widening in time with my mouth. "Wh-what?"

"It was one thing to slip into the canal and survive. It's another to jump in." His Adam's apple climbs slowly, then drops back even slower. "How do you think Marco would react if I went to Shabbe and pledged my allegiance to their queen?"

Annoyance tiptoes over my shock. "You can't possibly equate protecting serpents to swearing fealty to another monarch?"

"In Marco's eyes, the serpents are just as despicable as the Shabbins."

"You're comparing people to animals."

"Says the girl who considers them our equals."

I lock my lips and turn my eyes to the horizon, spy a coiling shape beneath the swells. Thankfully, the scales gleam orange and not pink. I don't want Minimus anywhere near a boat loaded with powerful Fae.

After a very long beat, I spit out, "Why would *my* act reflect on *you?*"

"Because I stood up for you, Fal." His hand plucks mine from the folds of my dress, cocoons it between his warm palms. "Because I want to keep standing up for you, but I can't do that if you deliberately put yourself in such situations."

I try to snatch my hand away, but he holds on tight. "I never asked you to pick sides."

The wind rises when we reach the middle of the channel and swirls my hair.

He snares a lock and presses it behind my ear, and although Dante knows me by heart, I flinch when his thumb grazes the blunt shell. "There are very few people in this kingdom who want nothing from me. I treasure the few."

Although my pulse doesn't slow, it settles into another rhythm. "Except I do want something from you, Dante."

His eyebrows slide close together.

Before his wariness can take root, I say, "I want that date you promised me. If you're still willing to take out the wild Serpent-charmer."

A smile crooks the corner of his mouth, which he moves close to my ear. "Once Marco returns and I hand him back Isolacuori, I will demand a few days' leave." His volume drops. "Stay out of trouble so we can spend my vacation time together, all right?"

His suggestion buoys my heart. "Just us?"

"Just us." His thumb draws circles over my knuckles.

Considering I have a crow in my bedroom and need to hunt down three more, plus grab the dish-shaped one in the trophy room, I deem it wise not to make any promises.

He tucks another flyaway behind my ear. "No trouble, all right, Fallon the Charmer?"

"You make me sound like a sorceress."

"Would explain why I'm under your spell."

I roll my eyes. "A minute ago, you wanted to strangle me."

"And now I want to kiss you."

My eyes widen as I angle them every which way to see if any of the other Fae on the boat are watching. The two steering are focused on the looming Tarecuorin islands, and the two at the rear have their backs to us, busy scanning the ocean for threats.

"Forget anyone's around."

Beyond his shoulder, I catch sight of another boat—Silvius's. "The commander's watching us."

Dante tosses a look over his shoulder before refocusing on me. "Creep."

One of the many things that man is... Others are nasty, disre-spectful, and sycophantic.

Dante clutches the sides of my face and tips it so it's perfectly level with his. "Forget him, Fal."

Easier said than done. "What of your reputation?"

"You're part Fae, not to mention the general's granddaughter. You're hardly an improper companion."

"So I don't need to be your dirty little secret?"

He smiles, then moves that smile closer to me. Scrapes it across my lips. "Only if you want to be."

"No."

He chuckles softly, and the sound hardens my nipples and shortens my breaths. When he slants his head and coaxes my lips apart, I toss all societal fetters and primness to the wind and open myself to him.

After all, I'm kissing my now and forever, the man who cap-tured my heart in the shadows of Tarelexo.

My lids flutter closed as my body softens against his. Although he doesn't scoot closer, he's all I feel, all I taste, all I smell. His breath becomes the air in my lungs and his hands the only things keeping my body from swaying into his. He cradles my jaw between his pillowy palms.

His skin is so soft.

So much softer than mine.

So much softer than Antoni's.

My blood heats and beats as the memory of what I almost did last night floods my irises. Thank the Cauldron I refused Antoni's advances, or remorse would be gnawing at my conscience. I decide that before Dante and I part ways, I will tell him about the kiss because I don't want there to be any secrets between us.

Any more than necessary, that is.

Although my body remains with Dante, my mind wanders to the crows. More precisely, to the one in the castle. If I asked him to retrieve the crow dish, would he?

A wave hits the boat, bowling our heads together and clinking our teeth. We break apart, laughing like two schoolchildren who've just shared an awkward first kiss.

His eyes are so blue, his teeth so white, his lips so full and pink. This man is the epitome of male perfection, the benchmark against which I've measured every other man in my life and will keep measuring them.

To think he's mine.

He caresses the curve of my cheek. "Marco won't depart for another hour. Would you like to see where I live?"

It takes my naive mind a moment to process the connection between Marco's departure and a visit of Dante's quarters. My cheeks warm as I consider his offer. On the one hand, I need to check on my newest houseguest before getting to work; on the other, this will be the last time I see Dante for a week. Perhaps longer.

I'm not ready to say goodbye. "I thought soldiers couldn't entertain civilians on the barrack islands."

The slow smile my words spark across his face rids me of any and all sense of responsibility. "Soldiers cannot, but I am no soldier, Serpent-charmer."

32

Dante commands the gondolier to change course.

As we glide toward the island of white tents, I look over my shoulder at the drawn curtains of my first-floor bedroom. "That garish dish... Do you think your brother would ever consider giving it to me?"

Dante glances away from a passing military vessel stockpiled with trunks and soldiers. "No. He's attached to his trophies. They fuel his ego."

I'm tempted to ask straight out for it but decide being pushy can only backfire. I'll wait to unearth the remaining crows before ransacking the trophy room.

As soon as we dock, Dante stands and holds out his hand to help me disembark. With a graceful hop, he joins me on the wooden pontoon and laces his fingers through mine.

The soldiers patrolling the garrison shores watch us with wide eyes. I'm glad the sight of the prince walking with a woman startles them so. After all, it can only mean it's not a habit of his.

"What are you all looking at?" Dante barks, jolting them from their stupor and jolting me in turn. The power he has over people, over me, over Luce...it's formidable.

We stroll down a narrow cobbled road that opens onto a

larger street lined on both sides by tents. Some flaps are drawn open; others are sealed shut. Heads swivel as we pass, and conversations dim.

I cross many Bottom of the Jug regulars; none acknowledge me. Do they fear Dante snapping at them for looking my way, or are they *that* flummoxed by my presence amongst them?

Dante nods to a sprite guarding the entrance of a tent twice as large as the neighboring ones. The winged male snatches the corner of the flap and soars upward, parting the unblemished material to let us through. "I'm not to be disturbed, Gaston."

For some reason, I wonder if this is the sprite who delivered my ribbon and dress. "Of course, Altezza."

As I step into Dante's quarters, unease whooshes through me, growing more insistent when the heavy material settles, shutting out the sunlight. Flattening my palm on my stomach to ease my nerves, I concentrate on the stark decor.

Everything is functional and immaculate, from the honeyed floorboards to the crisp bedsheets to the hammered copper tub. A table stands beside the empty bath, outfitted with stacks of fresh towels and a porcelain sink. Although there are no windows, light filters in through the fabric walls, making the metal sparkle and the buffed floors shine.

It's pleasant in an understated way, albeit a little cold.

I twirl slowly to face him. "How does it compare to your home on Isolacuori?"

He stands with his back to the doorway, blue eyes sparking like the furnishings. "It doesn't. My home on the royal isle is gaudy; this one is efficient."

"Which one do you like best?"

"Currently?" He steps forward. "I much prefer my tent because you're standing in it."

Butterflies carry my lingering qualms away on their beating wings.

His hands circle my waist, and he inclines his face until our foreheads meet. "No wonder the pure-blooded females loathe you so."

I recoil. I'm hardly a Fae favorite, but loathed?

His grip hardens along with another part of him. "You are *unreasonably* beautiful, Signorina Rossi."

His pretty words thaw me out. I'm far from gorgeous, but if Dante sees me as such, who am I to contradict him? I take his compliment and store it inside my heart, next to all the others he's peppered me with over the years, then palm his shoulders and press up on my toes to reach his mouth.

I almost land my kiss when he murmurs, "Stop working at the brothel."

I roll back onto my heels, perplexed. "I can't stop working at the *tavern*." I make sure to hammer in the fact that Bottom of the Jug is first and foremost a place to eat and drink. "My family needs the money."

"I'll give you a stipend."

I shake my head. "No. There'll be no money between us."

"I wouldn't be paying to spread you out on my cot. I'd be paying to make your life easier. As for Bottom of the Jug, you do realize most patrons go there to satisfy their sexual needs?"

"Most, not all. Some go for the drinks and the delicious food."

His eyes flick over my face, quick sweeps of blue darkened by indecision. "Have you ever"—his throat dips—"slept with a man for coin?"

"No."

His deep exhale warms the tip of my nose. "Good."

"Would it have been a deal-breaker?"

His grip widens until his thumbs and index fingers sink between my ribs. "No, but I prefer to be the only Lucin familiar with the shape of your body and the fragrance of your"—he lowers his nose to the delicate skin behind my earlobe—"cunt."

I break out in goose bumps. Never would I have imagined my

body reacting to that skeevy word with anything other than dis-taste, yet from Dante's lips, it sounds downright sensual.

As he trails kisses to the sharp bones of my shoulders, I confess, "The night of the revel, I kissed someone else because I thought you hadn't invited me." When his mouth stops moving, I add, "It didn't go any further than a kiss, though."

"Who?"

"No one you know."

He lifts his head. "So not a Lucin?"

"Because you know *all* the men in Luce?"

A nerve twitches beside his flattened lips.

"How many women have you kissed?"

He releases my waist. "It's not the same."

"Why? Because you're a man?"

His cheek flutters again.

"Have you lost count?"

"I've never kept count."

"Yet you frown on my trifling experience?"

"You're right. It's unfair." After a beat, he says, "Forgive me." His hands slide back around my waist, then up the length of my spine. "No more talk of other men."

I shoot him a pointed look. "Or of other women."

A smile softens his lips. "Or of other women. Just you."

"Just you."

He gathers me to him and kisses me long and hard, with teeth and tongue, as though to scrub away the traces of another's pres-ence. When we break apart for air, he rasps, "I like your dress, even though I'd have liked it better if you were wearing the one I purchased for you."

Thankfully, he misses my grimace because his eyes are fas-tened to the pulse point in my neck. He pushes away my hair, uncovering Antoni's hickey. I expect a scowl, but instead, Dante lays his mouth on the faded bruise and suckles.

Is it wrong that I like this small act of possession?

He walks me backward until my calves hit his cot, his deft hands working the buttons on my frock. A silent second later, my dress pools at my feet and I'm left standing in drawers so sheer, they reveal the auburn tangle of hair beneath.

Dante stares, his chest barely moving, his expression giving away nothing. I grow somewhat uncertain. For all his talk of me being unreasonably beautiful, the man's surely been with dozens of prettier women.

Females with pointed ears, skilled tongues, and lush curves.

I glance at the sealed tent flap.

"Fal?" He tilts his head, calling to my eyes with his. "Are you having second thoughts?"

"Are you?"

"No." His certainty renews mine.

If Bronwen hadn't predicted my future, I would've made Dante work for this moment, woo me, but whatever happens, he and I will end up together. "I love you too much to have second thoughts."

A graceful curve of lip illuminates his handsome face as he scoops up my hands and sets them on his jacket collar. "How about you undress me?"

My hammering pulse makes my fingers shake. After several failed attempts at threading the button through the slit, Dante covers my hands with his and guides them. Once unbuttoned, he tosses his jacket aside and carries my hands to his shirt. I untuck it from his slacks and roll it off him. Although he wastes not a minute towing my hands to the waistband of his pants, I pause to admire the muscles stacked between his razor-sharp waist and taut shoulders.

"We don't have much time," he murmurs.

"I know, but give me a minute to look at you." I slide my hands from his hold and glide them up his taut abdomen, over his rounded pecs, his dark nipples, his sharp collarbone. I don't miss the shudder that racks his body as I skim my hands back down his beautiful torso to his slacks and unhook the buttons of his fly.

As the crisp material glides down his narrow hips, I pull my hands away and return my eyes to his. Although I never imagined I'd lose my maidenhead in the middle of the afternoon in a tent in the barracks, I always imagined I'd lose it to this man. I suppose time and place are of little import when you're with the right person.

Dante takes my mouth in a kiss that makes butterflies soar past my stomach and into my rib cage and drags my body into his, smearing a trail of heat over my navel. Without breaking our kiss, he laces our fingers together and carries them to his taut length.

"Look at what you do to me," he rasps, nipping my lower lip before moving our entwined hands over himself.

He pulses against my palm, his skin satin soft and ribbed with bulging veins. Without being prompted, I glide my thumb over the glistening tip. His hand drops from mine to wrap around my neck.

I squeeze him. I must use too much force because his lips twist. I spring my fingers wide. "Did I hurt you?"

His grimace morphs into a smile. "No, Fal." He pecks my lips. "It feels good, but it'd feel even better if you moved your hand back and forth."

Here I thought I'd know exactly what to do thanks to Catriona, Phoebus, and Sybille, but clearly, I'm clueless.

I follow his pointers, and he groans, which I take as a good sign.

I increase both my speed and pressure. "Like that?"

"Just like that." His chest rumbles. "Just like that."

His lids close and his head falls back, his long braids slapping his toned back. He's beautiful everywhere. As I allow my gaze to roam over the flesh I grip, his hand snares my wrist and stills it.

I snap my gaze back up to his face, which is no longer twisted in ecstasy. "Did I do something wrong?"

"You were perfect. Everything was perfect."

"Then why?"

"Because I don't want to come in your hand." He thumbs my lower lip before tracing the plumper arc of my upper one. "I want to come inside your body."

He steps into me until my knees buckle and my ass meets his mattress. Instead of folding over me, he toes off his boots and kicks aside his pants, then widens his stance and aligns himself with my face.

I stare up into his hungry eyes, heat flooding my cheeks as I realize which place in my body he wants to penetrate: my mouth.

33

Dante strokes himself, waiting, his weeping tip a breath away from my parted lips. Battling back my squeamishness, I stick out my tongue and flick it over his engorged head. His body rattles like my serpent's when I pet his dorsal fins.

Two different species yet the same reaction. How Dante would detest the comparison.

I swirl my tongue over his skin that's as smooth as Tarecuorin silk and as salty as Mareluce. He groans, and I swear the guttural sound vibrates the walls of his tent. Emboldened, I ease him into my mouth.

"Your hands, Fal." His chin falls against his chest, his lids at half-mast. "Use your hands on me." He nods to my fists, which lay balled atop my bare thighs.

I raise one to his throbbing length and the other to his heavy sack.

As I knead and stroke him, his fingers thread through my hair and his hips begin to rock. He drives himself in so deep, my throat clenches. I choke and try to pull back, but his palm pins my head.

I smack his muscled thighs, and although I don't manage to shift him, I do manage to lean away and spit him out. "Don't push my head."

"Sorry." His fingers freeze before sparking back to life and smoothing down my hair.

"Or pet me." Who knew I'd have such strong opinions about an act I'm performing for the first time?

He raises his palms and holds them aloft.

Realizing I'm killing the mood, I murmur, "Sorry. It's my first time and—"

"You've nothing to apologize for, Fal." He leans over me, his palms skating down my neck and over the slope of my shoulders. "Absolutely nothing." He nudges my mouth with his and kisses me, softening me with each sweep of his tongue. When the line of tension in my shoulders finally drops, he disengages our lips and crouches before me. "Have you ever explored your body?"

I swallow deeply as his palms sail to my bared breasts.

"Have you ever made yourself come?" He squeezes the soft globes of flesh, electrifying every last blood cell in my body.

"Yes."

"Show me where you touch yourself."

I slide my lower lip between my teeth, cheeks prickling with heat. "Why? Do you suspect my erogenous zones are in peculiar places?"

A low chuckle shakes his chest. "You'd be surprised what some people like." He releases my breasts and slides his palms over my thighs, then cinches my knees and pulls them apart. "I think you touched yourself…" He runs the heel of his hand over my underwear, pupils dilating at the dampness he encounters. "Right. Here."

I hold my breath before gasping out a "Yes."

He repeats the motion, pressing a kiss to the inside of my thigh. "Hips up, Fal."

I dig my palms into the mattress and lift myself just high enough for him to roll down my underwear. Once it falls to the floor, he glides a finger to my opening and circles it before sinking in knuckle-deep. I blow out a ragged breath at the intrusion.

To think it's only a finger, and a rather slender one at that.

He drags it in and out until my walls squelch around him. "Look at how ready you are for me."

My heart beats as fast as my thighs shake.

After a few more thrusts, he tows his digit out and skates it back up my slit. To my regret, he skips right over my clit, caressing instead my hollow stomach and buttoned navel and the seam of my ribs. When he reaches my breasts, he toys with my nipple, rubbing and pinching it.

Although the friction is uncomfortable, I've craved the feel of Dante's hands for far too long to ask him to stop. He brings his mouth to the tender skin he's kneading and laves the sharpened point.

Although it doesn't light up my body, the sensation is tolerable. He licks my other breast, then peppers gossamer kisses across my collarbone, leaning over me until my spine unspools.

"Thank you," he murmurs.

"For what, Dante?"

He climbs over me, heavy cock flopping between our bodies. "For saving yourself for me."

"There's only ever been you."

I wait for him to return the words, but unlike me, Dante is neither a virgin nor a liar.

Keeping his gaze on mine, he nudges my thighs apart and pushes himself inside. There isn't any give. Gasping, I contract around him, the word *stop* stabbing the inside of my throat as he sheathes himself to the hilt.

Pinpricks of pain crackle where our bodies connect, yet all I can think is, *It's done.*

"Are you all right?"

I swallow and, talented liar that I am, nod.

As he pumps his hips, whispering how wondrously tight I feel, sweat breaks out along my hairline. In Mamma's books, the heroines experience such pleasure during the act that, without fail, it brings them to orgasm. I'm starting to think these anonymous publications were written by men, because I'm closer to weeping than I am to climaxing.

As the burning sensation spreads like Fae-fire, I try to catch my breath, but he plunges his tongue through my parted lips. Even though our minutes are few, I clap his hips to slow his fiendish tempo but fail at my task and merely end up holding on for dear life.

Thankfully, Dante doesn't last too long, and when he finally spills himself inside me, the blaze has subsided to a prickly warmth.

With a juddering breath, he drops his forehead into the crook of my neck and grows completely still. The relief I experience at that moment is so potent that I sigh. As he softens inside me, I coast my hands to the base of his spine, then skip my fingertips along the smooth beads woven into his coarse braids, over the mantel of his strong shoulders, and up the velvety shells of his elegant ears.

He inhales deeply, then levers his head to look at me. "Till my very last breath, I'll remember today, Fallon the Charmer." He closes his fingers around one of my hands and kisses my knuckles like the gentleman that he is when he's not taken over by his lust.

I find my mind wandering to Antoni, to how sex would've been with him, but flick him far and wide. How dare I taint this precious event with contemplations of another man. "I'll remember today always too."

I silently thank Nonna for that awful tonic she made me ingest. I may want Dante's children someday, but that day is far in the future.

He kisses the hinge of my jaw, then pries himself out of me and strides to the basin. As he washes himself, he trails his eyes down my body, halting on the sheets that stick to my backside.

I peer down, and although I expect the red stain, I bite my lip to have sullied his pristine sheets. I'm about to apologize when a look of pride seizes his features. Sybille warned me that some men consider it a great honor to deflower a woman. I'm uncertain as to why, but if Dante's pleased, then so am I.

As I sit, though, Nonna's warning about leaving traces of my blood around the kingdom clangs within me. I grip the sheet and wrap it snugly around my body before standing. Luckily, my blood hasn't seeped in deeper than the first layer of white cotton.

While my lover slips on his pants, I sashay to the basin and dampen a corner of the sheet to wipe down the insides of my thighs, then ball it up.

Before I can toss it into the washbowl, Dante lays a hand on my forearm. "Leave it, Fal. I'll have it taken care of."

Except I cannot leave it. Even if Dante isn't ill-intentioned, someone in his employ might be.

Before he can stop me, I submerge the soiled linen. Dante's lips pinch but he doesn't admonish me for disregarding his directive.

I pluck my drawers from the floor and thread them onto my legs, then scoop up my dress. He helps me with the buttons, observing me with an unsettling intensity.

I scrub at my cheek, worried about dried drool or some other bodily fluid, but feel nothing suspect beneath my fingertips. "What is it?"

"I was just thinking about how much I'll miss you."

A heady thrill tiptoes up my spine. "Invite me to the palace then." Not only would we get to spend time together, but I'd be geographically closer to the trophy room crow. A win-win.

He looks like he's contemplating it, but when he cups my cheek and sighs, I realize I'll need to find some other way onto the isle. "You'd be too great a distraction."

Is that why, or is he worried about my motivations?

He leans over and kisses me gently, then releases my arm to

pull open his tent flap. "Gaston, fetch Gabriele. I want him to escort Signorina Rossi home."

"I don't need an escort, Dante. Just a boat."

"You'll have both."

I sigh.

Gabriele mustn't have been forewarned of his task because his eyes grow wide when he enters the tent. "Fallon," he says by way of greeting.

Leaving Dante is harrowing albeit indispensable for I need to finish my treasure hunt and he needs to practice ruling the kingdom that will soon be his.

Ours.

As I step out of the tent, I find the commander poised on the other side of the cobbled road, hands clasped behind his rigid back, narrowed eyes affixed to me. Antipathy drifts off him like my blood off Dante's sheets.

Oh, how the male loathes me. Especially since he didn't get to pitch me into Mareluce and watch me sink. I'll have to tread extra carefully, because I sense the hateful man will be watching my every move as he waits for his sovereign's return.

34

Loud, raucous sobs echo against the frescoed walls of our house, distracting me from the dull ache throbbing between my thighs. I recognize the cries as Mamma's and sprint up the stairs, my heart clocking my ribs in fear of what I'll find.

If the crow sank its talons into Nonna…

If…

When I reach the threshold of her bedroom, I find my grandmother crouched beside Mamma's rocking chair. "Look, Agrippina. She's back. And safe. Our Goccolina's fine."

I kneel in front of my mother's chair and take her hands in mine, scanning every millimeter of bare skin for a weeping gash. "Mamma, I'm here. Look at me. I'm here. And I'm fine."

"Fallon. Leave. Fallon. Leave. Fallon."

Is this an observation or a warning? Did she think me gone, or is she telling me to leave? "I'm right here, Mamma."

She shakes her head, her copper waves scampering over her hunched, freckled shoulders. "Fallon leave."

"I did, but I'm back."

"Leave. Leave. Leave." The anxiety shading her tone combined with the intent luster in her blue eyes knocks the wind from my lungs.

"Are you telling me I need to go, Mamma?" I whisper, even though it isn't like Nonna will miss my words. She's standing right there, emerald irises spangling with worry.

Mamma stops shaking her head but only to start nodding it.

I glance at Nonna in confusion. "How long has she been like this?"

"When I got home from the marketplace, I found her on her knees, banging on her door. She crawled all the way to it. Thank the Cauldron it was closed."

Had I shut it before leaving? I remember checking on her and finding her asleep but nothing else, too panicked between the bird and my "arrest."

What if she shut it herself because she was scared of the bird in my bedroom? What if the bird dematerialized and passed through the wall separating our bedrooms? What if it's gone?

Goose bumps scamper across my collarbone and spill down my chest.

"What is it?"

I blink away from the wall. "Wh-what?"

"You're flushed."

I cup my neck, my palm clammy against my hot skin. "I've had a day."

Nonna presses a mug of rowan berry infusion to Mamma's lips. My mother shakes her head.

"Bibbina mia, you need to drink."

I don't think I've ever heard my grandmother call Mamma her baby, and it sends a bolt of pain through my heart. How devastating it must be for a mother to be powerless in front of their child's degradation.

Finally, Mamma stops rocking, stops repeating the word *leave*. She looks up at her mother and parts her mouth. Nonna helps her drink the sour berry tea, running a knuckle over Mamma's chin to catch renegade droplets.

As though it held actual magic, the concoction soothes my

mother and weighs down her lids. Her lashes, burnt umber like her thin brows, lower. I think she's about to fall asleep when her eyes flare and set on me.

"May the winds carry you safely home." And then her lids plummet, and she leans her cheek against the pillow Nonna propped behind her head.

Nonna and I blink at each other. It's the first time Mamma has articulated a full sentence. At least the first time I've heard one.

"Did she—did Mamma just—" My mind reels with her strange blessing, because that's what it was, right?

"She did."

"Have you ever heard her say…*that?*"

"When she was pregnant with you, I caught her whispering it to the sky. I assumed she was wishing your father a safe passage to wherever he'd sailed off to. I once confronted her about it. She told me we were all allowed our secrets." Nonna's lips thin as she stares between me and her resting child.

I think of the bargain Nonna struck with my grandfather, but speaking of it will necessitate an explanation as to how I found out, and she looks haggard enough. "You think my father was a sailor? *Is* a sailor?"

"I don't know, Fallon. She never did tell. I just know she met him during one of her trips to Rax. She used to go there every day to succor the needy." Nonna smooths Mamma's hair. "She had such a big heart. Wanted to save everyone and their sprite."

"*Has.* She has such a big heart. She's not gone, Nonna."

"A part of her is." Nonna sighs, staring down into the mug of tea as though to divine Mamma's future like Beryl does every time I brew her a cup of coffee.

Although Beryl's tales are always entertaining, she's never envisioned me as a queen. Then again, why would she? I'm but a lowly halfling. How glad I am that she's a conniving siren instead of a demonic one.

"Why did Dante's friend drop you off?" Nonna's offhand comment blows my mind off Beryl.

Did she also see my port of departure? I wait for her to say more. She doesn't make me wait long.

"What were you doing in the barracks?"

"Dante invited me over for a visit."

She squeezes the bridge of her nose. "And you went?"

"I did."

Her disapproval is as pungent as the smell of rowan berries. "Goccolina…"

Before she can call me a fool or whatnot, I blurt out, "You know where else I went today? To Isolacuori."

The mug falls from Nonna's hands and shatters in thick, sharp pieces. What little pinkish liquid remained flows between the shards and her slippers. The sound makes Mamma jump but somehow doesn't wake her.

Nonna's mouth opens. Shuts. Opens. Her irises darken as suddenly as the Racoccin forest during storm season. "Ptolemy…" The name of the marquess comes out no louder than the steam from our teapot.

Since I'm still on my knees, I gather the pieces of the mug, careful not to let the infusion stain the pretty pastel fabric of my dress. "He told the king about my sympathy toward the serpents, and the latter demanded a hearing."

"And?"

I layer the chunks of ceramic inside my palm like fallen rose petals and look up at her. "And King Marco would like me to use my gift to bring peace between land and sea dwellers."

Horror rearranges Nonna's lovely features, giving her the air of someone older. "You told him about your gift?"

"Of course not, Nonna. Besides, I don't even know if I actually have one."

"Was Justus—"

"Yes."

"Did he hurt you?" Her fingers are balled into such tight fists that her knuckles protrude.

"No, Nonna."

A little voice in the back of my mind adds, *Not yet.* I don't let that bout of insecurity escape. Nonna is anxious enough.

I finally climb back to my feet and turn my attention toward the window, toward the white army tents gilded by the setting sun and the neat row of military vessels bobbing along the narrow island.

Silvius's boat is empty, but does that mean he's stopped watching me?

"Justus is accompanying the king to Tarespagia for more betrothal festivities, so my hearing will resume next week upon their return." I turn back toward Nonna, whose eyes hold a far-away gleam, as though she's back at court, back in Justus's household, back in a time and place where my mother's ears were as sharp as her mind, where I didn't exist. "Do you think he truly wants peace, Nonna, or do you think he's trying to squeeze a confession out of me?"

Nonna blinks back to the present, to our little blue house in Tarelexo that has kept us safe until now.

"The Regios abhor animals almost as much as they detest humans, so do not confess to anything. And, Fallon, you never go to the court without me again, you hear? Never."

I make her the promise even though I won't keep it. I cannot. Because the only reason I have to return to Isolacuori is to gather the crow, and I refuse to involve Nonna.

35

As Nonna returns to the kitchen to dispose of the broken mug and start on dinner, I head toward my bedroom. My heart jolts as I reach my door, as Mamma's words clatter inside my mind.

Fallon. Leave.

The crow must've fled while I was away! That's why she was urging me to leave.

I shove the door open so fast I fall into my bedroom, managing to stay upright only thanks to my death grip on the handle. Although the light is thin, made thinner by the setting sun and my drawn curtains, everything is in sharp focus—the armoire, the desk, the vase of drooping peonies, the crow perched on my bedpost.

My theory sinks like silt, giving way to both relief and foreboding. Relief because losing a bird outfitted with iron appendages would've been most problematic, and foreboding because I'm back to square one on twigging Mamma's worrisome decree.

I close my door and lean against it, attempting to calm my runaway pulse. The crow watches me with its unnerving citrine eyes.

"I thought you were gone." I don't owe it an explanation, but since the bird understands me, I decide to give it one.

The creature's head doesn't tilt.

"My mother seems convinced that I must leave. Since she directed me to the vault, I imagine my leaving is somehow linked to you."

Am I really pouring my mind out to this animal? What exactly am I hoping for? Advice? A directive? The vault could very well have been a fluke. After all, my mother isn't right in the head.

What am I going on about? It was no fluke. She warned me Bronwen watched, and Bronwen was watching. She spoke of gold in the Acolti vault, and there were piles of it.

Some superior force is using my mother as its mouthpiece.

Is that superior force Bronwen herself?

What *is* Bronwen?

My bedroom walls spark out of existence. My ceiling and floor too. Suddenly, I'm peering down into a ravine. I snap my arms out and bang my knuckles against something hard—a wall of gray stone. The fingertips of my other hand spring open but meet no resistance.

I throw my weight to the side and clutch the rock even though I'm not falling.

I'm...I'm floating.

What the Cauldron is happening to me? My gaze slings wildly around for something...someone, but I'm alone in—Where am I? Monteluce?

The rush of a stream thunders beneath me.

Far, *far* beneath me.

Even though gravity isn't dragging me downward, I grip the rock, more lizard than woman.

I'm about to yell for help when something gleams on a narrow ledge below me, a black arrow protruding from its breast. My scream dies before it is born, and I blink.

The gorge vanishes, and I'm back within the confines of my bedroom, squatting in front of my bed, fingers curled around the wooden frame, knuckles white, thigh muscles drumming as hard as my biceps.

My lips flutter with breath after breath.

Was that a vision?

Am I having visions now?

Is this what assaults Mamma's mind and riles her up?

Even though I'm no longer dangling tens of meters over a gorge, I straighten with caution. I'm loathe to admit I glance at the floor to make sure it's still there. Sure enough, the slats of hardwood glint like raw honey.

I finally lift my gaze back to the crow and sigh. "I think I know where to find your next friend." I spear my fingers through my hair, pressing the locks out of my face, and glance toward the window. In two strides, I'm standing beside it, drawing the curtain open to peer at the smog-swathed peaks. "I think it lies in a gorge somewhere in those mountains."

A shudder rolls through my marrow. If Rax is reputed to be a perilous place, the chain of mountains that separates the two sides of the kingdom is reputed to swallow whole all those who dare venture into its rocky folds.

"Maybe Bronwen can assign this mission to someone else." I turn back toward the crow, scrutinize the citrines embedded into its head before trailing my gaze along its stubby neck and black wings. "Or better yet, why don't you fly out there and succor your friend?"

The crow's eyes seem to narrow, so I narrow mine in turn.

"I don't see why my suggestion merited such a look. It's not the least bit outrageous. In case you haven't noticed, I've neither wings nor magic."

My forehead prickles as though the skin has gone numb. I rub at it, attempting to expunge the strange feeling, when I find myself standing in night-soaked woods before Bronwen and a sad-dled horse.

I jolt. Slam my lids closed. When I pry them back up, I'm back inside my bedroom, clutching my curtains like a life rope.

What the Cauldron was that? *Another* vision?

And if it was, who sent it to me? One of our gods? Bronwen herself? Is Bronwen a goddess? An oracle? An enchantress? Is she an evil spirit? She certainly looks like something otherworldly with her melted face and unseeing eyes—something wicked.

Oh gods, what if she is an evil spirit come to destroy the world through me?

The history of Primanivi funnels into my mind, setting my enthusiasm awhirl. What have I done? What am I doing?

36

I eye my bed. Eye the crow, which eyes me right back. I lunge and crouch, hook the leather satchel I stuffed underneath and slide it out, and then I grip the obsidian spikes, one in each hand, and jump to my feet.

Before the crow can flit off its perch, I raise my arms and strike. Again and again. Every time I think my spikes will encounter flesh, they sail through black smoke.

Sweat glazes the nape of my neck and drenches my dress, my muscles drum, and the sting between my thighs has taken epic proportions, yet I don't stop my assault on the wicked crow.

I've never inflicted harm on an animal, never wished one harm either, but I'm now more than ever convinced that the bird I awakened is no animal.

"What are you?" I growl between hard pants, weapons raised.

The malicious thing has the audacity to scowl. What I cannot understand is why it hasn't flown away…why it taunts me so. Can't smoke fit beneath doors?

Exasperated, I unlatch my window and fling it wide. The breeze that wafts in cools the perspiration beading on my upper lip. "Get! Get, and find Bronwen. Tell her that I'm not her puppet. I neither need *her* nor *you* to capture Dante's heart. We'll be together, crown or no crown."

I'm still holding on to the pieces of broken black stone, but my fingers are loose and shaking.

"Go!"

The crow stares down at me from the top of the armoire.

Gods, this is the inanest evil spirit in the history of evil spirits. I'm giving it a way out, and it won't take it.

Without thought, I hurl the stakes into Mareluce. After the dark canal gulps them down, I lift my gaze and am about to turn back toward the bird when I spy a figure standing on the black shore of Rax.

Perhaps I'm imagining the turban and the snapping skirts, but it doesn't stop me from yelling, "Find someone else! I'm done with your fool's errand." My eyes sting. From sweat. From tears. From complete and utter frustration. *Why me?*

"Why me?" I whisper out loud.

Because you're a magicless silly girl whose will is as easy to bend as her heart, that's why. My mind is a pitiless critic.

I drag my burning gaze away from Bronwen or whoever stands on the other side of the canal, if it's even a person, and rake it over the gloomy corners of my bedroom. I'm expecting the assessing glint of golden eyes, but nothing shimmers.

Nothing moves.

The crow's gone.

It fled.

Finally.

In the old myths, there exists a tale the Fae enjoy whispering to their children to warn them against befriending curved-ear Fae. It's the story of how halflings lost the points of their ears. I never believed this perpetuated tale, that one impulsive girl could doom an entire race by opening a sacred box filled with Fae secrets and spilling them across the three kingdoms. But isn't that, in a way, what I've just done?

Released something that has the power to doom our race?

"Fallon, what in the Cauldron is going on up here?"

I whirl toward my bedroom entrance.

Nonna's tall, thin figure is backlit, yet I don't miss the furrows crosshatching her face or the direction of her eyes as she takes in my toppled desk chair, gaping armoire, rumpled bedsheets, and tipped vase dribbling water and peonies.

"Are you...redecorating?"

I snort and scrub the moisture webbing my lashes.

"Goccolina, what's wrong?"

"Have you ever done something stupid for love, Nonna?"

"I married your grandfather."

"You—you loved him?"

"Once upon a time. What's this about?"

As I stare at the stars swathing the cobalt sky, the desire to confide in my grandmother bloats my tongue.

"What is it you've done?" She must've padded closer, because her floral scent envelops me even though her arms don't.

And they surely never again will once she learns of my gullibility and complicity.

It's this fear that she'll stop looking at me as though I'm precious that pricks my tongue and deflates my rising yearning to unburden myself.

Because she's expecting me to say something, I murmur, "Dante will be taking some time off next week."

Nonna's eyebrows cant as she scrutinizes me and then my bedroom, obviously puzzled as to the connection between Dante's break and the disheveled state of my room.

"He's asked me to spend it with him. Just the two of us." I lick my lips. "I said yes."

Never in a million years did I picture myself sharing this with my grandmother, but it beats explaining the true source of my anxiety.

"I'm not asking for your blessing because I know you'll never give it to me, but I wanted you to know."

I yearn for her to stroke my arm and tell me to follow my heart. Speak a sweet lie like when I was a child, and she'd try to protect me from the harsh reality of life. But Nonna hasn't lied to me in years.

Nonna sighs. "Goccolina, the prince will never marry you, however many trips you and he take together."

I gasp as though she's staked me with those obsidian spikes. "You know nothing of Dante and how different he is from Marco!"

Nonna's mouth smooshes into a thin line.

"You're so jaded, Nonna. So...so..." My eyes prickle with heat that distorts the sight of her stern face. "I hate you."

She doesn't flinch. Either she doesn't care or she doesn't think I truly mean it.

"I'll prove you wrong." I start toward my door but backtrack, shove my mattress up, and grab the gold coin. "Here. Make sure the marquess gets this."

"Where did you—"

"It was given to me."

"By whom? Whose money did you take?"

"I didn't take it. It was *given*."

"By whom?"

"By a man who doesn't believe me a fool for loving a prince and who doesn't believe I will amount to nothing because I came from nothing."

A breeze blows a lock of my hair into my burning eyes. I wrangle it back.

May the winds carry you safely home.

Suddenly, I think it was Mamma's way of telling me that this decrepit blue house is no longer my home. That I must spread my wings like the crow and soar toward my true home— Isolacuori—by way of Rax and Monteluce.

Leave. Fallon.

I look toward the now deserted blackened shore and the jeweled greenness beyond. *I'm going, Mamma. I'll leave tonight and gather those five crows.*

Oh, the look Nonna will wear when she spots me sitting on the Lucin throne.

Empowered by the image of myself in a crown, I stalk out of my cage and away from the woman who's kept me trapped within it for the last twenty-two years.

37

Although I consider setting sail for Rax immediately, I head to the tavern first. Like the king said, I'm responsible, and I won't leave the Amari family in a bind just because my grandmother has wounded my pride.

Besides, I want to collect my pay so I have coin to trade during my journey through the Lucin wilds and inform my best friend that I'm taking off so she doesn't worry.

When I reach Bottom of the Jug, the tavern is bursting with diners, and both sisters look as though they've blasted themselves with their air magic. Their hair stands on end, and their collarbones are glossed in sweat.

"Finally!" Sybille blusters past me with a platter of drinks that she deposits on a table. "Where in the three kingdoms have you been?"

Guilt worms itself behind my breastbone at the idea of leaving them.

They'll replace me.

I'm replaceable.

That little voice, which has spurred me to act impetuously in the past, spurs me to stick to my plan. It isn't like I can go home. Not after the way I stormed out.

I look over my shoulder, the same way I've looked over my shoulder a hundred times since I banged the door of my house shut, expecting to find Nonna trailing me. The only person staring at me is a bearded fisherman scrubbing down his deck.

My grandmother is as prideful as I am. Expecting her to chase me is like expecting snowfall at the height of summer.

Swallowing back the lump in my throat, I roll up my sleeves and get to work. It's mindless, which allows me to plot my next steps. Even though, deep down, I presume Bronwen will be waiting for me with a saddled steed, if she isn't, do I set off without a horse?

It only dawns on me now that the clothes I wear are completely impractical. However much I hate my boots and overly washed frocks, I can't exactly trek across Monteluce in silk slippers and a dress as delicate as butterfly wings.

In Rax, clothes are sewn to endure. I'll trade with someone. Surely, I'll have no trouble rehoming such pretty frocks.

Sybille knocks her shoulder into mine. "First off, where did you get that dress? It's gorge. Second, what's eating you?"

"I borrowed it from Phoebus's sister."

Sybille's lids shoot up. "Flavia 'I hate halflings' Acolti lent you a dress?"

"Phoebus lent it to me."

"And he had one of his sister's dresses lying around because? Oh."

I'm not certain what conclusion she's drawn, but I leave her with it. Maybe Phoebus will tell her about our morning, but I won't. Especially not in a place filled with perked ears.

"As for what's eating me... I slept with Dante." Even though my afternoon deflowering is not on the front line of my thoughts, I want Sybille to hear it from me and not a random patron.

The copper jug she came to refill slips from her fingers and clatters noisily against the bar, catching the attention of the ten or so diners hunched in front of drinks and wooden boards of cured meat and cheese.

"Oh. My. Gods." She leads me by the elbow to a dusky corner of the tavern, her mouth still gaping. "And?"

"And you could've warned me it hurts." The ache has dulled to sporadic pangs.

"I can't believe you slept with Dante."

In truth, I can hardly believe it myself. The afternoon feels surreal. "I know."

"Was it everything you dreamed of and more?"

I hesitate, because no, it wasn't. As much as I want to confess this to Sybille, Dante and I will be married someday. It's in poor taste to complain about your husband's lovemaking. Besides, we were pressed for time. It's bound to get better.

"I'm leaving."

Sybille's head rears back. "Because of the sex? Was it that bad or that good?"

"Not because of the sex."

"Then why?"

"I need to get away from Tarelexo for a little while. Commander Dargento is breathing down my neck, and things at home have been tense."

She studies me. "Your mother?"

"No. Nonna."

She squeezes my arm. "I'm sorry, Fal." Suddenly, her sympathy morphs to eagerness. "Let's leave together."

I'd love nothing more, but it'd be unfair to drag her into my mess. Moreover, I'm genuinely worried the prophecy won't come to pass if I don't go at it alone, and I really need it to come true.

"I cannot take you with me, honey. It's something I need to do on my own. Besides, your parents and sister would never forgive me if I took you away from here. And then Phoebus will insist on coming, but now that he has a new boyfriend—"

"What? That weasel. He said it wasn't serious with Mercutio."

"I think he likes him more than he'll admit. Even to himself."

Sybille grins. "You should've seen them at the revel the other night. They were so—"

"Once you two are done gossiping, I'd appreciate some assistance." Giana swipes her glistening brow with her wrist.

"Sorry, Gia. Tell me who needs what." I dry my hands on my pretty skirt.

"Table ten wants a pitcher of wine, and the commander wants a platter of prosciutto."

The commander's here? My gaze zips toward the pointy-jawed man in white, sitting with another man dressed in uniform, not one I recognize.

He's not here to spy on you, Fallon. He's here for food.

"I'll take table ten." I return to the bar and snatch one of the ready-to-go jugs lined up on the counter, then swing around the bar toward the six Tarecuorins playing cards.

As I refill their cups, Catriona, who's just descended the stairs, bustles toward Silvius. The tavern is rowdy, and the commander's table is along the far wall, so I don't hear their exchange, but I'm guessing she's gauging his interest in a rendezvous. I pray he says yes, because when I make my grand escape, I prefer for him not to see me off.

I pour out the last droplet of fizzy Fae wine just as his gaze slithers off the courtesan and zeroes in on me. Catriona glances over her shoulder with a little sigh. Does this mean he refused her advances? And if he did, is it because he's "working" or because he's finally decided that sleeping with other women won't win him the respect of the one he wants?

As I wind my way back toward Sybille, I debate whether to tell her about Silvius's desire to marry her or her sister, but that would require a long-winded explanation about how I learned this, and I haven't yet informed her of my unfortunate date with the king. In truth, I'm somewhat surprised she hasn't heard about it. The Lucins do so love to gossip, and what better fodder than a halfling getting arrested for serpent charming?

"Pappa needs help plating something." Giana motions to the kitchen.

I shoulder open the swing door and am about to offer to help when I notice Marcello butterflying pigeons on a chopping board. The birds are featherless, but their heads are still attached. My stomach heaves and I swoon. I clutch the doorframe and wait for my vision to color and my insides to settle before even attempting to take a step forward.

It's not the first time I've seen Marcello prepare a roast, but for some reason, for a fleeting moment, it reminded me of the crow. And yes, admittedly I tried to skewer it earlier, but only to turn it back into a gewgaw, not into someone's supper.

"Fallon, are you all right?" Defne is at my side, arm laced around my waist in support.

"Sorry. Yes. I…uh…forgot to eat today." It only strikes me then that I have indeed forgotten.

She leads me to a wooden stool too close to the chopping board and unwraps a block of pecorino. After slivering it, she unscrews the lid off a jar of pickled vegetables and sets both in front of me.

Keeping my gaze on the grimy floor beneath my stool, I shovel down my meal. I don't feel any better once I'm done, probably because I ate too quickly, but I'm glad for the sustenance.

As I scrub my plate in the sudsy basin, I tell Defne and Marcello that I have to make an impromptu trip, and no, nothing bad has happened to anyone, but I won't be able to work at the tavern for the foreseeable future.

Defne's lips curve with a soft smile. "It's about time. Marcello and I were wondering when you'd fly the nest."

How appropriate…

"You should encourage Syb to do the same." Marcello's counsel shocks me into silence. "Maybe she could go with you. You girls have the grandest of times—"

"I can't." The words shoot out of my mouth, much brasher than intended. "I cannot take her with me right now. Once I'm settled, though…"

They look at each other, brows pleated.

"Settled?" Defne repeats.

"I'm meeting a friend. And, well, I want to see where it goes, but I haven't told Syb about him."

"Ahh…" Defne's forehead smooths. "So this is about some boy. The one we spoke about the other night?"

"Yes," I lie.

Marcello's wariness doesn't fade. If anything, now that he hears I'm going off to meet a man, he seems downright disappointed in me. I briefly wonder how he'd feel if he learned this man had wings and feathers and quite possibly isn't male at all.

"Has Ceres met this *friend* of yours?" His tone is strained.

"Do you really think he'd still want to rendezvous with me if he'd met Nonna? She just may be more frightening than Justus."

That gets a chuckle from Defne.

"Well, I'd feel better knowing his name," Marcello grumbles. "In case anything—"

Defne slaps her husband's arm. "Leave the poor girl alone. Don't you remember how we'd sneak around behind our parents' backs?"

I could kiss Defne. I actually do peck her cheek and whisper, "Thank you."

"Anytime." Defne removes her coin purse, but I tell her I'll pick up my wages at the end of my shift and to deduct a canteen, a block of hardened cheese, and some dried fruit.

"Won't this man feed you?" Marcello is tapping the flat edge of his butcher knife against his open palm as though ready to slaughter my fake lover.

Defne tsks. "I'm sure he will, mi cuori. Now set that knife down before you injure yourself and bleed all over Signore Guardano's meal. Pigeon in blood sauce might be a delicacy in Nebba but not in our civilized kingdom."

When he doesn't set the knife down, I say, "I'd rather leave prepared in case it doesn't work out and I must make my own way."

"Smart girl." Defne arches an eyebrow at her husband, who's still grumbling into his beard about boys not being raised like in the olden days. "I'll get your supplies ready before the night is through."

Chanting a chorus of thank-yous, I pick up a tray of food that's ready to be delivered and head back into the dining room. I'm crossing my fingers that the commander has downed his drink and left, but he's still there. And worse, he watches me weave around tables.

When I slide back around the bar, I want to scour my skin to remove the slimy goose bumps he's raised. Even though technically, I'm not running away from anything, I won't miss the obtrusive man.

Especially after Catriona slides into the seat in front of me and says, "That man is obsessed with you, micara. Are you sure you don't want me to negotiate a tariff on your hymen's behalf?"

I blush from the roots of my hair to the nails on my toes because she delivered those words loudly. Keeping my attention on the jug of water I'm wiping down, I murmur, "I'd rather move to Rax and abstain from sexual relations for the rest of my life." I could've confessed I had no more hymen, but that's really none of her or anyone's business.

She blinks, even though it isn't the first time I've hinted at my distaste for the man.

My firing nerves hurl a smile over my lips. "But thank you for thinking of me and my maidenhood."

She sighs. "A shame. Such a shame."

The exact opposite. The commander would probably wring my neck while fucking me to force a damning confession from my lips.

The rest of the evening, I silently will the man to leave before last call, but the stubborn ass doesn't budge from his seat, and although he isn't outright gawping, my neck prickles intermittently from his stare.

What if he waits for me until the end of my shift? How am I supposed to negotiate transport into Rax with a high-ranking officer on my tail?

When the penultimate customers leave, I finally head over to his table. "That'll be one silver and fifteen coppers."

He nods at his table companion, who seems more of a decoy than a live person considering how motionless he is. The younger man digs two coins out, both silver.

"I'll be back with your change." I whirl on my aching feet. To think my day isn't over…

"Keep the change, Signorina Rossi."

Over my shoulder, I toss, "I'll be sure to tell the Amaris of your generosity."

Before I can retreat, he calls out to me again. "Seducing the prince won't help your case."

I don't want to engage this man. I have places to be, crows to find. But I cannot help loosing a dramatic sigh. "Oh no. There goes my ingenious plan. Do say, who should I seduce then? The king himself? *You*?"

I think, or rather hope, my snark will shut the male up once and for all, but he decides to needle me some more. "Do you know what your prince charming is doing at this very moment?" Silvius's voice is so close that I spin around. He hovers over me, hands bound behind his back as usual, lips fashioned into a smirk. "He's dining with the Glacin princess." Silvius slithers around me like a serpent. "I hear they dated when he was stationed up north."

"Good for him."

"I can tell you don't believe he has any affection for her."

"Because he doesn't. Not romantically."

"Do you kiss men you're not romantically involved with?"

"No."

"My point exactly."

"What is your point?"

"Before coming here tonight, I had a meeting in Isolacuori. When I arrived, Dante's tongue was buried deep in the princess's throat."

"You're lying."

He removes an enameled snuffbox from his pants pocket and pinches out a single flake of salt, which he presses onto the tip of his tongue. After he's swallowed it, he repeats those words, and each one embeds itself into the fragile casing of my heart, causing the organ to ache. "The man won't sleep with whores because the Glacin princess won't allow him into her bed if he does. I'm guessing he hasn't told her about you, though."

He slides the snuffbox toward me, and although I don't want to play this game, I scoop out a fingerful of flakes, which I sniff.

Salt. It truly is salt.

He snaps the box shut and returns it to his pocket. "You look positively distraught by the news."

I roll my fingers into such tight fists that my nails tattoo small crescents inside my palms.

"Commander Silvius, the establishment is closed." Giana's voice clangs like metal striking metal.

He tosses something shiny her way. "I'll take a room. Preferably one without a roach."

Giana's nostrils flare as she watches the silver coin flip end over end to the ground, not even attempting to seize it. "I'm afraid all our rooms are booked for the night."

He stops his incessant circling. "Are they now? Catriona

251

mentioned business was slow for the doxies this evening when she propositioned me."

Giana doesn't gratify him with an answer. "Don't forget your coin on your way out."

"Careful, Signorina Amari. I could make or break this establishment's reputation." He snaps his fingers to showcase how easily he could ruin her and her family.

"I don't take nicely to threats, Commander. Now stop harassing my staff, and see yourself out. And perhaps quit returning. Like you said, too many roaches crawling around our establishment. It's time we run them out."

The glower he sends her way is frightful, yet Giana doesn't even flinch. However hard I want to wrap her in a hug and thank her for her support, guilt that I brought this on her and her family tacks my feet to the sticky floorboards and my arms to my ribs.

My departure may not have been ordained by any god, yet it's a godsend for everyone around me.

When the commander and his friend finally leave, I whisper, "I'm sorry."

"For what, Fallon?"

"It's my fault he threatens you."

She swipes a dishrag over the bar. "Dolcca, don't ever again take the blame for fatuous men. Now lock the door, and help me straighten this place before you leave on your adventure."

"You heard?"

"I hear all."

"All, huh? Did you hear about the way I spent my afternoon?"

Sybille emerges from the kitchen. "Finally. I thought the sprite-ass would never leave." One look between her sister and me has her frowning. "What did I miss?"

"Fallon was about to recount her adventures on Isolacuori."

Gods, Giana truly does hear all.

Sybille gasps. "You went to Isolacuori without me?"

"Trust me. You wouldn't have wanted to tag along on that trip."

As I tell them about Justus, the king, and the commander's suggestion to toss me into Mareluce, Sybille's mouth widens and widens until all her pearlescent teeth are on display. Her sister, on the other hand, displays not a gram of shock.

As we dim the glow of the lanterns that are strung up from fishing ropes helter-skelter across the room, I ask Giana, "Do you think it's true? About the princess of Glace?"

She side-eyes me. "Steel that sweet heart of yours, Fallon, or our world will end up licking away all its honey."

However poetic, it doesn't answer my question. "Does that mean yes?"

"No, I hadn't heard of their tryst. Am I surprised by it, though? No. Eponine comes from Nebba. It's only natural that Marco would seek an alliance with the last kingdom."

"Marco can't force his brother to marry if he doesn't want to."

"Perhaps. But what if Dante does want to?"

Anger gnaws at my insides like a ravenous animal, siphoning all that is sweet until I'm left with a writhing, rabid hunger to dethrone Marco immediately.

Perhaps in the end, Dante won't choose me, but the least I can do is make sure he gets to choose for himself.

38

After receiving bone-crushing hugs from Defne and Marcello, I head out with Sybille onto the moonlit pier, the note her parents inked and sealed with wax tucked into the satchel I've knotted across my drumming chest.

My heartbeats are so close together, they rattle the handful of coppers and jostle the food and water that'll keep me going during my mountain crossing. At least the food and water will. I may run out of coin before then if the vision I had of Bronwen with a horse was brought on by low blood sugar and I have to undertake this journey by foot. Here's to hoping it wasn't a hallucination but an augur of my future.

Although the wharf is still calm at this hour, many fishermen are already up and about, readying their lures and nets. As we walk toward the ferry's berth, the moonlight tangles in Mattia's shoulder-length mane. He's crouched on the deck of Antoni's boat, scraping barnacles off a cage. His movements slow as his head tips up and he sees us.

I wave. Antoni must not have told him we were already over because I get a tentative smile and a wave back.

Sybille leans into me and whispers, "You think it'd be weird if I asked him out on a date?"

"Why would it be weird?"

She arches an eyebrow. "Because I slept with Antoni."

"Over a year ago." I study the delicate lines of my friend's profile, the thick lashes, pert nose, and full mouth that's one shade darker than her deep-brown face. "I say go for it."

"What if he rejects me? Who'll hold my hand if you're gone?"

"Phoebus."

She pouts. "What about my other hand?"

I roll my eyes. "I won't be gone long."

"I wish you'd tell me where exactly you were going."

"Where the winds blow me."

"What if the winds blow you off a cliff?"

"I'll make sure not to stand too close to one's edge."

"You really should head to Tarespagia by sea. I've heard people disappear in Monteluce."

"There's *one* road, and it's constantly patrolled. Can you imagine the odds of getting lost?"

"You're good at defying odds."

Grinning, I knock my shoulder into hers. After we reach the ferry pontoon, I hand the blue-eyed canal captain Marcello's letter that explains my reason for crossing—gathering supplies for the tavern on his behalf—then extend a copper to pay for my ticket.

"Ferry's full," the man says.

"Um." Sybille frowns at the empty benches. "Looks pretty deserted to me."

"Ferry's full." He hands me back the note, which I unfold and read over quickly, worried Marcello asked the man *not* to let me board, but the squiggly curves and loops say exactly what he promised they would say.

"That's ridiculous." Sybille's cheeks puff in anger.

"Why won't you take me?" I ask him.

I catch his gaze flicking over my shoulder and turn. Although

I spot no one watching us, he's clearly not letting me cross on someone's orders. The commander's?

"Better get yourself home, Serpent-charmer, 'cause no man will risk his livelihood to help you escape."

I grit my teeth and turn, making Sybille whirl. "Silvius is behind this."

"Why would he—Oh. The turd."

She couldn't have found a more befitting nickname. Perhaps I'll start calling him Commander Turd from now on. It has a nice ring to it.

She pulls me to a stop. "You should ask Antoni. He'd surely take you."

The ferryman's voice rings in my ears, and I shake my head. "I don't want him to get in trouble."

"I suppose you could always *swim* across. You've already had a shitty day. What's a little more shit in your day?"

"Your humor knows no bounds, Syb."

Although the idea of wading through dirty water turns my stomach, I contemplate whistling for Minimus and diving into the rippling blackness. But two things stop me. First, Minimus may neglect the fact that I'm no serpent, and second, I may be playing into Silvius's hands.

I raise my gaze to the gauzy clouds twisting around the waning moon, wishing Bronwen would proffer a third option my way. When no rope or iron crow tumbles from the sky nor black bird swoops overhead, I lower my gaze back to the murky forest dotted with torchlight beyond the barrack island.

I'm aware it's an illusion, but Rax seems to be floating away from Tarelexo.

"I'll be right back. Don't move." Sybille untangles our arms.

As she leaves me standing alone on the wharf to contemplate my crumbling future alone, I lower my lids and think, but instead of ferreting out solutions, my thoughts stray to Isolacuori and the princess Dante's apparently courting. Here I thought he'd rejected Beryl and the others for me.

Why am I risking my neck and sanity to get him on the throne if he intends to sit a princess down beside him? He promised there'd be no other woman. After anger, jealousy pelts me, but then another wave of anger washes out my blazing rancor.

Why am I taking Commander Turd's word? Perhaps he too is resistant to salt. Perhaps he *thinks* he saw them kiss, and that's why he was able to speak the words under—

"Come on, person of great interest." A thin arm snakes around my waist. "I found you a solution."

My eyes open and settle on Sybille. "Which one?"

"You'll see."

When I do see, I dig my feet in. "I told you, I won't involve Antoni."

"That's why I asked Mattia. I even struck a bargain on your behalf."

"Sybille, no."

"Oh, chill. It's a win-win for me. Not only do I get to make my friend's dream come true, but I get a date with a sexy blond."

She drags me along while I list all the reasons I won't set a slipper on that boat. "Stop your mutterings, and climb aboard already."

"Sybille."

"Fallon."

"I've always dreamed of a three-way with the two of you." Mattia says this so loudly it gets the attention of a passing guard and a few sailors. He holds out his hands. Sybille grabs ahold of one, then nods for me to take the other. "Antoni will be so fucking jealous."

"What will I be so fucking jealous about?" The blue-eyed captain emerges from below deck in only a pair of slacks.

Like magnets, my eyes rove over his bare chest, widening at the sight of the row upon row of luminescent bands cinching his carved biceps. Does he strike bargains for sport? I count twenty on one arm and spy even more on the other.

Before he can catch me staring, I force my gaze to a neighboring bearded captain sorting through a box of tackle.

"Look at that timing, ladies. The cabin is all ours."

Sybille plucks my hand from my side and sticks it in Mattia's palm. Before I can react, he reels us both onto the vessel.

39

Antoni steps in between Mattia and myself, forcing his friend's arm to bend and his fingers to release me. "No."

"Antoni," Sybille hisses between clenched teeth. "Fine. A foursome!" she announces loudly, gripping my hand and tugging me into the cabin below deck.

Antoni's mouth pinches harder, but he follows.

The second we're inside, Sybille smacks the door shut. "Gods, subtlety isn't your forte."

"What the fuck is going on?" Antoni growls.

"You just woke up, didn't you?" Sybille looks him over, lingering on his sculpted torso.

Antoni scrubs a hand down his face. "Start explaining."

She opens her mouth, but I talk before she can. "Commander Dargento suggested I be tossed into Mareluce to prove I can tame serpents."

I'll tell Antoni exactly what I told Sybille, which isn't the story I gave her parents. So many lies I'm perpetrating. All to protect those I love, but still… The ease with which they tumble from my lips floods me with guilt.

"King Marco needed to leave for Tarespagia, so he postponed

my dip in the ocean until his return next week. I believe he or my grandfather decided to have me watched."

"I still don't understand why you're here for a threesome with my first mate." There's no pliancy to Antoni's voice.

"She's getting to it," Sybille huffs. "Gods, you're cranky this morning."

I wet my lips with the tip of my tongue, my fingers sliding along the strap of my makeshift satchel. "I don't want to be tossed into Mareluce, Antoni. I don't want to test out Silvius's theory, especially not in front of the king. Gods only know what he'd do to me if I did have an affinity, and the serpents only know what *they'd* do to me if it turns out I didn't."

"So you're looking to flee?"

"Yes." That's where the lies begin. "I told Syb's parents I was meeting a man on the other side and that was the reason I was leaving, but I'm not meeting any man. I'm trying to get away before I'm either turned into a serpent chew toy or into a new tool in the king's armory."

"And Prince Charming can't bail you out?"

The Cauldron only knows how I keep my calm. "He used up his ace after I fell into the canal ten years ago."

For a long moment, no one says a thing.

Then Antoni breaks the silence. "So your plan is to spend your life on the run?"

"No. My plan is to reach Tarespagia. My great-grandmother, Xema Rossi, lives there, and she's a very influential woman who I believe will protect me."

"You *believe*?" Antoni's mocking tone makes my fingers scrunch Marcello's letter.

Where Sybille gobbled up my lie, cooing that going to Justus's mother is brilliant, Antoni's clearly not convinced.

"Your plan is terrible, Fallon."

"I didn't ask for your opinion."

"Maybe not, but you're clearly here to ask for something of me."

"This was a bad idea." I turn and reach for the doorknob.

Sybille scuttles against the wall to block me. "I will not let you die because someone's pride is getting in the way."

Even though the cabin is dark, I don't miss the nerve feathering Antoni's jaw.

"This is a big ask, Antoni, and yeah, you can say no, but Fallon needs to get across that canal. I want to borrow your boat. I'll pay you for it of course."

"Sybille," I whisper, unaware that was what she'd devised.

"You want to—" Antoni sputters. "Do you even know how to drive a boat?"

She gives a one-shouldered shrug. "How difficult can it be? You two do it."

Mattia snorts.

"And how exactly will you get through the guard barrage with a wanted felon, huh?"

"I'm not a felon…" I swallow. "Yet."

Sybille snatches the note her father wrote me and pushes it into Antoni's hands. Because the boat is wedged in between others, the single porthole spits out very little light. Antoni squints to make out the writing.

"I know you're literate, so you must've noticed it says Fallon's name on there." He punches the spot on the parchment.

"Nothing a little ink smudge can't fix. Besides, it's signed by my father."

"What if they ask to search the vessel?"

"That's why I want to borrow *your* boat, Antoni." She taps her foot against the little round rug.

A long beat passes. I'm not certain why everyone's so silent and grim until I catch Mattia gnawing on his lip while Antoni scowls.

"How do you know about that?" the latter finally asks.

My eyebrows pinch together. *"That?"*

Antoni's Adam's apple jostles up and down the column of his throat. "Who told you?"

"I put two and two together. I know you and my sister aren't dating—or dating humans—yet you two spend an inordinate amount of time going back and forth to Rax together. I approve of what you're doing, by the way."

"What are you doing?" I find myself asking.

His gaze snaps to mine with such force, I take a step back and shut my mouth.

"That's really none of your business. As to borrowing my boat, that's a no."

"We're talking about Fallon's life! Do you really want her to die?"

He glares at Sybille. "I said no to borrowing it because I'll be driving the fucking thing."

"Not sure that's such a great idea, Cap." Mattia spears his fingers through his golden mop and nods his chin at me. "Word on the street is that whoever gives her passage will be tossed into Filiaserpens."

"So you're okay with letting Sybille swim with the serpents?" Antoni asks.

"She's a girl. She won't get caught."

"What sort of dumbass assumption is that?"

Mattia's hand falls from his hair and settles at his side.

"You really think Dargento would hesitate for a second to punish a female, Mattia? Not to mention that Sybille is Fallon's best friend. All of Luce knows it. She'll be the *first* person he'll look at. Which is why Syb won't be on this boat. You and Riccio either." Antoni's blue eyes finally settle on mine, full of shadows that have nothing to do with the ambient light. "I'll take her across."

I want to protest, but what other option do I have?

"We'll leave at dusk tonight."

My heart bangs. "I need to leave now," I whisper.

"You just told me the king won't act on Dargento's idea until he returns."

"I know, but...but I cannot go home. I got in a fight with Nonna about seeking out her mother-in-law." Oh, how the lies roll off my tongue, ringing with such truths I may start to believe them.

"You can stay with me," Sybille offers. "Besides, you could do with some sleep."

I have no doubt I look as frazzled as I feel.

She slides her hand through the crook of my arm. "So we meet here at nightfall?"

"No *we*. Just Fallon. And ask Giana to prepare her for transport. She'll know what to do."

Gods, what sort of illicit operations are these two running in Rax? Sybille opens the door.

Before she can tug me out, Antoni nods at me. "I want a minute with Fallon." When neither Mattia nor Sybille make any move to leave, he adds, "Alone."

I nibble on my lower lip, expecting he's about to ask me to grovel or to apologize for falling back into Dante's arms a heartbeat after I left his, since I imagine he knows. After all, I kissed the prince under the scalding sun for all of Luce to see.

Once the door shuts behind the two others, he says, "If you really think your great-grandmother can help, I'll take you straight to Tarespagia."

I lick my lower lip. "That's days at sea. Even if you hid me, it'll be too much of a risk."

"You can't honestly be planning to walk all the way there?"

"I'm going to get a horse."

"It'll still take you over a week to reach the other side of the mainland."

"I'm aware."

"But you'd prefer that to a few days on my boat?" There's a tinge of hurt in his tone, and I'm not sure what it's about until he says, "If you're worried I'm going to ask you to put out, I won't."

"I know you'd never take advantage of me, Antoni."

"So why won't you take me up on my offer?"

"Because I won't. I can't. Insisting won't alter my answer."

"I'm not scared of the commander."

I remember the feeling I got when we attended the party, of the familiarity between my four fellow outcasts and the humans. Now it all makes sense. "I imagine as much, considering your Racoccin activities." *Whatever they may be...*

The air leaving our lungs and the waves lapping at the hull become the only sound in the cabin for an interminable stretch of time.

"What happens if your great-grandmother refuses to help?"

"I'll board a vessel to Shabbe. Surely, they'll take me in seeing as how they hate our king."

"No boat will take you to the queendom."

"Then I'll swim there." My frustration grows roots.

"I thought you were doing all this to avoid swimming?"

I toss a hand up in exasperation. "Then I'll scurry back to Monteluce and hide there for the rest of my mortal days."

The sinews in his neck are as rigid as the mooring lines bolting his boat to the dock. "Monteluce's one of the most dangerous places in the kingdom."

"I'm not scared."

"You should be." His blistering tone must heat his skin, because his ocean-and-sun scent embalms the small cabin.

I place my hand on the doorknob. "Well, I choose guileless oblivion. It works for me."

Antoni makes a sound between a huff and a snort. Casting his eyes on the tiny window leaking insipid dawn light, he says, "I need to get the boat ready for the day. See you at dusk."

"I'm sorry."

He doesn't respond, doesn't even look my way, but I know he heard me. How could he not? The cabin is tiny, and I didn't whisper or croak.

Sighing, I walk off Antoni's boat feeling like smooshed dung and rethinking involving such a good man. Especially when I have nothing to offer him except my friendship.

You will be queen. Bronwen's words clang through my mind, reminding me that if I'm successful—No. *When* I succeed, I'll be able to give him all the riches he deserves. I'll buy him that apartment he wants.

A whole house.

I'll make him rise alongside me.

40

I stand in front of the oblong mirror pinned to Giana's wall, tightening the belt on a pair of pants.

Pants. Actual pants. The sort women are forbidden from wearing. The last woman who dared walk the streets of Tarelexo in a pair ended up wearing them to greet the serpents.

Fashion can be deadly in Luce when it goes against the monarchy's rules.

However much I like the beauty of gowns, there's no denying that pants feel like swaths of freedom. "How am I ever supposed to go back to wearing dresses?"

"Thanks to that half-baked scheme of yours, you may never have to. Crossing Monteluce on your own? It's foolish and reckless and—"

"You really know how to build up a girl's confidence."

"Fallon, I'm worried!" Giana pulls so hard on the fabric with which she's flattening my breasts that it strips my lungs of air.

I turn away from the mirror and put a hand to her shoulder. "I know your reproof is born from a place of love, but please, Gia, don't make me rethink it. I spent half the day scolding myself and the other half hyperventilating so hard Syb pried my eyes open to make sure I hadn't turned into an air-Fae, then built a fort of pillows between us."

Gia's slender jaw ticks, undoubtedly with more admonitions.

"Besides, I could turn all that criticism around on you."

Her pupils spread, blotting out most of the gray.

"Look, I'd prefer for your parents to keep believing I'm running away to meet a man behind my grandmother's back."

She heaves the sigh of a warrior surrendering his weapons before doing a very un-Giana-like thing. She steps forward and traps me in a hug. "Don't die, you crazy girl."

"Right back at you, Gia."

After another deep exhale stirs the tendrils of hair beside my ears, she releases me.

"So this is how you get me on Antoni's boat without anyone noticing?" As I slide my satchel over my flattened chest, I give my mirror image another once-over. She's managed to make me resemble a prepubescent boy.

"No. That getup is so you don't catch the eye of the patrols in Rax. Not to mention it'll make riding a horse much easier."

She talks like someone who's been there and done that, surely because she has *been there and done that*.

At my raised eyebrow, a twinkle lights up her eyes and spreads to her mouth. "Hope you're not the type to get dizzy."

Apparently, I'm very much the type to get dizzy. Then again, I'd wager the few coppers jingling in my belted purse that the organs of anyone stuffed inside a wine barrel and rolled across cobbles would rumple and spasm.

I scold myself for having gobbled down the bowl of raisin-flecked polenta Sybille carried up to me when I awoke in the middle of the afternoon. The softened cornmeal was supposed to stick to my bones, but it's not sticking, unless there's a bone in my throat I'm not aware of.

I clench my teeth as we go over another lumpy patch. Tarelexians really need to level their roads.

"Signorina Amari." Silvius's smarmy voice penetrates the curved slats that keep me hidden.

My heart jostles. Since I'm facing up, I squint to make him out through the slats, but the outside world is already thick with a darkness that rivals the one inside the barrel.

"Commander." Giana's voice is tight but steady, betraying no emotion except her tangible loathing for the man she threw out of the tavern last night.

"We're looking for your little round-eared friend who didn't make it home last night."

I work hard on quieting my breaths, grateful for the clamor of the wharf. I understand why they chose dusk to roll me out to Antoni. The fishermen and merchants are all out, getting rid of what they weren't able to sell in Tarecuori.

"I've many little round-eared friends. You'll have to be more specific."

I can just imagine Silvius grinding his teeth.

"Fallon Rossi."

"Fallon crashed with my sister last night. She was exhausted from her...*lively* day, so my guess is she's still lying in Morpheus's arms."

"*Your guess?* Don't you live with your sister?"

"We Tarelexians may lead modest lives, but we do have separate bedrooms, Commander. Now if you don't mind, I need to get rid of this wine that's soured instead of matured."

A pause.

"And how will you be disposing of it?"

"The usual way."

"Enlighten me?"

"It'll be brought to Rax, where all Tarelexian garbage goes."

It's hopefully no more than my runaway imagination that makes me think the barrel trembles beneath Giana's hands.

"Fetch me a glass!" I hear the commander shout.

My heart stops beating.

"I want to sample your soured wine, Signorina Amari."

Oh gods... Oh gods.

A ship horn blasts, followed by growls and grunts and splintering wood. I hear a man yelling he's going to kill another. I feel the rumble of footfalls as men race to intercede.

"For Cauldron's sakes, half-bloods are all crooks," Silvius huffs. "Toss him into the canal." He must speak the order to the guard beside him because he doesn't bark it.

The quay has grown quiet, save for a few muffled grunts.

"Commander, the man is clearly inebriated." Giana's voice is slightly shrill. "Hardly a reason to have him put to death."

"There's nothing quite like cold water to clear the mind."

"Don't do it," she grits out.

"Or what, Signorina Amari?"

"Or you'll lose everyone's respect and obedience." The barrel is definitely palpitating. "Think of the order you gave these men not to allow Fallon passage. If you send Mattia into that canal and he gets taken by the serpents, do you really think anyone would hesitate to work against you the next time you require their compliance?"

"I could only wish them luck considering the fleet of guards."

"Here I thought you possessed a modicum of political savviness, but I guess that isn't necessary to lead soldiers."

My pulse is so wild, my ears have started to ring.

"Perhaps you require a little swim to clear *your* head, Giana."

My mind begins to whirl as though the wine-soaked wood is liberating spiritous fumes, and the air grows oppressive to the point where I begin to panic because the oxygen feels worryingly thin.

Oh gods, I'm going to suffocate to death. The palms I have pressed against the sides of the barrel grow clammy and my spine damp with sweat.

I will the commander to walk away and leave Mattia be.

I will Giana to start rolling me again.

I will the serpents to rise from the water's depths and put on a show, splash dirty water on all the guards.

I will Minimus not to be part of the maritime assault.

The commander gasps. Or maybe it's Giana. Perhaps it's the both of them.

"What in the underworld is that?" Silvius asks, tone no longer bladed but almost fearful.

I must've prayed to the gods hard enough, because something is clearly coming.

"It looks like a cloud of birds," Giana murmurs as though she's sensed my panic and is trying to calm me by giving me a play-by-play of what's unfolding beyond my cramped hidey-hole.

Squawking pierces the moist, airless darkness surrounding me. From the ruckus the creatures make and Giana's comparison to a cloud, I fathom the birds number in the hundreds.

"Bloody Cauldron. Guards, ready your weapons!" Although loud, Silvius's voice seems to grow fainter as he gives the order.

And then I'm rolling, my head and bum alternately whacking against the sides of the barrel. Giana is running, no longer taking care not to bang me up. I know she has no choice, so I squeeze my eyes and steel my muscles.

"Fuck, that was close." Antoni's voice penetrates my hideout, and my lids flutter open, lashes damp from the swirl of emotion.

"He wanted to throw Mattia into the canal." Giana's voice is full of nerves.

"I suspected as much when they dangled him above it. Now quit gawking at the birds, Riccio, and give me a hand."

"Have you ever seen so many ducks and herons and—"

"Riccio, focus." Antoni sounds on edge and irate enough to snap my barrel with just his bare hands. "Giana, get back to the tavern."

A minute later, I'm finally set down.

"Untie the mooring lines, and get off the boat," Antoni hisses as the noise level decreases exponentially.

Two shallow thwacks, and the ring that kept the lid sealed pops off like a cork. Air—sweet, delicious air—penetrates my cramped lungs. I steal lungfuls of it as Antoni reaches down and grips me underneath my armpits to heave me up.

His gaze rakes over me in quick sweeps. My hyperventilation and complexion must display how I feel because he says, "The worst is over."

But is it? Don't I need to crouch inside another small hole? I really don't like tight spaces.

He motions to the open hatch. "Get in."

I swallow down another wave of panic along with a growing sob. "I don't think I can—"

"Fallon, please. If you don't, then all the risks Giana and Mattia took will have been wasted."

I flinch because the guilt he lashes me with feels like a whip.

As though the birds have awakened the serpents, the boat rocks hard and knocks into its neighbors.

I fall against Antoni as he mutters, "I need to get up on deck to steer." He grips my head between his palms, presses his forehead against mine. "Fallon Rossi, I don't know if you believe in omens and gods, but I believe everything happens for a reason, and those birds...they came out for a reason. Maybe that reason isn't you, but what if it is? What if they came to help you get away?"

My mouth goes dry, and my pulse rears to a stop.

Of course.

This is Bronwen's doing!

Or the crow's!

His rough thumbs are soft against my cheekbones. "Perhaps serpents aren't the only animals you can charm."

I swallow, and it feels like I'm trying to gulp down an obsidian spike. Have *I* done this? Has my panic somehow carried every bird in Luce to me?

I nod, my forehead slipping off Antoni's, then twist my face away from his and climb down into the hole. It's twice the length of the wine barrel but so shallow I need to lie down. Bolstered by Antoni's words, I slide into place.

Antoni stands above the hole and wastes precious seconds staring down at me. His eyes seem to gleam as though he's seeing someone else in my stead.

Or not seeing anyone at all.

The boat bucks sideways, tipping the barrel and stealing the trapdoor from Antoni's fingers. The slice of wood shuts with a deafening whack, pitching me in total, suffocating darkness.

Don't panic, I tell myself, flattening my palms on either side of the cubby space. *Don't panic. Bronwen is watching, and the crow is aiding.*

Or the Cauldron.

Or one of our gods.

I feel both discombobulated puppet and shiny fishing lure, flopping from a fraying string between calculating men and shrewd beasts.

Whoever is manipulating my fate should probably have toned down my allure to avoid their chosen doer becoming someone's choice prisoner.

41

W hat feels like a century later, Antoni's boat stops moving. I think we've arrived until I hear gruff voices overhead. Their words are muffled by the closed cabin door and the small rug strewn over the floor, but I don't miss the soft thump of someone jumping aboard.

The groan of wood makes my breathing falter. And then the door hinges creak and the voices become so clear that I know someone's standing on the threshold, peering down the three steps that lead into the cabin. What will they think when they spot the empty barrel? Unless Antoni has disposed of it or shut it?

"Commander thinks the girl's behind the birds," comes a voice I've never heard before.

"He's an imaginative man, the commander."

"You think it impossible? Word is she can communicate with serpents."

"So can most females who work at Bottom of the Jug." If I didn't know Antoni, I would've scowled at his sexual innuendo and being lobbed in with the doxies. "If she didn't favor pointy ears and crowns, I may have dropped her off with my next delivery of faerie dust."

I'm too busy wondering what faerie dust is to worry about Antoni discussing my crush on Dante.

"I've got the pointy ears," the man said.

"Just missing the crown, Simonus."

Simonus grunts. "The army blacksmith owes me a small favor. I can get him to finagle something resembling a crown."

"You do that, then sprite me your offer, and I'll negotiate on your behalf with Catriona, who's in charge of all the tavern girls."

"The commander doesn't get wind of this."

"Have I ever shared anything concerning you with Dargento?"

"No, but I hear he's got a thing for the girl."

"It's called bloodlust."

"Not just that sort of lust."

I'm so disgusted I let out a little squeak.

"Did you hear that?" The stairs creak.

Merda. Merda. Merda. I sandwich my lips and hold my breath.

"Did I hear what, Simonus?"

"The squeak." His voice trickles down from right above. Although floorboards separate us, my chest constricts as though he's standing on it. "Sounded like vermin."

"Sure hope I've got no mice, or I'm sending you the bill."

"Excuse me?" The man shifts, peppering me with dust motes. I don't dare breathe for fear of sneezing.

"I had to dock in Rax for hours the other day, waiting on Vee to fulfil your order."

"Not my fault your human friends are lazy."

Antoni heaves a deep sigh. "Fine. No bill if you'll let me be on my way. Vee told me about a brand-new way to cut the dust that'd make the high last twice as long. I'm picking up samples."

"Same price?"

"Maybe cheaper."

"Bring one back on your way home."

"Will do." After a beat, Antoni asks, "Since you're standing there, can you lift my mattress?"

"Why?"

"To check for mice. I'm no rodent fan."

Simonus grunts. "Check your own damn mattress."

The floorboards screech as he backtracks out of the cabin, and then the door thwacks shut.

Although my lungs burn, I wait to feel the boat bob before I release my breath and suck in a fresh lungful.

I'm still gulping down air when the boat comes to another standstill.

My impatience to emerge from the black hull is mitigated by my fear of getting caught by a passing patrol. So I wait.

Seconds slip into minutes before the rug finally rustles and the round hatch is lifted. Gasping in a breath that feels like pure sunshine after so much darkness, I sit up and almost knock heads with Antoni. He rises from his crouch, tension creasing every smooth plane of his face.

I pant as though I've just risen from the depths of Mareluce. "I'm sorry"—another pant—"I squeaked."

Antoni offers me a hand, which I greedily take, very much done with small cavities. "I would've squawked in horror too had I heard Dargento was sweet on me."

I shudder, my skin feeling dredged in cobwebs.

As I take in the empty room—Antoni must've tossed the barrel overboard...smart man—he says, "You mentioned crossing Monteluce on horseback. Where are you getting your horse from?"

"I...um...in the forest."

He cocks an eyebrow that gets lost behind a wavy lock. "In the—" He sputters. "You do realize Rax is all forest, and a large one at that?"

I swallow and nod, praying that vision I had of Bronwen and

the crow will come to fruition. And soon. Gods only know what monsters lurk in these woods...

He kicks the rug back into place over the closed hatch. "You're just going to wander the woods until a horse magically appears?"

I turn away from his cutting tone. "I'm fully aware of how daft it is thanks to Giana." Steeling my spine, I trudge up the stairs but stop and dig a copper out of my pocket that I extend to Antoni. "Thank you for the risks you took. I'll never forget your kindness."

He stares at my coin, then up at me. "What the fuck is that?"

"Payment. For taking me across."

"Put that away."

"You did me a favor. A dangerous one at that. It's the least I can do." It's also the only thing I *can* do. I've got nothing else to give him. Well, besides food, but I doubt he needs any.

Actually...

There is something else I can give him. Something Nonna has warned me against, but I trust Antoni not to use it wickedly.

I descend the three steps and rest my palm against his bicep. "Tiudevo, Antoni Greco."

He inhales a sharp breath that I attribute to the pain of my bargain sinking into his flesh. But then his eyebrows tip toward one another.

"Does it hurt when it appears?" I peek down at my chest, wondering if a glowing dot has materialized on my smooshed chest. I can't feel anything.

The slant of his eyebrows deepens. "It usually does but..."

"But what?"

"No bargain inscribed itself on my skin."

"How is that possible?" I hook my index finger into my crushing chest strap. Although I don't manage to pry it far from my skin, I do manage to cop a look at my cleavage. No dot glows.

"Are you certain you're Fae, Fallon?"

I roll my fingers into fists as doubt insinuates itself into me anew. I blast it away. After all, *both* my grandparents saw me emerge from Mamma. "Maybe it didn't take because I'm defective."

He steps toward me, so close his scent punches up my nose. "What if you aren't defective? What if you just aren't Fae? What if your grandmother stole a human child because your mother lost hers from the trauma of ear culling?"

I rear back from him, really hating this changeling theory. "My grandmother would *never* steal someone else's child." Gnashing my teeth, I whirl around.

He catches my wrist and reels me back. "I didn't mean to offend you, but one has to wonder—"

"One doesn't have to wonder anything." I pry my arm from his grasp.

"Why didn't you go to Dante?"

"Because I didn't want to cause a rift between him and his brother," I lie.

He snorts. I won't take the bait. I'll walk out of here with my head held high and my confidence in Dante intact.

As I put my foot on the first step, he says, "Know what I think?"

"I'm not interested in what you think."

I peer into the darkness, on the lookout for sprite patrols. Although Fae trust the winged pests as far as they can throw them, Fae trust humans less. Not to mention they prefer sacrificing sprites to the darkest parts of Luce.

When I catch no movement but the gentle sway of leaves, I step out onto the deck and climb onto the boat railing.

"I think you were afraid Dante would've refused to help."

Wrong. You're wrong.

I don't engage in a debate, merely jump toward the bank. The soles of the knee-high boots I borrowed from Giana skid on the cluster of slick, knobby roots knifing through the moist ground. I grab onto the nearest trunk to steady my footing, then carefully hop until the soil levels out.

"Fallon, wait."

I don't.

He follows me. "I'm sorry."

"You loathe Dante, so I highly doubt that you are." I will him to contradict me, but unlike me, Antoni isn't a liar. "You don't need to walk me through the woods. I'll be fine."

"I need supplies for the lieutenant."

"And those supplies happen to be in the direction I'm going?"

"Yes."

My jaw clenches. "Then I guess I better change direction." I turn and head the opposite way.

I wait to hear his footfalls, but none thud behind me. After I've walked a distance, I glance over my shoulder, finding only a murky legion of trees surrounding me.

Relief settles in the pit of my stomach, but the feeling wanes instantly. The forest is full of strange noises and shifting shadows and not a single pinprick of light.

A soft keening echoes through the obscurity, raising the fine hairs on my nape. I stop walking, trying to gauge where it came from so I can journey the opposite way. I hear it again and spin, heart clattering against my ribs. I dig through my satchel for the little knife Giana gave me earlier. Its blade is stubby but sharp. I doubt I could drive it through any being's flesh. In truth, I'd planned on using it to sliver my cheese and dried fruit paste.

My fingers finally meet wood, and I yank the knife out, cutting a hole into my bag. *Great. Bravo, Fallon.*

I'll probably end up stabbing myself. Regardless, I hold it out, squinting into the abounding darkness.

Although I probably should stay quiet, I murmur, "Antoni?"

Gods, I hope it's him. Sure, I'd give him grief for tailing me, but secretly, I'd be relieved he disregarded my demand to leave me be.

No one answers.

Between my clammy palm and trembling arm, the knife slips and tumbles onto the ground. I crouch to retrieve it just as branches rustle overhead. I look up so fast my neck cracks. I think I hear the flap of wings and pray that it's a bird and not a platoon of sprites.

I peer long and hard, but the foliage is dense, impairing what little light trickles from the veiled crescent moon. If only I had fire power... Any power at all, for that matter. The ground is humid enough that, had I been endowed with water power, I could've wielded its dampness, fashioned a screen of thick mist to shield myself, or softened the ground to bog down an attacker.

A branch snaps to my right, flicking my heart into my mouth. I pivot, arm extended, blade slicing the night like a streak of lightning.

A soft caw drives my neck backward.

Golden eyes gleam through the jumble of branches.

The crow spreads its wings, jumps off its perch, and soars away. I sprint after it, my pulse thundering so hard, the inside of my mouth tastes like a copper coin. Although I trip repeatedly, not only do I manage to stay upright, but I also succeed in keeping up with the feathered trailblazer.

The crow hooks a sharp turn, which sends me wading through a bush outfitted with a thousand needles. I curse like an inebriated sailor as they snag my sleeves and pants, nipping at the skin beneath while tearing up the exposed parts. I shoot my hands up to protect my face from the assault.

Moisture trickles down my forehead and cheeks. I don't bother wiping it off until the hedge finally releases me into a lit pocket of woodland.

As I attempt to catch my breath, I wipe my face on my shirtsleeve and absorb my surroundings. A hut slumps against a thick tree like a lumpy growth, its roof thatched with twigs and leaves, its walls a mixture of pale mud and brambles.

A soft neighing drags my attention back to the thick tree and the black horse that clip-clops out from its shadow, reins tucked in none other than Bronwen's hands.

If I had any doubts about prophecies and visions, they breeze right out of my head.

Lungs throbbing, I just stand there, aching from a stitch in my side, perspiration coursing down my temples and slipping into the corners of my eyes. I take another hard swipe at my face, soiling my white shirt.

Bronwen nods to the stallion. "Climb onto Furia, Fallon. We've not a minute to spare."

My horse is named Fury? Great.

As I approach him, she says, "He will take you where you need to go."

He looks like he will take me straight to the underworld.

"I've never ridden a horse." I tentatively present my hand to the horse.

"You will learn fast."

The horse lowers its velvety nose to my palm and snuffles, its delicate nostrils flaring like Minimus's the day we met during my impromptu swim.

Gods, I hope my serpent will keep himself hidden while I'm gone. I'm about to ask Bronwen to use her woo-woo skills to protect him when a deep voice hisses, "*Her*? You can't be serious."

I whirl around, a plausible explanation for this encounter tripping up my pulsating throat.

It's just about fully formed and ready to spring out when Antoni adds, "She's Lucin, Bronwen."

42

Antoni knows Bronwen.

He *knows* Bronwen.

Then why did she vanish when he showed up that first night in Rax?

Her white eyes gleam like serpent tusks. "Climb on, Fallon. You must depart—"

"How the fuck can *she* be the one?" Antoni glares, not at her but at *me*.

Gods, I don't like this version of Antoni. Where is the kind boat captain who stroked my heart with his caresses and sweet words? Does he even exist, or was that merely one of the personas he uses to fool people?

To fool me?

I pull my shoulders back and stick a hand on my hip. "What's wrong with me being the one?"

He jams his hand through his sun-stroked hair, dislodging a bramble or two. Unlike me, though, he mustn't have charged through the flesh-grater shrub because his skin bears no cuts. "That sob story you fed me about your great-grandmother and Commander Dargento. Was there any truth to it?"

"Silvius *is* after me, but the seeking out my great-grandmother part was a fabrication." I feed my foot into the stirrup and hoist myself up like the knights from Mamma's books. Thanks to my pants, the process is swift and easy. "I was told not to speak to anyone about the prophecy. If I'd known... Why didn't you tell me Antoni was in on"—I draw a circle in the air to encompass the crow, which is, oddly enough, nowhere to be seen—"everything?"

Bronwen hands me the reins. "Thank you for escorting Fallon across the canal, Antoni. You will be greatly rewarded for your valor and loyalty."

Is she evading my question because Antoni hasn't been informed of *everything*?

"Funny you should speak of loyalty, considering where Fallon's lies."

Bronwen turns her unnerving stare toward him. "What are you trying to say, Antoni?"

"That perhaps she's not the best person to entrust with gathering the king's crows."

So he does know everything...

"Fate picked her. Make your peace with it, and go play your part." Bronwen's tone was never sweet, but now, it's downright brittle.

"Fallon is smitten with Dante Regio. You really think she—" Antoni's head jerks back, and he peers into the darkness that stirs above our heads.

The crow has returned from gods only know where crows go.

"Lore," he breathes.

"Not so much a legend after all." I thread my fingers through Furia's long mane, stroking the gleaming ebony coat beneath, waiting on Bronwen to give me my orders. Perhaps they'll be to follow the crow, who seems to know where to go.

"How"—Antoni swallows—"how is he free?"

He? Is the crow male, or did Antoni use the pronoun like he could've used any other pronoun?

"Fallon liberated him."

I guess it is a *him*.

Bronwen's head is tilted and her eyes set on the heavens. Can she see the crow, or is she sensing his presence?

"Why would a Regio devotee agree to collect Lore's crows?" Antoni watches the crow land on the thatched roof of what I imagine is Bronwen's home. "And again, *how*? Obsidian is noxious to—"

"Devotee?" My fingers glide out of Furia's mane and settle on the saddle's pommel. How can Antoni liken me to some senseless zealot? I've got plenty of sense. "I may appreciate Dante, but I've *no* appreciation for Marco, which is *why*, Antoni, I've agreed to collect these legendary crows."

"You do realize that dethroning Marco Regio won't win you any brownie points with his brother, right?"

I'm guessing Bronwen hasn't told him the part of the prophecy where I become queen. I suppose he'll find out soon enough. "Dante and his brother don't have the best relationship. He'll see reason."

"Tà, Mórrgaht." Bronwen nods, pallid gaze fastened to the space the crow occupies.

Morrgot? Is that the creature's name?

Apparently, I've asked my question out loud, because Antoni says, "Creature?"

"The crow." When his eyebrows stay knitted, I add, "The mythical, winged thingamajig perched up there. Is Morrgot his name?"

"Thingamajig?"

Is he daft? "Oh my gods, Antoni. What is wrong with you? Why do you keep repeating everything I say?"

Although Antoni's mouth opens, Bronwen speaks first. "Yes. Mórrgaht is his name."

It's an odd-sounding name. "It's very...exotic?"

"Common in Crow tongue." There's a sardonic lilt to Antoni's voice that makes me think he's pulling my leg, but why would he? "Isn't that right, Bronwen?" He crosses his thick arms.

I frown at both of them. "So you can...communicate with him and his kind, Bronwen?" It would definitely make my interaction with serpents less outlandish if she says yes.

Although her steel-gray turban casts shadows across the rutted topography of her face, they don't dim the milky glow of her eyes. "I can. Now—"

"Can you communicate with crows as well, Antoni?"

"Fallon." Bronwen's eyes are wide and planted on me, twin mounds of snow. "You must depart immediately. Before the sprite sentries—"

"Sending her into this blind is cruel." Antoni's arms are still firmly knotted in front of his chest, his gaze firmly set on the crow, his brow firmly creased into a frown. "I'll accompany her."

"No. You have your own path to travel, Antoni." Bronwen's dismissal is as clear as an Isolacuorin summer day.

"He cannot protect her in his current—" He flinches as though slapped.

Has Bronwen spoken into his mind? If she has, then how come his gaze is on the crow?

"In his current...*what*?" I ask.

Neither answers me.

I cock up an eyebrow. "What are you two keeping from me?"

"I'll go with her, and then I'll set sail for—"

"No." Bronwen's voice brooks no argument. "We can't afford another delay."

Although not currently high on the list of people I'd have chosen to travel with, it would've been nice to have companionship.

"You can't send her off alone. It's too fucking dangerous."

"She's not alone." Bronwen rests her hand on the horse's neck in case Antoni missed the behemoth beneath me. "Have you forgotten about his talons and beak, Antoni?"

Oh...she's speaking of my feathered sidekick, not my hooved one.

Antoni's jaw ticks.

"I also have a knife." I reach into my bag to retrieve it and show it off.

Antoni doesn't spare my stubby blade a glance. "She's mortal and magicless. Not to mention wanted by the three most powerful men in Luce."

Bronwen shudders, which makes Furia jerk. I shove my knife back into my rucksack and list forward to clutch both the reins and mane between my clammy fingers.

I'm on a horse.

A giant horse that could toss me off any minute.

"You cannot go with her, Antoni, for if you deviate from your path, it'll alter Fallon's destiny, which in turn will alter Luce's."

"How?"

"Not now," Bronwen hisses.

Antoni glowers at the crow, whose eyes narrow right back. "Tell me why her and I'll leave."

"Please, Antoni—"

"Why her?"

Bronwen's lips pinch.

"I haven't worked my ass off and risked my life for Lore's cause to be treated like an untrustworthy idiot."

Their shouting match makes Furia prance sideways and back. I grip him with my limbs as tightly as my lungs are gripping each one of my breaths.

"Because she's immune to both obsidian and iron." Bronwen's tone whips Antoni like a jostled branch.

"She's Cathal and—"

"Antoni—"

"Kahol?" I repeat. "Who or what is Kahol?"

"How's that possible?" he murmurs.

Before I can make heads or tails of what is perplexing Antoni, the crow captures my attention with a low, guttural caw that sounds eerily like a warning.

"Sprite sentries are near." Bronwen's hushed timbre glazes my skin with goose bumps.

Here I thought the warning was for Antoni to shut his mouth in order to keep me in the dark. I'm so sick of the dark. I want answers.

The crow springs off the roof. As though a lead rope links his iron talons to Furia's halter, my steed wheels around and takes off. I gasp as the reins hiss across the inside of my hands, welting my skin, then grit my teeth and hang on to my horse's wild mane.

Before the forest swallows me whole, I glance over my shoulder at the tiny clearing and the shrinking figure of the ship captain. In spite of the growing distance and the teeming shadows, I don't miss the tight pucker of his mouth and the twin slashes of eyebrows darkening his irises.

He's displeased.

By what he's learned about me or because Bronwen forbade him from accompanying me?

I sigh and focus back on the road ahead, mulling over the new words I picked up.

Lore. The master of these crows I must find.

Morrgot. Crow number one.

Kahol. An ethnicity? A thing?

If only I could speak Crow. Maybe Morrgot will teach me in between rescuing his friends.

I crane my neck toward the canopy of leaves, on the lookout for my winged scout. After several heartbeats of squinting, I catch the flap of wings.

Diaphanous, featherless ones. I count two pairs.

The sprite sentries aren't near…

They're here.

43

The two sprites drop in front of Furia like winged pine cones, startling my steed. The stallion rises onto his hind legs.

Oh gods, oh gods... I squeeze my lids shut and grip the animal's mane for dear life. When his front hooves bang back into the earth, I'm miraculously still astride.

One of the sprites hooks an arm through Furia's halter and levels a hard stare at my stallion, pinning his hooves to the gummy forest floor. The small faerie displays astonishing audacity, seeing as he's half the size of Furia's head and could easily be tossed away or chomped on. Then again, pixies are more attuned to animals than their full-size counterparts.

Another sprite hovers over Furia's long neck, his beady green eyes leveled with mine. "Where are you riding off to so fast, lad?"

Lad? I may have snickered at his decidedly not very keen grasp of physiognomy had I not been so relieved to be mistaken for a boy.

Afraid my voice will give away my *un*maleness, I point to my lips and mouth words, pretending to be mute.

"Speak up."

Definitely not bright, this one.

I shake my head and point to my mouth again.

"I b'lieve he's sayeen he can't speak." Unlike his partner, the sprite holding onto Furia's halter has a strong Racoccin accent.

"A mute, huh?"

I nod enthusiastically, my shoulder-length locks rushing around my cheeks. Had I shorn them off, I would've attracted less attention, perhaps none. My heart pinches at the idea of putting a blade to my scalp. What would Dante think of me bald? He'd be disgusted. Not only would I look human, but I'd look...unlady-like. I'm too vain for my own good.

I will Bronwen to intervene. Or Morrgot. Where is he anyway?

I glance past the gesticulating sprite, hoping to catch the flut-ter of black wings, until I realize the crow showing himself would send the sentries soaring toward Silvius, which would surely put a damper on my illicit bird reaping.

"So what's a halfling doing running off in the middle of the night?"

I mouth, *Ailing grandmother.*

"For Cauldron's sake, what's he saying?"

I mimic writing.

"Methinks he's askeen fur an ink pin."

"Do I look like I have a quill and inkwell on me, lad?" The green-eyed sprite opens his arms wide as though to display his lack of writing accoutrements.

Or maybe it's to show off the hollow stick hooked into his baldric. I've heard sprite darts are dipped into a poison that will knock out a full-blooded Fae for several hours.

"We could tyke him to the seer's hut. She must 'ave some ink and pins."

"The only things that harridan's got are zany eyes and a zanier mind," the other mutters. "We'll take him to the garrison."

Stupid me and my ploy to come off as mute. I almost break and reveal I can talk, but that would only win me a one-way trip to the Tarelexian barracks instead of the Racoccin ones.

I gesture to the forest and mouth, *Must go. In a hurry.*

I twist the reins incessantly around my sweaty fingers while keeping my heels flush with the horse's briskly pumping body. If I give Furia a firm kick, he'd take off, and the momentum would fling the sprite holding on to his halter into the bushes. They may pursue us, but surely my steed could outrun them, especially under the cover of the night. But then what?

The sprites would report a rebellious boy riding a black stallion, and I'd have a whole battalion of Fae on my tail.

I blame Bronwen for putting me in this situation. If only she'd let Antoni come with me. If anyone could dig me out of this mess, it's the sweet-talking boat captain. After all, he's been working against the crown for years, and no one has been the wiser.

A full minute ticks by, and no one comes to my rescue, not Morrgot, not Antoni, not Bronwen.

Think, Fallon. Think.

My gaze drops to the dart stick hooked into the sprite's belt. Before I lose my nerve, I drop Furia's reins and snatch the unsuspecting sprite around the torso, pinning both his arms and wings to his body.

My hand is so slick that he almost slips out of my grasp, but I crush him harder as I pluck his hollow stick and carry it to my mouth. It takes me several attempts to thread the toothpick-sized reed between my lips.

The captive sprite squirms and yells, which makes his partner spring away from Furia's halter and jolt upward.

"I don't want to hurt anyone," I mumble around the dart stick, "but I need to be on my way."

The Racoccin sprite stops his ascent to the tangle of branches overhead. "The lad kain speak."

"Not." His trapped friend grunts. "Lad."

"You got me. Now please. If you promise not—" I hiss as the

wriggling male sinks his teeth into the fleshy meat between my thumb and index finger, shocking my fingers apart.

He shoots up and out. "Get her, you idiot! Get her!"

Furia prances backward, then forward. I shoot my bleeding hand down to his mane and latch on, then crank my neck back and blow the dart in the sprites' direction, praying it'll at least graze one of them, but my missile soars right past them.

I try blowing again, but no second dart lurks within the weapon. Furia jerks, and I think he's been hit by a dart until a dull whiz whispers past my ear. How? How did he know to move his body and, by extension, mine?

"Give that to me!" the green-eyed sprite roars, reloading.

I flick the piece of wood dangling between my lips at where they're huddled. Unlike my dart, my stick clocks one of my accosters right in the head. Unfortunately, it clocks the one not holding the projectile launcher.

"Assaulting the king's guards will cost you dearly, scazza." As his friend rises, rubbing his forehead, he barks, "Inform Commander Dargento of—"

Black smoke coalesces around their bodies, cutting him off midsentence. My polenta lurches up my throat as I realize it isn't the only thing the smoke has snipped.

I gawp at the halved sprite bodies lying on the slick ground in absolute horror, then blink back up at the smoke gathering into the shape of a crow. I raise a trembling palm to my mouth.

Santo Caldrone, Morrgot has just killed two innocent pixies. "What have you done? What have you done?" My tone is as frenzied as my stomach's pitching.

What sort of monster am I abetting?

Before I can swing myself off the horse and get away from the murderous crow, Furia begins to canter. I debate throwing myself off when I'm slammed with a vision that steals the breath from my lungs.

My wrists are bound behind my back, and my chest is heaving with sobs as Silvius holds a steel blade to Nonna's bobbing throat. Although the sky is a limpid blue, the ocean is dyed black and covered in floating chunks of pink serpent flesh.

I thump back into reality with such force that another strangled sob drops from my mouth. What the underworld was that? A snippet of my future had the sprites lived to tell on me?

I shudder as the sight of Nonna's ghostly face and Minimus's slaughtered body flash behind my lids. Although bile bastes my palate, resolve fills my veins, snuffing my lingering desire to forsake this mission.

I can only return to my robin's-egg-blue house once Dante sits on the throne, for only then will I have the backing and status to protect all those I love. Which isn't to say I approve of Morrgot's manner of intervention.

"You could've stunned them or knocked them out." I hope my words will reach the crow, who is, once again, out of sight.

Nonna's face flashes behind my lids, eyes pried so wide, her green irises bob amidst the white. Silvius's fingers are wound through her black hair, and the steel is biting into her slender throat. *"Her blood is on you, Signorina Rossi. All on you."* But her blood is on him. It flows in rivulets around his knuckles and penetrates into the fabric of his pristine white uniform.

"Stop," I whimper.

Although I can barely make out Morrgot's body against the pitch-blackness of the Racoccin woods, I don't miss the golden gleam of his eyes that peer down at me, narrowed. As though he's challenging me to complain again about his manner of dealing with the sprites.

Is *he* the one planting these gruesome images inside my mind? Does this homicidal bird hold such power?

44

The stars fade, and the sun cycles over us, and still, Furia gallops and Morrgot soars. The adrenaline of snaking through trees on horseback keeps me wide awake. Although my hands ache and my throat feels as dry as parchment, I don't ease my grip on the reins to fish out my canteen.

We haven't run into anyone since the sprites, which isn't surprising considering the treacherousness and compactness of the Racoccin forest. I doubt anyone in their right mind would venture where we do. Not only is the land steep and uneven, but the light is scarce, made scarcer still by the tangle of branches and the canopy of leaves.

When dusk sets in, my sit bones are numb, and my blisters have sprouted new blisters. Monteluce has always seemed far, but at the moment, it feels as though it lies in another kingdom altogether.

"Are we almost there?"

If Morrgot hears me, he doesn't answer.

I probably shouldn't be distracting him from mapping out our course. I'd really hate to end up embedded in a tree trunk.

If only Bronwen had allowed Antoni to come…

What I wouldn't give for someone to talk to. And a soft bed.

A warm bath. Strawberry gelato. Cool water. A bag of ice for the bruises blooming on my inner thighs.

My list is long.

For the next few hours, I add more things to my list, in part to keep my mind off the pain and fatigue and in part to keep myself alert.

Furia books a sharp turn, his body listing so far to the right, mine begins to list too. I grit my teeth and hold on with every last crumb of my energy. The forest vanishes, giving way to a wall of rock that seems to rise all the way to the heavens.

However hard I tug on the reins, Furia neither slows nor swaps direction. He forges on ahead at full canter. I try to reassure myself that he didn't run into any tree trunks, so there's really no reason he's going to hurl us against the mountainside.

Yet fear curdles my stomach as the sulfurous scent of Rax is replaced by the chalky aroma of twilit stone. I yank on the reins, angering my baby blisters, but Furia forges ahead. I crane my neck and call out to Morrgot for help, wondering if it's slipped the bird's mind that neither my horse nor I can transform into smoke.

Unless Furia can…

The crow veers to the right, and my steed, thankfully, follows, but then the crow hooks a sharp left, and so does Furia. My heart flattens itself against my spine, and I shut my eyes.

I hate this treasure hunt.

I hate *everything* about it.

Why did I accept? For a golden coronet and Dante's love? If I die, I'll have no head to crown and no heart to give.

I should've jumped off this mad horse while I still could.

Furia rolls his powerful shoulders and jumps. When hooves click against stone, I crack one eyelid open.

We're climbing up a steep and narrow passageway lined in moss and paved with stone. Is this the path land travelers speak about over pints of faerie wine in Bottom of the Jug? I expected it to be wider and festooned with sprites. From what I can see and hear, it's just me, a horse, and a crow.

The world grows quiet and dark as we progress deeper up the trench with only the steady clip-clop of Furia's hooves and the occasional scrape of wind against the dank stones for noise. Whenever I feel the walls around me pressing against my knees, I tip my head up and stare at the stars overhead, reminding myself that I'm not enclosed in a box.

I'm free. Sort of.

"How long until we reach your friend?" I ask.

The crow peers down at me and offers no response.

I wait a few minutes and ask, "So, Morrgot, any chance you know what Kahol means?"

Another look. Another stretch of silence.

I'm starting to think I imagined it was the crow sending me the visions when the stone walls around me stretch and stretch, Furia vanishes, and the twinkling firmament becomes obscured by timbered beams.

Footfalls resound on the other side of a wooden door inlaid with silver grommets. When it swings open, I jerk back, then take another step back as a giant of a man fills the doorframe, shoulders and head skimming all three sides.

Although there's a lot about him to take in, it's his eyes that call out to me. They are black as keyholes, made even darker by the black dirt smudged around them, as though he's dipped his fingers in mud and dragged them across his lids and cheekbones.

The man stares straight through me with an intensity that makes me flinch. I start to turn to see who he's looking at when he pants, *The king was just found dead."*

"The king?" I gasp, pulse clattering. What king are they speaking of? Is this a vision of the past or of the future?

The incensed stranger doesn't react to my utterance, which means he can't hear me, the same way he can't see me.

"They're saying it's you. I thought—I thought..."

"You thought what, Cathal Báeinach? That I'd murder the only person in Luce willing to support our people?"

The voice is so thick and velvety that I almost miss the two foreign words.

Kahol Bannock. Kahol is a man.

"Assemble the siorkahd, Cathal."

Although spoken with little volume, the command stirs my very marrow.

I spin around to catch a glimpse of Kahol's interlocutor but drop from the vision.

Before my next breath, I'm back on Furia, back in the trench underneath a dome of stars blunted only by the outstretched wings of a black crow.

My mind reels from what the crow has shown me. I've no more doubts that it was his doing. After all, I asked him what Kahol meant, and he presented me with the answer.

The first time I met Bronwen, she called me Fallon Bannock. And then tonight, Antoni said—

I can hardly complete the thought, yet my mind ties both ends until I'm left with a conundrum more baffling than statuettes that can shift into animals.

Even though the word *daughter* was never mentioned, what else could I be to this man?

"Kahol Bannock is my father?" I try to come to terms with the shocking discovery that my absentee father is a frightening giant with a penchant for eye makeup. I think of my mother with all her soft angles and bright coloring. The more I picture her and the man from my vision, the more I find it impossible that *she*, of all people, had intimate relations with a man who looks like he could crush a person's larynx and remove his head with a mere swipe of his pinky.

A chill vaults up my spine. What if it isn't the ear culling that broke her mind but this man? What if he was a monster who forced himself on her? Who destroyed her by putting me inside her womb?

I squint at the crow. "Did you know Kahol Bannock personally?"

Morrgot, who flies just above me, regards me with his citrine eyes.

"Was he—" I lick my lips. "Was he a good man?"

I wait for the crow to transport my mind someplace else. For Monteluce to fade and for Kahol to reappear. But none of that happens.

Perhaps my words got lost in the air that separates us.

"Did Kahol *hurt* my mother?" I cannot pronounce the word *rape*. It tastes too vile on my tongue. And the idea of being a product of such a union…

Cauldron, I'd prefer being a changeling a million times over.

I try another question. "Did you show me the past, or was that the future?"

I will Morrgot to send me another vision, but however many times I ask, my mind stays blank. Has he exhausted the number of images he can send me?

Unless he doesn't know which king died…

Left alone with my thoughts and the steady clicking of Furia's hooves, I replay the vision, and although Kahol is the man I see, the one I keep hearing is the male he rumbled at, the one with the tenebrous timbre that pebbled my blood.

You thought what, Cathal Báeinach? That I'd murder the only person in Luce willing to support our people?

Our *people*.

Who are these people? Revolted Lucins? Fae from a warring kingdom?

My father's hair was shorter than how halflings wear it but longer than humans are allowed. Is he human like I've always been told or a halfling? But if he is a halfling, then how come my magic hasn't made itself known?

I gasp.

The Battle of Primanivi was waged by a tribe of mountain dwellers assisted by crows decked with iron talons and beaks.

Morrgot has iron appendages.

Morrgot is leading me into the mountain to find another crow like him.

Lore's crows.

Santa merda…

I just got into bed with my people's enemy.

45

My heart has been pounding out of alignment since I made the connection between Morrgot and Primanivi. What if Morrgot isn't leading me to the other crow? What if he's leading me straight to his master? And what if this rebel leader takes me hostage and uses me in his war against the Regio dynasty? What if he has no intention of helping Dante take the throne? What if he intends to take it?

Gods, what have I gotten myself mixed up in?

Why me?

Just because I'm related to a man serving Lore's cause doesn't mean I'm on board with it. Not for the first time, I chide myself for rushing into something without analyzing its every facet.

I glance over my shoulder at the ribbonlike trench we've been traveling for hours now. I could jump off Furia and run down. It's not like we've taken any turns, which, in all honesty, is surprising. Wouldn't a tribe of rebels make the way to their land more difficult to reach? Then again, we haven't crossed paths with a single guard, so this trail mustn't be known.

I eye Morrgot, an ink blot against the lightening sky. Would he attack me with his armored talons if I renege on my offer to find his metal cronies or let me go unscathed? What if he chops me in half like those two sprites?

Their mangled bodies flare behind my lids, and I shudder. If only I'd had the prescience to carry an obsidian spike. I pat the satchel nestled against my chest to locate my knife, but my palms are so reddened and blistered I can hardly feel a thing. When nothing spiky pricks my fingertips, I release the reins to open my bag.

I slip a shaking hand inside and find the canteen, slick with a condensation that feels divine against my aching palms. I root around for the rest of my supplies—the bar of soap I swiped from Giana's bathroom, the logs of goat cheese, the wedge of hardened pecorino, the crackers, the fruit paste, the knife. My fingertips meet only coarse jute and the cool metal of my canteen.

I peer into the bag in case, by some miracle, my numbed fingers missed colliding into my provisions. But no. Everything's gone. Just gone.

Skin tingling with alarm, I feed my entire arm inside the bag to reach the bottom. When my fingers slip through a hole the size of my fist, I suck in a breath.

I want to rage at myself, but that won't miraculously replenish my rucksack.

Perhaps this is a sign I should abandon this mission here and now, before I starve to death and end up in a crevasse in Montcluce, lying beside that second crow I'm supposed to succor.

But then what?

I return to Tarelexo and behave like a model citizen so Silvius doesn't toss me behind prison bars or prematurely push me into Filiaserpens?

My forehead prickles from someone's scrutiny. Since Furia's concentrated on the arduous ramp ahead and no other being seems to inhabit this part of the kingdom, I deduce it's Morrgot. Sure enough, when I flick my gaze in his direction, I find him staring.

In that moment, I'm glad he's not a man, because a man would've judged me. However assessing the crow sometimes appears, he's an effigy come to life. Not even a real animal, which means he cannot possibly be endowed with true sentience or logical thought.

I fish out the canteen and take a swallow, hoping it'll tame my annoyance. As though to wind me up, my stomach decides to growl. I plug my canteen and eye the yellow moss peppering the sides of the trench.

I almost reach out and rip off a chunk, but many faerie plants have side effects, and I'm not in the mood to experience one of them.

Besides, I'm not *that* hungry.

Hours later, although Furia's the one doing all the exercise, cold sweat trickles between my squashed breasts, my stomach spasms, and I ache in places I wasn't aware *could* ache.

Before I black out from fatigue and low blood sugar, I take another sip of water, then reach out and tear off a clump of the moss. It's damp and stringy like wet hair and smells like musty fur. My throat closes.

Maybe it doesn't taste as foul as it smells.

My nose crinkles as I carry it to my mouth. Right before I can dart my tongue out to taste it, I'm slapped in the face by a wing. Morrgot snatches the moss, his talons scraping against my blistered fingertips, then flies off to dump it.

"Hey! That was lunch!" My scratches ooze a mix of blood and serum. I stare at the pinkish liquid, wondering if I could nourish myself off my own blood. Cauldron, my mind has gone the way of my cheese.

My stomach screeches like a wounded animal. As I reach out for another handful of moss, Furia vanishes from underneath me, and I'm standing in a meadow beside a narrow river. The water rushes down the mountain so fast its flow is deafening, yet I don't miss the grunts and cries of a child with rounded ears. The young boy is patting an abdomen that's so bloated, it looks like it belongs on the body of an overindulgent adult.

When his face begins to bubble with welts, I gasp. His eyes roll into his head, and then he collapses face first into the grass and his sausage-link fingers fall open, revealing a clump of yellow moss.

I thump back atop Furia with another gasp. Although the meadow and boy are gone, all I can see is him.

Him and his handful of moss.

The same moss I'd have ingested had the crow not seized it. It strikes me that the bird has just saved my life.

"Thank you," I whisper, appetite gone.

I settle for another sip of water, then stash it back inside my satchel and stare at the thickening mist that does away with what little sunlight reached the trench.

Soon, the darkness surrounding me is so absolute, the mountain so still, the air so quiet, save for the clip-clop of Furia's hooves on the stone and the occasional whoosh of Morrgot's wings, that my lids drift low.

Lower.

Lo...

I awake to the *drip-drip* of something warm along my fingers. I think it may be raining, but the dampness is localized. My spine groans as I peel my torso off Furia's neck, and my fingers ache as I stretch them open. I must've clamped Furia's coarse mane all night considering how rigid my knuckles feel.

When I catch the bloodstain reddening my fingers, my lids jerk as high as my pulse. I swing my gaze around to see what bled on me only to find Morrgot hovering an arm's length away, a limp rabbit clutched in between its talons.

I wrinkle my nose as I realize he's about to make a snack of the bunny. He dips lower, nodding his head to the rabbit. Is he—is he offering me his kill?

Stomach shriveling from the scent, I shake my head. "I'm sorry. I don't—" Bile jumps up my throat. I swallow hard to send it back down. I croak out the rest of my sentence, concentrating hard on keeping down my two-day-old polenta. "I don't eat meat or fish."

I figure it'll probably seem ridiculous to a crow. I'm not even certain why I'm explaining my dietary preference.

Morrgot doesn't drop the bunny on my lap or roll his eyes at me—can crows roll their eyes?—yet I sense his exasperation. He probably thinks me a dumb human. After all, I need sustenance. I know it. He knows it. Yet here I am refusing to eat food that would sustain me.

"How much longer till we find your friend?"

His black wings stir the air once, twice, and then he flies off. It feels like a full hour slips by before his blackness blunts the white sky. Perhaps it has been one hour. Or two.

Although the sun barely splinters the smog, the air seems brighter, hinting at midday.

He flaps his wings, easing himself back into the trench, interrupting the one-sided conversation I've been having with Furia. Horses are, regrettably, rather aloof creatures. I wonder if Morrgot can plant images inside the stallion's mind.

Morrgot sinks lower and extends one metallic talon.

I stare at the branches ornamented with large berries, then up into his jeweled eyes. "For me?"

His head dips.

I take the branches and, without wasting a single second, pick a berry and pop it into my mouth. It's sweet, so very sweet, like the candy Giana used to bring back from Tarecuori. The juice slips down my tongue, a puddle of pure delight. Perhaps it's because I'm starving, but I anoint these berries most exquisite crop in all of Luce.

I pick off every pink pod, even the shrunken ones, and then contemplate gnawing on the branch in the hopes that the sap is as sweet as the nectar. In the end, I forgo acting like a rabid animal with a bone. I do, however, pull on Furia's reins and offer the leaves and branch to the horse. The horse sniffs it once, then takes it from my fingers and chomps.

Although I've caught the horse licking the high stone wall to gather the moisture beading between the rocks, I haven't seen him eat anything. Unless Morrgot has fed him while I was sleeping?

I cannot believe I slept while riding a horse.

I cannot believe I'm *riding* a horse.

Only soldiers and purelings ride horses.

It was one of Mamma's favorite pastimes when she was a girl growing up in Tarespagia. She'd ride her precious gelding down the beach or through my family's kingdom-renowned grove.

Furia stops walking so suddenly that my body pitches forward. Frowning, I glance around the man-made ditch, then attempt to see beyond its lip, but only standing atop the saddle would allow me a glimpse.

The crow cycles dizzyingly above my head while Furia's pointed ears flick back and forth. Clearly, something is happening.

Something only the animals, with their unequaled senses, have picked up on.

"What's going on?"

The vision of the gorge slams into my mind, complete with the din of rushing water, the mineral scent of wet earth, and the glimmer of an iron crow.

We've arrived.

46

Morrgot lands on the side of the ditch. He must beckon Furia because my horse nears him, berthing his big body against the damp wall speckled in moss. I take it I'll need to stand on the saddle and pull myself out of the trench on my own.

How I regret Furia doesn't have wings.

I regret it harder when I attempt to coax my leg out from between his flank and the wall, and a cramp seizes every muscle in my thigh.

I groan as I lever it in slow motion and then groan louder when I tug my other leg up and plant my foot on the saddle. Sweat salts my upper lip. To think all I've done to acquire such aches and pains is sit.

As I press my palms against the wall and pivot to face it, I lick my lips, and then I grit my teeth and heave my sore body to standing. How is it that all I've eaten is a handful of berries, yet I feel like I weigh as much as a beached, century-old serpent?

Neither Furia nor Morrgot move or make a sound as I scrabble to better my grip on the stacked rocks so I don't swoon off Furia and crash onto the trench floor. I'm not sure I'd be capable of peeling myself up if I fell.

How in the three kingdoms and one queendom am I supposed to venture down a ravine in my advanced state of decomposition?

I'm going to fall into that stream and get carried down all the kilometers we've traveled. With my luck, I'll wash up right at Silvius's polished black boots.

Tugging my lower lip into my mouth, I scan the wall for a nook to use as a foothold. Once I find it, I lift my leg, and holy mother of Fae, I see stars. They glimmer on the edge of my vision, usurping every color but white and gray.

Are white and gray even colors?

I breathe in and out until the moss turns marigold again, my clamped hands a reddened peach save for my bone-white knuckles. Gnawing the life out of my lip, I feed my other foot into a higher nook, then scuttle higher and higher.

What feels like a decade later, I crawl out of the ditch onto a loamy embankment that's cool to the touch. I could lie here a fortnight, but of course, Morrgot won't let me. He hops until he's standing right by my face, his molten eyes leveled on mine.

I sigh. "I'm getting up. I'm getting up." I roll onto my back, my bones cracking like the wooden floor of Bottom of the Jug.

My desire to pry myself up rivals my desire to succor a mystical crow from a ravine.

"I've got an idea, Morrgot. A brilliant one. How about you fly down there, grab your friend, and carry him up to me, then I'll remove the obsidian arrow that felled him?"

When I get no answering vision, I tear my gaze off the gauze of clouds and set it on the large black spot beside my head. The crow neither looks amused nor enthusiastic about my suggestion.

"Should I take your complete apathy as a no?"

An image flashes behind my lids of a hand, a very beautiful, masculine hand, skimming an obsidian spike and turning to iron.

I frown out of the vision. If he's trying to prove he'll become iron-plated upon touching the spike, then why use a hand? Sure, crows don't have human appendages, but he could've prodded the spike with his wing, and I would've understood.

I loose a deep sigh and begin the arduous task of standing. I roll onto my side and push myself up, my arms quivering like our windowpanes during the squalls that assault Luce when the temperatures drop too suddenly. It takes me almost a full minute of panting and teeth clenching to seat myself and then another few minutes to get my legs underneath me.

I peer down into the trench at Furia, who stands motionless, eyes closed. Even though I'm not looking forward to this part of my trip, I'm glad that the stallion gets to rest. I do worry about food and make a note of collecting leaves or handfuls of grass. What do equine behemoths, able to travel almost two days without rest, eat?

Perhaps Bronwen gave him some magical oats that can last him a week? The more I think of it, the more it'd explain his energy. If only I could eat some magical oats…or some more berries.

I turn away from Furia toward the crow, who's taken flight and is circling me again. "Where to, Morrgot?"

The bird takes off, gracefully soaring through the marbled sky. It strikes me that he too probably hasn't slept, but since I know he's magical, I'm guessing he doesn't need sleep.

I trail after him, the cramps in my legs easing as I walk through verdant fields filled with wildflowers and grass as tall as my knees. I plan on collecting bushels of it on my way back. Butterflies as yellow as Flavia Acolti's room flap around my hands. One even lands on the tip of my nose, eliciting a laugh from me.

Here I imagined Monteluce barren and inhospitable, but it writhes with life and color. Why have purelings painted the environment as so hostile when it's anything but?

I crane my neck to check on the crow's direction, find him drawing lazy circles over my head, golden eyes trained on me. "Are we almost at the ravine?"

He soars forward. After another long while, the grass begins to thin and the air to fill with the thunder of streaming water. I slow, keeping my gaze riveted to the orange earth beneath my boots, watching for the imminent drop-off that comes more suddenly than I've anticipated.

Morrgot seems to think I've missed it because he slams into my body with an astounding amount of force for such a slight bird. I hobble backward, my boot catching on a rock that sends me tumbling onto my ass. *Great.* Exactly what I needed.

"I'm not blind, Morrgot." As I wobble back to standing, I add, "But I appreciate you looking out for me."

My assurance doesn't stop the crow from hovering close. His every wing beat stirs the hair framing my face. I push a hand through my shoulder-length locks that are so knotted the crow may mistake them for a nest. I decide to worry about it later.

Keeping a full boot's distance between myself and the edge, I peer downward. I don't notice the statue immediately, my gaze affixed to the bottom of the gorge, which is so far below, I actually gulp.

If I slip, it's game over for me. No crows. No crown. No Dante.

Even falling into the stream wouldn't save me, considering the carpet of boulders protruding from the foaming water. "You better have a backup crow collector, Morrgot, because this is a suicide mission."

The crow, as usual, doesn't make a noise. He merely drifts beside me, observing his skewered twin on the ledge below.

Could I craft a tool to fish out the bird without scaling a rock facade as smooth as the Isolacuorin pontoon?

I could tie stalks of grass together, but even if I manage to snare the bird, the weight of its solid body will snap my makeshift rod. Since it can't hurt to try, I turn away from the gorge to hunt down sturdy stalks.

With hands hardened by blisters, I braid bushels together, then knot each plait until I've finagled a satisfyingly thick and long rope.

Morrgot has been watching me in silence. I wonder what's

going on inside his little head, if he deems me a curious two-legged specimen or an ingenious one. After fashioning a loose snare like my neighbors taught me when I was a child and would try crab fishing from the embankment between our houses, I return to the brink of the ravine, crouch, and feed my rope into the void.

"Wish me luck, Morrgot."

He doesn't wish me anything. Doesn't even send me an encouraging vision. Does he already know whether it'll work? Can he see the future like Bronwen?

It takes me four tries to loop my snare around the crow's neck. I'm tempted to pump my hand in the air but won't rejoice or pat myself on the back until the crow darkens the earth beside me.

Barely breathing, I tighten the snare. And then, only then, do I start tugging.

Slowly.

Slowly.

The odds of this working are about as good as Phoebus dating a woman, but this is a magical quest, and I'm a prophetic crow seeker, which must—hopefully—increase my odds of success.

When the creature's torso begins to lift, so does my optimism. If this works, I want a medal.

I put one hand over the other, again and again. The effigy's talons roll off the rock, and although it's probably in my mind, the scrape of metal against stone seems to echo across all of Monteluce.

I stop to breathe. In and out. In and out. This is it. The pivotal moment that will decide whether I become queen, a blood spatter at the bottom of a ravine, or Marco's future prisoner.

Holding my breath, I pull.

The statue lifts.

One centimeter.

Two.

Three.

I start to smile, my captive inhale rising up my throat.

The crow dangles halfway between myself and the stone shelf. Emboldened, I reel it in faster.

If only Phoebus and Sybille could see me now. How proud they'd—

Crrrr.

I freeze.

One of the braids is fraying.

Tongue thrashing with heartbeats, I tug gently.

A stalk snaps.

Sweat runs into my eyes, and it stings, but I don't dare blink.

You've got this, Fal.

In slow motion, I slide one hand over the other, then repeat the movement until the crow's head is within reach. I stick the braid beneath my knee and lean forward. My fingers skim the top of the creature's metal head.

My throat fills with heartbeats. I fist the rope again and pull and then reach out, but the crow swings, and the only thing I manage to snag is the arrow's teal fletching between my middle and index fingers.

Crrraaaack.

The rope tears.

I tighten my knuckles around the fletching, sweat salting my upper lip, and hold on with everything I've got. My knuckles strain and my biceps vibrate as the crow's solid iron body slides and tows the arrow.

I grit my teeth, dig my knees into the earth for balance, and swing out my other arm. Just as the fletching tears from my clamped knuckles, I clasp the shaft and slam back onto my heels.

The crow plummets, bumping into its former perch before dropping. All. The. Way. Down.

Drenched and trembling, I carry the arrow to my face and stare at it, then stare down into the ravine where the iron crow teeters on the crest of an oblong boulder. Why hasn't the bird blackened yet? Did a piece of obsidian stay inside the crow? I rub the sweat out of my eyes and scrutinize the weapon so hard, I see double. I blink it back into focus.

The gleaming black arrowhead is chipped.

If a sliver of obsidian remained inside the crow…

With a frustrated wail, I reel my arm back and launch both the arrow and my torn rope into the ravine. I watch them fall, unable to meet Morrgot's stare.

The ravine wobbles in and out of focus as my eyelids swell with heat, yet the metal crow below is in perfect focus. I remind myself that this is a magical animal and not a real one. That his shape can't be dented or his organs scrambled.

His…

What if it's a *her*? What if I've just knocked down Morrgot's paramour?

The statue tips and crashes into the foaming stream, beak first, splayed wings keeping it from gliding between the rocks and sinking, or worse, getting carried off into Mareluce.

I swipe my knuckles beneath my lash line to catch errant tears. "I'm sorry, Morrgot. I'm so sorry."

I avoid looking at him, inspecting the walls surrounding the ravine for a path down. The flutter of black feathers beside my cornea drives my lids lower still.

I cannot look at Morrgot. Not until I've fashioned a new plan.

Morrgot doesn't let me ignore him, though. He flaps his wings so close to my face that he brushes my cheek. Since his feathers are as soft as silk, it doesn't feel like a slap, even though that was surely his intent.

Heaving a sigh, I finally look up at him.

He swoops into the ravine, not low enough to touch his friend but low enough for me to note with trepidation the absence of shiny metal amongst the foam and rocks.

47

Where—
Out of the foam rises a sooty cloud. I drive the heels of my hands into my eyes, blinking wildly, because this mustn't be real.

Was the arrowhead whole? Did I imagine the blemish? Or did the stream carry the residual obsidian from the crow's body?

The smoke coils to the top of the boulder and hardens into flesh and feathers. Lore's second crow.

Oh my gods. I've managed to free Lore's second crow!

Since Morrgot cannot touch obsidian, I'm left with two theories—either the black arrow broke during the bird's collapse, or the current dislodged it.

However it happened, joy and relief make every one of my extremities tingle.

I did it.

I. Did. It.

The magical relic tucks its wings in and rolls its neck before tipping it upward. Instead of staring toward his friend, the crow stares at me with eyes as luminous and golden as Morrgot's.

After a couple of heartbeats, it spreads its wings and takes off.

Two crows down, three to go.

"Where to now, Morr—" The last syllable in his name withers in my throat as the crows dematerialize and meet, their shadows melding, giving birth to a larger blot.

When they solidify, they are no longer two but one.

A single bird that's twice as large...*everywhere*. Its iron talons are almost the size of my fingers, and its beak looks like it could slip through my throat and come out the other side.

I live amongst people who wield magic, yet I'm astounded.

After I collected Morrgot, I realized Bronwen had been miserly with details. But now...now I'm wondering what else she's kept from me. And why? Will this symbiosis occur with each crow? And if so, how large will Morrgot become? As large as the crows who killed Dante's father and attacked our people? Will Morrgot end up dwarfing me?

The only thing that makes more sense now is how five crows will get Dante on the throne. Any Fae faced with a monster bird outfitted with an iron beak and talons will shake in their boots, the king of Luce included.

Morrgot soars out of the ravine toward me. I scrabble to my feet and back away so fast, I trip over my own boots. My arms windmill, trying to keep my body upright, but in the end, it's the pressure of Morrgot's body against my shoulders that keeps me from falling. Once steady, Morrgot circles me, flapping his wings to remain level with my face.

As I stare at the black crow, I once again wonder if what I'm doing will doom my kingdom or better it but then remind myself that once Dante is king, he'll take me as his queen. There's no one to swear an oath to in this empty field, nevertheless I utter one beneath my breath.

"When I sit on the Lucin throne, I swear to be a beacon for justice and equity."

The throne? What an ambitious woman you are.

I freeze and gawk at Morrgot before pivoting and scanning the field in search of the owner of the voice that just rumbled through the air. "Who's there?"

My heart has deserted my rib cage and is crawling slowly up my throat. If I'm caught with magical crows, I will neither sit on a throne nor live to see another day, no matter how ambitious I may be.

The light has thinned, rendering the field a patchwork of leaden grays and ashen lavenders. I squint to make out a human shape, but besides the crow and the occasional winged insect, no other being blights the dimmed landscape.

Did I imagine the voice? Was it my conscience reminding me to be humble? If it was, my conscience has a mighty husky timbre. Rather masculine.

Unless it wasn't a person but a—

"That voice...it came from you?"

The crow doesn't answer, yet I take his silence as a yes.

"How—how are you speaking to me right now?"

You've given me back my voice.

"I've..." I lick my lips. "How?"

By uniting two of my crows.

Goose bumps coat my collarbone. "This is insane."

I take it Bronwen told you little about me.

"Bronwen told me *nothing* about you. I thought I was collecting statues, not magical birds that can send visions and speak." I swallow down my rising pulse. "Your beak doesn't move, so how are you making noise? Are you—what are those court entertainers called again? A ventriloquist?"

A ventriloquist? A snort resonates inside my skull. *I'm no ventriloquist.*

"Then how?"

I'm speaking inside your mind.

My mouth parts a little, then a lot.

Have I flummoxed you, Ionnh Báeinach?

It's silly, but I'm not a fan of his term of endearment or being called a Bannock. "I'm not that young, and my last name is Rossi, not Bannock."

There's a moment of stillness, scarred only by the churning of the air around Morrgot's wings. *You are Cathal's daughter, which makes you a Báeinach, but if you prefer to wear a punishing general's name, then I will abide by your wishes.*

My lips pinch. "I prefer to wear my mother's name."

There's a lengthy pause, one that resonates with unspoken words.

"Will all five of your crows do what those two just did?"

Yes.

"And all their names are Morrgot?"

Yes.

"And Lore is your master?"

A beat of silence slips between us and then the word, *Yes*.

"And this Lore, are we looking for him as well? Is he currently a statue spurting water into the king's bath?"

The crow doesn't smile, yet I feel his smile. How? I cannot explain it. Perhaps it's the slow churn of citrine ringing his pupils, which are fastened to me. Perhaps it's my imagination.

He's not spitting water into anyone's tub, no.

Although I have a thousand and one questions for him, I stockpile them for a time when my mind isn't reeling from the sound of a man's voice inside my skull.

Studying the landscape cloaked in veiled starlight to map out the course back to Furia, I do ask a final one. "So where is your next crow?"

In Tarespagia. Buried in your family's grove.

My gaze veers back to him. "My family's grove?" *How convenient.* Unease dampens my palms. I wipe them against my pant legs. "Tell me, Morrgot, is the prophecy real, or did Bronwen orchestrate this *hunt* because of my heritage?"

A beat passes. Two.

I start to wonder if he heard my question when he says, *Your princeling sits at the base of the mountain, surrounded by a battalion of men.*

"A battalion of—Why?"

Why...to apprehend you.

48

My heart pumps so fast that it strips the moisture from my tongue. "He kn-knows—knows that I've f-freed you."

I swing my gaze around the field, expecting to find Dante advancing toward me, long braids whipping around his crisp uniform, golden beads sparkling.

He's in the valley, I remind myself.

I rush up a rising slope and peer down. All I can make out through the thready clouds are colored globs like paint on an artist's palette—Racoccin green, Marelucin blue dotted with reflective copper rooftops, and at the very edge of the world, a latticework of Isolacuorin white and gold.

I was so focused on my task that I hadn't taken a moment to gaze out over the kingdom that'll someday be mine. It's wondrous. So much so that I almost forget why I'm standing on top of a hill.

When I recall Morrgot's words, I squint down into the wooded valley. Sure enough, a squadron of white-garbed Fae ring the mountain like a moat of salt.

The commander reported you missing and was ordered to find you. Dante decided to spearhead the task force, which got under Dargento's skin.

My pulse is slowly ebbing. Not that being declared a runaway is good news, but it's preferable to being chased for freeing a winged foe. "How do you know?"

I can hear them.

"I'm sorry. Did you just say you can hear them? They're a thousand meters below us."

Sound carries upward.

"I'm standing right here, and *I* can't hear them."

My senses are sharp, Ionnh Báeinach.

Sharp is an understatement. It must be an animal trait. A *magical* animal trait.

"It's Fallon, or Fallon Rossi, or Signorina Rossi. Your pick. As for young, I'm twenty-two, so I'd appreciate not being addressed like a child."

Ionnh means Miss in our tongue.

"Oh." I scrape my fingers through my hair, feeling a little foolish about my outburst. "Call me Fallon. After all, we're on a first name basis, aren't we, Morrgot?"

The crow appears blacker against the last splash of daylight.

Very well, Fallon.

He unspools the syllables in a way that makes my name sound foreign and inexplicably more lyrical, as though it's been mispronounced my entire life. Perhaps it has.

What if the man who fathered me whispered it to my mother, who stamped it between my upper lip and nose upon my birth? The baptismal groove may stem from Lucin folklore, but my name just may stem from Crow lore.

I stride back down the knoll, following the trail of crushed grass away from the gorge. I walk almost a mile, lost in the tumble of my thoughts, before I glance up at the sky to make sure my silent companion is still shadowing me.

His gold eyes are fastened to me, which makes me wonder if he's even looked away.

I pluck a fistful of long grass for Furia. "Tell me about Kahol Bannock."

I'm expecting Morrgot to soar higher to evade my question, but instead, he asks, *What would you like to know?*

"Everything. How did he meet my mother? How long were they together? Is he dead?"

Morrgot doesn't answer me right away. Is he sifting through his memory of the man to figure out which parts of his life are safe to share with a stranger? I would most definitely think twice about sharing anything about myself with this bird.

Your father and Agrippina met through Bronwen, and since Bronwen trusted her, Cathal did too.

"And you?"

I trust very few people, Fallon.

"Do you trust me?"

No.

I bristle that he doesn't hesitate, especially after all I've done for him.

You're offended.

I stare straight ahead at the endless field of silvered grass and harvest another bunch. "I'm risking my life to save yours."

You're risking your life to conquer your beloved prince's heart. I'm merely a stepping stone on your path.

My cheeks blaze that he's aware of my reasons for agreeing to collect the iron crows. "Bronwen's the one who told me of the prophecy. I didn't come up with it." Not that I owe him an explanation.

The tension that lingers between us blots out any and all camaraderie that may have developed between this talking bird and me.

After a long while, I finally shatter the silence. "So, Kahol. Is he dead?"

No.

"Then where is he? Why did Bronwen seek me out instead of him? Why did he abandon me?"

Because he's imprisoned.

"Where?"

Morrgot stares at the shimmering ocean that spills out from beneath the mountain like the train of a pureling gown. *Beneath the ocean.*

My skin prickles. "In the galleon? The one that Marco sank." My whisper is so loud, I worry the Lucin troops chasing me will have heard it.

You know of the galleon?

"Antoni mentioned it the night he told me about the Battle of Primanivi."

And Bronwen believes he's trustworthy . . .

I snap my neck back to glare at Morrgot. "The man's done nothing but fight for your cause."

Do you really think he's doing it out of the kindness of his heart?

"Perhaps his fight isn't completely selfless, but I can assure you, Morrgot, he didn't touch on any great, forbidden secret when he told me about the battle waged before my birth." I'm breathing heavily, partly from my pace and partly from my annoyance that this suspicious creature thinks so poorly of all those risking their livelihoods to bring him back to life. "You know what? I *hope* he has something to gain."

Bronwen promised him heaps of gold.

"Gold from the Regio coffers, I presume."

No.

"Are you saying the diviner has riches of her own buried somewhere in Rax?"

No.

"Then where, pray tell, will the gold come from?"

From me.

319

"*You* have gold?"

Why is this so shocking?

"Because you're a bird! How can a bird possess coin? Did your master give it to you?"

No one gave me a thing, Fallon. Morrgot's eyes gleam darkly against the pitch-black sky as though maddened I've relegated all he is to his physical nature. *I earned every coin of my wealth through lucrative treaties and hard work.*

I snort. I cannot help it. I'm picturing Morrgot tapping on doors with his beak, rolled parchments clamped between his talons. And then, more ludicrous still, I imagine him dragging a plow through a field. "Are you telling me that you used your built-in iron extremities to amass wealth in honest ways?"

You got me. Thanks to my arsenal of Crow powers, I've managed to loot, eavesdrop, and murder to my heart's and people's content. A beat of silence. *How else could a bird commandeer so much loyalty?*

The stories Headmistress Alice recounted may have been spoken by crow-fearing Fae, but all stories are based on fact, and the fact is Morrgot's a dangerous creature. One who can murder in the blink of an eye.

The memory of the two sprites floods my throat with bile. I swallow hard to slide it back down.

You should be terrified of me, Behach Éan.

Beyockeen? I stifle my curiosity because I don't care for malicious nicknames, and I cannot imagine the awful-sounding words meaning anything kind after our inimical exchange.

"Tell me, Morrgot, will you be halving me like those sprites once I've freed your five crows?"

He answers without hesitation. *I'll have no more use for you.*

Either he truly is the most detestable being or his sense of humor needs work. "Some would say having a queen in your corner would be useful."

Depends whose queen she is.

I frown, for if he's heard the prophecy, then he's aware I'll be Dante's. Oh gods, does he think I'll be Marco's?

Before I can set him straight, he distances himself from me until he's no more distinguishable from the firmament than the water from the sky. Not only is this crow sensitive, but his temper is worse than Sybille's around her blood cycle.

Although the wind ruffles the boughs of the conifers dotting the field, the abounding silence swells to the point where I stop and whirl on myself to locate Morrgot. I begin to believe he's abandoned me to this mountain, which embitters my already tart mood. What if I'm advancing toward a cliff? Sybille mentioned Monteluce was full of them.

"Unless you have more candidates with an immunity to iron and obsidian who don't mind having their kingdom's army chasing after them," I hiss, "you may want to tell me whether I'm going in the right direction."

These mountains are in your blood, Fallon.

Do I correct him and explain that heredity doesn't work that way? I decide to skirt another battle of words and focus my dwindling energy on hunting the abundant obscurity for the crow.

Since his voice echoed inside my mind, I've no direction to follow. He could be perched on the mountain summit hundreds of meters over my head. Unless he can't broadcast as far as he can hear?

"How much farther, Morrgot?"

My answer comes in the form of a whinny, as though Morrgot pawned the answer off on Furia. Unless Furia is whinnying in distress...

I'm not yet familiar with equine sounds.

In spite of the bruises lining the insides of my thighs, I pick up my pace, impatient to climb on my horse and have him do the walking. I prefer bruises to blisters. Although Giana's boots are comfortable, the kilometers I've walked to and from the ravine have irritated my already raw skin. If Phoebus was disgusted with the state of my feet before, he'd be utterly horrified now.

If only we could find a stream, one not lodged at the bottom of a ravine. What I wouldn't give for a long soak. Plus, my canteen is running on empty after my brisk promenade.

"Any chance we'll come across a brook or river on our way to Tarespagia?"

Yes.

A single word has never made me happier. "Is it far?"

When I catch sight of Furia's peaked ears, a sigh escapes me. I kneel and am about to toss my armload of grass into the trench when horror stills my arms. "This isn't toxic, right?"

No.

Relieved, I throw my offering onto the dewy stones at his hooves, then maneuver my sore body back into the saddle.

As Furia makes quick work of his meal, Morrgot says, *We should reach Tarespagia in the morning.*

Morning can't come soon enough, yet when first light creeps onto the horizon and pries my clasped lids open, I'm wholly unprepared for the sight before me.

49

As far as the eye can see, the ochre summits have been carved into dwellings so vast, they resemble islands suspended in the sky. The illusion is strengthened by the thready clouds that drape around the rows of soaring pillars that support each abode like table legs.

I blink.

The bone-smooth columns and three-story dwellings remain.

I rub my eyes because surely, *surely* I'm hallucinating. Although devoid of luxury, these man-whittled peaks can't possibly be real. If they were, I'd have heard about them.

When my lashes sweep upward again, there they stand, dark against the rising sun, solid amid the brightening blue.

I lap up each detail, jaw so wide I may just end up choking on clouds if I don't choke on my shock first.

Unlike typical Lucin homes, these don't shine, save for the small windowpanes dulled by so much dust that they blend into the stone facade. There are no copper shingles, no gilt detailing, no inset cut stones, yet I am blinded by this architectural wonder's understated magnificence.

If only Phoebus and Sybille were at my side. If only I could've shared this discovery with them.

"What is this place?" I find myself whispering.

Morrgot's answer ripples inside my mind, deep and quiet, like a brick tossed into placid water. **Rahnach bi'adh.**

I roll the foreign words over my tongue. "And what does Rawnock Byaw mean?"

The sky kingdom.

My jaw snaps shut with an audible click. *Kingdom?* "Which Regio monarch built it? And why have I never heard of it?"

It was built long before Costa Regio's reign.

My gaze runs over every ancient curve and sharp edge, slides down the smooth shine of the pillars. It must've belonged to one of the early ruling dynasties, men who considered themselves kings even though they acted like savages.

The wind blows harder the farther we climb, its howl so fierce, it scatters goose bumps up and down my limbs. "Is it still inhabited?"

No.

That explains the buildup of grime and the barren feel of this city. It also explains the absence of stairs or ladders or whatever else was used to access the city. Unless stairs are hidden inside the pillars? As Furia's hooves click up the trench, I study the columns, on the lookout for a hidden doorway, but no telltale groove jumps out at me.

And then I get sidetracked because the sun rises right in between the columns, a blinding sphere of orange, red, and gold. I'm familiar with beauty and with the sun, yet the sight is so glorious that my jaw grows slack again.

I glance over my shoulder at the damp, moss-covered wall I've gazed on for days on end. How high we've climbed. The altitude explains the cooler temperatures and why my ears have popped at least four dozen times since I awoke from my doze atop Furia.

As I roll my shoulders and stretch my neck, I cast my gaze off the derelict palace and onto the crow whose eyes are, for once, trained elsewhere than on my face. "Are the Regios unaware of this place?"

Oh, the Regios are aware of its existence. Why do you think they've buried it beneath clouds?

"Buried? Are you saying…" My voice is drowned by the song of the wind twisting into my hair and icing the dried sweat along my spine.

That they've kept it purposely hidden from their people? Yes.

"Why?"

Spite. Fear. Jealousy.

I frown. "I'm not sure I follow."

What cannot be destroyed or occupied needs to be concealed or it will undermine the ruler's power. Can you imagine if the Lucins got wind that there exists a place in Luce the Regios have yet to breach?

"How *did* the former inhabitants breach it?"

The former inhabitants could fly.

I crank my neck back and gasp, "Fly?" No one, not even the Fae with an affinity for air, can levitate, much less travel without their feet touching the ground. "People could once fly?"

Morrgot doesn't answer, just flaps his wings to rise higher, eyes fastened to this neglected city.

"You aren't speaking of people, are you? This was your…*bird-*dom?" Kingdom sounds too human for a nest.

The word wins me a hefty side-eye from Morrgot, who clearly disapproves of being zoomorphized. I'd have snorted had nostalgia not rolled off him and into me.

Every hour that passes makes me more attuned to the crow's feelings. The same way I can sense Minimus's pain, I can now sense Morrgot's.

Me and my odd affinity to animals…

I stroke Furia's neck, trying to get a read off him, but the stallion's mind and heart remain impenetrable, which just adds to the conundrum that is my relationship to animals.

A thought strikes me then. One that has to do with animals but not with me. What if the den Minimus inhabits is as magnificent as this giant rocky nest? What if, like the Crows, he and his brethren have built an underwater empire?

I'm about to ask Morrgot when he breaks off into two crows. I'm just as startled as I was the first time I saw it happen. Well, the first time his two crows became one.

My pulse ticks faster, the sound drowned out by a low, liquid whoosh—water.

The trench we've been traveling narrows and turns shallower. Furia stops, snuffles, then paws at the damp rock.

"What is he—"

Before I can finish my question, the stallion backs up and then breaks into a canter that has me folding my torso over his neck.

He's going to try and make the jump!

Again, we're racing toward a wall, except this time, there are no turns to make. He leaps, and my heart leaps in time with him. I don't breathe until Furia clears the stone obstacle that's as tall as he is and his hooves clatter on the esplanade. Like the pillars, the ground is as smooth and shiny as ice and refracts every speck of sunlight.

"You crazy beast." I clap and stroke Furia's neck, and he halts and lets out a satisfied whinny.

As my pulse quiets down, I look for the water I heard but cannot find its source. Is my body so weary and my tongue so parched that I imagined it?

Perhaps a cascade flows on the other side.

I cluck my tongue and wiggle the reins, but the stallion doesn't penetrate the deep shadows lurking between the pillars.

I hesitate to tap my heels into Furia's flanks but worry the stallion might take off at a canter and spring right off the stone esplanade. Unlike Morrgot, Furia isn't outfitted with wings, and unlike purelings, I'm not quasi-unkillable.

"Should I get off?"

When I receive no answer from our merry leader, I turn in the saddle, my spine cracking from the abrupt movement. Morrgots One and Two are nowhere to be seen.

They better not have abandoned me in their *bird*dom... I'm two-legged and two-armed and far from skilled enough with either set of limbs to scale mirror-smooth pillars.

"Morr—" The last syllable of his name gets lost in the deafening grind of stone against stone and the shuddering vibrations that shoot into every pillar.

Into the ceiling and walls they hold.

Into Furia.

Into me.

50

I scream for Morrgot, certain the pillars are about to crumble and his dwelling is about to fall, certain I'm about to be crushed beneath it all.

At my scream, Morrgots One and Two shoot out of the trench like fireworks, dragging twin streaks of black smoke in their wakes. The crows slam into each other like percussions, and I swear it makes the entire mountain shudder harder.

"Wh-what's happening?"

Furia's ears are pricked up and flipping back and forth, but otherwise, the stallion isn't perspiring from every pore like I am. I clutch his mane as water shoots out from beneath the esplanade and courses down the trench, liters upon liters, as though the mountain has siphoned up the entire ocean.

Relax, Fallon.

"Relax?!" My tone is strangled. "The whole damn mountain just trembled, and you're telling me to fucking relax! What did you do, Morrgot?"

I restored nature's balance and bought us more time.

Droplets spray upward, glittering like tossed tinsel against the brightening sky. "How exactly have you bought us more time?"

By flushing down our tail.

It takes my addled brain a moment to understand what he means. What he *did*.

My face must go as white as the blouse glued to my flushed skin because Morrgot adds, **Your prince will be fine. A little wet, but he'll live. After all, pure-blooded Fae can't die from drowning.**

"What if there are halflings down there? *They* could drown! And horses? You may not care about my brethren, but you care about animals, don't you?"

The horses know how to swim, and no half-bloods are riding with Dante. The prince, like the king, doesn't allow runts in his regiment.

"Because purelings have an unlimited supply of magic. Not because he deems them better fighters!" I yell over the unceasing rumble of stone and water.

Of course.

Morrgot's mocking tone isn't lost on me. I glower as he sweeps around me, fluttering my hair with a beat of his wings. Silence films the air between us, thick as the humidity.

"If you murder Luce's future king—"

You have my word that your princeling will be unharmed. Does that settle your nerves?

I suck in breath after rickety breath as the trench fills and fills, as water as clear as air flows down. "What about the humans living in Rax?"

What about them?

"This'll flood the forest."

The water knows the way to the ocean.

"What does that even mean?" I toss a hand in the air, then think better of releasing Furia and snatch a clump of his black mane.

It means that the land won't be inundated.

"And the toxic moss? What will happen to it? Will it poison the serpents? The crops? The wells?"

Salt nulls the toxin. The second the stream meets the sea, the

moss carried down with the torrent will become no more toxic than a mint leaf.

My anger recedes like a tidal wave. "So that poisoned child could've been saved with salt?"

Morrgot's chest pumps hard beneath his blue-black feathers. **Yes.**

I fall silent as the earth continues to rage like a fitful child. Only when the tremors beneath Furia's hooves ease and the gush of water is replaced by a fast-moving current do I sweep my leg over my steed's rump and jump down.

Not that there's anyone to watch, but my landing is inelegant. It could've been worse, of course. I could've gone *splat* and bled out all over the stone.

I press a steadying palm against the saddle as cramps rattle my thighs, attempting to upend my body. I wait for the ache to vanish, but all it does is dwindle. I sense I'll have to live with it for the time being.

Hesitantly, I remove my hand from Furia to fish out my canteen. I drink the last of the water, then start for the source. May as well make use of Morrgot's dirty tactic.

He flies into my path. ***You cannot drink this water. Not until I find a solution to eradicate the moss from the stones.***

"Right. No salt." I turn away from the forbidden source, my insides wilting. Gulping down my own saliva, I ask, "Did you plant that moss to keep away intruders?"

He scoffs. ***And poison my people?***

His *people?* Antoni mentioned mountain dwellers domesticated crows, but Morrgot makes it sound as though it's the other way around. "I suppose poisoning your human followers and their pet birds wouldn't be all that smart."

Pet birds? He spits the words inside my mind.

"My apologies. I shouldn't have called them pets." *Note to self: refer to his crows as people.*

Nibbling on my lip, I study the smooth ceiling that looms three stories high. "Did someone plant the moss, or did it just start growing on its own?"

Costa Regio planted it in the hopes it would kill off the half-bloods. The only thing he succeeded at was poisoning the inhabitants of Racocci.

Horror drives my gaze back to Morrgot.

Thousands died before we managed to erect the dam and squeeze the antidote out of the vile man. Yet it's still deemed one of his most brilliant ploys. Timbre dropping, he adds, *The start of the Magnabellum.*

My lashes skim my brow bone. "You were—you were around then?" Why I'm surprised by anything concerning Morrgot is beyond me, but still…

Yes. I was.

I replay his words, wondering if they're true or if he's feeding me a sob story. "The Magnabellum was a war between Shabbe and Luce."

No. It was a war between the Crows and the Fae. The Shabbins were our allies.

"But that's not what the history books say."

Because history books are written by the victors, Fallon. His gruff tone vibrates my skull. *Costa's blame incensed the humans, who were, until then, loyal to the Crows. Your father suggested I take the fickle Fae out, but I refused, because Costa had the backing of both Nebba and Glace, and I feared they'd come to our shores to aid his coup.* He grows quiet, but it isn't a calm sort of quiet, it's a tempestuous one. *If I'd listened to Cathal when he told me Costa learned of our obsidian curse, Luce would still be ours.*

"How did he learn of your curse?"

From Meriam, his Shabbin lover. The one he later sacrificed to create the wards around the queendom.

The great Fae king who detested Shabbe had an affair with a Shabbin?

Morrgot has single-talonly destroyed everything I know about the dawn of Luce.

A bird kingdom… How crazy.

Once word of my growing aviary reaches Marco and my grandfather… I shudder as I picture Justus scaling the other side of the mountain to greet me with the steel blade of his jeweled sword.

"My grandfather is going to murder me," I muse out loud.

The dead can hardly murder.

The blood deserts my upper body. "My grandfather—he's… You—you killed him?" Is that what Morrgot stole off to do in the middle of the night? I cannot decide if I'm relieved or appalled.

Not yet, but rest assured, Fallon, that anyone who so much as wishes you harm will be dealt with accordingly.

I blink at the crow, who flutters his dark wings with the languor of a nectar-sated butterfly. I've come to know Morrgot enough to realize that his calm is an illusion and that *dealt with* is a euphemism for *killed*.

"I suppose I should be grateful that you'll act as my weapon and shield, but I'd appreciate if you didn't mete out murder impulsively, especially on my behalf. Because once we part ways, those deaths will reflect on me." Dante will forgive a traitor, but he's too wholesome to forgive a murderess. "It's one thing to have feathers on my hands, Morrgot. It's quite another to have blood."

The crow stops beating his wings, yet he remains suspended, drifting like the clouds ringing the mountain. The ensuing calm is harsher than the earlier uproar.

The heat will become stifling soon, and the stream I promised is still a ways away. We should go.

"I don't get a tour of your city?"

And run back to your princeling with all our secrets? I think not. Besides, you don't have wings.

"I have two functioning legs." *Somewhat* functioning.

The only way into my city is by flight. He's already floating away on a breeze that carries the scent of the tropics—hot sand, wet fronds, and sweet fruit.

"Then how do all your human followers get up there?" I scan the ceiling for a latch before chasing his darkness amidst the gilded blue and lush green.

I thought the view of the east was breathtaking, but the view of the west beyond the clouds…it's unlike any landscape I've ever laid eyes on. The emerald is carved into giant fronds instead of small leaves, the aquamarine froths against crescents of sand so pale they resemble spilled sugar, and the bright hues—magenta, tangerine orange, and sunshine yellow—battle to outshine each other.

Tarespagia glistens from its lacquer of clear sunlight and sways in the tepid air.

A velvet muzzle nudges my shoulder, startling me out of my contemplation. I stroke Furia's nose, and the horse leans into my touch.

I sigh. "It's beautiful, isn't it?"

The horse flutters its nostrils. I take it as an agreement.

Any day now, Fallon.

"I'm glad you're not as moody as he is. I don't think I could've dealt with two grumpy companions."

Dragging my hand from the hinge of his jaw to the cusp of his shoulder, I put my foot in the stirrup and heave myself up. My skeleton creaks like a boat hull in rough seas, eliciting a fathomless groan from my lips.

I'm glad we're heading to a stream, but what I wouldn't give for a feather bed. "Hey, Morrgot, you mentioned the sun was hot." Furia takes off at a brisk trot that jangles my sitting bones. "Any chance we could stop in a patch of shade for a nap? Or better yet, at an inn with bedrooms?"

We'll rest.

"At an inn?" I will him to say yes, but willing Morrgot to do or say anything is like expecting a sprite to unhand a stolen copper.

Because I'm violently optimistic, I decide to take his silence as a strong maybe. And then, as my body sways like the thickening tropical forest, I start dreaming of this inn, and I swear I can smell oil sizzling beneath bubbling eggs and taste sweet buns browning in a nearby oven.

Please let it not be a figment of my starved imagination.

Although the scent of bread and eggs lingers, I realize it's in my mind as we traipse through luxuriant groves cloaked in mist and find neither hut nor human for kilometers on end. Unlike in the east, the cloud cover doesn't lessen the heat, which feels like a damp cloth pressed against my mouth and nose.

Soaked in sweat and mist, my sunny mood begins to gray. "You said we'd reach the stream in the morning, and it's way past morning."

I said we'd reach Tarespagia.

"What about the stream?"

Rest, Fallon. We're almost there.

"Rest? Where?"

Where you sit.

There goes my daydream of inns and beds. Although he brings me more berries, they hardly stave off my hunger, but I don't complain. I've not the energy to do so, and soon, I drift. And when I awake…

I think I may be dreaming again.

51

Water crashes.

I can feel the wetness on my nose.

And sunshine, glorious, bright sunshine.

Morrgot delivered.

It isn't that I doubted he would, but—No, I wholly doubted it.

He's been so sullen since we left his abandoned sky city behind that I thought he'd try to steal some of my happiness to even out the playing field.

The stream he promised is so much more than a stream. It's an oasis with a waterfall. No pale sand cinches the diamond-clear water, yet I've never seen a place more idyllic in my entire life. Rounded boulders shaded by taller ones and giant palms surround a shallow pool that glimmers in the bright sun.

I don't wait for Furia to stop walking before I dismount. I just swing off the saddle and stagger toward the oasis, dropping to my knees as though it were an altar and I a devout person. I scoop out a handful and splash my face, then drink until I cannot hear the water dropping into my empty stomach. Until the hunger pangs recede and my head clears.

Sated, I stand, throw off my satchel and boots, then wade into the pool fully dressed and crouch to immerse my body. Keeping my knees bent, I open the ties of my shirt, then drag it off my head and scrub it between my sore hands. After I lay it to dry on a hot stone, I tug on the firm knot of the brassiere. When it loosens, my rib cage spills open like an umbrella, my bones reconquering the space that was stolen from them.

I worry I won't be able to stuff them back inside. Then again, I only wore the breast trap to pass as a male during my brief trip through Rax. Until we reach civilization, I've no need to deceive anyone.

Morrgot watches me from the highest rock where he stands guard like a Fae sentry.

My bliss radiates out of me in the form of a smile that transforms into a contented sigh when the brassiere plops into the pool. "I'm so happy right now, I could kiss you."

Morrgot turns his head as though the idea is so preposterous he can't stand to look at me.

His disgust merely makes me want to taunt him further. Especially since I have no one else to talk to. "Have you ever had a crow girlfriend?"

His eyes return to me. *I had many female friends.*

"Because of your status, or is there actual charm beneath that gruff exterior of yours?"

His pause is so great that I sense that I've either baffled him or piqued him. *What need would a king have for charm?*

I'm not certain whether to laugh or frown. Is he serious? "I suppose you're right, even though it makes me sad for you."

Why would it make you sad?

I stare at him a moment longer before salvaging my brassiere and setting it to dry beside my shirt, then pluck off my socks and roll down both my pants and underwear. "Because of the type of friends power brings you. They're not always the honest or loyal type." After using the rocks as a scrubbing board, I lay my pants and underwear flat, then crouch anew and rub my skin and hair until I've scoured off every last ounce of sweat, dirt, and dried blood.

Wringing out my hair, I crane my neck and look back up at Morrgot, whose eyes are, like always, fastened to me. I'm starting to think he worries I'll make a run for it and leave him to find his missing three crows.

Speaking of which... "Does obsidian shatter?"

Why do you ask?

"Because of the bowl Marco made with one of your crows. I was just wondering how to free him. I was thinking I could drop it when I'm brought to the trophy room. You know, after I'm arrested and dragged to the dungeon." I tip my head to the side. "Right before Dante saves me and makes me his queen."

Morrgot studies Furia, who's happily munching on a palm frond.

"How exactly will you dethrone Marco?"

How are kings removed from power, Fallon?

My head snaps straight. "You're going to kill him?"

I should for what he's done to me and my people, but Priya has asked me to deliver the man to her shores so she may deal with him as she sees fit.

"Priya?" Beads of water trickle down my arms and around my breasts, running down my hollowed stomach. When it releases a low, short growl, I palm it and scan the trees for something to eat.

The queen of Shabbe.

"You're friends with— You know her?" I'm half-awed, half-perplexed. "I hear she dismembers men, starting with their most private parts." I picture Marco at her mercy, but the thought is so horrid, I force it away. "I hear the sand in Shabbe is pink because of all the blood spilled."

Impressive.

"What is? Her manner of torture or her ability to take lives without a care in the world?"

Neither. I'm impressed by how the Fae have turned the Shabbins into veritable creatures of nightmares.

"Are you saying it's all hearsay?"

Not all of it. The Shabbins are ruthless and formidably powerful, but they're also clever and fair.

"If they were clever, then why let the world believe they're monsters?"

What choice do they have? They've been prisoners of their island for over five centuries, and the few brave or foolish souls who dare penetrate the wards become stuck right alongside them.

"I hear they turn them into slaves."

You've heard wrong.

"How would you know?" I snap.

Why so peeved?

My forearms dig into my abdomen, which rages, but no longer for food. "Because you're implying I've gobbled up lies my entire life."

It isn't your fault, Fallon. You didn't know any better.

His answer cools my simmering frustration until I realize that I'm licking up his words the same way I licked up my professors' teachings and the rumors spilled at Bottom of the Jug over tankards of faerie wine. "How do I know *you're* not the one lying?"

I suppose you don't. You'll have to visit Shabbe to make up your own mind.

I snort. "Oh, you're good. You're *really* good. But the thing is, Morrgot, I'm not the dumb girl you believe me to be. I'm not taking a one-way trip to a land you claim is pretty and fair." I notch my chin higher. "And if you try to drag me there, I'll stake every last one of your crows and drop them into Filiaserpens where they'll rot for all of eternity."

The gold in Morrgot's eyes churns. *Once you make me whole, I will owe you my life, Behach Éan. You'll have nothing to fear from me.*

Again with that nickname… If he's calling me names, then I demand he shares their meaning so I can make up some of my own. "What does *Beyockeen* mean?"

Are you averse to coconuts?

"It means *that*?"

A distinct snort resonates through my mind as the crow takes off toward a palm tree and latches onto something. Something that whooshes through the air and thuds against a boulder with a loud crack. Milky water spills out from the broken husk and bleeds down the gray stone as the two sides of the split coconut seesaw precariously.

After recovering from my surprise, I swim toward the rock dripping with juice, poach one of the hairy brown shells, and tip it to my lips. The nectar coats my throat and tongue, and although I try not to waste a drop, I'm drinking with such unbridled thirst, the coconut water dribbles off my chin, scoots across my collarbone, and beads between my breasts.

Another coconut cracks against a rock and then another.

Morrgot is gifting me a veritable feast. Probably to shut me up, but I'm too ravenous to care.

Using my nails, I claw at the creamy flesh lining the shell but get nothing because my nails are so blunt. I use my teeth next but almost crack a molar on the outer shell. I'm about to ask Morrgot if he can spot some nifty tool I can use to spoon out the meat when I find him perched in front of me, a chunk of white hanging from his beak.

I expect he's going to wolf it down, but instead he lengthens his neck to offer it to me. I take it from him with a slow "Thank you."

As I chew it, he says, **Cúoco. That's how we say coconut in Crow.**

I swallow, then try out the word, "*Coowocko*."

He peels out another chunk, which I pluck carefully from his beak, careful not to graze the razor-sharp iron.

"And those delicious pink berries you brought me earlier?"

Beinnfrhal.

"*Benfrol.*"

Literally, mountain berry.

"And *Beyockeen*? What does that mean? Annoying one?"

His beak can't twist into a smile, yet it feels like he's smiling when he asks, **However did you guess?**

I fake glower at him. I'm certain it means something not great, but I really doubt I guessed correctly. "You're such an ass." The chuckle that resounds between my temples widens my eyes. "Did you just…*laugh*, Morrgot?"

A charmless ass like myself laugh? You must be hearing things.

I stare at him for a full minute. Not only did he most definitely laugh, but now he's teasing me. I dip my hand into the pool and, quick as a hummingbird's wingbeat, flick a handful of water onto Morrgot.

I note, with much glee, that water rolls down his feathers and drips down his metal beak because I, Fallon Rossi, halfling not very extraordinaire, managed to catch a lethal, magical crow unawares. "Not so gloatful now, huh?"

He spreads his wings and shakes them out until they're as dry as the trench before he opened the floodgates. **Gloatful? Is that some new word added to your language in my absence?**

"No. But it should be added." I lie back on the water and float like a starfish. "It's a really great word. Phoebus would love it. Sybille too, although she'd surely give me grief about it." Gods, I miss those two. I close my eyes and dream up their faces so that they're a little bit with me. "Back to *Beyockeen*. What does it mean?" I'll admit, I'm slightly one-track-minded.

When, after a full minute, I don't hear an answer, I crack open a lid. Morrgot's no longer on the rock. A quick look around my oasis doesn't bring me any closer to figuring out where he went.

He's gone. Or hiding.

Though Morrgot doesn't strike me as the hiding type, so I imagine he went to do a crow thing. Maybe hunt down some poor jungle rodent to snack on. Furia is still around, though. The sight of my stallion is strangely reassuring, as though Morrgot didn't up and abandon me to the wilds of Monteluce without an escort.

I pull myself out of the water and sprawl out on a rock.

Forget *close to divine*. This place *is* divine.

If the overworld exists, then I pray it's like this, a series of private oases with sweet water, vibrant skies, and warm rocks.

Although…will I be granted entry inside the realm reserved for good Fae, or will my crow aiding send me straight to the underworld?

Deciding it's thoroughly useless to worry about my fate at the present moment, I shut my eyes and let myself drift off.

52

I wake because of an incessant buzzing. Although I've never wished harm on a creature, I'm a little miffed with the insect that's decided to pull me out of my slumber. As I blink the world into focus, I realize with great surprise that I'm covered in palm fronds.

Did a windstorm sweep through Monteluce while I slept? I push up onto my elbows, the fronds slipping noiselessly off my warmed, rested body and gliding into the limpid pool. For a windstorm, the palm fronds are very localized, all of them on my body. No, someone put them there. Even though a person who shields you from the sun shouldn't inspire dread, my pulse ramps up as I squint around my private oasis. The only living beings I see, besides the hordes of buzzing insects, are my stallion and my crow.

Well, not *my* crow.

The crow I happen to be helping out.

The crow whose eyes are presently shut. As I wonder if he's the one who covered me in palm leaves, I'm sucked into a world with no light, save for a handful of stars and a faraway bonfire.

I stand on a hill a few paces away from a woman garbed in red silk and a man dressed all in black. They don't see me, too busy staring at the people amassed around the bonfire, so I study them openly.

The woman's coiled locks reach her narrow waist and snap in a breeze I cannot feel, the same breeze that flutters the man's cloak and the black hair that curls around his rounded ears.

"My father wants us to marry." The woman turns, and I get an eyeful of her profile. Straight nose, pale eyes, skin as brown as her hair, and lips so full they look like Ptolemy Timeus's silken boat cushions.

"I'm aware." The man glances at the woman, and I catch the black smudge of charcoal smeared all around his eye. It reminds me of my father. I'm guessing the man I'm staring at is another Crow follower.

"You don't have to worry. You and I won't marry, Lore."

Lore. I suck in a breath. This is the man who owns the winged quintuplets. The master of the crows. Which decidedly is a strange concept considering Morrgot considers himself king. Maybe this man is the rebel *human* king of the Crow supporters while Morrgot rules over the animal part of the tribe.

"How harsh you are." It strikes me that Lore sounds a lot like Morrgot, but people who spend a lot of time together start acting and speaking similarly.

The woman laughs, a breezy, beautiful sound. "Save the theatrics for those who don't know you."

Lore smiles, a curve so subtle I may have missed it was it not for the gleam of his teeth.

"Cian is my mate."

"I've heard. He hasn't stopped speaking about it since you penetrated his mind." They both turn back toward the bonfire. "Has your father heard?"

"My father wouldn't hear it even if I yelled it into his ear. He wants you and me to marry. Marriages are power plays, not love matches." After a beat, she adds, "He wants your kingdom, Lore. If I were you, I wouldn't trust him."

"You know this better than anyone, Bronwen, but I trust no one."

343

I clap my lips. This is the same woman as the blind soothsayer who forecast my future?

"You trust me, don't you?" she says.

"You've yet to give me a reason not to."

I step closer, absorbing her features. The woman standing on the summit of the hill is gorgeous, her skin as smooth as melted chocolate, and her eyes, although pale, have color in them. I cannot tell which one from where I stand, but I can tell they're not white.

"What happened to you?" I whisper out loud.

Where she doesn't turn, Lore does. He looks down at me, eyes smudged in so much black that his bright irises stand out like coins. "Fallon?"

I freeze.

He knows my name. *Lore* knows my name!

"Bronwen!" I yell to capture the woman's attention and demand why she passed herself off as a blind, deformed crone.

She turns, but not toward me. She turns toward the valley and the bonfire that shoots sparks into the night air. And then she's gone and so is Lore. And so is the hill and the abundance of shadows.

I'm sitting upright on my boulder, blinking wide eyes at Morrgot. "What the underworld was that?"

Morrgot just stares back, awake now. *Obviously*, since he sent me a vision of Bronwen and Lore.

"What happened to Bronwen's face?"

Morrgot keeps staring and staring, and I'm tempted to dig my pinkies into my ears in case water's lodged in there and I missed his answer, but Morrgot doesn't speak out loud, so that'd be rather pointless.

"She was so beautiful. What happened to her? And Keeann? Who's he? Besides her mate. Wait, does mate mean husband?" Silence. "Why are you gawping at me as though I've lost my mind?

Didn't you—" I look around, gathering some of the fronds and pressing them against my bare breasts, suddenly self-conscious. "Didn't *you* send me that vision?"

A twig snaps and my heart pinwheels. When I see Furia walking around, my pulse slows.

We need to get going.

The sky has deepened and darkened while I slept. It's now streaked in liquid golds and velvety oranges, the color of the fire crackling in the vision of Bronwen and Lore.

Sighing, I gather my clothes and drag them on. Although they don't smell any nicer, they look brighter. How I miss the scent of soap, the slide of it across my skin. Perhaps once we reach Tarespagia, I'll get the chance for a proper bath.

As I stuff my brassiere into my satchel, not caring all that much if it ends up slipping out, I ask again, "So what happened to Bronwen? And to Keeann?"

It's her story to tell, Fallon.

I growl in frustration. "Well, she's not here to tell it, now is she?" Morrgot circles me.

I blow away a piece of hair that is molded to my cheek. "She knows *everything* about me. It's only fair I know *something* about her."

More silence.

"I won't get on Furia until you—"

Cian is Cathal's brother.

I'm so stunned that he's indulged me that it takes my mind a full minute to wrap itself around that kernel.

"That makes her my… Oh my gods, Bronwen's my aunt?" I yell this so loudly that I startle two scarlet birds from a tree. I'm sort of surprised they hung around, what with an enormous, scary crow lording about. I suppose Morrgot isn't in the habit of attacking his own species.

I gave you something. Now please, get on the horse.

I don't move because I *cannot*. I'm still processing that I have a relative I've never heard about. Although women claim themselves capable of doing two things at once, this skill obviously passed me by, same as my Fae power. My family line really gave me the short end of the stick. Maybe my father's Crow affiliation nullified all the good stuff.

Furia hooves the grass and huffs.

"I'm hurrying. I'm hurrying." I slip on my boots and sling my satchel around my chest, and then I grab ahold of the reins and pull myself up with ease. Furia must sense my newfangled adeptness because he starts walking before I'm seated in the saddle.

We'll reach Selvati by sunrise, spend the day, then set out for Tarespagia.

Selvati is the equivalent of Racocci on this side of Monteluce, except four times more populated, poorer, and dirtier. I hear most humans live in squalor and racketeer unsuspecting Tarespagians for a living.

"Where will we be spending the day?" I'm praying he doesn't suggest under a piece of rusted metal.

In the home of a friend.

I'm tempted to say, *you have friends?* but swap it for a more pleasant question. "With walls and a roof and a bed?" I almost add a bathtub to my list but don't want to come across as demanding or prissy. Which is odd, really, because it isn't like I actually care what Morrgot thinks of me.

With walls and a roof and a bed.

I take in a deep lungful of dusky air, the tightness in my chest easing. "Now I'm actually excited to discover Selvati."

Don't let excitement run away with your gumption. The Regios have smothered humans for so many centuries that they've become wretched.

The tightness returns tenfold, as though I've slipped the brassiere back on and wrapped it twice around my breasts before knotting the laces. "Then why are we spending the day with them?"

Because it's easier to move about unnoticed in the dark than in the light.

"Are Dante and his army still behind us?"

No. They're ahead of us.

"Ahead of us? How?"

They boarded a ship this morning and will be docking in Tarespagia by nightfall.

"How do you know all this?"

I caught a few sprites discussing it while you were sleeping.

I blanch because by caught, he must mean— "Are they still alive?"

Morrgot swerves around a tawny-trunked tree with sprawling branches dotted in rubbery green leaves no larger than children's palms.

"Did you kill them?"

I had no choice, he finally says.

"Everyone has a choice!"

Would you have preferred I let them fly off with the information of your whereabouts and the company you keep? Do you know what Marco would do then? He'd launch his whole army after you, and not to abduct but to kill.

"Dante wouldn't let him kill me. As for the sprites, you could've"—I toss a hand in the air—"I don't know, strapped them to a tree until we freed the rest of your crows."

Dante is powerless. As for strapping them to a tree, they'd have been eaten before dusk by the wild cats that prowl this side of the mountain.

The blood that had started to return to my cheeks drains right out of them. "Wild cats?"

Or Selvatins.

Bile bastes my throat as I swing my gaze from side to side, on the lookout for bloodthirsty animals and humans. "Selvatins are cannibals?" I whisper, afraid my voice will carry and alert them to a fresh meal traveling their way.

Not all of them.

That does *nothing* to reassure me. "I slept enough to last me a full week. No need to laze about Selvati. I'll just get a cloak with a hood and—"

You have nothing to worry about, Fallon.

"You just told me Selvatins chomp on people. I don't want to be chomped on! I don't know about you, but my extremities and limbs don't regen—"

With a feverish whinny, Furia rears back, then lifts his forelegs off the ground, sliding my body and most of my organs so far back, they smack my spine. Clamping my thighs around the saddle, I seize a handful of the stallion's mane.

When Furia's hooves collide against the jungle floor, I catch sight of a woman tattooed in brown ink from hairline to cuticle.

She grins at me, exposing a full set of blackened teeth. "It's her."

53

The woman swings like the pendulum of a clock from the liana wrapped around one forearm and one ankle, her long dreads swinging in time with her agile, muscled body. A bib of layered chains hooked to both her neck and waist shivers against her hennaed torso.

"Her?" I hunt the dense foliage for Morrgot, but all I see are dozens upon dozens of men and women crouched on branches, chained and inked from head to toe like the black-toothed woman before me.

"The girl who talks to animals," the woman continues.

Furia twitches, dancing from one hoof to the other.

"Whole kingdom's buzzin' about you," a boy adds. He's gangly, with more ribs poking out of his decorated chest than from my corseted dresses.

I swallow. "You shouldn't believe every rumor you hear."

"So you were talkin' with a real person back there?" another branch hugger asks. I think it's a woman from the pointiness of her nose and chin and the delicateness of her cheekbones, but her exposed chest is all male.

"Um. No. With my horse." My hands are so clammy they dampen the leather reins. "But he doesn't answer me or anything."

I shrug. "Lonely people and their quirks. Anyway, I should…um… get going."

Several people cackle, and I realize with escalating anxiety that everyone's teeth are black and feathers poke out from behind their shoulders. Although I'm hoping the feathers trim their dreads, my hope is rapidly squashed when one of the women extricates a long arrow that she feeds into a bow and whose ivory tip is fantastically sharp.

"Morrgot," I mutter beneath my breath.

"No need for swearin', girl. We ain't planning to kill you."

Just eat me toe by toe…

"We don't get paid if you're dead."

"Paid?" My heart, which has been clocking my spine since the woman dropped from the tree like a coconut, holds still.

"A bounty's been placed on your head." It's the delicate-faced male who answers.

"Who—" I swallow the squeak from my voice and try again. "Who's put the bounty on my head?"

"The king heself."

Well…merda. Where the underworld is my trusty crow bodyguard? Is he keeping away, worried I'll go off on him if he murders all these tree people?

I mean, I would absolutely be angry, but better an angry sidekick than a captive one, right? I will him to stir up some chaos, saw through a few lianas and branches, so Furia can hoof it out of here.

"Get down from the horse or we shoot it down," the woman says.

My heart drops, then bounces so high I clamp my chattering teeth shut to keep it from flailing out. "Morrgot!"

Ask them how much gold the king has offered.

Is he serious? "Are you planning on ransoming me?" I mutter under my breath.

The woman embracing the liana arches an eyebrow, which

pleats the whorls of ink adorning her forehead. "Are you thick? Did you not hear us say we are?"

No, Fallon. I'm planning on paying them off so we can be on our way.

"I really doubt I have enough on me to match a king's bounty," I murmur.

"What'd she say?" someone asks.

"Just chatting with my horse." I lean over and pat Furia's sweat-slicked neck. "How much is my going rate?"

"A hundred gold pieces."

Oof. The price on my head is jarring, especially considering halflings are reminded daily of their worthlessness.

Offer them a hundred.

Between gritted teeth, I say, "I don't have—"

I have it.

I frown because I don't remember a purse strapped to his talon. "Where?"

"Off the horsey, girl." The woman drops noiselessly to the ground.

Furia backs up before wheeling on himself because we're surrounded.

Give them my offer!

"I'll match the king's reward if you let me pass."

The jungle goes quiet as though the leaves and insects are also holding their breath.

"You've got a hundred gold pieces?" the woman asks.

"Yes." I glance upward, urging Morrgot to make it rain, but no coins drop from the sky.

Chiseled Face clucks words in a language I don't understand.

"Lyrial thinks you're bluffin'."

I'm taking Morrgot's prolonged silence as him gathering the coins. "I'm not."

"Then a hundred for you and another fifty for the horse."

"What?" My fingers slip along the reins. "That's—"

Fine. Tell them that's fine.

I cannot decide whether I'm more glad than worried that he's around and not scrounging up money from his coffers. "You've got yourselves a deal. Now…"

More clucking erupts. Liana Hugger says, "We talked amongst ourselves, and we've agreed that you accepted too easily."

"Because I have places to be." *Crows to collect.* "You know what, my offer is one twenty-five. Take it or leave it."

What are you doing, Fallon?

"No deal." Lyrial steps up to Liana Hugger's side and seizes Furia's reins, not hard enough to yank them from my hands but hard enough that my stallion can no longer shift around restlessly. "But me and my brothers and sisters wonder, how is a round-eared whore so rich?"

"Whore?"

"We heard where you work, girl." Liana's lips are curled in disgust.

I huff in annoyance. "I work in a tavern, not a brothel." Why does everyone believe Bottom of the Jug is a pleasure house? It's not like it's called Bottoms and Jugs. The only bottom most patrons ever see is that of a bottle.

Fallon, Morrgot growls.

I disregard his growl. I'd like to see his reaction if anyone referred to his sky city as a dirty nest full of libidinous birds doing the naughty, however it is crows copulate. I'm still uncertain.

The whorls on Lyrial's face rearrange themselves again. "How is a girl who works in a *tavern*"—I appreciate him insisting on that word—"so rich?"

"Affluent friends."

"Affluent?" The curls of ink on his brow move.

Even though I want to be on my way, I clarify the word for the savages' sake. "Affluent means rich."

"How rich?"

"Rich rich."

Fallon. Morrgot's growl snaps me out of this decidedly ludicrous conversation. *Just tell them you will get them their hundred and fifty pieces of gold, and let us be on our way.*

One hundred and fifty... I daydream of all the things I could buy for one hundred and fifty, all the wares that would make Nonna's and Mamma's lives more comfortable, all the ways I could help out the Amaris. Move Bottom of the Jug to Tarecuori and rebrand it with silver calligraphy instead of chipped black paint. Maybe they'd call it Top of the Jug or the Silver Carafe.

"Since your friends are so rich, we want two hundred." Lyrial's head is tipped to the side. "And we want it immediately." There's a taunt to his voice, as though he doesn't believe I can actually procure it.

Will you please get rid of them, Fallon? Say yes and move on.

Yes to two hundred? The fact that he's willing to part with so much money makes me regret not having negotiated a treasure-hunting fee or at the very least a severance package if the going gets too tough and I have to bow out.

"Fine, but not a cent more!" I cry out because the hubbub around me has grown to dizzying levels. There's so much clucking of tongues that it sounds like every tree on this side of Monteluce is crawling with chickens.

Lyrial tips his head. The air whooshes behind me, and then arms come around my waist and seize the reins, caging me.

"No move," the skinny boy from earlier says, his breath so rank it makes my eyes water.

I hope they use some of Morrgot's gold to do something about those rotted teeth of theirs. "What do you think you're—"

He snaps my satchel from around my shoulders with a blade he then drags up to the underside of my jaw. The satchel lands at Lyrial's bare feet. The male crouches and digs through it, pulling out my filled canteen and my brassiere. He tosses both aside, then upends my bag. To his disappointment, however hard he shakes, nothing else falls out.

"No coins. Check the saddle!"

Two others press around me and run their hands over the saddle and in turn over my legs. I'm very tempted to kick them, but that wouldn't end too well for me, what with a rusted blade digging into my neck and having only that one neck.

When they report back with a cluck of tongue that no gold is sewn into Furia's saddle, Lyrial lifts his head up, and from his dreads, ears poke out.

Very pointed ears.

As pointed as the rest of his features.

As pointed as the pureling commander who sparked this whole Fallon hullaballoo.

"You're a pureblood." I sweep my gaze around the ones I can see. "You're all purebloods!" Their hair is so long that I should've put two and two together but was misled by their blackened teeth and habitat.

Unless they do live in a mansion in Tarespagia and only dress like doxies with horrid dental hygiene to scare passersby out of their purses.

"You're Fae—way higher up than halflings on the Lucin pyramid of wealth—so how come you're hanging out in the jungle with the likes of me? Aren't purelings treated as demigods on this side of the kingdom?"

"Where's that money, girl?" Lyrial asks.

They're obviously not your typical purelings, Fallon.

Obviously. Eye twitching from a spike of adrenaline, I take in the darkening shadows around me, hunting for the shape of a bird.

I fathom they've been ban— Is that a fucking knife at your throat?

Through barely parted lips, I grit out, "Certainly feels like one."

So he was absent when the boy dropped onto the saddle...

The temptation to demand he not leave me alone again withers as the metal nicks my skin and a bead of blood rolls down my neck like a rogue pearl.

Morrgot lets out a slew of foreign words. Each sounds worse than the nickname he's scrounged up for me.

A clinking jangle followed by a low *oompf* sounds right behind me. The boy, who dropped by uninvited, goes as limp as an overcooked noodle and lists to the side. A slight shift of my hips, and he topples off Furia along with a fat coin purse.

Hisses erupt along with the straightening of vertebrae as all the tree Fae stare between the purse that clocked their fellow heathen and the patches of purpling sky.

"Nice aim," I grumble.

"How did you— How—?" Lyrial's green eyes gape as wide as his blackened mouth.

"Magic," I say before wondering why he and his people—*pure* Fae—haven't launched magical warfare on me. I don't taunt him, preferring he keep it that way.

I fold and refold my fingers around the reins. "Our deal is done. Move."

Neither he nor the female move.

"Did my voice not carry to your broad ears?"

"We heard you, girl." The woman's voice is as jarring as the purse one of her people has upturned. "We must count."

At their speed, I'll be here until sunrise. "They're all there."

"We. Count."

I blow a piece of hair off my face.

The bookkeeper looks up after a half hour and says something that makes the corners of Lyrial's lips hook upward. Did Morrgot cheapen out? I don't have magical math powers, so I cannot tally up the spread of gold with a blink of an eye, but I can tell there are *a lot* of coins down there.

More than I've ever seen in one place at one time.

"What?" I snap.

Although Lyrial is still holding on to the reins, Furia begins to prance.

"Send us another bag from the heavens, and we let you leave."

54

You heard the pointy-eared swine ask for something to be sent from the heavens, right, Behach Éan?

"I know you believe me part Fae and part daft," I mutter with as much aplomb as I can muster for one encircled by irrational forest folk, "but I assure you, my senses are wholly adequate."

At this point, I don't much care if the jungle Fae assume I talk to myself.

No need to bristle. I was just making certain you and I were on the same page.

Before I can ask what in the world Morrgot's trying to get at, smoke rips past Lyrial's eyes and detaches the man's arm at the elbow. Like, clean off. No tissue or bone connect the appendage now dangling off Furia's bit.

My stomach lurches in time with Furia, who grasps his freedom between two hooves.

The last thing I see are Lyrial's eyes rolling back into his pretty face and his female companion catching him with a shriek.

Arrows are launched. Since Furia seems to know where he's heading, I pivot my upper body to keep my attention on the feathered missiles in order to duck and lean accordingly. Nonna taught me to never turn my back on the enemy, for one has far more chances of dodging a blow they see coming.

Although I react fast, Morrgot reacts faster. His shapeless blackness seems to swell as he zips left and right, up and down, batting away the hail of arrows. I almost relax enough to turn back around but catch a white gleam just as an arrow sails past my smoke shield.

I flick my head to the side, knocking my ear into my shoulder, and the arrow whizzes past my temple.

Fallon! Morrgot has turned solid and is gaping at me with such shock, like it's the first time something has gotten past him.

I'm glad I didn't let my guard down, or I'd have an arrow planted in the middle of my forehead. *Wise Nonna.* "I'm good, Morrgot."

An arrow clicks into a neighboring trunk, snapping him from his trance. He doesn't speak as he buffers me from the last ones. Only when Furia foams with sweat and we've put a kilometer between us and the bad Fae does he morph back into feathers.

Did the arrow—Were you hit?

"No."

Nonetheless, he circles me to check.

I want to ask him why my word is never good enough for him, but Morrgot has trust issues galore, and he seems genuinely worried, so I let him hover.

"Your gold!"

What about my gold?

"We need to go back and get it."

Why?

"Because one, there was a lot of it, and two, those hooligans will surely put it to terrible use."

It'll keep them away from you. That is all that matters. Besides, there's plenty more where it came from.

"Where *did* it come from?" And no, I'm not planning on

stealing from him, which isn't to say that if he hands me a coin or three, I'll turn any down. I have endured *a lot*.

From—how did you put it?—my nest full of libidinous birds.

I freeze because I don't remember saying that out loud, but I must've. I change the subject. "I cannot believe you severed Lyrial's arm."

Morrgot takes his time answering. *He's lucky he still has his head.*

I swallow down the lump of acid crawling up my throat. Morrgot's appendages are all made of iron. "It won't grow back, though, will it?" The thud of my heart matches Furia's fast trot.

You have to admit, I was on my best behavior. I left the others unscathed. If it had been up to me, you wouldn't have had time to chitchat with the lot, and they wouldn't have had appendages enough to spring arrows your way.

I decide to overlook his latter comment and focus on the one that isn't making my coconut lunch attempt to flee my stomach. "Chitchat? Is that honestly what you think I was doing?"

Well, you were *discussing the status of Fae in Lucin society.*

"To buy you time to get me out of the rotten situation! Which, by the way, was entirely your fault to begin with."

I don't recall putting a price on your head.

I crank my neck back and glare into the canopy of starlit branches. "I wasn't speaking of the rewa—"

Furia leaps over a felled tree, effectively snapping my mouth shut. His pace turns manic again. Either he senses more evil Fae, or Morrgot is telling him to go faster so I can no longer argue with him.

I spend the rest of the night clinging to Furia as he blazes across the vertiginous uneven terrain and marveling at my twilit surroundings. I'm aware this isn't a sightseeing journey, but I'm calm enough again to appreciate the splendor.

Until I hear a branch breaking over my head, followed by a scratchy hiss.

Morrgot sweeps low.

"What was that?"

I get my answer a half second later when two wide-set eyes gleam at me from a large head full of speckled fur.

"Is that a...leopard?" My whisper is as tense as the lines of the predator's body, which I note with a swallow is almost the same size as Furia's.

Morrgot lets out an ear-shredding squawk that startles the spit down my airway. As I wheeze, the leopard's shoulders unbunch, and he lurches onto his paws and spins on himself, vanishing into the brush.

"I didn't know you were capable of such a sound." Hacking out a lung has thinned and roughened my voice.

I favor mind walking.

"So, mind walking. Is that a Crow power?"

No. Only I am capable of this.

"How come only you can penetrate animal's and people's minds without their consent?"

That will be a story for another day.

"Why keep it for another day? We still have a long walk ahead, haven't we? May as well keep chatting. It'll make the time pass faster."

It will also alert any lurkers as to your whereabouts.

I press my mouth shut and scan the land and trees. Only the chant of nocturnal creatures blunts the silence, which seems to thicken like the humidity the closer to the ocean we get.

As the adrenaline drains, every sore spot on my body makes itself known, the sorest being my chest. I lift a hand to my breasts, and the mere graze of my palm against my peaked nipples makes me whimper.

Morrgot swoops low. *What? What is it?*

"You know how women have something called breasts?"

The gold rimming his pupils becomes no thicker than the wiry wedding bands Sybille's parents wear. He stares fixedly at my face. No lower. Either he's unfamiliar with the female anatomy, or he's very genteel.

What about your...breasts? He must've inhaled an insect or a grain of sand, because his voice sounds raspy all of a sudden.

Wait. He mind speaks or walks or whatever it is he calls his ability. His words aren't produced by his vocal folds, are they? Maybe he's just flummoxed about discussing female body parts.

I press my forearm beneath said body part to keep it from bouncing. Now that I've noticed the burn, it's all I can focus on. "Those hoodlums took my bag. My brassiere was inside." I wished it gone, but now that it is... I sigh, hearing superstitious Giana remind me not to make wishes I do not want granted.

I'm struck by an idea. It isn't great, but it could bring me some relief.

When I release the reins and untuck my shirt, Morrgot dips lower, having seemingly forgotten to use his wings. He morphs to smoke right before colliding with Furia's peaked ears and shoots upward. Once in the clear, he solidifies again.

What are you doing? He sounds peeved, as though his flight lapse was somehow my fault.

I pull the rumpled hem taut around my ribs and knot it. "Trying to lessen the friction." My solution isn't ideal, but it helps. "Shoot," I murmur as I take hold of the reins again.

Now what?

Signore Moody seems moodier than usual. It's been a long night, one that is finally coming to an end. Although the shift is slight, the jungle has quieted, and the blacks are melting, graying, reviving the contrasts that the night had flattened.

"I don't think I can pass as a boy without a brassiere."

Morrgot's eyes flick to my bare midriff before fixing on my knotted shirt. His nose cannot wrinkle, yet his distaste for my niftiness comes through loud and clear.

"Relax. When we reach town, I'll untie my shirt." I skim the burnt-orange petal of a dangling orchid that reminds me of Mamma's hair. "You think everyone knows about the bounty?"

I believe that if a mountain tribe has heard of it, then yes.

"We should push on, then. Head straight to my family's estate."

No. Not in broad daylight, and not before you rest.

I lift my gaze. "In spite of the reward, you trust your Selvatin contact not to take me hostage and deliver me to the king?"

Yes.

"Why?"

Because this person knows he has more to gain from my return than a hundred pieces of gold.

Ah. Of course. Bronwen must've promised him a bucket of coins for aiding the future queen in ridding Luce of its current ruler.

"Does this person know about"—I gesture in his vicinity—"*you?*"

He does.

"Do many people know about you?"

Of me, yes. Of my return, no. And we need to keep it that way, or the price on your head will inflate considerably. He gives me a pointed look.

Does he seriously think I'm going to trot down the streets of Selvati and proclaim I'm bringing a bunch of lethal crows out of hibernation? When he returned two decades ago, he started a war! Even if the Lucins aren't fond of their monarch, they undoubtedly prefer peace to bloodshed.

Andrea Regio was willing to negotiate. We agreed on dividing the kingdom, but his son intervened.

I frown at the change of topic. Then again, we *were* discussing war and politics. "So why did the Crows kill Andrea? Because he changed his mind?"

We didn't kill Costa's son.

"Then who did?"

Andrea was killed by his own flesh and blood. By his own son.

55

Morrgot has stunned me into complete and utter silence. *After accusing us of his father's murder, Marco gathered all the humans in Racocci inside a cave. He told them it was for their protection against the Montelucin rebels and their iron-taloned birds, when in truth, it was to lure me and my people out. He gave me an ultimatum: a ceasefire, or he would crumble the cave walls.*

It takes my reeling mind a minute to understand all Morrgot is saying. I had no love for the monarch but now…now all I have is pure odium.

After murdering his own father, Marco almost sacrificed thousands of innocents?

"I imagine you chose the ceasefire since you were turned to metal?"

Morrgot's molten eyes roam over mine, over my face, as though hunting to see where my loyalties lie before releasing any more details about Primanivi. *I did, but he still ordered his earth Fae to shake the land.* He pauses, eyes on the horizon, which is rapidly filling with color. *I ordered my people to succor the humans, who misunderstood our intent and attacked us with the obsidian-tipped weapons Marco had given them.* He swallows. *I underestimated how deeply the Regios had brainwashed humans during our five-century-long absence. Bronwen tried to warn me.*

Another lengthy pause, followed by a full body shudder that bristles his inky feathers.

That afternoon, we became harbingers of death and Marco a prodigious savior. He gathered all my men who fell to our curse and two of my crows, gave one to Justus to dispose of and staked the other himself, and then he warned me he would kill one human for every hour I didn't surrender my final crows. I didn't think he would, but the death toll started to rise.

Goose bumps scurry over my skin, pebbling more than the slice of stomach bared to the elements.

He left the bodies in Racocci for me to find, made certain the cadavers appeared mauled by an animal and not murdered by their fellow man. The hatred for my kind rose to a point where bands of humans went up the mountain to try and capture the evil king themselves. The crow in the ravine was taken down by a human.

Part of me wants to stroke Morrgot's wing because rehashing this battle is clearly taking a toll on him, but another part keeps piping up to say: *this is his side of the story.* Can I picture Marco assassinating his father? Honestly, I never saw them interact, so no. Can I picture him using and discarding humans? Yes.

But I've also seen how callously Morrgot inflicts death. He is far from innocent.

"And your final two crows?"

What choice did I have but to surrender them?

His choice of pronoun is odd, since I imagine Lore *made* him surrender. Unless Lore was also apprehended in the cave and turned to metal?

I could've either doomed every human in the kingdom or cursed my people for a few more years.

"What do you mean, *curse your people?*"

My people's magic is tied to mine. When I fall, they all fall. I was made from five crows to prevent such a fate, yet twice...twice I've failed them.

"Maybe you should ask your avian god to turn you into a hundred crows next."

That earns me a robust side-eye.

"Sure, it would make your next crow collector's job tedious, but it *would* greatly increase your chances of escaping your curse. Imagine how small you'd be if divvied up into a hundred crows. I've never tried driving a toothpick into a wasp, but I'm guessing it'd be quite tricky."

He snorts while I smile, but too soon, my mind veers back to the Battle of Primanivi, and the uptick of my mouth wanes.

I pat Furia's sweat-soaked neck. "Does that mean that now that you're back, some of your people have awakened?"

They can only break out of their obsidian form once all five of my crows join.

"Stone? Don't they turn to iron like you?"

No. Only I turn to metal.

I squint at the brightening, shimmering sea. To think that beneath it lies a ship filled with stone statues of men and birds. The distant white caps catapult an idea inside my skull.

I whip my gaze toward Morrgot. "Can serpents touch obsidian, or does it affect them like it does your species?"

It doesn't affect them. Why?

Thank the gods, because I threw those spikes into the canal. The breath I loose could tip a ship. "You know how I can sort of communicate with animals? Well, I'm friends with a serpent."

He eyes me warily.

"I could maybe teach him to remove the spikes from your people and crows? Or tow the ship closer to shore? Or something. He's massive and very strong."

I nibble on my lip as I think logistics. First, I'd have to lead

Minimus to where the ship sank off the southern coast of Luce. It would tack on a few days to my overall mission, but if it worked—

Antoni and his crew are dredging the ship to shore so you can free my last crow.

My eyes grow as wide as my mouth, and I suck in too much air. "Every boat that wanders those waters sinks! You've condemned him to death."

He won't die.

"Why? Because Bronwen foresaw he'd be fine?"

Yes.

"What if she's wrong?"

She never has been.

"How come she has this power? No Fae I know can foretell the future."

She struck a deal with a Shabbin sorceress. Her sight of the present for the sight of the future.

My blood runs cold at the idea that the Shabbins possess such power. "What did she give the sorceress in exchange?"

Her eyes.

"No, I got that. I meant…coin, jewels, her firstborn?"

Her eyes. The Shabbins can see everything she sees. She's become their eyes.

Oh… *Oh!* "They're spying on us?"

They're our allies. All they desire is to help us rise and take back what's ours so we can help them shatter the wards.

How strange to think that Luce will be divided between two monarchs. "She can truly see the future?"

Truly.

I sit up straighter in the saddle as though a crown already graces my head. I'm curious to know when and how Dante will propose. I dream of a lavish affair with music and flowers but decide I'd prefer a simple one.

I hope he'll ask Nonna for my hand before getting down on

one knee with a really beautiful ring. I would really like to own something pretty. Something that didn't belong to anyone else. Something made only for me.

Cauldron, I'm old-fashioned.

After what feels like an hour of painting the perfect proposal inside my mind, one worthy of gracing the pages of a book, I flick my gaze to the sky to make sure Morrgot is still around. It takes me a few sweeps of the dawn sky to spot him.

He soars high, eyes on the horizon, large wings slicing through the inert heat. I cannot read his mind yet feel he's contemplating his future also. Once he's achieved all his and Lore's political ambitions, will he settle with a female friend? Or five female friends, one for each of his crows?

He slants me a droll look.

I guess a heart that has beat solely for revenge won't beat for anything else until all his Crows have returned, and I'm not speaking of the ones that make up his body but the ones that make up his... What is a group of crows called again?

I remember the class snickering about the term and Headmistress Alice reminding everyone it was no laughing matter.

A murder!

A murder of crows.

A shiver drags up my spine like nails on a chalkboard, and I grimace. Oh, how Headmistress Alice will scowl once the blue sky blackens with birds. Gods, I'll start my reign by being loathed by all the Fae.

As long as I'm loved by some—Phoebus, Sybille, Mamma, Nonna, and Dante—it'll be all right.

Flat rooftops appear in the distance, quieting my thoughts. Although I heard Selvati is as much a shantytown as Racocci, dipped in dawn, it resembles a magical city from one of Mamma's stories.

Don't speak of Bronwen's exchange, not even to your

princeling, or she'll be put to death. I'm about to tell him that I'm no snitch when he adds, **Understand that I'll stop at nothing... nothing** *to protect her, Fallon Rossi.*

I mash my lips together. His threat comes through loud and clear, especially since he called me by my Fae family name.

"Don't betray me, and I won't betray you." I kick Furia, urging my stallion into a gallop. I want to get away from Morrgot even though I know that until my task is done, I won't be rid of him.

How would I betray you?

I can sense his body soaring over mine but keep my gaze pinned to the rambling town.

"By being too greedy and eliminating not one but two Regios." The hot wind snatches my words and hurls them at him.

56

Y*our shirt.*

Morrgot and I haven't talked once since our spat, if the heated words we exchanged could be considered a spat.

"Ask nicely and I might unknot it." I thought we'd arrived at an understanding, he and I, but the only place we've reached is another impasse.

He doesn't trust me; I don't trust him. What a team we make.

I think he swears, but unlike Lucin, which sounds melodious even shrieked, every word in Crow sounds guttural and angry.

"And keep your voice down. My brain hurts."

That makes him quit his muttering.

I wait for him to ask me to unroll my shirt.

And wait.

How proud can a bird be?

If you don't untuck your fucking shirt, I'll inflict bodily harm on every Selvatin who leers at you. Is that truly what you want?

I pick open the knot and let the shirt drift back in place over my stomach. "That wasn't *nicely.*"

I'm not a nice person.

You're not even a person.

Sewell's house is four streets away. Furia knows when to stop. Keep your head low, and stick to the shadows.

Selvati is a mishmash of wooden houses with either thatched roofs or tarpaulin ones or a mixture of both. It may have been quixotic way back when, a quaint fishing village of sorts, but now the reigning hue is drab ochre, and the nicest houses are nice only because they possess front doors, unbroken windows, and a hat of thick thatch.

In spite of it being the crack of dawn, Selvati is already bustling with human and equine traffic, so I glide into the hubbub effortlessly. Although I sense a look or two cast my way, all in all, humans are too busy getting to work or school or wherever it is these people are rushing toward to notice the dusty, sweaty girl riding a dustier, sweatier steed.

Or so I think.

A man trots up alongside me. "That's a nice horse you've got."

Furia does stand out in stature and gait. No other horse on this sandy street is as broad or tall as my stallion. Wouldn't it be ironic if I get stopped not because of my identity but because of my ride?

I stroke Furia's neck to sink my restless fingers into something solid. "I agree."

"You're a girl?" The man's gaze snaps off Furia and onto me.

"No."

The man's eyes drift to my chest and don't move. *Rude.*

What part of keeping to the shadows didn't you understand, Fallon?

"But you've got titties," the observant bloke says.

"I'm top-heavy. We've all got our flaws," I deadpan.

The man's features crinkle in confusion. He can't seem to decide if I am, in fact, a boy with a sizeable chest or a girl pulling his leg.

Like most humans, he's thin. Like all humans, he's got ears like mine, except his stick out because he's got no hair to tuck around them.

"You're not a boy," he finally says, but he doesn't sound all that certain.

Will I have to intervene, or can you lose your admirer?

"He's admiring Furia," I mutter.

The man's forehead furrows. "What?"

"I'm late." I egg Furia into a trot with my knees, not bothering to wish him a pleasant day.

The crow's grumpiness is rubbing off on me. It better wear away soon.

My sit bones ache each time they meet the saddle, and my nipples are on fire, but a long scrutiny of my surroundings dries up my pity party. Most of these humans are sacks of bones with hollowed cheeks and lifeless eyes, worn thin by the roughness of living. At least the young man back there had a spark about him.

The spark of hope and youth.

My first order of business as queen will be to fan that spark and help it catch on every human face. I will be the humans' queen—their eyes, their ears, their hearts.

Furia halts in front of a door, which I think must've been turquoise once upon a time. Now it's a weathered gray flecked with patches of greenish blue that barely stand out against the dulled wood siding.

We've arrived.

I hunt the rooftops for the crow, but his feathered form is out of sight.

As I dismount, I squint up and down the sandy street for a puff of smoke but find none. When Morrgot doesn't want to be seen, he's eerily inconspicuous. At least I won't have to worry about being caught with a crow.

I loop the reins over Furia's neck just as the front door swings open and out strides a man with a smile full of crooked teeth and skin as brown and brittle as rye bread. His expression draws my gaze away from his leathery skin.

I didn't realize how much I missed genuine smiles until I find myself gaping at this friendly, open face. I quickly glance over my shoulder to make certain I'm its recipient before letting myself return it.

Breathing easier than I have in days, I say, "You must be Sewell."

He tips his head to the side of the house, to a little alley that separates his wall from his neighbor's. I lead Furia into the narrow passageway that smells dank—of piss and seaweed and grit. Where a chilly humidity drapes across Racocci winter like summer, here the air is hot and muggy.

A bucket of water awaits Furia, as well as a bale of hay. My horse—yes, Furia feels like mine—tugs frantically to reach it, but with deft hands that are as sun-browned as the rest of him, Sewell works the halter off Furia's head.

Guilt swarms me as I realize I never thought to remove the metal bar or the saddle back at the oasis.

Sewell drapes the reins over a stubby tree that looks as desiccated as this place and its people, then proceeds to remove Furia's saddle, revealing layers of frothy sweat and sticky sand. All this is done in silence. He hoists another bucket from what I assume must be a well, because there's a system of ropes and pulleys, and showers Furia, who shakes himself dry, nickering happily, head buried in his bucket of hay.

Sewell stands back and watches him. "What a beautiful creature."

I nod my agreement.

"I imagine you desire a bath as well."

I lick my parched lips, darting a glance toward the well.

Sewell laughs. "Relax, Signorina. I wasn't contemplating tossing a bucket to wash you down."

In all honesty, I'm not sure I'd have minded it all that much. I don't voice this, afraid he may swap a long soak for a brief spray.

He leads me through the back door of his house. Right as he shuts the door, I say, "We forgot to tie up Furia."

"That horse isn't going anywhere." He sounds so certain that I imagine Morrgot told him he mind-controls the animal.

Unlike the man on the horse from earlier, Sewell doesn't have an accent. Or at least not a strong one. He doesn't roll his *r*'s or drag out his *s*'s as much as I do, but I attended a Tarecuorin school, so I learned to speak like the Fae nobility.

"Thank you for harboring me for the day," I say as I look around his house, which is sparser than mine. There are no flowers, no seashells, no plethora of wicker baskets hooked to the wall or hand-stitched curtains. It's a man's house, I think, although I could be wrong. He could be sharing it with a woman who doesn't have any time or interest to decorate.

"It's an honor."

I note he uses the word *honor* instead of *pleasure*, as though I'm someone worthy. He must have a lot of respect for Morrgot.

Sewell fills a glass with water from a pitcher and hands it to me. "I've got biscuits. They're a little dry but filling. Would you like some?"

"I'd love a biscuit." Like Furia, I greedily gulp down my water, then wolf down three biscuits and another glass of water.

The man is still smiling at me, and I'm suddenly hit by a bolt of guilt. What if I ate his daily ration?

The man sinks into a bow, which draws my eyebrows together. I'm about to tell him I'm not yet queen when smoke drifts through the rafters and hardens into the shape of a bird.

"Sire, it's been too long."

Morrgot must tell him to rise, because Sewell straightens from his inclined posture.

"Yes. Both are ready. Come." He ushers me through the only other door into a room that's a little smaller than mine, made even more so by the presence of a copper tub beside the bed.

Clapboard blinds obstruct the window, pushing the sun away, yet the heat is already stifling. The sun must bake these houses to a crisp at noon. Morrgot perches himself on the wooden bed frame.

"Can I bring you anything, sire?"

"A bird bath and a bowl of seeds, perhaps?" I suggest pleasantly.

The smile drops from Sewell's face. "What?"

Don't taunt this man. He is good.

My cheeks warm. "I was taunting you, not him." I turn to Sewell and flick my wrist in the general direction of the crow. "Morrgot and I aren't on good terms at the present moment."

The color drains from Sewell's face, absconding with its ruddiness, turning it as ashen as his walls.

Morrgot must reassure him that I'm jesting because his complexion slowly brightens.

"The week has been long," I say by way of apology.

"Well, I best let you rest. You have much to do still." He crosses the threshold and starts pulling the door closed.

Oh yes, don't remind me. With a weary smile, I say, "Thank you again for your hospitality."

"No need for thanks. A friend of Lore is a friend of mine."

"I'm not—"

The door clicks.

"—a friend of Lore's," I finish, but he's already gone. I turn on Morrgot, who's still present. "Why did you tell him I'm friends with your master?"

He assumed.

I huff in annoyance, but the bath beckons, and in seconds, I'm nude and stepping into the water. It's cold yet feels divine. I shut my eyes and fold my legs to maneuver as much of my body as I can fit inside.

There's soap on the dish.

Eyes closed, I grumble, "You're still here?"

I promised to guard you, remember?

I open my eyes and peer up at the crow. "You also promised to murder me."

That wasn't a promise, Fallon. It was a warning.

"Same difference."

I fish around the sides of the bath for the bar of soap that's worn so thin, it melts inside my palms, a pale pink buttery mess that smells like a desert rose. I stand so as not to let my precious handful slip into the water, scrub my scalp until it no longer feels grainy and oily, and then I wash under my arms and between my legs. I'm careful not to make contact with my nipples, which have morphed from dusty pink to an alarming crimson purple.

I lower my body back into the bath and rinse by indolent soaking.

Fallon. Bed.

"Hmm…"

Fallon.

My lids pull up. The rods of light poking from around the window are brighter, whiter.

Don't fall asleep in the bath.

"Why not?"

You could drown.

"In this much water?" I brush my palms over the sudsy puddle, popping the lingering bubbles. "I may like defying the odds, but—"

Please.

That single word makes me heft myself out of the bath and crawl into bed. I moan when the sheets kiss my skin and my cheek meets the pillow. "I'm broken, Morrgot. You broke me."

I think I hear him sigh, but that sound could very well have come from my lips.

Rest, Behach Éan.

"You still haven't told me what that means," I mumble against the pillow.

If he does give me the answer, I'm too deeply gone to hear it.

57

I wake to the most divine feeling in the world—soft hands kneading the sore muscles of my back. I think I've died and gone to the overworld. Or I'm still asleep and this is a dream. Or Sewell is in my room.

That last one jars me awake. I turn, but there is only darkness behind me. I let my lids drift shut again and groan, willing the fantastic dream back.

As though by magic, the fingers reappear and trace the shape of my bones before dipping into knotted sinews and manipulating them until they soften like cocoa butter.

I'm sorry for being so harsh on you, Behach Éan.

Not only do I get a massage from a fantasy therapist, but I get an apology from my winged companion?

Best. Dream. Ever.

I sink into the straw mattress.

Sink into the phantom fingers plying my sore skin and the cool haze buffeting my nape.

"I'm not your enemy, Morrgot," I murmur before untethering myself from the real world with all its artifices and hurts to penetrate this dream world where only the pursuit of bliss and pleasure exists.

The hands coast down my back, drawing small, slow arcs along my spine. I stretch out onto my stomach to let my fantasy masseur have easier access, although fantasy masseurs probably don't require easier access. They're made of air and starlight—or something divine like that. I've no doubt their ethereal fingers could slip right through my rib cage and caress my heart.

The stroking halts at my waist, as though my illusory well-being attendant is hesitant to slip farther down my body.

I appreciate gallantry in real life, but gods...these imaginary hands have carte blanche to do whatever they please with my body.

"Don't stop," I whine.

I'm pretty certain I sound like a doxy and that every one of my moans is resonating throughout my kind host's house, yet I cannot seem to care.

The palms that had yet to move lower finally glide across my waist, then past it, slipping down, down, down. In one smooth stroke, they reach my ankles and dip into the arch of my foot before sweeping back up the hills and hollows of my calves, thighs, and buttocks.

"Oh gods," I moan.

This dream is almost better than the one I had about the canal water transforming into strawberry gelato.

The fingertips breeze across the outline of my body, gentle... gentle.

Scratch my previous contemplation.

This dream has my ice-cream kingdom beat.

Although I never want it to end, I slide into a vortex of pitch-darkness anew.

⌣ ℯ ⌐

When I awake, it's to the sight of Morrgot perched on the beam over the closed room door. Although his lids seal out the gold and his wings are tucked into his body, he seems poised for an attack.

For once, I study him. His innate and at times overwhelming pride wafts off his midnight feathers even in slumber. It's the way he holds himself, I think. Or perhaps it's something deeper, some tenebrous strength that billows about him like smoke, that ricochets off his shiny beak and razor-sharp talons.

I remember how neatly they sliced through flesh.

Mine.

The sprites.

Lyrial's.

He is dangerous, formidable. A force to be reckoned with. A force to be feared.

Sire.

I'm aware he considers himself a king amongst his kind, but how odd it was to hear a grown man use such a grand title on a bird.

His wings twitch, and I think my staring has awakened him, but his tufted feathers relax until they lie smoother than Mamma's hair after my morning ministrations.

To think Mamma slept with one of his followers. A man who Morrgot seems to admire and trust. One of the few he trusts. I wonder what it'll take for him to trust me, because truth be told, I don't want to make an enemy out of this winged king.

And not because I fear him, even though he is plenty frightening with those bladed appendages of his, or because he can penetrate my mind—I need to set up firm boundaries—but because he's attentive, caring, and whip-smart. Qualities I seek out in my friendships. His sense of humor and charm need work, but all in all, I want this bird, who doesn't look at my rounded ears as flaws or my violet eyes as smudges on my Fae nature, in my corner.

He needs you, Fallon, I remind myself. *His true nature will shine through once you've exhausted your purpose.*

Gods, I really dislike my conscience at times. It's so dour and realistic.

I bat my lashes to whisk it away, but it's not the only thing I whisk away. I manage to whisk away my shadowy bedroom.

I now stand in one as wide and tall as my entire house. Although the windows are small, they breathe light into the space, gilding the tall wooden rafters and the stone walls that aren't straight or buffed smooth like my people prefer. This room is odd and coarse, with a massive bed set on a wide stone esplanade covered in dark pelts and a standing bookshelf hewn from twisted branches held together by slabs of gray rock.

A slight shift in the air draws my gaze off the thick leather spines toward the imposing silhouette of a man standing by one of the windows, hands clasped behind his back, black hair gleaming navy like Morrgot's feathers. The male's shoulders are straight and incredibly wide, made wider by the taper of his waist and the leanness of his hips.

I try to glimpse the shape of his ears, imagining they will be round since his hair is cropped well above his shoulders, but the blue-black locks screen them off from my sight. Curiosity shuffles my feet—bare, I realize, soon realizing the rest of me is bare as well...*odd*.

Another dream, I surmise, since it's neither a memory nor reality. I'd remember showing up naked in the bedroom of a complete stranger.

For an instant, I worry it may be a glimpse into my future, but my future is a monogamous relationship with Dante in Isolacuori, and although the man has his back to me, I can tell he's not Dante.

Dante's shoulders are narrower, his biceps firm but leaner, and his hair mahogany instead of midnight black. Not to mention my prince's skin is a rich brown and this man's skin is pale, as though he doesn't often stand in broad daylight.

Emboldened by the assurance that this is another figment of my entertaining imagination, I pad closer. The rock is chilly beneath my bare toes and, to my utmost surprise, unsegmented.

The whole floor is one single slab of rock. I find that fascinating. So much so that I forget I've set sail toward the stranger and only remember because his boots come into my line of sight, toes pointed toward mine.

I whip my neck back, sucking in a startled breath when I recognize the face staring down at me. It's the man Bronwen called Lore in the vision Morrgot sent me. This must be another vision.

I tilt my head to the side, waiting for the crow master to speak, since I really doubt Morrgot shipped me into this scene without a goal in mind.

But the crow master doesn't speak. He just stares.

So I stare back.

It's quite unfair that he got to wear clothes while I popped over in my birthday suit. Not that I want to see him disrobed.

To break the awkward silence, I say, "Your eyes are the same color as your crow's. I mean, crows'." I drag out the *s*. "Unless you deem him *one?*"

I don't comment on the makeup or the tattoo on his bladed cheek. I'm guessing both are a show of fealty toward their animal companions. The way the black is smeared around the eyes resembles wings, and the feather, well…it resembles a feather.

"Fallon." His jaw, I note, is as hard as the walls surrounding us. I also note that it's ticking. "Fallon Báeinach."

"Rossi. But I guess I'm a Bannock too. You're Lore, then?" I stick out my hand. "I'll admit, it's a little odd meeting like this"—I nod to my unclothed body—"but still a pleasure."

"How are you here?" Lore doesn't make a move to shake my hand, merely watches it, stiff jaw ticking away.

"Your bird sent me. I guess he wanted to introduce us. Not sure why he shipped me over naked, though. Perhaps it's symbolic?"

His gaze rises and falls over my body. "Symbolic?"

I feel my body pinkening. "You know…"

"I'm not certain I do."

I snag my lip between my teeth, then pop it free. "I can mean you no harm since I have no weapon on me." I nod to my still outstretched hand. "My fingers aren't made of obsidian, Lore."

His eyes snap back to mine, pupils distended against the sunset irises.

Assuming it mustn't be Crow custom to shake hands, I lower my palm and scrape it down my hip. My skin is clammy even though my body is hot, made hotter by the intensity of Lore's black-rimmed stare. It wouldn't surprise me if his irises were made of actual flames. I'll have to ask Morrgot once he carries me back to reality.

Since he hasn't yet, I fill the silence with idle chitchat. "It's a nice grotto you have here. Very"—I gesture to the austere decor, trying to come up with a word to encompass it—"crowish."

"Crowish?" A side of his mouth lifts, which is a welcome change from all the ticking.

I shrug. "Au naturel. Rugged. Devoid of Fae artifice. Masculine."

The corner of his mouth turns up a little more. "You detest it."

"Detest is a strong word. Would I choose to live here? Probably not, but that's rather irrelevant since it's your home, and although we might become fast friends once I revive you, you probably won't want to hang out in your private quarters with me." I'm tempted to grab a pelt from his bed to toss over my shoulders but figure it'll fall through my fingers. "So, what was it you were looking at?"

I approach the window and peer out, and my breath...it's snagged from my lungs because the view is spectacular. Crystal blues, pearlescent sand, and foamy waves spreading into an ocean that shimmers like a carpet of cut sapphires toward an island pinkened by the sunset.

"Is that Shabbe?"

"It is."

Which means... "We're in the sky kingdom!" My gaze hurtles back to Lore's. "I cannot believe Morrgot allowed me inside these walls. He was so adamant about keeping me out."

Lore is quiet, contemplative, and it isn't the land that he contemplates but me. I suppose that if a naked stranger pranced around my bedroom, I'd be observing them as well. Not that I'm prancing, per se.

With his face in full light, I can make out his lashes against the black makeup—alluringly thick and soft, like velvet. His nose is long and sharp, not beak-like, just really straight. I bet it'd indent my skin if he ran it along my cheek.

Which...why the underworld would he?

My face grows so hot I'm tempted to press it against the stone wall, which I'm certain will be cool, but that would surely strike him as odd.

I turn back toward the window and cross my arms, concentrating hard on the view below. "So...um...what do you want to talk about?"

"You tell me."

My gaze flicks back to his. He's no longer smiling, but his features aren't half as hard as they were when I first showed up.

Except for his cheekbones.

And jaw.

And nose.

What is this fixation I have with his nose? It's not *that* different from most noses. It probably just stands out more because of the makeup, like an island in the middle of an ocean. "How should I know?"

Tendrils of smoke lift from his hair, as though he's about to wink out of existence. "Because you're the one who penetrated my mind, Behach Éan. Again."

58

I blink at Lore, but when my lids drag up, he's gone, and in his place is the low ceiling of Sewell's house and my ever-faithful crow sidekick.

I take a breath. Two. Wait for the oxygen particles to clear the shock waves racking my body. But then my brain replays Lore's words, smiting the cleansing effect of lungfuls of air.

Because you're the one who penetrated my mind, Behach Éan.

I can penetrate minds now? Minds of total strangers to boot? It makes no sense.

I'm the halfling with no power. Resistant to iron, salt, and obsidian, but those are hardly powers.

I sit up so suddenly that the sheet pools around my waist. "Guess what?" I yank it up, then tuck it beneath my armpits, aching nipples be damned.

What?

"I think your power rubbed off on me, because I just penetrated someone's mind. And you'll never guess whose!" Lore's face with his strange makeup and piercing eyes scores my lids. "Oh my gods, this must be my Crow side awakening!"

And if my Crow side awakens, then perhaps my Fae side will follow.

I shoot my gaze over to the bathtub and attempt to move the water.

Not even a ripple forms. I squint at it again. Again, nothing.

Our powers don't rub off *on each other, Fallon.*

"But I *saw* your master. I *talked* to him. And I can assure you, he saw me." The memory of his heated gaze on my bare flesh warms my cheeks. "He talked back." My voice loses strength as my certainty wanes. "He even called me by that nickname you…" I stop pouring out my thoughts.

The only reason Lore would use the same nickname as Morrgot is because *I* put that word in his mouth.

Our encounter was a fabrication of the mind, a consequence of my high level of exhaustion.

"It was just a dream," I mumble, my pulse dropping back into alignment and then dropping some more. I swear, it turns downright listless.

Not that I wanted it to be real, but I wanted to have powers.

Morrgot must think I'm a serpent short of a den. Oh, why did I need to go and overshare?

Keeping the sheet tucked snugly around my torso, I dig my fists into my eyes and rub my disappointment away. When I lower my hands, Morrgot's still staring.

"Is it time to leave?"

The silence stretches. And stretches.

Then finally, his mind walking shatters it. *It is.*

Why did he hesitate? Because he's worried about my mental wherewithal affecting this next segment in our journey? If anything, the combination of frustration and rest is flooding my veins and lending me a sort of manic vigor.

"How deep will I need to dig?" I'm hoping he says deep. My newly invigorated muscles thrum in time with my pulse. I need an outlet, and plowing through sand sounds ideal.

The noise of Selvati at night leaks through the thin walls,

invigorating me further. I scoot my legs to the edge of the bed. I'm about to drop the sheet to grab the clothes I discarded before my bath, but they no longer grace the wicker chair in the corner.

"Um, do you have any idea what became of my things?"

Sewell is laundering them.

Oh. "That's kind of him. Should I"—I gesture to the door—"go collect them?"

No. He's coming.

I make sure all my bits are covered. I may walk around naked in my dreams and in front of birds, but it's not a habit of mine in real life. I rake my hand through my hair, which has acquired a lot of volume while I slept. And I do mean *a lot*. I stand, sashay over to the bathtub, then bend over to observe my reflection. Even though there's hardly any light, I catch the swell of locks atop my head in the mirror-smooth surface.

I scoop water and dump it on the chaos to smoosh it down, and then I finger comb the mass. As I untangle, my mind wanders back to the deft fingers that ran over my skin, to the crow master who I managed to conjure in fantastic detail after one brief glimpse. My mind is a strange place.

A knock startles my fingers out of my hair.

"Come in."

"Slept well?" Sewell asks, smiling. I think he may be teasing me, that he heard me moan or talk about penetrating minds with Morrgot, but the more I watch his face, the more his smile strikes me as genuine.

"Yes. Thank you for lending me your bed." I look at the fabric draped over his arm. It's yellow and velvety. Unless he laundered my clothes with pollen, what hangs over his arm isn't mine.

"I hope this'll fit." He holds it up.

A dress unspools, honeyed velvet with an outsize black floral motif. The skirt is long and full, made fuller by the narrowness of the bustier top.

"That's...um..." I stare at Morrgot, hoping he'll pitch in. When Sewell keeps presenting it with that bright smile of his, I think my crow is letting me handle this one. "A dress."

"Sure is." Sewell's grin grows.

"Is it the best outfit for...tonight?" I don't utter my plan for the evening out loud, uncertain how much Sewell has been told.

"Six silvers, this gown cost. Never bought anything as pricey in my forty-four years of life."

Forty-four? Huh. I estimated my host was in his sixties. Time strikes human faces so very fast.

Nibbling on the pillow of my lip, I venture, "I don't have six silvers on me."

"Oh, that's all right. His Majesty paid before sending me to the market on Cliffside."

My eyes must bug out because Sewell's grin fades and he shifts from boot to boot, the velvet dress rustling in time with his sideways bobbing.

"Have I chosen badly? I don't know much about women's wear, but the salesclerk assured me it'd be perfect for tonight."

"No, it's lovely. Truly. I guess I was expecting pants."

"You cannot attend a revel in pants."

"A revel?" I swing my attention to Morrgot. "You're sending me to a party?"

I am.

"I thought—I thought I'd be..." I mime shoveling and almost drop my sheet in the process. "Not to challenge your decision, but don't you think a girl in a ball gown handling a shovel will raise more eyebrows? At least in slacks, I may be mistaken for a boy."

Sewell will be doing the shoveling.

"Ah. Okay..." I'm glad for the extra set of hands yet can't help but frown.

You, Fallon, will be distracting Marco and your prince.

I sputter, then choke on my sputter. "You're handing me over to them?"

I'm handing you over to no one.

"If they see me, Morrgot, they'll take me. There's a—" I shift my eyes to Sewell. If he doesn't know about the reward, then I'm certainly not going to test his allegiance to Morrgot by spouting an amount of money that would alter his life without needing to risk it for a crow. "I'm wanted," I say simply.

Because they assume you've run away. You'll tell them you came to Tarespagia to seek your great-grandmother's counsel and weren't aware of the upheaval your absence caused.

I lick my lips, tasting the salt the king will surely slip me to ascertain I'm speaking the truth. "What about the trench?"

What about the trench?

"It filled and dragged down a regiment."

They don't suspect you. Don't take offense, Behach Éan, but releasing the barrage isn't in the realm of your capacities.

I cross my arms and lift my chin, taking offense. "I'm strong."

I swear Morrgot chuckles. *Your grandfather himself tried to break the barrage and failed.*

Oh. The knot of my arms loosens, but my chin stays high. "Well. Good." I stamp out the words.

Sewell lays out the dress on the bed. "Do you want help dressing?" His head snaps backward, and his ever-present smile shrinks before winking out of existence. "Apologies. I only meant to help."

I glower at the crow, who must've scolded him. Gods only know why since I'm not some piece of obsidian that'll poison humans if they touch me. "Help would be greatly appreciated. Unless you plan on lacing me up with your talons and beak, Morrgot?"

Sewell bows his head and backs up. "I'll get Furia saddled."

After the door clicks shut, I scowl some more. "You obviously don't wear gowns all too often, or you'd know they're a pain to do up." The fancier they are, the more eyelets and ribbons and teeny hooks made for teeny fingers they have. Then again, women who wear fancy gowns have a staff of sprites and halflings dedicated to dressing them and are never in a rush to get anywhere.

Sewell has no female companion. Unless you care to become his, then I suggest you attempt to dress yourself. If you prove incapable of lacing your own gown, I'll assist you.

"Usually, it's the undressing that leads to companionship, not the dressing," I mutter under my breath. "Not that I expect a bird to know anything about people courtship." I slide the sheet back onto the bed, pick up the dress, and drop it over my head. The silk lining feels like cool lotion against my clean skin. "He didn't get me any underwear by any chance, did he?"

I'll fetch your laundered ones.

Morrgot melts into a shadow that slips through the doorframe. What a neat trick that is. I wonder if all Crows are capable of changing consistency or if that's another power possessed only by the king of their species.

When he reappears, having managed to open the door with his talons, my underwear is clutched in his bill. He drops it onto the bed as though it were rotted carrion, then presses his body into the door, shutting it with a resounding click.

I slip one foot in, then the other. The fabric is warm and dry, and although the detergent has hardened them, I'm glad for their clean feel. Once in place, I start on the laces that hold the stiff bustier in place.

My shoulders ache from all the twisting and tugging, but I manage relatively well. Could it be snugger? Yes. Do I care? As long as it stays up, no.

Tighter. I can see your breasts.

I smooth my palms over the rich fabric and peer up at the crow. "Why are you even looking at my breasts?"

Morrgot flocks down from his perch and vanishes behind my

shoulder. Seconds later, a chilly gust presses against my spine. The sensation is vaguely familiar. Is it the feel of his feathers or of his smoke?

I twist my head. Black wisps paint the velvet bodice and curl around the thick black lace.

A firm tug squeezes the air from my lungs and flattens my chest, jabbing my bruised nipples. Another tug costs me another breath. The crow works quietly, diligently, using a dexterity I would never have suspected him to possess, neither in bird form nor in cloud form.

Done. The cool smoke of his body slips over my shoulder blades, and I swear it feels like fingers dragging over my skin, gentle yet strong, delicate yet solid.

I shiver before growing very, very still, because the hands that kneaded my body in my dreams felt alarmingly similar. A blush devours my flesh, followed by heady confusion.

Did *he* give me that massage? The question tiptoes onto my tongue but never plunges off its tip. It's too absurd and completely preposterous.

I may have tightened your top, but not to the point of ridding you of breath. His smoke curls around my earlobe, drawing another shiver from my body.

"Wh-what?"

You've stopped breathing.

I've felt embarrassment before but never like this. I whirl away from the velvet chill of Morrgot's body, confusion crashing through my veins. He's back in feathers. I whisk my gaze away from his before he can glean my insane train of thoughts.

Something on your mind, Behach Éan?

A million things are on my mind, and most have to do with the crow and my dream. Although I didn't feel like going to a ball, I'm suddenly glad that I'll be amongst my kind. "Will Dante be at the revel?"

The princess of Glace's ship docked in the harbor a little over an hour ago. Your prince was on it.

My eyes widen. "He came with *her*?"

Why so surprised? Rumors abound in Luce of their involvement.

My ribs feel like they've splintered and are now poking my heart. "And rumor has it I can converse with serpents," I snap, striding toward the door. "But we both know that's utter beetlepoop."

Is it?

I stop in the doorway and shoot Morrgot a glare. "The only animal I can converse with is *you*."

His pupils shrink.

However petty, he hit me where it hurts, so it's only fair I return the blow, and there's nothing this creature hates more than being reduced to his primal nature.

As I streak through Sewell's house toward the backyard where Furia awaits me, Morrgot says, *You forget you're Cathal's daughter, Fallon, and he was just as much a Crow as I.*

Chest heaving, I spin, my heavy dress billowing around my legs. "And what? He could morph into a yakking black bird with iron appendages?"

Morrgot soars over my head, lifting the fine strands of hair framing my upturned face. I'm expecting him to answer since he so loves to speak his mind. But he doesn't say anything as he sails past me and dissolves into the darkness.

His silence bugs me.

Humans can't possibly shift into animals...can they?

59

I sense Morrgot even though I haven't laid eyes on him since Sewell and I left his home. The kindly male has been riding beside me for the last hour, but we haven't spoken much because the streets are filled with busybodies.

Or so he warns me.

Most bodies look too busy and exhausted to be eavesdropping, even though almost all peer at us as we ride past them. I cannot help but clutch Furia's reins a little tighter.

What they must think of me in this velvet dress...

Thank the Cauldron, my companion is one of them. Whispers still trail us, but they're tinged with more curiosity than covetousness.

Women look up from their laundering, wringing the brown river water from their piles of clothes. The foamy runoff snakes toward the groups of bathing men scrubbing the grime from their faces with more grime while swatting away hovering flies and splashing children.

The younglings are the only bright spots in Selvati. Everyone else is grim, wary. A red ball rolls right in front of Furia, who rears back.

"Sorry, miss." A needle-thin boy scoops his ball up before pitching it back toward other children dressed in rags.

Some have distended bellies; all have toothpick legs.

I haven't wandered deep enough through Racocci to know whether the situation is better or worse or equal, but the abounding squalor coils my insides. How could Marco let these people subsist in such filth and with so little? Even if he didn't go so far as to distribute riches, it would cost him nothing to send Fae to sanitize the water or grow crops.

I grit my teeth, trying to contain my rage before it bursts out of me, and I charge toward Tarespagia to put an end to Marco's days without Morrgot's help.

The horrid spectacle does comfort me in my recent choices. I feel zero guilt that the Crow king plans on dropping his fellow monarch on the queendom's shores. Let him be mistreated and starved. It'll serve him right.

As we weave deeper down the crooked, sandy lanes, the air grows heavy with the scent of wood fire, ale, and stew. Smoke curls through whichever opening it can find, be it a missing windowpane or a tear in the roof. It fills the torchlit darkness with the scent of boiled rice and beans and sizzling animal grease.

Dogs, as scrawny as the children playing ball by the river, poke their heads into dilapidated homes. One even runs off with a chicken, which earns him a sputtering pursuer armed with a broom.

Most of the establishments in Selvati are open to the elements. Either the inhabitants can't afford walls, or the weather remains warm enough year-round to allow people not to immure themselves.

Because the roads are narrow, Sewell must often ease his mangy mare behind Furia. Although I'm bursting with too much anger for there to be much room for any other feeling, each time a human grazes my horse or velvet frock with more than just their eyes, unease pierces through my rage and reminds me that although my ears aren't spiked, my hair rests at my shoulders, and I've meat on my bones.

The deeper into Selvati we ride, the fewer the people and the quieter it becomes, as though the dwellers bordering Fae territory fear making noise.

Sewell sidles up to me, his bald head gleaming from the light of a fat candle melting on a neighboring sill. "We're almost at the checkpoint. When the guards ask who I am, tell them I'm your horse's steward."

I stare beyond the flickering flame of the candle into the house where a gnarled man is hunched over a book, a quill in his hands. I imagine he's drawing since humans aren't literate.

I roll my shoulders, which are tense again. What I wouldn't give for another phantom rubdown. "Horses have stewards?"

"Every Tarespagian animal has an attendant."

I imagine Morrgot with a maid to fluff up the twigs in his nest and another to replenish his birdbath. "A vestige of the Crows' legacy?"

Sewell's Adam's apple jumps in time with his eyes that scan the street. "It's best not to mention them, milady."

The sand gives way to cobbles lined with a golden gate that stretches farther than the eye can behold.

Tarespagia.

We've arrived...

"I've never met my great-grandmother."

Sewell glances at me before returning his attention to the uniformed guard standing at one of the checkpoints. "She's... something."

"Something?" I smile for the first time since we left his house. "Something fearful? Sprightly? Warm?"

"Most definitely not warm."

"My grandmother raised me, and she absolutely detests her mother-in-law," I say as we near the guard, whose eyebrows have slid toward his nose.

He steps toward us, spiderwebs of green magic glittering from his raised palm. "Halt!"

Did he think we were going to try and jump the gate topped with spikes that carry the same lethal shine as Morrgot's talons?

Speaking of…where is the crow? I flick my gaze skyward, hunting the star-sprayed firmament for the twin golden orbs that have tracked my every movement since I stepped into the Acoltis' vault.

"State your business," the guard barks, the hand not crackling with magic resting on the pommel of his baldric's sword.

"We're guests of Xema Rossi."

"Not we," Sewell breathes beside me.

I frown until it dawns on me why he's hissed the correction. "By we, I meant my horse and me. The human tends to my stallion."

The guard squints at me, Furia, Sewell, then back at me. I'm waiting for recognition to flare across his face, but there's only suspicion. "Names!"

I thought everyone and their sprite was looking for me. I wonder if I should make up an alias.

"Her name is Fallon Rossi." Like always, the deep voice steals some beats from my heart.

I scour the darkness for Dante, find him riding a white horse as tall and muscular as Furia, flanked by four men also on horseback, two of whom I recognize—uncouth Tavo and discreet Gabriele.

It's been only a handful of days since Dante and I last saw each other, since we lay together in his tent, yet it feels like years have gone by since that afternoon.

I almost speak his name but swap the two syllables out for three. "Altezza." My voice sounds breezy. I'm hoping only to my ears. "What brings you to Tarespagia?"

His blue eyes gleam as brightly as the golden beads adorning his long braids. "You."

60

D ante's answer reverberates against the golden gates separating us from Tarespagia.

His horse is soaked in sweat, as are the horses of his close guard, as though they've been galloping through Selvati.

"The entire kingdom is looking for you." His tone is as tight as the fold of his lips.

"Really?" Furia prances a tad nervously. I smooth my palm over his black coat to help settle his nerves. "Why on earth is the whole kingdom looking for me?"

"Because you ran away." He says this quietly, as though he doesn't wish the others to hear our exchange.

I coax my eyebrows into an exaggerated frown. "Why would I run away?"

Tavo gestures between Sewell and me. "Who's your new friend, Fallon?"

A briny breeze bends the tall palms planted along the gates and flutters my loose locks. I tuck the frolicking strands behind my ear. "He's my horse's steward."

"Is he now?" Tavo's eyebrows spike. "Since when do you have a horse?"

"Since I decided to ride to Tarespagia to meet my

great-grandmother before the king tosses me to the serpents. I thought it'd be nice to see her at least once in my life."

Every last bit of tightness leaks out of the prince's beautiful face. "Fallon," he breathes out my name, and it feels like a caress, like a sigh. "You're not going to die."

No, I'm not. But that's because I'm not planning on swimming in Mareluce. "Did you ride all the way here, Princci?"

Furia paws the ground, apparently impatient to get going.

"I—" He swallows. "I came by way of sea." He probes my face with his keen eyes. "The footpath the commander uncovered flooded."

"That must be why the land trembled after I crested the mountain!" Although Dante and I will soon have no more secrets from each other, it's necessary I keep some from him until Morrgot is whole.

Dante scrutinizes me with such thoroughness, I worry he'll catch the too-rapid flutter of my pulse.

After an agonizing minute, his gaze retreats from mine and alights on Sewell, whose eyes are cast downward in the deference expected from humans. "Did this man accompany you in your travels?"

"Yes." I've always been a skilled liar, but lying to Dante feels wicked. How I wish I could pull him away from his entourage and let him in on the secret that's three crows short of changing our lives.

Tavo's long red hair snaps wildly around his shoulders. "Did you see anything interesting during your voyage?"

Is Tavo asking about the sky kingdom no one speaks about? "Trees. Clouds. More clouds. There are a *lot* of clouds in Monteluce." I almost make the mistake of speaking of the ambush, but that would lead to me confessing my awareness of the bounty.

"Is that all you saw?" Suspicion sets Tavo's amber eyes alight.

I slide my lips together. Should I let on about the *bird*dom, or should I play dumb? I glance upward again, hoping Morrgot will ferry over his opinion on the matter.

Mention it. It's too imposing not to have been seen.

Awesome. I'm about to tell Dante when everything inside me stammers to a violent halt. I didn't ask Morrgot out loud, which means... *You can read my thoughts?!*

Speaking into someone's mind is one thing, but eavesdropping on someone's thoughts without their knowledge of it? That's... that's— I feel duped. And stupid. And angry. Oh, *so* angry.

We'll discuss the matter later, Fallon.

Oh, you bet your feathery ass we will.

"What are you looking at?" Dante's question yanks me out of my seething.

I may not be the crow's number one fan right now, but I still need him, so I grit out, "The stars. They're blinding on this side of the kingdom."

The prince's jeweled eyes level back on mine. "Brighter than on our side?"

My jaw is still so tight that the words come out clenched. "Probably not from Isolacuori, but certainly brighter than from Tarelexo."

Dante studies me as though trying to see past the walls of my mind. I make sure to buttress them.

"May we continue this conversation at my family's ranch? I forgot my cloak, and there's a bite to the air."

His gaze drops off my chin to travel over my collarbones and bare shoulders. Even though I'm still reeling over my discovery of Morrgot's clandestine talent, I cannot help but shiver from Dante's prolonged scrutiny and the ensuing sparkle that touches his eyes.

He may have come with some other woman, but I affect him.

His fingers travel over the gold buttons of his white jacket, undoing each. He spurs his horse toward mine, shrugging out of the elegant garment, then releases the reins and leans forward in the saddle to drape the heavy white fabric over my shoulders.

The scent of him rises from the collar—mineral with hints of salt and musk...*familiar*. I inhale deeply, letting it reach into me and mollify my mood.

Dante lingers beside me, his leg and eyes pressed to mine. "You scared me, Fallon."

The heat of his murmur razes everything around us, every sound, every color, every onlooker.

I suddenly don't care an iota about Morrgot's deception. As long as he makes Dante king and me his queen, the crow can mislead me all he wants.

Furia bites the rump of Dante's horse, eliciting a pained whinny.

"Furia," I chide my stallion. I'm about to ask what's gotten into him when I realize it's probably not a *what* but a *who*.

Although tempted to glare in the general direction of the sky, I avoid casting my eyes upward and settle on thinking a few terrible thoughts about the crow.

Better get on your way, Behach Éan, for you have no throne to sit on until you make me whole.

His pet name is really starting to get on my nerves.

"Fallon?" The groove between Dante's eyebrows tells me it isn't the first time he's called out to me. He nods to the open gate.

I don't have to touch my heels to Furia's flank or shake the reins. My stallion, as always, knows the way.

As we cross over into Tarespagia, my jaw begins to relax and my petulance to wane. Which isn't to say that I'm feeling forgiving.

Keeping my gaze on the sandstone ramparts cinching pureling estates, I decide to take full advantage of the crow's intrusion. **Since you can read minds, Morrgot, tell me what thoughts are scrolling through Dante's. Does he suspect I'm lying?**

"Why didn't you come to me?" Dante eases his horse beside mine.

Unlike in the streets of Selvati, a herd of horses could stampede down this avenue shoulder to shoulder.

I fasten the top button of Dante's jacket so it doesn't fall off. "Come to you with what?"

"With your desire to travel to Tarespagia."

"I heard you had company and that I wasn't to disturb you." Who knew the princess of Glace's presence would be so convenient after all?

Bronwen... A little voice that isn't Morrgot's answers. Bronwen surely orchestrated this. My skin prickles with renewed awareness of my puppethood. *Did Bronwen invite the princess, Morrgot?*

Dante's jaw clenches. "You promised—"

I wait for him to say more. "What did I promise?"

"Not to get into any trouble."

"And you promised not to kiss another woman."

I wait for him to tell me he didn't, but the words never come, and his silence is a punch to the heart. "Is she nice?"

Please say no.

He shifts his gaze from my face to the road, but I don't think he's seeing the flagstones or the line of palms that hems them in. "She is."

Battling down my jealousy, I stare at the trees. They're so straight and thick and tall that they resemble solemn giants with their massive, waving fronds. I've no doubt they were nurtured by earth Fae, the same way I've no doubt the vines of flowers icing the top of the ramparts are Fae-made.

"But she's not you." His belated answer hooks my sinking heart and reels it back up.

Its thuds, loud as the thrashing waves, must penetrate his ears because a tentative smile reshapes his lips.

Yet he still kissed her, comes an unsolicited voice.

"We're here." Dante tugs on his horse's bridle, leading the way down a path paved with the same shimmering sandstone that adorns the rampart-like walls and the broad roads between them. "The revel is in Marco's honor. He'll be in attendance."

"That's fine."

If he's surprised by my willingness to spend time with his brother, he doesn't mention it. "Does your great-grandmother know you're coming?"

"No. It's a surprise."

"She isn't the type of woman you want to surprise."

His counsel doesn't irk me, because in my head, I've built her up to be the feminine version of my grandfather. Just as callous and ashamed of Mamma and me.

Gods, if she knew who my father was…if anyone knew who he was…

Even Dante would look at me with stark horror.

I chase the thought away immediately. Dante has always accepted me the way I was, round ears and all. He'd never think differently of me if he found out the origin of the blood in my veins.

Which he will find out.

Soon.

We come to a stop in front of an estate that puts the Acoltis' to shame. Unlike the homes in Selvati, this one is made of a mosaic of turquoise glass and mother-of-pearl that shimmers like the Isolacuorin canals.

Dante reaches up. Although I can now swing off Furia with a modicum of grace, I still seize his hand. Any excuse to touch him.

He releases me the moment my boots meet the ground. Yes, I wear boots. Sewell, in his haste, forgot fancy shoes. Without a doubt, they'll attract many a sneer from the crowd within. I don't much care if my fashion faux pas sparks whispers, because I'm not here to make a favorable impression or to form bonds with relatives who couldn't care less about me.

I'm here as a distraction.

I turn to Sewell and hand him Furia's reins. "See that he's fed and given water."

Our eyes lock for a long minute.

"Of course, milady." He lays a Selvatin accent on thick.

The temptation to look up is harrowing. *What now, Morrgot? Now, you dazzle the reveling Fae with your charm.*

Since Morrgot finds me as charming as a wet sock, I snort.

"Something the matter?" Dante offers me his arm.

I school my features. "Just imagining the look on everyone's faces when I walk in."

A smile edges over his lips.

"On your arm no less. Will you be requesting the bounty?"

His tendons shift beneath my fingertips, and I realize I've just put my foot in my mouth, and deep at that. I pretended not knowing I was on the king's most wanted list, yet I'm aware of a reward?

Merda. Merda. Merda.

Yes, this deserves three shits. Before Dante can say anything, I pile a lie atop my previous one. "Am I wrong to assume money was offered for my retrieval?"

"You're not wrong, but—"

"I'm curious…" I plow on. "What was my worth? At least one gold piece, I would hope."

As two turbaned servants heave open a double-wide door with the same insets of mother-of-pearl and glass, Dante turns me toward him. "He offered a hundred gold pieces for you, Fallon."

I fake gasp and smack my palm over my heart. "For *me*?"

"Marco's dream has always been to take the island of Shabbe."

My hand slips, coursing over the velvet. "You mean the queendom?"

"It's an island with a self-proclaimed monarch. Hardly a kingdom."

Even though his insistence on refusing to call it a queendom bothers me, I avoid contradicting him in order to hear the rest of Marco's dream and how I play into it.

"Our ships cannot sail near the wards without those savages commanding their serpents to sink us."

"*Their* serpents?"

"It's rumored serpents answer to the Shabbins."

My heart flounders around my rib cage like a trapped fish.

"The same way they answer to you."

61

My open-mouthed shock is not an act this time.

"My brother believes your mother had an affair with one of the Shabbin males who breached our shores when the wards weakened two decades ago."

Oh. My. Gods. *What?!*

I almost tell Dante that can't be true since my father is Kahol Bannock, but thankfully, I'm physically unable to shift my lips. Explaining my mother lay with a Crow is assuredly no better than with a Shabbin.

"Of course, it's impossible, or the wards would've thrown you out of Luce, but if you *can* communicate with serpents, we could approach their shores and"—he leans over until his mouth is flush with my ear—"begin *negotiations*."

Negotiations?

"Do you understand why you're so valuable to him?"

Glass shatters, its tinkling sound overpowering the white noise buzzing between my temples.

I jump. Dante straightens and releases my arm as though worried what people may think of seeing him touching the halfling with the odd eyes who may or may not be able to speak serpent.

Still reeling, I trail my gaze over the seesawing shards of the wineglass to a hem of pomegranate silk and then upward to a pale, oblong face framed by waist-long black hair.

I feel like I'm staring at my grandmother, except Nonna is in Tarelexo and has green eyes and furrows around her mouth and eyes. This woman's eyes are blue like Mamma's, and her skin is as smooth as my mother's.

"Xema!" the woman screeches.

Perhaps she isn't my aunt. But the family resemblance…

Someone mutters from inside the giant reception area packed with gaudily attired guests, who all slowly twist around toward the woman in red.

"What now, Domitina?"

So the woman is my aunt…

Xema's voice isn't shrill, yet it booms across the room, which has fallen so quiet that I hear Dante swallow slowly.

The crowd parts around a woman with a puff of silver hair, lustrous pearls running up the shells of her peaked ears, and a brilliant-hued bird on her shoulder. She hobbles forward, leaning heavily on an ornate cane.

Although her hair isn't flaming red like I imagined it would be, her irises are. As they settle on me, they flare brighter than the firepits peppering Selvati. "What stray have you dragged inside my home, Princci?"

I blink. I didn't expect a hug, but really? A stray?

My fingers ball into fists. "Correct me if I'm wrong, but strays are homeless. Since I have a home, one I love terribly much, I'm afraid the term you're looking for is visitor. Or guest. As for being dragged, I assure you, I came willingly."

My great-grandmother's eyes blaze. I suspect she's two seconds away from incinerating me.

"Scazza."

I'm so used to the derogatory term that I don't bristle at being called a street urchin, but I do bristle at being called that by my own family. Insults may roll off our round ears, but they also trickle inside and round other parts of us.

I will not be rounded.

Nonna warned me Xema was unpleasant, yet I hadn't envisaged that she'd be the love child of a fire poker and a cantankerous sprite.

"Quiet, Beau," she hisses to the bird on her shoulder.

Wait...the insult came from her parrot? Can she also hear birds, or did it just talk out loud?

Dante must sense my shock because he leans over and says, "That parrot insults everyone, princes included."

Xema stops beside Domitina, and both look me over, lips curling in time with their noses. I feel like I've dropped into the pages of one of Mamma's books, the one about the girl with the awful stepmother and evil stepsisters, the one in which the girl, considered no better than vermin, becomes queen.

How fitting.

My thoughts drift to Morrgot. Is he witnessing this from some shadow, or is he busy overseeing Sewell's digging? I wish he'd flock to *my* shoulder and stare down these horrid people. Maybe even run a claw down their pretty gowns and nick their skin.

What am I thinking? I blow out my wickedness, ashamed. Nonna taught me better.

Although I will never sit on your shoulder, once I'm whole, we can revisit teaching them some manners.

"No," I breathe.

"No?" Xema raises an eyebrow that is jarringly black.

"No...offer of a drink?" I swipe my tongue over my parched lips.

Domitina crosses her arms. "We don't serve round ears in our establishment." Her eyes fall to the short-haired blond gathering the broken glass by hand.

The kneeling girl, a halfling like me, flinches. I hate to imagine the staff's quality of life.

I paste on a confident smile. "I didn't expect you to serve me, Bisnonna." Considering Domitina doesn't even call her Nonna, I sense calling Xema Great-Grandma will irritate her to no end.

Sure enough, she hisses as though I've prodded her wrinkly skin with an iron ingot.

"In case you haven't heard, I work at a tavern, so I'm quite adept at pouring wine into goblets and gullets. Or wherever it is our customers want their wine poured." I let the innuendo hang. However often I refute anyone who implies I'm a sex worker, the paling of my grandmother's and aunt's faces is much too satisfying.

Dante makes a choked sound beside me.

"I promise to leave after one drink," I say sweetly, taking in the fancy revelers.

I spot a slew of familiar faces: the Acolti parents and daughter, Flavia's soon-to-be husband, Victorius Surro, who is as ancient as her father and just as patronizing, and many Bottom of the Jug regulars. Some hold my stare and give me lengthy once-overs that make my skin crawl; others look away, as though worried I'll acknowledge them and thus tarnish their reputation.

The women all stare unabashedly, though, and whisper just as shamelessly. The few words I catch are about my ears and the prince's coat draped over my shoulders.

"I see Ceres's gaudy sense of fashion rubbed off on you." Xema holds her head so high that I can see up the narrow slits of her nose.

Gaudy? My grandmother's frocks are as plain as the ones humans wear in Rax. "Sadly, the money she makes from selling tea and poultices doesn't allow for gaudy gowns. Not that she'd have anywhere to wear them. You know, what with her being persona non grata for not turning her back on her daughter or me, however sordid we both may be."

Fallon, play nice. We aren't quite done.

They're wretched.

I know, Behach Éan.

I don't miss the sigh in his voice, and although he must be halfway across the property from me, hearing him brings me a little solace.

"Out! Get out of my house, you filthy little…little…"

"Halfling?" I supply.

"Bastard!" she shrills, loud enough for all of Tarespagia to hear.

The crowd grows so quiet that I can hear the bubbles pop atop the crystal carafes of faerie wine. I can also hear the white cotton slide over Dante's skin as he crosses his arms.

"Bastard," her parrot repeats.

"That's enough," Dante says.

I lift my chin, glad for Dante's solidarity, even if it's the parrot he's scolding.

"That's enough, Fallon," he repeats quietly.

As I swing my gaze up to his, I catch the smirk painting Domitina's red lips. Dante siding with my hateful relatives feels like a slap to the face.

"Thank you, Princci." Xema stacks her palms atop the pommel of her cane.

The crushed shell inserts between the slabs of sandstone blur. I blink the blur away, then raise my fingers to the collar of Dante's jacket and undo the button. "I'm suddenly too warm, Altezza."

He doesn't extricate the military coat I dangle between us. Does he consider it dirty now that it's touched my skin?

"Shall I have it burned, or will laundering it be enough?"

"Fal, stop. You're acting—you're acting unlike yourself."

Except I'm not. I'm speaking my mind and heart. "I'm sorry you preferred the doormat version of me best."

"That's not what I said."

I hear Victorius murmur that I must be having my monthly, which wins him the glare of a whole slew of women, including his wife-to-be. I may have smiled if my ego weren't smarting.

I end up tossing the white jacket on a wind-sculpted piece of wood beside the door. *I'm sorry, Morrgot, but I cannot stay here any longer.*

I start to turn when the crowd, which had hemmed itself together after Xema's passage, parts anew, this time around two men, one of whom wears a crown and a lipstick smudge on his jaw and the other a look of utter revulsion.

"Fallon Rossi!" Marco exclaims, Justus in tow. "I thought I heard your spirited voice."

Both men skirt my unwelcoming committee, and although the king smiles, my grandfather doesn't. He stares daggers at me, his hand resting on the pommel of the sword he no doubt wishes to drive through my body.

What a family I've been born into…

"Where was she hiding?" Marco asks his brother.

"Beside the gates." Dante shifts as though the amount of attention he's currently receiving is making him uncomfortable.

"The gates? Which gates?"

"Of Tarespagia."

Marco's jaw squares with a grin. "A most terrible place to hide, Signorina Rossi."

"I wasn't hiding."

"Then what in Luce were you doing at the gates?"

"I was waiting to be let through. I wanted to meet the Rossi women I've heard so much about before my upcoming dip in the sea."

His eyes taper on my face before sliding to Dante's. I'm tempted to put another step between his brother and me. Many steps.

"Thank you for your help, Brother. I'll take it from here. Go enjoy the party and Alyona."

I clench my jaw at the mention of the Glacin princess.

Dante's shoulders square and his body grows still. "I'm certain

Alyona is quite capable of entertaining herself at the present moment."

Marco steps close to his brother and whispers something that makes Dante's spine straighten. If only my hearing were as sharp as Morrgot's.

Can you hear what they're saying?

I receive no answer.

Morrgot?

Still nothing.

Dread coalesces beneath my skin and makes it break out in goose bumps.

I stare at the darkness twinkling beyond the open doors, pulse striking my throat. Something's wrong.

Unless our new means of communication has run its course? I pray to all the gods, including the Crows', that this is the reason for Morrgot's sudden muteness.

But my conviction withers when I catch two guards sprinting down the walkway.

"I'm sorry to interrupt, Your Majesty," one of them pants, "but we have a problem."

62

The king raises his blazing gaze to the two perspiring guards. "Well, speak up!"

Dante turns toward the messengers. "What's the problem, Roberto?"

Roberto's gaze pinwheels around the room, lingering a beat too long on me.

Morrgot? I screech inside my mind. I'm about to sprint to the grove, even though I haven't the faintest clue where it might be, when I make out a series of disjointed words through the adrenaline-induced trilling inside my eardrums: *Isolacuori. Attacked. Sprites just arrived with the news.*

Marco's livid stare veers off Roberto and his fellow soldier and smacks his brother. "I gave you one job, Dante. One. Fucking. Job. And what do you do? You fucking botch it." Under his breath, he mutters, "Useless."

A lesser man would've flinched, but Dante stands his ground, chin held high. "*Who* did this?"

"Humans." The other guard spits out the word as though it were the vilest one in the Lucin dictionary.

"Humans?" Marco repeats, as though stunned they have it in them to revolt.

Dante pivots fully toward the guard, and the beads in his long braids ding. "How did they get past Dargento and the royal guard?"

"A distraction, sire. A bank of serpents attacked the boats in the harbor. It was mayhem. They sank three vessels before the commander managed to chase them away."

All eyes veer to me. Do they think I ordered the hit? I'm standing right here.

My grandfather steps around the king and barks, "If I learn this is your doing, Fallon..." He lets his threat hang in the deathly quiet reception room.

"Please." I roll my eyes. "If I sank the royal fleet, Nonno, I'd make sure you were aboard one of the boats."

Justus's ponytail swings like a pendulum as he rears his head.

"What type of demon did your daughter birth, Son?" Xema shrills.

The insult reverberates against every faceted crystal and dangling shell of the dozen or so chandeliers swathing the grand room in faerie light.

"Did you order the hit, Fallon?" Dante lowers his gaze to me.

Nothing, not even his previous backing of the horrid women in my family, prepares me for his inquest. "Of course not!" How could he think such a thing? "I'm standing right here."

Roberto clears his throat. "It happened this morning."

"And what? Do you think I was on the other side of the kingdom this morning? My horse may be quick, but he's just a horse."

"Maybe she rode in on a serpent." Domitina's intimation sparks whispers about my connection to serpents amidst the rapt spectators.

My temper hollows my cheeks. "However convenient that would've been, Zia, I can assure you I didn't come by way of sea."

As deeply awed as I am by your backbone, Behach Éan, perhaps curb it, or my distraction will have been for naught.

I jump at the sound of Morrgot's voice. Even though a part of me wants to strangle the crow for having abandoned me in this nest of pointy-eared vipers—apologies to snakes, kingdomwide— another part wants to congratulate him for his cunning.

Though could you have picked another animal? One not associated with me? Maybe ordered a militia of termites to chew through the wood?

"Feed her salt!" Xema says at the same time as her parrot squawks, "Traitor." He is the first animal I dislike, and I picture him becoming Minimus's snack.

Dante fishes a snuffbox out of his pants pocket, pops it open, and holds it out.

Without removing my gaze from Xema and her loutish pet, I grab the box and shoot back the contents so no one can accuse me of ingesting too few flakes. I gag but gulp.

And then I state loudly and clearly, "I did not order a hit on the royal harbor. I cannot control serpents."

Eyes widen, mouths too. I've stumped them all.

I scan their flummoxed faces. "Any other query you'd like a genuine answer to while I'm under oath?"

Although my family members' expressions remain suspicious, Dante and Marco drop their death stares. It's only a lull in the storm that will beat back down on me eventually, but it's a lull nonetheless.

"What did they take from Isolacuori?" Marco's knuckles whiten around the pommel of a dagger strapped to his waist.

"According to the sprites sent by the commander, they breached the throne room and doused your eternal flames."

His intake of air is sharp, as though the guard announced the entire castle had been demolished.

"Anything else?" Dante asks.

"That's all, Altezza," the second guard says, wiping his brow.

Marco sputters. "Anything *else?*" Smoke drifts off his gold brocade tunic. From his clenched knuckles as well.

Since he isn't Crow, I suspect he isn't about to burst into an amorphous blob.

Blob?

I smile at Morrgot's reaction. Until I remember he can literally read every thought in my head.

"It's a direct attack on the crown!" Marco exclaims.

Even though Dante stands between us, the heat radiating off the crowned monarch suffuses my skin.

"Justus, ready my ship! We leave tonight. I want to gut the traitorous rats myself, then burn their carcasses and have their ashes blown across Racocci."

My hands drop to my stomach, which gives a violent kick at his disproportionate retaliation plot. I look toward Dante, willing him to slake his brother's thirst for murder by reminding him that putting out flames may be insulting but hardly worth snuffing out lives.

Marco storms toward the door but halts at the guard's softly delivered, "Maezza."

"What?" he barks.

Roberto seems suddenly fascinated by his sand-crusted boots. "No one was caught."

The relief that hits me is so heady, I almost swoon.

"What do you mean, no one was caught?" the king snaps.

"Meaning they got away."

"Who did you fucking leave in charge of my kingdom, Dante?"

Dante's jaw clenches. "Like I mentioned earlier, I left Commander Dargento in charge."

Marco's crown slides across his sweat-lacquered brow. He shoves it back in place before ripping it off his braided tresses and lobbing it to one of the guards, who just manages to catch it. "Dargento is an impotent imbecile."

I never expected to see eye to eye with the king on any matter, but I must admit, he has Silvius down pat.

"I hope you're proud." He pokes Dante's chest, and smoke curls from the white shirt. Then he grips a handful and heaves his brother toward him until his mouth is flush with Dante's ear and hisses words I fail to catch. When he shoves him away, the fabric of the prince's shirt is charred. "Tell my fiancée that I'm going home so that my kingdom doesn't fall to imbeciles because of an imbecile." And then he thunders out the door, Justus and a fleet of soldiers in his wake.

The imbecile he speaks of, is it his brother or Silvius?

I'm still angry at Dante yet can't help but touch his arm. "Are you all right?"

He glowers at me as though *I* singed his shirt, then plows forward toward the throng of revelers. He's intercepted at the front by a young woman with skin as white as snow and a dress that seems woven from snowflakes.

She touches his wrist, raising eyes as silver as her dress to Dante. Although his nostrils still flare, he doesn't flinch away from her touch. She asks him something I don't hear over the loud chatter, and I catch his chest lifting in a sigh.

She touches his cheek with a gloved hand, and although he catches her wrist and tows it away, my chest tightens with jealousy. Her gaze slips past Dante and lands on me. Alyona and I haven't been introduced, yet we clearly know about each other.

Dante's hand glides up her arm, settling on her elbow. He tugs, spinning her away from me and leading her into the crowd. Because he's taller than most, when his head turns toward me, our eyes lock. Can he see the pain he's caused me? And if he can, does it bring him any guilt?

The scent of potpourri overwhelms me as my aunt comes to stand before me. "Best you leave now. You've outstayed your welcome, Fallon." She smooths hands adorned with twinkling yellow diamonds and pointy red nails down the satiny folds of her dress. They're the hands of a woman who has everything done for her.

"Funny you should use that word seeing as there was nothing welcoming about the moment we spent in each other's company." How I hope Morrgot and Sewell are finished. I'm very ready to leave. "Any message you'd like me to carry back to your sister and mother?"

"What sister?"

I frown.

"And what mother?"

Although my heart doesn't break, it crackles. Especially considering all the anecdotes Nonna shared with me over the years of how close her daughters were. Domitina used to revere Mamma, who would take her baby sister everywhere.

I back away from the beautiful woman with the ugly heart and cross the threshold. Outside the front door, I peer around the grounds. *Where's the grove, Morrgot?*

Follow the torchlit path.

I walk fast, casting glances over my shoulder. No one follows me. *What a rotten family I have. It's a wonder I turned out the way I did.*

You mean humble and compliant?

I snort at his humor. *How in Luce did you wreak all that chaos? Did you fly back to Isolacuori while I slept?*

I'm hoping he says yes. Then at least he wouldn't have observed my lively slumber.

I did not.

Well, damn. *Bronwen?*

Not Bronwen, but the people she entrusted with recovering the piece of me locked in the throne room.

I stumble on the hem of my dress and catch myself on one of the golden torches. I hiss as my fingertips connect with the flame.

What's wrong?

Nothing. Clumsiness. I grip the folds of my heavy skirt and hike it up as I break back into a run. *Did they manage to get the bowl?*

They did.

And? I ram my shoulders back to prevent as much bounce as possible in the front area of my torso. *Did they free your crow?*

Only you can do that.

My heartbeats swell and invade my mouth. *Why is it that only I can do it?*

Because of your immunity to both obsidian and iron.

How come I'm immune?

After a full minute of silence, I call his name through the bond. He doesn't answer, so I concentrate on the path that keeps twisting to the point where I wonder if I'm running in circles.

You're not. Look up.

The sight of his darkness soaring over me settles my jangling nerves. *Go to Sewell. In case—*

Sewell's fine, Fallon.

You told him not to touch the obsidian, right?

He knows, Behach Éan. His voice is as gentle as the rush of wind through my hair.

I really despise running.

You've almost arrived.

I hope he's not pulling a Nonna. Whenever I complained that something dragged, she'd tell me it was almost finished. It was never even close to being done.

There's a definitive smile to his voice. *I'm not pulling a Nonna.*

Since Morrgot's being exceptionally forthcoming, I ask, *Now that we've made up, why don't you tell me what Beyockeen means?*

Made up? Were we fighting?

Even though I've tried to keep up my pace, I'm lagging. *I was mad at you.*

You're often mad at me.

Stop deflecting.

We've arrived.

Although the flagstones transform to moss, his answer, *again*, feels like an avoidance.

But why?

Is his pet name that awful?

63

J ade stems shoot skyward, bursting into clouds of foliage strung up with faerie lights that drip like dewdrops, lending the grove a mesmerizing glow.

I can picture Mamma standing where I stand now, gazing at the lush greenery that seems impervious to the arid sands of Selvati. I wouldn't be surprised if faeries erected an invisible shield around the pureblood estates like they built clouds around Monteluce.

Don't touch anything in this garden. Morrgot barely flaps his wings as he soars over my head.

Why? Will it set off a magical alarm?

Water ripples in shallow ponds on which float lilies that glow like miniature moons, and lianas dotted with bloodred flowers strain around tropical trees that shoot up higher than the bamboos ringing the grove.

The deeper we penetrate, the thicker and broader the trunks become. One tree is so titanic, its base has been hollowed into a passageway. Phosphorescent plants dapple its belly like faraway galaxies. Galaxies that move. When one unspools to touch me, Morrgot launches himself straight for it and releases that startling shriek cry.

The timorous stalk rolls back in on itself.

Why is this grove the most toured place in Tarespagia?

"Because of its biodiversity and luxuriance?"

Because of the hallucinogenic nature of these plants. Most contain toxins that will scramble Fae brains for days. Do you know what happens to non-Fae?

I nibble on my lip as I duck out from beneath the trunk and follow the mossy land. *They never recover?*

They die.

I suck in a breath. *You mean humans?*

No, Fallon. I mean any and all of mixed heritage. The moss they planted in my stream was cultivated here.

I raise my palm and press it against my chest to ease the sudden pressure. I attribute the discomfort to Morrgot's caveat, but what if…what if I've been stung? I freeze on the cusp of a bamboo bridge suspended over a shallow gulley filled with tropical flora.

You haven't been stung. Morrgot's crow swoops around me, his feathers grazing my bare shoulders, pebbling my chilled skin. *I wouldn't let anything happen to you, Fallon.*

Of course not. Delirium or death would thwart his reunion with the rest of his crows and master. When my panic subsides, I shuffle onto the bridge, desperately trying to avoid touching the rope banisters, even though Morrgot insists those are safe. *If I die, who will remove the obsidian from your crows?*

You won't die.

My fingers skip along the rope in time with my pulse as the plant tributary sparkles and rattles several meters beneath me. *But if I did? Could you still break free?*

No.

Seriously? *Only I can do this job? Why?*

Because you're the last of your line.

The last? More like the first, no?

Your father is a block of obsidian.

Oh right. He's out for the count. *But couldn't humans equipped with heavy-duty gloves free you?*

For our protection, neither Fae nor humans can separate the obsidian from our bodies.

His voice is as somber as the sky hanging over the grove that's starting to feel more like the dome of an arena in which I'll have to fight for my life and his crow's.

So only half-Crows? Before he can answer, another question hurtles into my brain. *How come I'm not a block of obsidian?*

Because your powers were bound in your mother's womb, Fallon.

The bridge feels as though it swings beneath my feet. I grip the rope, my worry about toxic plants superseded by something way bigger. "Bound?" I exclaim.

Before you were born, a Shabbin witch penetrated the weakened wards and bound your magic. He pauses, waiting for his revelation to settle, but how in Luce could such a truth settle?

Twenty-two years, I've wondered why I had no magic. *All right*, not twenty-two, but definitely a full decade.

I'm not faulty. I'm suppressed. Because of a Shabbin witch.

I'm not defective.

Great Cauldron, I'm *not* defective.

I'm sorry to press you, Fallon, but we must hurry.

"*Why?* Why stifle my magic? And did my mother—" A lump is forming in my throat. "Did she accept, or was I spelled against her will?"

Your mother was aware it had to be done. It was for your safety, Fallon. What do you think the Fae would've done had they realized your heritage?

I would've been a block of obsidian, so I'm pretty certain they'd have tossed me into a canal.

I'm not defective. My lids burn. My chest hurts from how chaotically my heart beats.

420

I'm not defective. I want to cry I'm so relieved, but I also want to rage for having been tampered with.

If my powers are repressed, how come I can talk to you?

Movement in the grove was just reported to your aunt. I promise to explain everything to you after—

He stops speaking so suddenly that my eyebrows bend.

"What?" I scrutinize his feathers, fearing they're about to morph back into iron, but they remain black and downy. His eyes shut, and the absence of gold drop-kicks my heart. *What's wrong?*

Something tall and dark appears at the end of the bridge. A man. *Sewell.* He's wrapped strips of his turban around his face, leaving only his eyes apparent. His stare is round, glassy, haunted.

He takes a step.

Falters.

Takes another.

Stumbles again.

And then he reaches for me, mouth gaping around a mouthful of smoke.

64

What's wrong with him? I shout through the bond.

Morrgot's second crow streaks across the bridge, slams into the one guiding me, then together, they morph into a wall of smoke that presses me backward. *Turn around.*

"Why?"

Turn, Fallon. Turn. Around. The gravity and vigor of his timbre are the only reasons I concede. *And don't look.*

What's happening to— A wet rip followed by a copious gush make my eyes squeeze in time with my throat. I pray the noise came from the humid grove.

You can turn.

I pivot slowly, scanning the night for Sewell. He's no longer on the bridge or on the opposite embankment.

Morrgot hovers beside me. *Walk.*

Stunned and shaking, I put one foot in front of the other. *What happened to him?*

He must've touched the obsidian.

Must've? Weren't you with him?

The grotto within which my crow is buried is carved in obsidian. I could only stay a handful of seconds at a time.

When my gaze slopes to the dense web of plants beneath the bridge, cotton-candy-like fingers press my chin up, forcing my attention upward to the billowing cloud that is Morrgot.

Don't.

I take Morrgot's command to mean *Don't look down.*

Gliding my palms over the rope to support my jellied limbs, I inch across the bridge. When my fingertips meet something viscous and warm, I freeze, then jolt my hands off the guardrail.

Although Morrgot still has my chin in a vise, I incline my eyes. The night is dark but not dark enough to camouflage the crimson stain on my palm.

Blood. I swallow hard, jamming back the bile surging up my throat. Through clenched teeth, I mutter, "Why did you involve him, Morrgot?"

Because it was necessary.

I rear my head back, unhooking it from its perch. **His death was necessary?**

No, Fallon. Morrgot sounds angry.

Bronwen told me not to speak of the prophecy with anyone, and here he is, involving people.

He seethes through the bond. **His death was a misfortune, one that will forever weigh on my conscience, but Bronwen insisted he needed to dig out my crow or you wouldn't be able to free me in time.**

I'm not that useless.

That's not— A frustrated rumble pours through our unfortunate mind link as he snaps back into his crows. If he'd been a man, he probably would've had both hands buried in his hair, yanking at the roots. But he's not a man; he's an animal. A magical one, but not magical enough to preserve lives.

I half expect him to leave me to fend for myself on the bridge, but he stays close. After all, he has much to lose if something toxic pervades my blood.

Sprites are coming.

I shrug a shoulder. *You'll just murder them like you murdered Sewell.*

I put him out of his misery, he growls. *I didn't murder him. It's the same act, just worded differently.*

He's silent, but not the quiet sort of silence. No, Morrgot is quiet like the sea is quiet before a squall. *If I could've saved him, I would have. But I couldn't. I fucking couldn't.* He flaps his wings once, his down fluttering in the humid breath of the ocean. *Hate me, fine, but don't waste his death.*

Hoofbeats sound, and horses whinny. Since sprites don't ride horses, I imagine Xema Rossi has dispatched guards. I roll my blood-soaked fingers into a fist. Grief and anger fueling my steps, I march forward and leap off the suspended bridge onto the moss-covered footpath.

The black dome. Morrgot's voice is low, edged in as much stirring darkness as his bird form.

I squint until I catch sight of something smooth and as black as a half-buried marble. The entrance to the obsidian cavern is wide and tall, large enough to accommodate a rider, even though it's just me. Before crossing the threshold, I squint into the darkness, trying to make out the hole Sewell dug, but it's like looking at a piece of solid black fabric—completely opaque.

Chest tight, pulse spiking, I step inside. Although I'm on solid ground, the air is so dense and black, I feel like I've penetrated an underwater cavern.

I take another step, my lungs squeezing, squeezing. "I can't— breathe." I wheeze. My eyelids begin to prickle. "Can't—see."

Get out. Get out NOW.

Winded, I turn and stumble. My arm bangs the obsidian wall, and I sag against it.

Fallon!

I jolt at the sound of my name, my smarting lids bouncing up.

OUT. NOW.

Hissing erupts all around me as the air turns solid with smoke. I press away from the wall and teeter toward the entrance, but the world wobbles, robbing me of my balance. I open my mouth to yelp Morrgot's name but don't even manage a squeak.

The memory of Sewell's gaping mouth and extended arm slams into me in time with something else. Something cool and wispy yet powerful enough to propel my body. It shoves me out of the dome and pushes me onto my knees.

My airways are on fire. My eyelashes burn. My blood boils. I rake in breath after breath, desperate for one that doesn't taste like soot.

Focá. Morrgot's wingbeats are as frantic as the foreign word he keeps repeating. *Focá.*

My throat fills with what feels like liquid fire. It streaks from my nostrils and shoots out of my mouth, and I swear, it tastes like hot embers.

I pry my lids up. Tears blur the moss that seems to have blackened. I cough again, and smoke curls from my mouth.

Oh my gods, my lungs are literally on fire. How is this possible?

Faerie smoke. Sewell must have tripped a hidden trigger.

Cauldron, my family is devious.

My elbows wobble and my thighs drum. I slam my lids shut, trying to ease the irritation.

When they open again, the sky is racing over my head, a hazy embroidery of stars, silvered fronds, and inky feathers.

Breathe, Behach Éan. Breathe. Morrgot's wings brush against my collarbone, my cheeks, cool as silk, soft as rose petals. *Breathe.*

Before I die, I want to know what Beyockeen means.

You're not going to die.

Sewell did.

Sewell was human; you aren't.

The stars churn, their sparkle dimming before brightening.

Slowly, my lungs and throat stop spasming. My nostrils and eyes stop boiling. Although my mouth tastes like ash, my throat lining no longer feels like it's being scooped out with a fiery spoon.

Morrgot hovers over me, his velvety feathers sweeping over my collarbone, my neck, my shoulders, my cheeks. He may only be soothing me for his own sake, but it's nonetheless nice not to lie here alone.

My mind clears long enough for me to realize that the sprites and guards must be closing in on us.

Neither is coming.

My eyebrows scrunch. **Did you kill them all?**

No.

I press my palms into the moss, catching the steady pulse of the earth. *Ba-boom. Ba-boom. Ba-boom.* Unless I'm feeling my own heartbeat, someone is coming.

A high-pitched whinny echoes around me.

Furia.

I roll my head to catch sight of my beautiful stallion, but the horse prancing around me isn't black; it's white. And someone sits in the saddle. Someone with waist-long hair and a white uniform.

The rider swings off his horse and lands beside me in a crouch of crisp white and black leather. "I believe you and I need to talk, Fal."

65

The way Dante stares at me raises the fine hairs on the nape of my neck. "Start talking."

I press up into sitting, the acrid taste in my mouth replaced by that of metal. *He doesn't know what you're up to*, I tell myself.

"I've got nothing to say to you, Dante Regio," I wheeze.

His gaze drifts to the gray smoke billowing from the obsidian dome, then back to me, a muscle quivering above the gilt collar of his unbuttoned white jacket. The same one he lent me and that I suggested burning. Apparently, no flame was needed to cleanse the fabric.

I scoot away from Dante and proceed to stand with as much grace as I can muster. "Not after you shut me out and left with your princess."

"If I'd left with her, I wouldn't be here with *you*." Dante rises from his crouch, looking me over from forehead to fingertip and back. "Besides, she isn't *my* princess."

I shouldn't care, not after his callous words from earlier. Nonetheless, his admission is a balm to my battered ego.

"Where's that squire of yours?" overly attentive Tavo asks. "Shouldn't he be *squiring* you?"

"He's keeping an eye on my horse while I visit my family's famed gardens." I cough, my lungs still feeling as though Marcello has speared them onto a spit and placed them in the kitchen's hearth.

"What's wrong with your voice?" Gabriele asks, his nervous steed turning in circles.

"Faerie smoke inhalation. She triggered the shield," Dante says with no hesitation. "That's what's wrong with her."

Gabriele's silver eyes grow wide. "But that can only happen if—"

"How many, Fallon?" Dante's palm hovers over the pommel of his sword. "How many?"

For the first time in my life, I wish Dante was with that other woman. "How many what?" I feign innocence.

"How many crows have you found?"

"Crows?" My raspy voice goes a little shrill.

"Stop playing dumb!"

I choke on the intensity of his tone and the ensuing rush of heartbeats. Dante has never raised his voice at me before tonight. I understand he's jittery, but he doesn't get to speak to me like I'm something stuck to the bottom of his boot.

"Even if she did find them, she can't unstake them. She's Fae." Gabriele finally manages to calm his horse.

"Part Fae." Dante's eyes are as cold as ice chips. "Part something else."

Tavo snorts. "Yeah. Human."

"No, Tavo," Dante says somberly. "Not human."

Tavo's sneer topples from his lips.

A sprite in full military regalia trundles toward the ring of brawn that prevents me from fleeing. I recognize him from my visit to Dante's tent—Gaston. "Xema Rossi's sending her," he pants, "parrot, Altezza. Doesn't trust us."

"Start talking before the pest arrives, or I'll have no choice but to report you, Fallon."

"Everyone has a choice, Dante."

He dips his chin. "Let me rephrase that. Tell me what you've done with the crows, or I'll let the parrot report back to his mistress that her great-grandchild is shoving her nose in places it doesn't belong."

Tavo and Gabriele press their horses so close to me that the animals' brisk exhales warm the sides of my arms.

"Last I checked, I was a Rossi, and this is Rossi land." I clear my aching throat. "So if anyone's trespassing, it's the lot of you."

Tavo leers down at me. "Spoken like someone with the delusion of a noble birth."

I will the Fae to fall off his horse and break at least six bones.

"Has the shape of your ears slipped your mind? *Again.*"

"That's enough, Tavo!" Dante snaps.

You hold the man in too high esteem.

My molars clench. *And you hold him in* no *esteem.* I wipe my face clean of any and all emotion, but my heart thuds riotously and floods my mouth with the taste of copper. *What should I do? Run?*

Do nothing.

Nothing? My heart halts its marathon. *Dante just threatened to alert my great-grandmother, who will gladly run me through with a steel blade. Or set me on fire.*

Shh, Behach Éan.

Don't shush me! My life is on the line.

You have such little faith in me.

That startles a bitter laugh from my singed larynx. *It's not a question of faith in you; it's a question of knowing the loyalty of the males around me. They'll do anything to protect their prince. Anything.*

And I'll do anything to protect you.

Obviously. I give a slight eye roll. *You still need me.*

I hear a sigh flutter through the bond at the same time as Tavo quips, "Following in your demented mamma's footsteps, I see."

I spin around. "Don't you *dare* talk about my mamma."

His horse lurches in time with his body, and he flops out of the saddle, whacking the ground with an extremely satisfying *oomph*.

Gabriele's mare rears while Dante murmurs, "What the—"

Gaston latches on to Tavo's reins and holds them up. "His reins were severed, Altezza."

I smile to myself. Well, to Morrgot and to myself since I imagine it's his doing. *Nice.*

Next time, I'm aiming for his wrists.

I suck in a breath at the same time as Dante. Did he also hear Morrgot?

The prince's blue eyes widen a little, then a lot. Although they're turned toward me, they're glazed over.

Shock parts my lips. *Wait...are you sending him a vision?*

Dante's eyes jerk to the fronds over my head. He unsheathes his sword and swings, the tip trained on the hollow of my collarbone.

I attribute his aim to a knee-jerk reaction. For all his recent annoyance with me, Dante would never slay me.

I take a step back...just in case.

Tavo bounces to his feet and, before I can move farther backward, locks one arm around my neck and the other around my waist. "What have you done?" he hisses into my ear. "What have you fucking done?"

Gabriele brandishes his sword, his jerky movement unsettling his horse. "She cut the reins? How?"

"Not her." Dante's gaze lowers back to me, and his cold stare turns downright frosty.

"She brought him back," Tavo growls, the heat of his skin becoming unbearable. "She brought the fucking Crimson Crow back from the fucking underworld!"

66

The scent of charred fabric curls up my nose. Is Tavo burning my dress?

I stare in horror at Dante, willing him to do or say something, but the prince is transfixed by a spot over my head. I imagine Morrgot. I roll my head as far forward as I can get it with an arm clutched around my neck, then let it fly backward. I expect to make contact with Tavo's nose or chin, but the back of my head meets air.

I whirl around, then jerk my head up to where Tavo squeals like a sow in heat, dangling from the iron talons of Morrgot's two crows.

Dante tosses his sword onto the ground. "All right!" He raises his palms. "I agree to your terms. Gabriele, toss your sword."

Gabriele throws it.

"Now, put him down."

Morrgot soars higher and then, only then, releases the detestable Fae. Tavo's body smacks the moss with a satisfying crunch. Finally…something broke. Probably his ego. Hopefully his dick.

Reality presses the slight curl of my lips back into a grim line.

As much as I wanted to share what I was doing with Dante, I wanted to inform him of it only once the five crows became one. Once I was closer to fulfilling part one of the prophecy.

Why would you show yourself?

Because I don't tolerate men assaulting women.

Dante would've intervened. I knead my neck, the memory of Tavo's grip clinging to my skin like a spiderweb. *Eventually.*

Morrgot is polite enough not to contradict me. Or maybe he agrees with me. That would be a first. Or possibly he's distracted and not picking up on my thoughts.

Gabriele's trying to calm his jittery steed. "How did she— She's half-Fae, and Fae can't—"

"Look at her damn eyes." Dante is still shaking his head, gaze on Tavo, who's slowly peeling himself out of the shallow indent his body has left on the moss. "Fucking look at them! Who has violet eyes?"

Gabriele frowns. "Fallon."

"Who. Else?" Dante bites out.

Gabriele's eyes go so wide, his silver irises are fully outlined in white. "The Shabbins."

"Don't those female savages have pink peepers?" Tavo sits now, one hand rubbing his forehead, the other whisking away clumps of dirt from his white jacket.

"Only the pure-blooded ones," Dante spits out.

"But the wards?" Gabriele exclaims.

"Mustn't be as impenetrable as Marco believes," Dante mutters.

I guess it's better to let them believe I'm Shabbin, right?

Black smoke drapes over my shoulders, cool and slick, like mist and somehow also like feathers.

"No harm will come to Fallon, Corvo." Dante snarls the Lucin word for crow, making it sound like an insult.

So what terms did you and Dante agree to, Morrgot?

I have something your princeling wants.

I'm shallow enough to think *me* but not foolish enough to believe Dante would accept working with Morrgot for my sake alone. *What is it you have?*

His answer takes a moment to come, and when it does, it's spoken with a heavy coating of acrimony. *The power to put him on the throne.*

"Beau's here!" Gaston soars toward Tavo.

Although the dark wisps of Morrgot's body don't vanish entirely, they shrink. I understand why when something thumps at Dante's feet.

A headless parrot.

I swallow at the sight of another dead body. Not that I'll miss this one, but still...

The prince lurches back in time with Gabriele's frisky mare. The sprite gasps, then projectile vomits over Tavo's cheek.

The redhead slugs the small, winged man, knocking him out cold. And then he stares at the life leaking out of the bird, probably imagining himself lying there. "What terms did you agree to?" He raises eyes that glitter with both dread and anger to me and the smoke stole wrapped protectively around my bare neck.

I want to tell Morrgot that he's wrangled the overconfident Fae into submission, that his protectiveness is a little over the top, but until I hear Dante swear to me he'll play nice, I'll take Morrgot's protection.

My winged guardian snorts.

What?

Nothing, Behach Éan. Nothing.

Liar, I whisper.

Our beginnings may have been rocky, but I feel as though Morrgot and I have reached a good place. Not quite friendship but a certain camaraderie.

Tavo eyes me, a glop of sprite vomit dripping off his ticking jaw and onto the rigid collar of his uniform. "What. Terms?" Tavo repeats since Dante still hasn't gratified him with an answer.

Dante scrutinizes the shadow cloaking me. "We're going to aid Fallon—"

"Are you out of your fucking mind?" Tavo shrugs his shoulder against his dirty cheek, wiping away more glistening bile.

"—in exchange for—" Dante continues, lips barely shifting over his teeth.

"Marco will kill you, Dante." Gabriele sounds calm, but his white-knuckled grip on his reins betrays his anxiety.

"He won't kill me."

Tavo finally pries himself upright. "He will, Dee."

Annoyance glosses the prince's cheekbones. "Gods!" He tosses both hands in the air. "Will you both be quiet and listen?"

Silence.

"We're going to aid Fallon, in exchange for which Lore will depose Marco."

I stare at the coalescing shadow of Lore's crows, wondering if Bronwen foresaw this moment, this deal between Fae and Crow. And then I wonder if she warned Morrgot about it. But then something else flicks those questions out of my mind.

Lore? I thought you would be the one deposing Marco.

"How do we know he won't depose you—and us—too?" Tavo's amber eyes burn as hot as his anger.

Although Morrgot's presence is reassuring, it fails to calm me. "Because he's not some crazed assassin!"

"The man was known as the Crimson Crow." Tavo seizes the saddle of his horse and swings himself atop it, then grabs either end of his reins and knots them together. "And let me tell you, Rossi, he didn't earn his title because he favored the color red."

My heart flaps wildly within the confines of my chest. *Is that true?*

That I've spilled blood? Yes.

But how much?

As little as possible, as much as necessary.

The memory of the two sprite bodies from the forest inflames my still-stinging eyelids. Did I really expect the master of lethal birds to be kind? *Swear to me that Dante will be unharmed.*

The roiling shadow weaves into two crows with two sets of golden eyes—one pair on me, the other on the three men and the sprite who's regained his wits. *I swear to you, Fallon Báeinach, that your princeling shall live.*

I don't bother correcting his use of my paternal last name. It matters too little at the moment. *And be unharmed*, I insist. *By you* or *by Lore.*

And be unharmed by us both.

I wait to feel the burn of his oath twine around my biceps, but the same way Antoni's skin didn't react to my words, my skin doesn't react to Morrgot's.

Crow blood must incapacitate bargaining. Wait…he struck one with Dante, didn't he?

Before I can ask if the flesh beneath his feathers bares the mark of their deal, Dante says, "Tavo, go start a fire in the stables to buy us time."

"Not in the stables!" My chest heaves. "Not anywhere there are living beings."

Dante crosses his arms. "Fine. Not the stables."

Tavo's jaw ticks. And ticks. "I can't believe we're trusting her."

"We're not trusting her." Dante dips his chin, eyes darker than a starless ocean. "We're trusting Lore."

A steel blade to the heart would've hurt less than Dante's avowal.

67

"Gabriele, air out the grotto." Dante juts his head toward the black dome as he shrugs off his jacket, the one he lent me when our years of friendship still meant something to him.

Clucking his tongue to force his horse past me, Gabriele holds out a palm webbed by silvery threads of magic. Pale tendrils fluttering around his shoulders, he arcs his arm and sends a bolt of wind so potent it lifts the heavy folds of my dress.

"Here." Dante rolls his singed shirt off his back and saturates the fabric with water. "Hold this over your mouth and nose."

I never deemed myself a particularly prideful person, but I refuse his shirt and his help.

I wish he'd never come to Tarespagia.

I wish I hadn't glimpsed this callous side of him.

Mind whirring with glum thoughts, I march back toward the grotto entrance.

"Fallon!"

My barked name doesn't magically spring my balled fingers open. If anything, it makes them curl harder.

Dante releases a low growl as he tramples the moss after me.

I stop on the threshold, testing the air for the sulfurous scent of faerie smoke. "Is it safe to enter?"

Gabriele peers down at me from where he sits atop his horse. "I'll keep fanning it."

When Morrgot doesn't yell at me to take Dante's wet shirt, I step past the threshold. The air is dark and heavy. Although it stings my flaring nostrils and eyes, it doesn't smother me.

"Will you please take my damn shirt already?" Dante shoves it against my chest.

I don't reach out for it, so when he removes his hand, it plops to the ground between us. I step over it, then circle him. "Don't need it."

"What happened to you, Fallon?" Dante speaks so close to my ear that I feel the barbed shape of his words. "What made you so bitter?"

Letting my gaze adjust to the darkness to spot the hole Sewell dug, I say, "Since when does refusing some soggy cloth make one bitter?"

"I'm not talking about you snubbing my help. I'm talking about your lies and your attitude. The girl I knew before going to Glace was sweet and soft."

As I scan the dome, I spot him making a vague gesture.

"The girl I returned to is calculating and barbed."

I tilt my head back and hold his gaze. "Tell me, Dante, who has the best odds of survival? A pink, newborn porcupine with lax quills or an adult with hardened ones?" Hoping I've made my point, I turn and squint into the darkness, seeking the glimmer of Morrgot's crow.

The soft brush of feathers along my knuckles carries my attention downward. *Hold on to me. I'll lead you to him.*

Should you be in here?

It's uncomfortable, but I'll live.

You're immortal, so that's a nonissue.

I spread my fingers, expecting to feel Morrgot's head or talons. Instead, his misty form glides between my fanned digits and enfolds them like a ghostly hand.

That sensation… *Focus!* I chide myself. *Now's not the time to weigh the odds of Morrgot being at the origin of your rubdown.*

Crouch.

I do.

The hole isn't deep.

I sigh in relief. At least I won't need to ask anyone for a hand up.

I'll have to let go now.

Okay.

He slips through my fingers like a warm current.

Inhaling deeply, I grip the rim of the hole, then slide in. Like Morrgot predicted, my boots hit earth fast. I squat, then run my hands over the bottom until my fingertips hit something hard and cold. Something that shimmers in spite of the obscurity and the thin coating of dirt.

I drop to my knees and dust off the shawl of grainy dirt, lightening my touch around the crow's head and the dagger protruding from its chest. I seize the hilt, feeling an inscription beneath my thumb full of curves and curls.

I yank my elbow up. The dagger slips free like an oar from water. Instantly, the iron crow vanishes into the darkness. Slipping the dagger into my boot, I heave myself back up and out, then stride past Dante, whose eyes track my every movement.

As I step past the threshold, I gulp in a breath of fresh air, ridding my lungs of the noxious stench lingering within the obsidian grave.

"Gabriele, toss the parrot into the hole, and cover it up," Dante barks.

Gabriele grimaces, but Dante joins me at the grotto's entrance. His gaze slides to where Morrgot's third crow is joining with the other two, girth swelling until the bird blots out the moon.

The beast he must be when whole... *At this rate, you'll be able to carry me home on your back.* I smile to myself, and I swear I feel Morrgot smile back, as though daring me to straddle him. *I'd love to see Luce from way up high.*

Then you best learn to fly, Behach Éan.

I snort because growing wings is sadly impossible. A defiant smile sharpens my lips. *If you don't tell me what Beyockeen means, I'll hop on your back when you least expect it.*

Have you forgotten that I can morph into smoke?

Fine. No riding you. I'll just have to get one of your bird friends to allow me to ride them.

Morrgot's pupils become pinpricks as though my suggestion has enraged him more than the prior one. Cauldron, he's a moody one.

He's also a large one now. Best not to get on his bad side. Or backside.

The dagger... His gaze darts to where Gabriele is sealing the hollow by gusting the gritty earth atop the parrot.

Ahead of you for once. I tucked it inside my boot. I walk back to the bridge and bend over to grab the hilt of the weapon. My thumb meets the grooves of the engraving—an *R*, for Regio or Rossi?

Rossi.

The letter cements my hatred for the family I was born into. Perhaps I'll adopt the name Bannock after all. Until I marry, that is, after which I'll take my husband's name.

Regio...

I'm suddenly not so certain about wanting to marry him. What had been Bronwen's exact words? *"Free the five iron crows, and you will be queen."*

I wish she'd added, *Should you wish.*

I grip the hilt harder, then pull my arm back and let the dagger fly into the dense jungle below. I stay there a moment, gaze skimming the dense vegetation, then, heart swelling like Morrgot's crows, I murmur, "Grazi, Sewell. May you rest in peace."

When I turn around, I find Dante blocking my path.

"You should've kept the weapon."

I scrutinize his hooded eyes, then fling him a provocative smile. "Not much point considering obsidian doesn't turn Fae to iron or stone." Childish, I know, but his behavior tonight...his words, they've cut me deeply.

Dante's mouth thins. "You trust too readily."

"I'm aware."

Hoofbeats clack against wood, and the bridge sways as Tavo advances back toward us on horseback. "We need to leave now. Xema's deployed all her personnel to look for her little parrot."

I brush my palms along my velvet skirt, which has picked up so many moss stains that if any guard did arrive, I could lounge on the jungle floor and blend in.

Morrgot sighs. *You, Fallon, are incapable of blending in.*

I pay his dig no mind because in truth, he's right. I don't blend. My last name may be Rossi, but my ears are round, and let me not get started on my odd first name that isn't Lucin. Why Nonna allowed Mamma to baptize me Fallon is beyond me.

Your name is Crow. It means raindrop.

My lips part. *Nonna calls me Goccolina, which means raindrop in Lucin. Does that—does she—*

She does not know.

Then how—

Furia's here.

I spin to find my beautiful black horse circling the black dome. He arrows straight for me, shouldering past Dante—*good horse*—stopping only when his flaring nostrils hit my collarbone. I cradle his head and press a kiss to his muzzle before hoisting myself atop him with surprising nimbleness.

"Serpent-charmer. Horse-charmer. Crow-charmer." Tavo's

face is glossed in sweat, like his horse's maroon coat. "Is there an animal that can resist your charm?"

"No. I control them all. Better watch your back." I throw in a saccharine smile that makes his eyes narrow. "And your front."

The sky rumbles and marbles with lightning, stealing my attention off Tavo. Wind whips my hair as clouds rush across the stars and tear. Rain lashes the jungle and whips my skin, blurring the darkness until I can hardly see past Furia's ears.

I'm sorry about the storm, Behach Éan, but it'll hide your riding party and wash away your tracks.

I suck in a startled breath and squint around me. **You can create storms?**

It's my newest—what is it you called my abilities again? Party tricks?

My awed gaping transforms into a smile, but falls from my lips when a hand snakes beneath my forearms and latches on to my saddle. I blink waterlogged lashes at Dante, who swings himself behind me.

"Gaston, be my eyes and ears in the Rossi household. Report back if they visit the grotto and notice the crow's been dug up. Gabriele, Tavo, we ride south."

Through the driving rain, I catch a vein stuttering alongside Tavo's temple. "South?"

"To the galleon," Dante barks through clenched teeth, gusting away his friend's furrowed brow. He reaches around me, attempting to pluck the reins from my fingers. "Let me steer."

"If you want to steer, climb atop your own horse."

His chest hardens against my spine. "Stop, Fallon. Stop fighting me. Not only am I your best bet for getting out of Tarespagia alive, but also I'm on your side."

He must dig his heels into Furia's flanks, because my stallion whirls before streaking off like a launched firework, skirting the dome and continuing on the path. Gabriele's and Tavo's horses gallop close behind, Dante's horse tethered to Gabriele's.

"I'm not taking that chance, Corvo." Dante's snarl vibrates my eardrum.

"What chance?"

"That you and your winged companion leave without us."

I attempt to put some distance between our bodies, but between Furia's speed, the narrowness of our seat, and our rain-slicked skin, it's an impossible feat. "So you're going to keep me hostage until he sets the crown atop your brow?"

"Precisely." His Adam's apple slips against the back of my head.

My lips pinch. That he lacks faith in Morrgot is one thing, but in me?

"You're a worryingly talented liar, Fallon," Dante breathes into my ear as we cut through the rain-soaked grove, across sinuous trails framed by stalks fledged with glossy, heart-shaped fronds that brush against my legs.

Although I miss my pants, I'm glad for the length and thickness of my dress. Perhaps the plants aren't poisonous in these parts, but I prefer not taking any chances. "What lie are you accusing me of now?"

"Let me see... Cresting the mountain without noticing the flooded riverbed or that pretty nest his species calls a castle. That you came to Tarespagia for a social call. That you slept with me when all that interested you was Isolacuori and the crow imprisoned in my brother's trophy room. Shall I go on?"

I turn my head as far as my neck will allow, hooding my eyes to protect them from the pelting rain. "I slept with you because I was crazy about you, Dante, not because you were my ticket onto the royal isle."

It strikes me that I've used the past tense. Did it strike him?

We emerge from the grove, but it takes us another fifteen

minutes to reach the Rossi gates. Dante commands the Fae guarding them to let him pass, and they do, because he's the king's brother.

Our horses' hooves clack against the slick sandstone as they race down the broad avenues, away from the ocean, away from the pureblood district. Before we've even reached the checkpoint, the gates are flung open.

After cantering past the same guard who let us through earlier, Dante drops his mouth to my ear. "If you cared at all for me, Fallon, you wouldn't have brought back the greatest Fae killer behind my back."

"That Fae killer will fetch you a throne."

Dante slides his nose down my damp cheek, and although my skin pebbles, it isn't with lust. "Until my brother's dead, I'll hold my breath."

"Dead?" I sputter. "Morrgot said he'd carry him to Shabbin shores and let *them* deal with Marco."

"I may hate my brother, Fallon, but I'm merciful enough to give him an honorable death rather than a sadistic one."

Merciful? I'm so shocked by his admission that my lips part, but a lungful of rain reseals them. I cannot believe Dante's ready to end his brother's life. That he speaks of it with such detachment.

"Where will your loyalties lie once the deed is done?" he murmurs.

"With you. They've always lain with you." Did Morrgot not show him the vision of me at his side, wearing a matching crown? "How can you ask me that?"

"Because you called that crow Your Majesty. Which makes me question your allegiance."

"What are you talking about? When did I call him His Majesty?"

"What do you think Mórrgaht means?"

"It's— That's his name!"

Dante laughs, and the sound is despicable because he's laughing at me. "Fallon, that corvo's name is Lorcan. Lorcan Ríhbiadh."

"Lorcan?" I sputter as we streak past broken homes and broken people. "But—I—"

"Also referred to as the sky king or, by his intimate circle, as Lore."

68

My brow knits. "The crow is named after his master? That must get confusing."

"His master?" This time, Dante's the one who sounds baffled.

"Lore. The master of the five crows."

"Don't you know anything about the Crows?"

I know my father was one of them. I now know they have a king, whom I've been calling His Majesty.

I glower up at the steel-gray sky, hoping Morr—I mean Lore intercepts it. *How could you let me call you that? Did you need your ego stroked? Is that why you didn't correct me?* Not for the first time, I feel duped.

I wasn't trying to mislead you, Fallon.

Then why? Why did I have to learn of your true identity through Dante?

In case you spoke my name out loud, which you did, on multiple occasions. Few people have heard the term Mórrgaht, but everyone is familiar with the name Lore.

If you'd told me the truth, if you'd explained it to me… Gods, I feel so stupid.

You are anything but.

I press my palms against my ears. "Stop. Just stop!"

"Is he trying to feed you more lies?" Dante's question slips through the web of my fingers.

My throat stings from the tidal wave of anger mounting within me. Slowly, I lower my palms. "Tell me. Tell me everything about Lorcan Reebyaw and his Crows."

You realize he will tell the Fae version of our story?

I'll take the Fae version over the fake version.

Fallon...

Don't.

If Dante wasn't trapping me in the saddle, I would jump off and pace the drenched sands of Selvati until my rage subsided.

"Once upon a time, when Luce was still divided between warring tribes, one of the mountain clans struck a deal with a Shabbin demon to become more powerful than all the others. To become unkillable."

Morrgot—I mean *Lore*—growls, *That wasn't—*

Don't.

Dante's long braids tinkle as we ride, the gold beads slapping against one another. "The demon demanded payment, and against many of his clan's wishes, Lore paid. And dearly at that."

"With coin?"

"No, Fallon, with something even more precious. He paid with his humanity. With his people's humanity."

I frown. "I don't—I don't understand."

"They gave up being men. They gave up being men and accepted becoming monsters, mammoth birds with weaponized extremities that can be turned to stone or iron but cannot be killed."

"So Lore was once a man?"

Dante tugs on Furia's bridle, angling the stallion toward the south. "Lore is *still* a man. One who can shape-shift at will into a hideous crow or into a puff of noxious smoke that can choke pure-blooded Fae."

My skin prickles. "And his master? Can he also…shape-shift?"

I feel the curve of Dante's mouth against my temple and hate that he's getting a kick out of my naivete. "The sky king answers to no one, Fallon. He has no master."

Lore's golden eyes spark behind my lids. I remember thinking how they looked strikingly like Morrgot's. Oh, the irony. They weren't similar; they were the same eyes! Eyes in front of which I paraded around naked.

My embarrassment is flattened by fury. *You're a man?*

I never hid the fact that I was male, Fallon.

No, just the fact that you're a two-legged one! I seethe. *This may be a joke to you, but it isn't to me. How dare you, Lore?* I choke out, on the verge of a meltdown. *How dare you?*

It's not a joke to me, Behach Éan. He may have softened his voice, but it doesn't soften me.

"Do you understand the Crow tongue, Dante?"

"I'm familiar with their dialect. Why?"

"What does *Beyockeen* mean?"

He repeats the word, breaking it up into two distinct sounds— *beyock* and *een.* "It means dumb bird. Why?"

Dumb bird? That's what he's been calling me? *Dumb?* Although I suspected it was unkind, I'm wholly unprepared for the surge of hurt that crashes atop the tide of my anger.

Behach does not mean dumb, Fallon; it means little. The word for dumb, in case you ever fancy using it, is bilbh.

Why should I believe you?

Why would I call the woman helping me dumb?

Because I swallow pretty lies like Fae swallow wine.

Fallon, I swear on Mórrígan that Dante's translation is wrong.

I don't know who this Mórrígan person is but imagine she's some Crow deity or he wouldn't be invoking her name in an oath. After minutes of mashing my molars, I ask, *Why little bird?*

Because that's what you are.

I'm neither sprite-size nor a bird.

By little, I mean young. And thanks to your heritage, you will one day be able to transform into a bird.

The idea of shifting forms, of shedding skin for feathers and growing wings, of flying, buffs the sharp points of my emotions. I'm still angry but I'm also staggered. *What if I don't want to shape-shift?*

Then you won't, but I've yet to meet a Crow who doesn't crave the freedom of flight.

I dwell on that as we travel through the rain-soaked, derelict human land, across endless planes of sand, toward the sweep of green that is the jungle. Although the storm halts when we breach the canopy of palms and other tropical plants, the air remains moist, preventing my hair and dress from drying.

Minutes turn into hours before we come across anything other than exotic creatures not quick enough to camouflage themselves. I wouldn't call the ride relaxing—it isn't—but it gives me time to parse through the new information I've acquired.

My mind is so adrift that when we pass a house woven from bamboo shoots, I almost miss it. But then we trot past another and another. Unlike in Selvati, the edifices are large and shiny, with windowpanes, thatched rooftops, and plots of cultivated land.

"Is this still Selvati?"

"No. Tarescogli. The western equivalent of Tarelexo."

"I've never heard of it."

"Because it's a new settlement that hasn't been added to our maps. In truth, its name isn't even official, but people call it Tarescogli because it sits on the cliffs."

"The Land of the Bluffs. It's pretty."

"In case you ever tire of Tarelexo, you could move here."

Dante's words travel from my ears to my heart by way of my ego. Even though I'd expect a comment like this from Marco or Tavo, I didn't expect Dante to suggest I stick to a place crowded with people like me, with rounded ears but magic in their blood.

69

Bronwen's prophecy clangs through my mind, reminding me that the only place I'll settle will be the royal isle. "Maybe I'd prefer an estate in Tarespagia." I wouldn't. I merely want to observe Dante's reaction.

He exhales slowly, deeply. "No one will sell you land in Tarespagia. It would be illegal. Not to mention expensive."

"Once you're king, you can make it legal."

"I'd have a revolution on my hands. Is that really how you wish me to begin my reign?"

"Of course I don't wish you uprisings, but there's so much to change in Luce. Humans need better living conditions, and half-bloods should have the right to use their magic as often as purebloods."

"I agree."

"And serpents need to stop being hunted."

My suggestion is met with silence.

I twist around in the saddle. "Did you hear me?"

"I heard you, but as long as they attack us—"

"If we stopped attacking them, they'd stop attacking us."

"We're not all Shabbin."

"I'm not Shabbin, Dante."

"You can talk to serpents. For Cauldron's sake, stop denying it!"

I gnash my teeth at his tone. "For the last time, I *cannot* talk to serpents, but I do feel a connection to them, the same way I feel a connection to most animals."

Because you're Crow, Fallon. Animals scent what we are through our blood.

My lids pull up as I remember Minimus's reaction to my wound. Morrgot too had—

I'll never get his name straight. *Lore. Lore. Lore.* I hammer the word into my mind, evicting the other.

Lore has finally solved one mystery. How *I* failed to elucidate it the moment he showed me who fathered me is beyond me. Is it because I hadn't yet come to terms with my heritage?

Not that I have accepted it yet.

"How do you know you're not Shabbin?" Dante's rough timbre scrapes over the side of my head. "Have you met your father? Is that another secret you hoard?"

Even though I bristle, I remind myself that Dante must still be in shock. "I know I'm not Shabbin because Lore—"

"Is your father." The noose of Dante's arms loosens, undoubtedly from disgust. "That's why he's so protective of you."

"What? No. I am *a* Crow's daughter, but not"—I nod to the sky—"his. Lore's just protective because I'm the only person who can free him."

"The only person, huh?" Tavo says, right before his face contorts with such pain that I think Lore planted his iron talons in a soft area on his body. "I wasn't planning on killing her, you gods-damned psycho."

Gabriele is looking at me too, but he has the good sense or the good manners not to speak.

"A Crow..." Dante murmurs, eyes slightly glazed.

Since his grip stays slack, I mutter, "It's not contagious."

He glances at my face, something hard and guarded in his eyes. He'll eventually see past it, but in the meantime, it hurts.

"I'm still me." The silence becomes as thick and sticky as the humidity. *Ugh.* I shouldn't have told him.

Never be ashamed of who you are, Fallon.

I'm not ashamed, I growl. *And butt out of my head. You aren't welcomed!*

As the distance between houses shrinks, Dante asks, "How have you hidden your shape-shifting for so long?"

His query sounds like an accusation. "I haven't hidden it. I *cannot* shape-shift, the same way I *cannot* control Fae magic."

"And why is that?"

I lick the salt of the sea and the frustration of my impotence off my lips. "My magic was bound in utero."

"So you wouldn't transform to obsidian…" He says this almost with wonder, but then all traces of awe drop from his tongue. "The Crows were no longer *present* when you were born, so who bound it?"

Dante is wary of me enough as it is that I decide not to share the Shabbins' involvement. "Like I said, they bound it *before* my birth, *before* they were all cursed."

"Sounds like Shabbin magic to me." Gabriele glances up at the sky. "The wards were weak back then. One of them could've snuck in."

"To bind my magic? A waste of their time and competence if you ask me." I snort, uneasiness crawling up my breastbone.

"Not if you're the beasts' only key to return to the land of the living." Tavo rubs the back of his head as though it still aches from his fall. "If you hadn't intervened, those Fae killers would've been gone another five centuries."

"If I hadn't intervened, Marco would've ended up killing Dante to keep the throne, just like he killed his own father!"

My revelation causes the loudest hush to fall over my entourage. Even the horses go still, stopping in the middle of a darkened road.

"The vulture king tell you that?" Tavo finally says. "'Cause the real story—"

Lore must be showing him the *real story*, because the Fae's eyes glaze over. Dante's and Gabriele's too.

"Every coin's got two sides, Corvo." Tavo's grumble makes his horse flick his ears back and forth.

"If what he just showed us is true…" The moonlight that drizzles through the trees hits Gabriele's face, highlighting the male's sudden pallor. "If Marco—"

Tavo tosses his hand in the air. "Marco may be impulsive, but if he'd beheaded his own father, it would be known."

"Would it?" Dante's pupils have dilated, eclipsing the blue. "Lazarus once told me…" His words are quiet. So quiet. "That my father wanted to make peace with the Crows." He licks his lips. "And that Marco never allowed him to perform the traditional Fae burial rites on our father. Instead, my brother set fire to our father's corpse right where it lay in Rax."

Gabriele's intake of air is so swift, it disturbs the pale flyaways edging his face. "Because a healer would've been able to tell what had caused the lethal wound."

"Fuck." Tavo, for once, seems browbeaten. "His own father. *Your* father."

I twist in the saddle. "I'm sorry, Dante."

He acknowledges my empathy with a nod. "Let's find a place to spend the night. The cliff roads are too treacherous to travel without light."

With barely any nudging, Furia sets off again. Two streets down, we come to a two-storied structure that glows in spite of the late hour. The words TAVERNA MARE are shaped in seashells above the door. An ocean inn sounds like an idyllic resting spot.

Dante releases the reins. "Gabriele, help Fallon down."

"I don't need help."

Tavo hops off his mare. "Planning on flying down, are you?"

I flip him off as I swing my leg over Furia's neck and dismount in a heap of velvet.

The male smirks.

Gods, I really hate him.

Gabriele's attention is leveled on the sky. "Did he follow us here?"

"What do you think?" Dante nods toward the glued seashells where a sooty drift breaks off into three separate puffs.

It's been hours since I've spoken to Lore, and although my anger hasn't waned, something bothers me too much to keep up my cold shoulder. *You can morph into a man, right?*

I can.

I think of the hands I felt along my spine last night. *Have you? Turned into one?*

I need all five of my crows for my flesh to turn solid.

I cannot help the wrinkle that pleats my nose. *You mean I'd see your insides?*

A chuckle comes through our bond. *No insides. Just a shadow that, with every crow, grows more solid.*

"Care to share what he's telling you?" Dante asks.

Keep the fact that you can walk into my mind our secret, all right?

I chew on my lip, curious as to why I should keep it to myself since Dante and his friends are now part of the team, but I suspect Morr—Lore has a good reason.

Morrlore? It has a nice ring to it.

Don't get used to it. I'm trying to forget the majesty part, but you know what they say about a bad habit?

Enlighten me. What do they say?

That it's like parchment tossed in water. It takes a while for it to sink.

"They're probably conspiring against us." Tavo tries to walk Furia to the trough, but my stallion refuses to follow where the Fae soldier leads.

"Definitely sleep with one eye open tonight." I pluck the lead rope from him. My quip leaches some of the amber from his irises.

"If anything happens to me," Dante says, voice low and slow, "he will never walk the earth."

I frown at Dante. Is he implying he'd command me to stop reviving Lore's crows?

Not command. Lore's deep timbre strokes my mind like a finger gloved in velvet.

He'd imprison me? When the crow offers no response, I look at Dante, who's rubbing the soles of his boots against the doormat. "How would you stop me, Dante?"

His gaze stays locked on the bristly pad beneath him. "I'd hope an oath would suffice."

Instead of mentioning that oaths don't take to my skin, I ask, "You'd *hope?*"

He sighs. "Fal, don't make me say it. It'll only anger you, and you're already in a wretched mood."

My eyes go as wide as my mouth. Is he saying—is he saying... "You'd kill me?"

"I'd prefer not to but my kingdom—"

I raise my hand to shut him up.

Dante would kill me.

He'd kill me.

My anger shifts from the crow to the Fae, then back to the crow who started all this, before swinging back to the Fae who cannot love me enough if he's willing to end my life.

Dante keeps polishing his boots when what needs polishing is his cold, cold heart, because that part of him has wholly lost its luster.

Mood soured, I tie Furia to a water trough on the side of the inn, then swipe a finger across my collarbone that comes away coated in umber sludge. Not that I care so much about what anyone thinks of me at the moment. I pass my hands through my damp hair and shake out more grit.

"What's our story?" Gabriele's hand rests on the doorknob, which he's yet to twist.

Dante palms his wet coat sleeves, then his trousers. "We're riding home."

Tavo tilts his head and eyes me. "What about ransom girl? Should we be seen with her?"

Dante's eyes are hard as marble as they look my way. Mine are harder. "Marco asked me to keep an eye on her, so it serves us all to be spotted together."

"Don't know what your plans are," Tavo says as he shoves past his friends, "but I'm done camping on the doormat. I want food, a bath, and a broad. Especially since I hear the girls are prettier in these parts. More exotic." He waggles his eyebrows before shouldering open the door.

The smell that escapes would normally make my wilted insides clamor for food, but they're tied in too many knots to so much as growl.

Unlike his brutish friend, Gabriele holds the door open for Dante, who climbs up the three front steps, then ducks beneath the low doorframe but not before looking over his shoulder at me. "Come, Fallon."

There's no place I'd like to be farther from than this man's side. "I'll come when I'm ready."

He looses a sigh. "I'm not going to kill you. Our interests are all aligned."

But if they weren't... Gods, I thought I hated Lore, but it pales to how I feel about Dante.

I'd murder him first, Behach Éan.

I snort. Of course he would. Anything for his precious Crows. My lashes sag under the weight of my harrowing disappointment.

You forget that you're one of them, Fallon. One of my precious Crows.

I'm only precious because I'm your tool, Lorcan Reebyaw.

And that is exactly what I am. A tool. A pawn. A thing to be used and discarded by these men.

I stare between the sky king and the earth prince who both need me, Bronwen's prophecy thudding through my skull: *Free the five iron crows, and you will be queen.*

Bronwen never mentioned I'd be Dante's queen, only that Luce would be mine.

My anger turns to shock. Shock and confusion. Lore was going to put *me* on the Isolacuorin throne. I shake my head, fists clenching. What a marvelous puppet I would've made.

That isn't—

I raise my palm to quiet him. I don't want to hear any more sweet lies or unsavory truths. Not tonight. Not ever. ***After this, Lore, after I've brought you and your Crows home, I'll be leaving Luce and the two of you idiots. You can murder each other for all I care.***

Resolve drying my eyes, I stomp beneath Lore and past Dante.

70

Our arrival knocks open a fair share of mouths and eyes. Although wet sand dulls the splendor of my sopping gown, I still stick out like a Fae at a sprite carousal. Thankfully, the three males in full military regalia stick out more.

I shiver as heat envelops my body, pimples my skin, and loosens my joints. I hadn't even realized how nippy it was outside. Fire is a truly wondrous element. As I stare around the small, rustic establishment, I compare it to Bottom of the Jug.

Here, there are no chairs, only benches, the bar can barely fit the two women behind it, and the tables are all communal. Nevertheless, the bare-chested doxies are present. Young men and women with hair down to their shoulders straddle laps, feeding patrons drinks and food using fingertips, teeth, and cleavage. None have spiky ears, but also, none have shaved scalps.

I count three pairs of spiked ears amongst the patrons, and that doesn't include the men I've come with.

The room is silent. Even the giggling harlots have grown as gap-mouthed as the fish smoking over the fire in the large hearth.

"Oh my gods, it's—" One of them stands so abruptly that whatever food she'd smeared on her collarbone for her customer to lick off drops to the floor. "Princci Dante." She curtsies, a glob of brown sauce rolling down the channel between her breasts.

"Sit, please." Dante waves a hand. "No need for any greetings."

A woman with sharp green eyes and cheeks rouged by heat and manual labor walks out from behind the narrow bar. "Altezza, what a surprise. Welcome." She can't help herself from inclining her head. "What can we get you and your riding party?"

"Hay and an attendant for our horses. Food, board, and a bath for us."

"Of course, sire. I'll get one of my lads to watch over them." She whistles, and a young boy in patched-up blue coveralls pops out of what I assume is the kitchen. "Orian, see to our guests' horses."

Tavo sizes him up with a hiked-up lip. "Not much meat on this one. Are you certain he's big enough to fend off potential thieves?"

The woman winds a protective arm around her youngling's neck. "There are no thieves in this part of the kingdom, signore."

Even though she's two heads shorter than Tavo, she holds herself with such dignity that she wins my full admiration.

Tavo mutters, "You're lucky. Our side of Luce is infested with filchers." He looks straight at me as he says it.

I narrow my eyes. What exactly is he accusing me of having stolen? The crows? You can't steal something that doesn't belong to the person who had it. "Just mortals trying to survive, Tavo."

"What about beds and baths?" Dante asks, probably to defuse the tension.

"We have three rooms available. Do you suppose that will suffice? Otherwise—"

"We'll make it work." Dante drops a heavy arm around my shoulders and reels me into the crook of his body. Unlike in the past, my body goes as rigid as a day-old corpse.

I don't say anything as the little boy goes out to our horses and the matron of the house bustles about, clearing the end of one table by shoving diners off benches. Once we're seated, though, I hover my mouth by Dante's stud-lined ear. "One of those rooms will be mine. *Only* mine."

"You must be watched." He grabs a bread roll from the fabric basket a serving girl deposited between the four of us.

Even though my appetite is nonexistent, I take a piece of bread and chomp into it as though it were an apple. "Afraid I'll make off with your enemy and your crown?" I throw him a saccharine smile.

He stiffens so suddenly that his bones creak as he shifts his torso toward me.

I drop the fake smile and the attitude and concentrate on the bread, which is delicious and fills one of the holes inside me. "Luckily for you, I'm uninterested in the Lucin crown."

To plug more of the holes the prince and the Crow have torn, I think of everything I love, everything I'll get back once this is over—Phoebus's squishy heart, Sybille's contagious laughter, Nonna's unwavering affection, Mamma's fiery hair, the crackle of old books, the sweet tartness of berries, the temper of storms, the color of rainbows, the sparkle of stars, the fragrance of the ocean.

I'm sorry, Behach Éan.

I slip more bread between my lips, then chase it down with some water. **Don't hurt the boy tending to the horses.**

His answer seems to take forever to reach me. **I would never hurt a child.**

A pitcher of faerie wine arrives, along with another basket of fresh rolls. And then the food. Although Nonna taught me manners, I heap vegetables and stewed grains onto my plate and dig in before the prince has even served himself.

Stomach blissfully full, I ball my napkin on the table and rise. "I'll see you in the morning. Wake me when it's time to leave."

Tavo shakes the empty bottle of wine over his glass. "Fetch us another jug before you leave, eh."

Is he speaking to me?

He glances past the girl straddling his lap, seemingly perplexed by the fact that I haven't done his bidding. "Oh right... I forgot to add the magic word. *Pefavare.*"

As though tagging a *please* onto his demand makes his request more palatable... "I know this may be confusing, what with this being a tavern and me working in one back home, but I'm not employed by these kind folks." I keep my voice low enough not to stoke up any gossip fires. "But I'll ask Rosa for one on my way up."

Rosa is the grown daughter of our hostess. Together with her mother and four younger brothers, they run the inn her half-blooded father built before he ran off with a Tarespagian pure-blood. I learned all this from a loose-tongued neighbor, who's been scooting closer and closer to our group since we sat down.

Tavo's been jesting that the man will end up climbing atop Gabriele's lap if his friend doesn't set boundaries, but Gabriele is affable, and although he doesn't strike me as someone who'll let another walk all over him, much less sit all over him, he's kept his elbows firmly atop the table.

I stroll away with reinvigorated spirits. "Hey, Rosa, my lovely companions would like another jug of wine."

Rosa, who's three years older than I am—again, a fact I learned from our chatty dinner companion—glances over at them, then back at me. "I'll bring one over. Do you need anything, milady?"

I startle at being called milady when my ears are as round as hers. "Fallon." At her frown, I add, "That's my name. As for whether I need anything, if you could show me to a bedroom and bath, I'd be eternally grateful."

She smiles and grabs a filled jug that she carries over to my riding party. Dante glances away from me long enough to thank her, but then his wary gaze is back on me. It would be a lie to say I don't miss the way he used to look at me, but that gondola has sailed.

One day, I'll find someone who'll love and admire me for who I've become. My mind drifts to Antoni as Rosa returns. Is he thinking of me?

Rosa wipes her fingers on her skirt. "Follow me." She escorts me up a set of narrow stairs and down a corridor that's just as thin. At the very end, she opens the door of a small bedroom with a round, wooden tub. "My brothers filled them with warm water from the village well."

"Your well has warm water?"

Even though she hasn't touched anything, she wipes her hands again on her skirt. "They didn't use their powers."

Her defensiveness tells me that her brothers—probably a water-Fae and a fire-Fae—used their elements to fill and heat the bath. "If I had power, I'd use it for *all* menial jobs. Even if it prematurely depleted my limited stock."

A frown mars her smooth forehead, which is partially hidden behind blond bangs. "Aren't you a half-blood?"

"I am." I sigh. "My power never manifested. I'm still hopeful, though."

"I've never met a half-blood with no magic."

"Well, now you have."

She presses aside a lock of hair tangled with her eyelashes. "I'm sure you know this, but using magic is illegal."

"Ridiculous, if you ask me."

Her pupils widen at my candor.

"The prince agrees with me. Not that you should wield your magic in his presence."

She doesn't talk for a full minute, but then she slides her lips together. "Spiky ears don't frequently travel to these parts. What brings the prince here?"

"We're heading back east."

"This isn't the usual route."

"We wanted a scenic one."

The door hinges groan, making Rosa jump.

I'm half expecting to find Dante or one of his two friends standing in the doorway, but there is only dark air. *Very* dark air. I narrow my eyes on a particularly obscure patch. **Lore?**

Yes, Fallon.

Get out of my room.

What makes you think I'm inside?

My eyebrows rise. Did I imagine the shifting shadows?

Rosa turns toward where I stare, then walks over. "Cobwebs are a real problem in these parts. You're not scared of spiders, are you?" When she swipes her hand through the air, my heart stills.

Sure enough, the shadow disperses. **I can see you.** Lips pinched, I say, "I don't fear spiders."

"The small red ones sting, but as long as you're a halfling, their venom shouldn't have lasting consequences."

"I'll make sure to watch out for small, red, spindle-legged creatures. Thank you for the bath." I try to shoo her out of the bedroom to have words with Lore and shoo him off in turn when I remember one more thing I need. "Any chance I could trade this dress for clean clothes? Preferably trousers and a shirt?"

Her head rears back as though I've asked her to fill my bath with red creepy-crawlies. "Trousers?"

"Perhaps one of your brothers would have a pair?"

"I—I—" She looks me up and down. "I'll see what I can find." I smile at her but receive no smile in return. "Thank you, Rosa."

Forehead pleated, she scurries out the door.

Once the wood settles, I pivot toward the darkest part of the ceiling. **Out. Now.**

The sly king morphs into his bird. One bird, from the size of him. **Lock your door.**

Once you leave.

Because you think a lock will keep me out? His tone is tinged in amusement.

No, because I'm still holding out hope that you're a decent man who doesn't leer at women while they bathe.

He sounds taken aback. *I don't leer.*

My hand slips to my hip. *Oh really?*

You're my curse breaker, he says with a hint of exasperation, as though I'm being childish. *I watch over you.*

I snort at how he justifies himself. *Well, no need to watch over me at the moment. I won't drown in a foot of water.*

If you want to get rid of me, lock your damn door.

Fine. I'd meant to do it anyway. Once the lock clicks, I say, *All done. Now leave.*

Those golden eyes of his linger on my face as he transforms back into smoke. And then they vanish in a dense shadow that slithers toward me.

The room is small but not so small that he can't maneuver around me, yet as his smoke curls through the divide between door and wall, it brushes against my crossed arms, raising a slew of goose bumps.

"Ass," I mutter.

Once he's gone, I turn around and contort my pebbled arms to reach the fastenings of my dress. For someone who doesn't care to be touched, he doesn't seem all that bothered with touching others.

A smile flips up a corner of my mouth as I imagine myself petting him. I bet that would keep him away.

You must truly work on your intimidation tactics, Behach Éan.

What I *need* to work on is guarding my thoughts. But aside from that… *You'd enjoy being petted?*

It depends by whom. And where.

My devious smile warps off my face as my mind tumbles into twisted places. *I'm about to rouse your stone friends. I'm certain one of them will be only too glad to pet her king wherever it is a king enjoys being petted.*

I joust with the laces on my dress, but instead of loosening them, I feel as though I'm tightening them.

Sweat coats my brow as I *finally* manage to shed the dozen or so kilos of damp velvet. Sadly, I fail to shed the image of Lore—the bird—fornicating with one of his other bird people. I squeeze my eyes shut, hoping to squeeze the image from my lids, but that only drives it in deeper.

71

L oud rapping on my door pulls me out of my bath before I'm ready to leave it.

Groaning, I grab the thin towel folded on the chair, shake it out, and wrap it around myself. I'm expecting Rosa with my clothes, but it's Dante with no clothes.

He steps inside and runs his gaze around the room as though he expects me to be entertaining company. Probably a certain crow.

"See." I flourish one hand, keeping the other on my towel. "I'm still here."

Dante's gaze skims my wrapped body.

"Did you need something?"

He closes the door, sealing us in together. "Confirmation you hadn't fled."

"The only place I'm fleeing to tonight is my bed." When he eyes it, I add, "Alone."

He snorts. "Have no fear. I'm not planning on getting into bed with a Crow."

Although I've made up my mind about Dante, I deadpan, "He doesn't sleep in my bed either."

"I wasn't speaking of him."

"Oh, I know." I prop my chin up. "Good thing for you, I don't much desire lying with a man I disgust, so I guess it works out for everyone." I skirt the prince and yank open the door. "Now that you've ascertained my whereabouts, kindly show yourself out, Princci."

His jaw squares as he works it from side to side. "My intention wasn't to cause you pain."

"Perhaps not, but the more you look at me like I'm a monster, Dante, the more you make me feel like one."

"How am I supposed to look at you?" He tosses a hand in the air in exasperation.

"Like I'm still me! Still a fucking girl."

He flinches.

"Still your friend, or whatever I was to you."

He takes a step toward me, looming over my smaller figure, and I think that maybe he'll grip my neck and kiss me. And that maybe, for closure, I'll let him. But then his nostrils flare and he pivots and pounds back into the hallway and into the room across the hall. In a manner unbecoming of a future king, he smacks his door shut.

Then again, the throne was never meant for him.

After closing my own door, I look down at myself, at this body that causes him such disgust, even though my nails haven't hardened into iron talons and my skin remains feather-free.

The lock, Behach Éan.

I slide my lip between my teeth. *He's not coming back.*

Perhaps not, but there are a dozen men downstairs, and although their odds of getting past me are nonexistent, I'd prefer not to soak any floors with blood.

Stomach swishing from the picture he paints, I spin the lock, then pad over to my bed. *Not all conflicts need to be resolved with murder, you know.*

Men don't only bleed when they're dead.

Keeping the towel around me, I sit on the mattress, which is a mixture of soft and lumpy, then lift the sheets that smell like sunshine and tropical bark and burrow beneath them. Since I slept the day away, slumber doesn't wash over me. Not to mention anticipatory nerves are firing everywhere in my body.

Tomorrow, Lore will be almost complete.

What of your fifth crow? The one from the palace? I dim the lantern on the nightstand and watch the play of shadows on the smooth lacquered-wood ceiling.

Its carrier will reach the southern shores just after sunrise.

I picture Giana toting the bowl, because who else could be involved?

It's not—

He stops speaking so suddenly that I sit up in bed and spin the dial on the faerie light. *Lore?*

Nothing.

"Lore?" I whisper before shouting his damn name. "Lore!"

Heart walloping my rib cage, I lunge to the window and prop it open, then stick my head through. The little boy, Orian, sits on a bale of hay, whistling as Furia and the other three horses graze the pale stalks he's scattered around.

My shout or the creak of the window must've alerted the child, because he glances up. "Everything all right, miss?"

"Yes," I lie.

Adrenaline rattles my bones. *Lore?*

I rush toward my door, tripping on a corner of my towel. It takes me three attempts to unlatch my damn door and two to pump the handle and get it open. I'm about to lurch toward Dante's door, but Rosa stands there, eyes wide, arms full.

"I brought you clothes." Her eyebrows hang low over her eyes. Like her brother, she asks, "Everything all right?"

I lie to her as well, forcing a smile and grabbing the clothes from her arms. And then I shut the door in her guarded face and dress, forgoing the sodden underwear drying on the side of the bath. The pants are a little tight and a little short and the shirt a little rough, but I'm too wired to worry whether my pant seams will burst or my nipples will bleed.

Lore? I shout through our bond.

Still no answer. All three of his crows can't possibly have been staked with obsidian.

Since my socks are dripping water beside my underwear, I stuff my bare feet into the boots and lurch out of my room. My fists come down on Dante's door. A gruff, "What?" explodes through the wood.

"It's me."

A moment later, he pulls open the door, a towel knotted around his trim waist, his brown skin glistening with water. To think that chest was pressed against mine a week ago. Not the time for reminiscing, I chide myself.

"What is it? Why are you dressed? In pants, no less."

I blink away from his hard body into his hard eyes. "Lore isn't answering me."

A nerve twitches at his left temple. "And I should care why?"

I rear back. "Because something must've happened to him. That's why you should care."

Just then, footfalls sound on the stairwell, and both Tavo and Gabriele appear, the tops of their heads grazing the low ceiling.

Gaston the sprite weaves between them, chest heaving. "Altezza, Xema Rossi had the dome dug up." He pants fast and hard. "She knows! She knows and has sent sprites to warn the king."

"I told you something was wrong," I hiss at Dante.

Tavo simpers at me. "Who's the boy?"

I roll my eyes, really not in the mood for his brand of humor. Not that I'm ever in the mood for it. "Shut up, Tavo."

The king sails south.

My gaze whirls in time with my heart. *Don't vanish like that!*

I'm sorry, Behach Éan. I had to send my crows in different directions, and I cannot speak unless two of me are near each other.

My heart is still beating out of alignment, but knowing he's not a lump of iron makes me feel infinitesimally calmer. *Well, next time, send me a vision!* Okay, calmer may be a stretch.

Tell them everything I tell you, Fallon. You need to set off tonight. I'll guide your way. Commander Dargento realized my crow was stolen from the palace and has sent a sprite to inform Marco, who's already changed course thanks to Xema Rossi's messengers. He's sailing back around Tarespagia now and should be on the southern front before daybreak.

My jaw has grown so slack, it takes me precious minutes to relay his words.

"Merda," Gabriele whispers.

The Acolti maid reported that you and Phoebus visited the estate recently, so Dargento had your friend picked up and then he forced him to open the vault.

I raise my palm to my mouth as cold fear swamps my chest and moisture floods my lids.

Also, a white-haired soldier rushed to your home.

Cato. That must be Cato. He's a good man. Did he reach Nonna? Did he get them out?

Bronwen and Giana had already gotten them away to safety.

My palm drops to my pounding heart.

They are safe, Behach Éan.

"But Phoebus… Phoebus is not." I whimper.

Lore doesn't deny it. After trembling with adrenaline, my body now shakes with fear.

"What about Phoebus?" Dante says.

"Silvius took him. Took him to-to-to—"

"Can you finish a godsdamned sentence?" Tavo snaps. "Fuck you too, Crow."

Dante sets a hand on my shoulder and squeezes. "Where did Silvius take him?"

"To the vault." I snag my wobbly lip with my teeth.

"What vault?" Gabriele's voice is quiet but tense as a halyard.

"His family's. Where one of Lore's crows was kept," I whisper.

"No more loyal a family to the crown than the Acoltis," I hear someone say.

I don't know who and don't care where the Acoltis' loyalties lie. All I care about is the fact that Silvius has my best friend. The second he discovers that the safe is empty, that Phoebus helped me…

The words he'd spilled inside my ear the day he escorted me to the castle hurtle back into my mind, along with one of the visions Lore sent me. I picture the commander holding a knife to Phoebus's neck instead of Nonna's.

Oh gods, I'm going to be sick. I rush to the bath and throw up my dinner. *Lore, don't let anything happen to Phoebus. Please.*

I've left one of my crows in the east to watch over him.

I scoop out water that hasn't yet clouded with the contents of my stomach and splash my mouth.

You must set off now, though, or Antoni's efforts will have been for naught.

My spine straightens at the mention of Antoni. I spin around. "We leave now. Right now!"

72

The hum of adrenaline grows to a deafening crescendo inside my head, pounding against my skull like the waves beyond the cliffs. I keep picturing Phoebus in shackles. How scared my friend must be. And all because of me.

Cauldron, if anything happens to him, I'll—I cannot think this way. Lore said he'd keep him safe, and I choose to believe he will.

I rush past Dante and jostle his friends.

I hear Dante order Gabriele to follow me and Tavo to settle our bill. As I streak out of the tavern, my vision narrows to a single point. *Ahead.*

Before the day is over, a new order will fall on Luce. One that I will fight to bring about alongside a Crow king and a Fae prince.

I march through the humid darkness, already imagining myself on the southern coast of Luce, freeing Lore's crow from its underwater prison and then smashing the bowl trapping his other.

The boy startles as we come around the corner and springs off the bale, a stick whittled to a point held high.

Gabriele lifts his palms. "At ease, little man. We've just come for our horses."

The boy lowers his arm, which I notice shakes. "You're leaving already?"

I walk toward Furia, my body palpitating as though my heart tore into a thousand pieces and drifted into all my extremities.

"Duty calls." I'm glad Dante sent Gabriele out here with me, because where Tavo is the open sea, Gabriele is a cove. His placid tone manages to calm even me. Not much, but enough to steady my hands as I strap the saddle around Furia.

Dante, thankfully, doesn't take long to arrive. He steps around the corner just as I've swung atop Furia. I think he'll ride his own horse, but instead, he bequeaths Tavo's to the stunned child and latches onto the pommel of my saddle. He nods at my foot. I remove it from the stirrup so he can spear his through and climb on.

I don't make a fuss about having to share, too anxious to head out and sort of touched that the child got a horse out of all this. "That was nice of you. Giving him a horse."

"I didn't do it to be nice."

Right. He did it because he doesn't trust me.

"This better not be a trick, Crow," he grumbles from behind me as Furia leaps forward, wood chips and sand flying every which way.

Thanks to Lore, my stallion knows the way.

There is no give to the circle of Dante's arms. He may not particularly want to touch me, but he also doesn't want to lose me, because I'm the girl who can free the king, who'll make him one in turn.

As we gallop through a landscape lacquered in moonlight, I think of Phoebus and Nonna. I hope they'll forgive me. I remember the disgust in Dante's eyes and suddenly imagine both my friend and grandmother wearing that same look. Where it hurt coming from Dante, it would destroy me coming from them.

I lift my gaze to the deep blue canvas of night, spot a flash of gold and a smear of black high above me. The Crow king is wind and shadow with a touch of starlight.

"How long will it take?" I ask over the roar of the waves crashing against the cliffs.

"Several hours." Dante's voice is tight with nerves.

"Are you ready?" I ask him.

"For what?"

I turn to glimpse his face. "For all this to be yours."

His eyebrows hang so low that his irises appear like pools of ink. "Luce won't be mine, Fallon." At my frown, he adds, "I've agreed to relinquish Monteluce, Racocci, and Selvati to Ríhbiadh. That's half my kingdom."

I blink because this is the first I'm hearing of their deal. "Why?"

"Did you really think the sky king was helping me out of the goodness of his heart?"

"I–I—" The truth is I didn't actually think.

"Crows are selfish, devious creatures, motivated solely by the lure of profit. He's only keeping me around because he wants peace with the Fae, and our people—*my* people—would never answer to a Crow."

"*Your* people? I'm still your people."

"Are you?"

"I roused him for you, you pointy-eared dimwit. I roused him so you could sit on a throne, so stop questioning my allegiance!"

He's quiet for a while. But then he says, "For me?"

"Yes. Hard to believe for a girl who's part Crow, right? Since—how did you put it?—we're all greedy and devious."

His chest rises against my back, his thudding heart fluttering the skin between my shoulder blades. One of his hands lifts off the pommel of the saddle and settles on my stomach. "I'm sorry," he murmurs into my hair. "Be patient, Fal. I've had mere hours to come to terms with all this."

I suck in a breath when his thumb begins to draw arcs over my navel. Just as I curl my fingers around his to tow them down, Lore swoops in front of Furia with a cry that makes the stallion stop so suddenly that my heart and body pitch backward. Both of Dante's hands are on the reins again.

"What the ever-loving Cauldron is wrong with you, Crow?" Dante roars just as the patch of rock we'd been hurtling toward crumbles into the sea.

He's just saved our lives.

Well, mine, because falling a dozen meters onto jagged rocks wouldn't have killed Dante.

Tell the princeling to fucking concentrate on the road instead of on your body, Fallon.

73

Our near spill into the ocean has made our riding party extra vigilant and extra silent. Rock doesn't crumble because of sound, yet no one speaks, not even the sprite perched on Gabriele's saddle.

Since sprites are only quiet when they're asleep or dead, his silence speaks volumes on the precariousness of this road. Especially considering that he has wings, and we do not.

The cliff is so chalky and slick in these parts that we've had to slow the horses to a walk, and still, the rock disintegrates like dried leaves more than once. It feels as though we're teetering on the brink of the very world as we move deeper south.

I'd heard this area of Luce was inhospitable, but I'd never imagined the extent of nature's hostility. I hold my breath when the passage narrows and only release it when my lungs begin to scream for breath.

Are we almost there? I cannot bring myself to use my voice to ask Dante, too afraid it'll affect the solidity of the path.

Almost. Lore's voice is sharp as a blade with not a hint of its former suppleness.

I suppose that he's as tense as the rest of us. He's so close to regaining his humanity. His people. His kingdom.

I cannot believe he bartered to keep so much of Luce for himself, the same way I cannot believe Dante accepted. Then again, did the prince have much of a choice? What will the neighboring monarchies think of a realm split between a Fae and a shifter? Will they accept its new geography? Will they ally themselves with both kings?

Two kings.

The sky has grown brighter, the rising sun having sucked the shadows from the world and painted it in grays and blues. Lore's twin smudges of black are so vivid in the light that I worry a passing ship will spot him.

"Look up."

I jump when Dante speaks because those are his first words since he yelled at Lore before understanding the crow's intent.

"Lore has blown our manufactured cloud cover away and unveiled his city for all of Luce to see."

What a bold move.

Dante's voice is barely above a whisper when he adds, "Marco must be livid."

I crane my neck and look up.

And up.

And then I blink slowly, because windows are carved into the cliff face. This must be another part of the sky kingdom. How far does Lore's home reach?

I must've asked my question out loud because Dante says, "They've built their nests inside every summit on this longitude. This peak is said to house Ríhbiadh's personal quarters."

"I'm surprised it still stands."

"Marco tried to destroy it, but the stone is magicked to be unbreachable. Ropes and Fae-made vines turn to ash. Arrows and cannon balls bounce off. Fae-fire doesn't crack the windows."

I glance away from the windows that shine in spite of the salt coating toward Lore's crows. *You're almost home.*

Both crows pin me with their golden stares. I frown at the intensity and the anger seeping from him. I assumed Lore was tense, but seething?

I won't fail you, I whisper through the bond.

His eyes hold mine a heartbeat. Two. And then his lids swoop low. When they rise again, he's no longer looking at me. He's staring past me at the ocean draped in morning gold that bangs against the craggy walls of Luce as though to shake us off.

I watch it too, my gaze lingering on the pink shores of Shabbe in the distance before traveling back to our shores, to a beached ship whose wooden bow darts out from the foam while the rest of its coral-crusted body remains immersed beneath the surf.

My eyebrows tilt because Antoni has managed to dredge up the ship!

I look for him, catching sight of Mattia's blond mane first, then the baked skin of the sea captain's arms and shoulders, Riccio's deep-brown locks plastered to his head as though he's just emerged from the ocean, and...

And...

"Sybille?" I yell.

74

All four turn their faces skyward.

Oh my gods. Sybille knows about the crows? Since when? Although I've no reason to feel betrayed, I cannot help but wonder why and *how* she kept it from me.

Look at me calling the Cauldron black.

Bronwen must've frightened her into silence the same way she frightened me.

I don't breathe once during Furia's trek down the sinuous path that leads to the cove below, and not because I'm frightened—although admittedly, the path is too narrow for comfort—but because Sybille is here.

Because the galleon is near.

Because we're about to change the course of history.

The second we reach the beach, I jump off Furia and race toward my friend, clasping her in a hug. "What are you doing here? You shouldn't be here."

Antoni's arms are folded, his biceps bulging with both muscle and bargains. "My thoughts exactly, but this one stowed away on my ship. Imagine my surprise when our boat hit that reef, and she popped out of the hull."

"Sybille," I chide her, even though I should probably be more focused on the fact that Antoni's boat sank. That boat is his life. His livelihood.

"Puh-leeze. You fed me a story about bonding with long-lost Bisnonna Rossi. Imagine *my* surprise when I learned what utter serpent doodoo it all was." She sounds angry, really angry, yet she's hugging me back. "You crazy, crazy girl."

"Not to interrupt this heartwarming reunion," Tavo says as he hops off his mare, "but Gaston's just spotted a ship coming around the western point flying the royal flag."

"Fuck, it's going fast." Riccio shoves a wet lock off his brow. "Did the king gather every air-Fae in the kingdom?"

I unclasp my arms and step around Sybille, squinting. Sure enough, the royal vessel is carving up the ocean alarmingly fast.

"Another one's coming from the east," Gabriele announces. "Traveling fast too."

Time to get to work. "Where's Lore's crow?"

"All the Crows are inside the hull." Antoni scrapes a hand through his hair, eyeing the prince and the other two men I've arrived with warily. "Altezza."

Dante gives Antoni the faintest nod. "Greco."

"Oh my gods, that's really him." Sybille's whisper stirs the hair beside my ear.

I tip my gaze up to the source of her awe. "That's really him."

She sucks in her bottom lip, eyes so wide her curled lashes skim her brow bone.

"Can you sense your crow, Mórrgaht?" Antoni asks.

Hearing him speak the Crow title sends me back to the night in the woods when Antoni snapped at Bronwen that I had a right to know. Was he speaking of the fact that Morrgot wasn't the crow's name? That Lore was his own master? That there was an actual man beneath the feathers?

Lore's two crows fly low over the galleon. I hold my breath when a serpent jumps, horn gleaming like fresh snow. Lore shifts to smoke, and the serpent falls right through him. We may have a connection with animals, but the serpent doesn't seem to have gotten the memo that Crows aren't the enemy, which makes my skin prickle.

Minimus's affection must be a fluke. I search for his pink body amidst the reptilian ones writhing around the submerged part of the boat but spot only yellows, oranges, and teals. Lore spins in a circle over the stern of the ship, the farthest point from where we stand.

The wood creaks as the ocean rolls the marooned vessel, tugging on the rigging Antoni and the others hooked between the bow of the boat and the boulders cinching the cove.

They've locked my crow in a cage of obsidian in the captain's quarters. Lore nods to the hull. ***Here.***

I gulp as I measure the length and depth I'm going to have to swim.

"How did four halflings manage to dredge a boat that was way off the shore into this cozy cove?" Tavo asks.

"Using our boat," Antoni says, but a look passes between one of Lore's crows and the captain that hints at something else. Another tool. Another source of help.

"Which is where?"

"On that reef." Sybille jabs her thumb toward the farthest outcropping of sharp boulders jutting from the sea. "Didn't you hear we crashed?"

"What's on your ear?" Dante's squinting at Sybille's earlobe, which bears a hoop speared through with an emerald bead.

The same bead decorates Mattia's and Riccio's ears. Only Antoni doesn't wear one.

She combs her hair forward as though to hide what the prince has already seen.

"It looks like one of Lazarus's healing crystals." Gabriele's gray eyes skip between Sybille and the others.

Lazarus, who healed my arm the day I disembarked on Isolacuori.

Lazarus, who lied about the iron contamination of my blood. Who knew about Marco's involvement in Andrea's death.

Tavo frowns. "The old crone's working against the Regio family?"

Sybille's cheeks puff as she blows out a breath. "He's not working against the Regios. He's working against Marco."

Dante watches the two black birds, which are still circling the area in the ship where their brother rests imprisoned.

"Marco is approaching fast, Fallon." Gabriele's voice cuts through the sudden quiet that's fallen over us.

"Time to get your feet wet, Serpent-charmer." Tavo removes a dagger from his belt and begins to pick at his nails with its point. He better not be contemplating using the blade on the serpents. "Or should I say Crow-girl?"

"Crow-girl?" Sybille's eyebrows are tipped toward each other.

"Haven't you heard?" Tavo points his dagger at the ship. "One of the Crows on that galleon fathered Bottom of the Jug's favorite barmaid. Apologies, Syb. I'm sure the customers like you too. It's your sister they're not too fond of."

I don't think Sybille registers the utter nonsense that came after the fathering bit. "You're part Crow?"

I sigh. "Apparently."

"So, now that we got that out of the way, explain how you hauled that boat"—he gestures to the galleon again—"onto this shore."

"We've been using our combined magic to drag it," Sybille confesses, daring him to tell her they've broken the law.

Tavo twirls his dagger. "Didn't know round ears possessed so much magic, combined or not."

"We've got quite the stock, what with not being allowed to use it on the regular." Sybille flings a dark smile at the spiky-eared soldier.

"With the help of purelings, we should be able to uncover the full ship." Riccio's arms are folded in front of his torso. Like Antoni, he wears only pants. Unlike Antoni, his biceps do not glow with stacked favors.

"Why would we deplete our magic when Fallon's not only a water-Fae but buddy-buddy with the serpents?" Tavo's forehead pleats, and then his neck snaps back. "You don't need to fucking shout inside my mind." Under his breath, he mutters, "Fucking Crow."

"What did he say?" Gabriele asks.

"That the ship's too unstable to swim through," Tavo mutters.

Antoni nods. "It is."

Dante's attention is on his brother's ship. "Too fast. Marco's coming in too fast. We need to hurry." He spins his head toward the ship sailing from the east, the gold beads in his hair clinking. "Dargento's vessel is coming in slower."

I should've known the commander was on the other boat.

"But he's closer."

Antoni claps his hands. "Let's do this!"

"My element's fire, Greco." Tavo holsters his dagger. "So I'm out."

"Riccio is a fire-Fae too." Sybille sweeps her hand toward the dark-haired half-blood whose eyes are so slitted, they appear more black than red. "And he's been key to keeping the serpents away. So I'm sure that for once, we can find you some added value."

Tavo steps up to her. "Careful, little halfling."

"Or what?" Sybille stands her ground, her straight ebony hair gusting around her face as though her magic is seeping from her very pores. "You're going to roast me?"

"Tempting."

She plants her hands on her hips. "Once a bully, forever a bully, huh?"

"Sybille," Dante says gently. "Please. Not now."

Sybille and Tavo glower at each other.

"Tavo, you're going to accompany Fallon on deck and keep your fire at the ready in case the serpents attack," Dante says.

Although the idea of hurting serpents twists my insides, the idea of being swept out to sea by one knots them tauter. Maybe they'll be as sweet as Minimus. A girl can hope.

Tavo's Adam's apple slips up and down his throat. "What about Riccio?"

"He'll go with the two of you." Antoni stares at the circling crows. "Lore's crow is in a cage. She'll need help getting it open."

"It's in obsidian, Antoni! Riccio can't touch obsidian."

Riccio flicks his lobe, making the little emerald bead twinkle. "Thanks to this little trinket, I can."

"It counters the effect on our blood," Sybille explains.

"How nifty," Tavo says. "Lazarus is so full of nifty magical baubles. Where did he claim he gets them again?"

Dante's lips thin. "We'll discuss it later. First, we need to get the crow."

Tavo's unbound hair flutters at his back like a crimson streamer. "How about we set fire to the galleon? Once it's ash, the iron crow statue should be easy to spot."

Antoni shakes his head. "The wood is too damp to catch fire. We tried."

"You tried with halfling flames. Pureling flames—"

"We don't have time to experiment," Antoni growls. "If Marco shows up before we can reach Lore's crow, he'll make sure to bury the galleon so deep, the Crow king will never again be a man."

I suck in a breath.

"That may not be the worst thing," Tavo quips.

Dante's jaw clenches. "He'll only get rid of Marco if he's made whole."

Tavo studies his friend a long moment, and I cannot help but wonder what goes through his mind. Ways to get rid of

Marco without Lore's help? Or perhaps Tavo's contemplating which position he wants in Dante's regime. I bet he'll ask for my grandfather's.

Come to think of it, what *will* become of my grandfather?

The serpents are under Shabbin control. They won't harm you, but don't let on you know they're harmless. The Shabbins don't want the prince to know of their involvement.

I lock eyes with one of Lore's circling crows. Ah...so that explains the look that passed between him and Antoni. *Did the serpents help drag the ship?*

They helped. There's a smile in his voice.

Like a string of paper dolls, Antoni, Sybille, Dante, Mattia, and Gabriele line up, while Riccio and Tavo come up on either side of me. Wind sweeps around my body and whips my hair, pressing against the foaming waves. Slowly the ocean retreats, revealing more of the galleon.

Splintered masts. Bashed decks. Algae-cloaked ropes.

"You're going to have to go fast," Riccio says.

I nod and walk forward, the heat crackling off my two escorts warming the skin through my shirt. "Wouldn't it be faster to swim to the submerged end?"

"Too much current, Fal."

"And serpents." Is Tavo shaking? I didn't think he was scared of anything, but apparently, he *really* doesn't like serpents.

"Follow me." Riccio scales up the figurehead.

"If they don't attack you, Tavo, don't attack them, all right?" I start my climb, using the pointy-eared female figurehead like Riccio did.

He holds out his arm to me, and I clap my hand around it. He yanks me atop the deck that's slick with corals and sea water.

"Hold on to what you can," he instructs, leading the way as Tavo hoists himself onto the vessel.

I close my fingers around the pieces of railing that weren't chewed away by the sea as I follow him across the sloping deck, crushing seashells beneath my boots.

A renegade wave hits the side of the boat, knocking me off-kilter. I begin to slide, but Tavo, of all Fae, grabs my arm, and although he singes my shirtsleeve, he manages to right me. He mutters under his breath how he got stuck with the worst job.

"Soon, you'll have a better one," I tell him. "Focus on that."

I want him to focus on you, Lore growls.

Motivation goes a longer way than threats.

As we head farther down the deck, I soften my knees and drop onto all fours like Riccio. Hand over hand, we scale along the lopsided deck. Another wave bangs against the boat. I shut my eyes and brace myself as the galleon seesaws.

"What the—" Tavo, who's still standing, preferring to hop from one broken mast to the next, shades his eyes.

When his eyes bulge, both Riccio and I twist our necks in the direction of Marco's ship.

"Fuck. Fuck. Fuck," Riccio whispers. "Fuck." And then he scrambles right over me, flattening my body against the deck. "Sorry," he has the decency to mumble.

"Get off the ship! Fallon, get off the ship!" Sybille screeches.

But I cannot get off the ship, and not because I'm frozen in fear of what's coming but because what's coming is about to smash more than just this galleon.

It's about to smash the hopes and dreams of all those on the beach and in the sky.

75

*L*eave my crow! We'll find him again. Lore's two crows fly low, trying to push me back the way I came. *Leave him!*

The cabin's so close. If I sprint down the deck, I can reach it in three seconds flat. I just need to calculate the trajectory so I don't miss the opening and topple off the ship.

Don't even think about it.

But I am thinking about it. How could I not? It's within reach.

"Get off me, Antoni!" Sybille snarls. "There's a fucking tidal wave coming. I'm not leaving without Fallon. Fallon!"

I peer over the edge of the ship at where she splashes in the ocean, Antoni at her heels. "I'm coming, Syb. I'll be right behind you. Go!"

"Not without you!"

I exchange a look with Antoni.

He acquiesces, then grabs her around the waist and slings her over his shoulder, carrying her kicking and screaming away. "Get Fallon off the ship, Mórrgaht!"

I think I hear Lore snarl something, but I could be misattributing the animalistic sound, for a whole slew of them are still pouring from Sybille's mouth.

The boat groans and tips as the water around it is sucked out to sea.

*Fallon... **Get off the fucking boat! Now!***

I eye the captain's quarters, eye the approaching tidal wave, eye Lore's crows. Before my nerves can desert me, I crawl to the middle of the deck.

That's it. I'm flying you off.

Flying me—

His two crows plunge for me, iron talons open as though to snatch my arms.

I scramble to my feet. "No, I'll run. I'll run."

It's not that I think he'll mistakenly spear my skin, but I cannot risk the cage vanishing at sea. Even if Lore can sense his birds, the ocean floor drops off to depths that no Fae, not even purebloods, can swim down to on a single lungful.

The second he pulls up, because for all his talk of not trusting me, he does trust me, I sprint.

Fallon! Lore's cry pierces my eardrums. ***No!***

I tuck my knees against my chest and slide through what once must've held a door but has long since become a gaping opening. The cabin is half-submerged, so my fall is short but wet. My feet hit first. I think it may be the floor, but when I try to stand, one of my boots slip right through what I've landed on.

Fallon! Lore's birds hurtle in after me. One of them reaches out and snatches my flailing arm, its cold talons encircling my bicep. A hiss escapes its beak, and it springs its talons wide.

I must've landed on the cage. Eyes wide, I crouch and stare around, find I'm standing on a black cage inside which an iron bird swings indolently from a chain fitted with a giant black hook.

Anger and horror for what Marco did to Lore pump my veins full of adrenaline. I close my fingers around the cage and yank on my foot to free my boot, then pop my head out of the water, take a deep breath, and dive under.

I swim around the cage until I locate the door. Bracing my feet on either side of it, I grab onto the handle and pull, but it's locked. I glance around the cabin for a key, but if one existed, it's been washed out to sea with everything else in the cabin.

"Merda!" I growl, letting precious air bubbles snake out. I break the surface, take in another lungful of air, and dive again. If my foot slipped through the bars, then my arms will fit.

Lore is screeching inside my mind to get out. Even underwater, I can hear his voice.

How long until the wave hits? My voice is surprisingly calm.

Two minutes, maybe three, but I want you out in one. Let go of the obsidian so I can carry you.

But I do the exact opposite of letting go. I press both my arms, all the way to my shoulders, through the thick black bars. I seize the hook with one hand and the iron crow with the other, and I pull.

And pull.

Until I can feel Lore's crow begin to glide. I scoot my fingers lower on the hook, at the base of where it connects with the iron bird's back, and tug so hard my shoulders scream.

Fallon! Out!

I'm not leaving without your crow.

The crow's body shifts another centimeter, and then another. I reangle the hook and push with both hands on the heavy metal body. Although my eyes burn from the salt, I keep them on Lore's open golden ones. I can feel him watching me. From underneath the water but also from above it.

There's anxiety in his gaze, but there's also pain. So much pain.

I'm sorry if I'm hurting you, I whisper to him, wrenching on his neck while pushing against his wings.

A pop as faint as an air bubble ripples from the metal crow as it slips free from the black spike. I snatch the statue's metal wing before he can sink and hold him aloft. Heart wedged inside my throat, I wait for him to morph back into feathers. Or better yet, smoke.

Until I recall the crow's hiss at the contact of my skin and release him. He stays suspended a moment and then he begins to drop. If his body hits the black bottom of the cage, he won't be able to morph.

Come on. Come on.

The heavy iron drifts lower. Lower.

My lungs squeeze and my vision grays. Keeping one hand on the cage so Lore's other crows can't swoop in and pull me away before I've saved the trapped bird, I stick my head out of the water and gulp in fresh air, then dive back.

The sunbeams slanting through the blown-out hatch window catch on the iron feathers and rain tinsel across the cabin. He still hasn't shifted!

Come on, Lore.

The wave is going to hit in under a minute, Fallon. Don't tell me to calm the fuck down.

I said come, not calm—

Suddenly, the crow stops falling, and the iron tinge of his feathers blackens.

Oh my gods, it worked.

It worked!

The crow's golden eyes stare at me through the metal bars.

Smoke. Become smoke, I urge him.

Get away from the cage, and I'll morph.

I spring my body as far as I can get it from the cage. Lore's outline blurs, clouding the water like ink, and then he carefully slips through the bars of his prison. The second he's free, Lore billows out of the water and slams into his other two crows, which must've already come together, considering the size of the bird that forms.

As I try to hoist myself out of the cabin, the water begins to ripple around me, the boat to shake.

Lore's enormous talons open. Without breaking skin, he cinches my biceps, flaps his wings, and floats me out of the cabin.

A shadow rushes over the sun, over us.

A shadow cast by a wall of water as tall as a boat mast.

My pulse stutters.

Lore's wings beat harder, faster.

Just as it hits me that I'm flying, the wave crests and droplets plummet.

And then something heavier hits us, something that shrieks as it drops from the curl of foam, something that drags Lore's great body down. The serpent smashes against the deck of the galleon, impaling itself on the stump of a mast.

I gasp as blood spurts from its wound and sprays upward.

When I feel it sprinkle my cheeks and lids, I know we're too low. The sky darkens, and still Lore beats his wings.

Even though fear lances up my spine and my heart feels as though it's dissolved into smoke, I whisper to myself, "You know how to swim. You'll be fine."

Lore huffs. *If you land on that broken mast, you will not be fine. Nor will you be fine if you smash into that rock wall. You're not fucking immortal yet, Fallon!*

Such a killjoy, Lore.

The whorl closes in on us.

The shackles of Lore's talons vanish, and I think he's been ripped from me until what feels like arms curl around my waist and something soft presses against the length of my back.

Roll yourself into a ball, I hear him murmur.

I tuck my chin and hoist my knees into my chest, and I swear the pressure around my body increases as though somehow, a shell has formed around me. Soft yet firm. Ethereal yet pulsating with life.

Deep breath, Behach Éan.

I gulp in air that tastes like brine and wind. Like the ocean and the air. Like my world and Lore's.

I squeeze my eyes shut and brace myself for the brutal slap that's about to swallow me whole.

This isn't the end.

This cannot be how it ends.

The wave collapses over us, a mountain of water that feels like an avalanche of snow and a landslide of rock, like Marco Regio brought down the entire mountain on top of us.

76

I spin and spin, get sucked in one direction, shoved in the other. The pressure around my abdomen falls away as the side of my head bangs into something hard before I'm hurled and wrung anew.

I keep my arms locked around my knees and my lips pressed as tight as my eyes.

I'm rolled again and again, jostled and smacked. Sand whips my cheeks and forehead, tangles in my wild hair as the water yanks at my roots like a giant hand. Over and over, I somersault until I don't think I'll ever know the difference between up and down. The pressure against my eardrums grows. I don't want to unpin my arms and risk a limb snagging or breaking, so I thread my wrists through my knees and plug my nose. The pop is instant but the ensuing relief fleeting.

The ocean is still towing and tossing me. Soon, the depth presses against my eardrums again. I squeeze my nose, waiting for the pop, but the only pop I get is that of my back banging against something jagged.

Another lurching undercurrent flows against me, pushing, pushing, but I don't roll this time. Whatever I hit must've snagged my pants. Thank the gods.

The ocean roils and rages around me. Debris flies. Something sharp jabs my cheek. I feel my skin split, burn, and the pain...it almost blackens my mind. But I hold on because passing out will be the death of me.

My lungs squeeze like balled fists as my heart spins, tossing heartbeats like handfuls of sand against my ribs and spine. Mareluce squeals and clanks, bangs and ticks. It feels like forever before the din quiets, before the cacophony is replaced by slower keens and gentler groans.

Only then do I dare part my lids and look at where I've landed. All around me, sunlight dances off floating sand and paints the splintered, ragged edges of wood and corals in color.

I press my palms into the hard surface beneath my back, feeling the smoothness of metal. I push, and something tears. I think it's only fabric until I catch the crimson bloom of blood. I turn to look at what I hit and find the statue of a black bird.

A giant black crow. Hundreds lay scattered around me. Lore's silent, hibernating army.

Whatever part of my body I impaled on the crow's beak mustn't have been too vital because my mind remains sharp. Still, I press my palm into my side. My fingers slip past torn fabric and land against torn skin. I trace the seam of the wound. It's as short as my knuckle but possibly as deep.

My lungs spasm, shifting my worries. I crouch to push off the ocean floor when a shadow slithers over me. I freeze, barely daring to crane my neck. My lashes rise, and I glimpse yellow scales.

The serpent's body brushes across my forehead, my cheeks, against the curved shells of my ears. My lungs begin to cramp. I need to shoot up to the surface. I wait until it swims past me, but the creature's so large and long, it takes him forever to glide out of my path.

The corners of my vision soften. I blink the underwater world back into focus.

I don't know if this serpent will try to attack me. The only thing I know is that I need air. And I need it now.

Without wasting another second, I shoot off the ocean floor, kicking my legs and pushing down the water with open palms. The water stirs around me, flickering yellow. I pump my arms faster, kick my legs harder. The serpent matches my speed before overtaking me. And then it begins to wrap its body around mine like a ribbon. Tighter and tighter. Until I can no longer scissor my legs. My fingertips graze the surface. I'm there. Almost there.

Don't do this, I tell the serpent. *Let me breathe. Let me live.*

But the serpent isn't like Lore. He cannot understand me.

His body becomes a noose as his equine face levels on mine, his eyes, black from lid to lid, holding me in their stare. I'm twelve again, in the Tarecuorin canal, but instead of a juvenile serpent with pink scales, I'm in the presence of a full-fledged adult.

The serpent drags his nostrils over the top of my head while I dig my fingers into his body, trying to glide up and out.

Fallon. My name skates toward me, liquid like the current, pliant like Lore's smoke, soft like his feathers.

Here! I shout back through the link before pushing harder at the body wrapped around mine.

My lungs are on fire, an inferno that's chewing me up from the inside. My squirming only makes the serpent's body stiffen.

I change tactics because the beast will end up breaking me, even if he doesn't mean to. I raise my palms to his face and stroke down either side of it.

The creature opens his mouth, his teeth shining like needles. I stroke down his long face again, never staring away from his eyes. I shape the word *please* with my lips. His body rattles, and I'm not sure if it's from pleasure or if it's a warning he's going to snap my bones like the ocean snapped the galleon.

Fallon!

The roar of my name makes me jolt. The creature yanks his

face from my lax grip and hisses. At first, I think he's hissing at me, but he's scanning the depths as though seeking out the source of my agitation.

I palm his hard cheek, attempting to calm him, and for a second, I think I succeed because his body stops crushing mine, but then something cuts into the water beside us, and the beast drags me down to the smashed galleon so fast my ears begin to throb.

I frame the beast's large head between my palms and force him to stare at me, and then I nod to the surface. The serpent jerks to a stop. I nod to the surface again. A small crab sails between our faces as he blinks. In understanding? Please let him have understood me.

My name resonates again, but it sounds faint, like it's coming from the other side of Luce. From the other side of the world.

The serpent's tongue darts between his lipless mouth and glides up one side of my face, then up the other. He rattles once, and then…and then he finally releases me. I try to tip my head toward the surface, try to kick, but I've no strength left. I stare at the yellow beast who has remained at my side and reach out for him, hoping he'll carry me up, but before my fingers can close around his scaled body, something cold and hard cinches my wrist and biceps, something that gleams pewter in the sandy sunlight.

Panic seizes me anew until a familiar timbre bites into my skull. *You never, ever disrespect a direct order from me again.*

The serpent watches me float up, his black eyes gleaming in the gold of his scales.

Never.

When cool air smacks my cheeks and forehead, I gasp in a breath that burns. *Although I appreciate you coming back for me, you aren't my master, Lore.* I don't say this to anger him, only to remind him. *I'm not one of your Crows. I don't belong to you.*

O ach thati, Behach Éan. Inky smoke coalesces around me,

knitting into a gossamer face before unraveling and hardening into black feathers and eyes that hold an unfair amount of power. *Thu leámsa.*

"What in Luce does that mean?"

Lore's beak doesn't curve, yet I can feel his dark smile. *That you, Little Bird, belong to the sky.* The crow emerges fully from the rocking surf, dark and huge, larger than I've ever seen it, a monster of down and iron. *And the sky...it belongs to me.*

77

A wavelet socks my face in time with Lore's arrogance. I gag on both salt and his words. No one *owns* the sky, the same way no one *owns* the sea, the same way no one *owns* me.

His great wings, which span the length of my body, flap as though to disprove my claim. As he rises from the surf, he swirls around my body, and I swear I feel the brush of fingers along my neck, the stroke of a thumb along my jaw.

I grit my teeth. I'm not sure what game he's playing. I've already promised to free all his crows. What more does he want from me? Subservience? Allegiance? He may be a king, but he's not mine, and he'll never be mine. ***Let's get this over with before I change my mind about making you whole.***

He clicks his talons into place around my arms, and I wind my fingers around his legs harder than necessary. I doubt it hurts him, what with his legs being made of solid metal.

As we rise, I keep my gaze on the ocean, on the winding serpent bodies and the approaching vessels that look no bigger than the model ship we built with Phoebus when we were children, the one Tavo knocked off our shared desk and crushed beneath his shoe.

Not that I was beginning to appreciate the male, but the memory burnishes my dislike of him and reminds me to warn Dante against making him part of his new regime.

I search for the prince amidst the line of bodies darkening the cliff's edge, my eyes widening when I find him tucked in the shadow of a giant male garbed in black robes. *Is that—is that Lazarus?*

It is.

What is he doing here?

He brought you my last crow.

How on earth did Bronwen sway him?

It doesn't take much to sway a man whose ruler killed his lover.

Killed his...his lover?

Andrea Regio.

Oh. Wow. I wonder if Dante's aware.

He isn't, and Lazarus would appreciate it staying that way. I won't speak a word of it.

Sybille's sudden howling of my name interrupts the chat I'm having with Lore in the middle of the sky. Her cheeks are shiny with tears that she keeps swatting away.

Antoni has one hand on her shaking shoulders while Mattia and Riccio stand behind them, eyes on the sky, on us. Sybille yowls that she's done being my friend.

I smile because I know she doesn't mean it.

Lore flies us a little to the right of the group, toward a wider area shaded by a single tree. I brace myself for impact, but our landing is gentle. Still, when my bare feet touch the ground, pain flares along my side, and my knees buckle.

Lore tightens his talons around my biceps as though sensing my lack of strength and eases me onto all fours before releasing me. I hunch over, glad for the firmness of dry land, glad that this endless day is almost over, because all of me stings, chafes, and spasms.

The pain worsens when Sybille barrels into me, girding my crumpled body in an embrace. "Don't you dare tell me how to handle my friend, Lorcan Ríhbiadh! She was stuck in that ship because of you! She almost drowned because of you!" Although her voice hurts my ears and her hugs hurt my skin, I don't push her away. "I don't think you understand how many years you knocked off my existence with that stunt!"

I smile into her neck, breathing in the sweet scent of air that forever lifts off her skin. "I'm sorry."

She snorts as though she finds my apology ridiculous, but then she's crying again.

"Not to interrupt," Tavo's voice grates my eardrums, "but Marco's boat will reach the bay any second, and you still have one crow to go."

I pull away from Sybille and follow his nod to something wrapped in several layers of jute and fabric, then look beyond Tavo's legs at the titanic healer whose ears gleam red and blue and green from all the earrings fringing the tall shells.

"Lazarus brought it. He arrived just as the wave—" Her lip wobbles. Although she snags it with her teeth, a soft whimper drops out.

I cup her wet cheek. "Look at me. I'm fine."

"You don't look fine. You look horrid. Like you wrestled a boulder and lost."

A laugh bubbles out of me. "Thanks for the kind words, Syb." She grins.

"And for your information, although I didn't wrestle any boulders, I did tussle with a giant wave before being impaled on one of Lore's friend's beaks, and then a sea serpent took a liking to me."

Her jaw drops open. "Oh my gods," she whispers.

A tusk pokes from the water, followed by a large yellow head. The beautiful beast who licked my face jumps, the coils of his long body cutting through the water that now cloaks the beach and outcropping of rocks.

Lazarus approaches, cutting off my view of Mareluce and my serpent. "I hear you have wounds that need mending."

I bite my lip, wondering who he heard it from. A glance over my shoulder shows a crimson stain on my wet shirt. I guess he saw it.

He crouches. "May I?"

I nod, and he rolls up the hem of my shirt.

Sybille hisses at the sight. "Is that her—is that her bone?"

Antoni, who's walked up behind Lazarus, presses his lips together so hard they vanish. I'm guessing my flesh must look pretty mangled.

The healer touches one of his beads, then presses the pads of those fingers to my wound.

My skin burns, crackles. I grit my teeth and ball my fingers.

"Apologies, Mórrgaht, but pain relievers will slow the healing process. I imagined you preferred to expedite it."

I lift my gaze to Lore's. "Yes. Expedite it."

Lore, who broke into four crows upon landing, circles us, restless and impatient.

Wasn't his fourth bird protecting Phoebus? Does that mean Phoebus is safe?

He's alive.

Except alive doesn't always mean safe. Since Lore seems preoccupied, I decide not to pester him. My friend is alive, and soon, he'll be safe. That's all that matters.

As Lazarus rubs another healing crystal and brings his fingers back to my blistering flesh, I ask, "That day on Isolacuori, you knew there was iron in my wound." It's not a question; it's a deduction. "Did you know it had come from Lore's crow?"

"I guessed it when I smelled obsidian on your skin." He kneads my skin as though coaxing the tissues to knit faster. "Bronwen warned me a girl would come when it was time, so I was expecting you."

"Did you know who I'd be?"

"No. That woman guards her secrets more ferociously than serpents guard the riches lining their den."

"Do they really hoard riches?"

"When the glowing jellies flow across the channel in the dead of winter, you can see all the way down into their lair, which resembles a vein of gold and diamonds. Have you never witnessed it?"

I shake my head.

"It's spectacular." He touches another bead on his ear, then moves his fingers toward my temple, but instead of pressing them to my skin, he brushes away a lock of my wet hair.

"What is it?"

Lazarus lifts his gaze to the halo of black crows. "The wound on your temple. It has already healed. His Highness says it's a serpent's doing."

Oh. Warmth floods my chest at the memory of the beast's ministrations and at the realization that I truly do have a special connection with the beasts who inhabit our waters.

I look toward the man who nicknamed me Serpent-charmer. He hasn't moved from where he stands on the edge of the cliff, attention riveted to his brother's ships. Is he second-guessing his decision to have Marco killed?

No. He's impatient for his reign to begin.

I understand that you don't have much love for the male, Lore, but Dante's not completely unfeeling.

He's willing to have his own brother beheaded.

As though he feels his name on our minds, Dante glances over his shoulder, first at me, then at Lore's airborne crows, before turning back toward the two ships incising the frothy sapphire.

Although no one tells me to hurry, I push myself up.

Slowly, Lore growls, flying dizzyingly fast around me as though to make sure one of his crows will be there to catch me should gravity fail me.

Sybille winds her arm around my waist.

Lore's crows flock higher, giving us space to maneuver, but his eyes, all four sets, stay on me.

To think that soon, those eyes that have tracked me for days across forest, jungle, mountain, and ocean, from dusk till dawn, will no longer look my way. For all our verbal sparring and our inability to see eye to eye on essentially every subject, I'll miss the stormy sky king.

I kneel in front of the package. Although Sybille wears a bead that protects her from obsidian, I make her stand back as I unwrap layer after layer. The bowl appears, its iron and gold shine dulled beneath pooled wax.

"How do I pry you out?"

Turn the bowl over.

I do, and my jaw clenches. Obsidian nails are hammered through the iron. Dozens upon dozens of them. I clamp my fingers around one and tug.

It doesn't slip out.

Twist it.

I twist and it loosens. What I assumed were nails are long obsidian screws.

"Maybe you should start twisting, Syb," Tavo suggests. "You know...what with this being a race against time and all."

I hiss at him. "She can't touch iron, you fool."

He sighs before copping a look at Lazarus. "Maybe Luce's favorite healer has a special earring to counteract iron?"

Lazarus folds his thick arms and raises his chin. "Only Fallon can break the curse of obsidian."

"Well then, I guess we're fucked."

I hurry, but not for Tavo's sake. I hurry so as not to draw out the crow's suffering.

Perspiration coats my brow by the time I call out, "Last one."

"That's what you said the last three times!" Tavo exclaims, pacing.

I nod, combing over every millimeter of iron, first with my eyes, then with my fingertips. The only things I feel are the holes that have yet to mend. As I toss aside the last screw, Lore's crow slips off the gold dish and lands on my lap. I scoop him up and hold him aloft, willing the perforations to fill and the iron to blacken.

He watches me through the wax still clouding his citrine eyes, weight slowly lightening, shell slowly softening. His rapid heart-beats fill my palm and mingle with my own feverish ones.

A tear rolls down my cheek at the magnitude of what I've just accomplished. Me, a girl from the wrong side of the canal with curious blood and no power.

I press my shoulder against my cheek before the tear can drip onto Lore.

"She's done!" Tavo screeches, tearing me out of the moment. "She's finally done!"

I'm tempted to silence that one before I take care of the king. He retracts his wings, dragging his velvet feathers across my clammy palms.

I snort. *Rein in the temptation.*

A feat you're asking of me, Behach Éan.

"Dante!" Gabriele shouts, tearing my attention off Lore and flinging it to the sky, to the giant fireball coming straight for us. "Watch out!"

Lore slips out of my hands and slams into his crows. Before my next heartbeat, a bird the size of a man streaks through the air, right for Marco's missile. I stagger to my feet and race to the cliff's edge.

He better not be about to do what I think he's about to do.

Large hands wind around my biceps and tug me back, but I drag my feet, fighting the person's hold. "My apologies for restraining you, but His Majesty threatened to return me to Isolacuori if you receive so much as a scratch, and I've no desire to return to Fae court."

Nothing he says makes sense. Which Majesty? Dante?

I must speak the prince's name out loud, because Lazarus bends his head nearer mine and whispers, "No, Signorina Rossi. Lorcan."

78

I glance up at Lazarus with a raised eyebrow for a half second, but then Sybille gasps, and my eyes are back on Lore.

Lore, who has plucked the ball of fire right from the sky and holds it between his talons. He whirls and releases it. The screams that rise from the king's vessel threaten to derail my heart and shatter my eardrums. Every air-Fae on deck must be blowing wind into the sails, because they bloat and shoot the vessel out of the fireball's path.

Arrows rise. Some gold, some black.

I scream.

"Shh, child. Don't distract him." Lazarus presses his meaty palm against my quivering lips as Lore breaks into his five crows and ascends so dizzyingly high that I lose track of him behind a thin cloud.

The arrows plummet like toothpicks just as a wave smashes into the ship's hull. It's nothing like the one Marco had his air-Fae fashion, but it makes the boat list and the mast skim the water. When it rights itself, half of the Fae on the deck have vanished into Mareluce while the other half are scrambling around a man dressed entirely in gold and another garbed in gilded burgundy with unbound orange hair.

"Why hasn't the Crow army risen?" I hear Sybille ask Antoni.

Both stand beside me, eyes riveted to the spectacle, while mine remain locked on Justus Rossi. Even from this distance, I can feel my grandfather watching me, reviling me.

"Because he must voice the old words out loud," Lazarus explains. "Which he can only do in his human form."

"Maybe he should take a minute to shift, then," Sybille says before gasping as more fireballs surge, this time from the vessel commanded by Silvius Dargento.

As though he sees the attack as a game, Lore's crows bat the flaming spheres with their wings, sending them hurtling into the sails of both ships.

One scorches the mast of the king's vessel; another tears through the sails of Silvius's. Although the Fae stream water onto the fire, the boats become flaming rafts.

"How many purelings do you suspect are pissing themselves?" I hear Riccio ask Mattia, who murmurs, "Not as many as halflings."

"There are no halflings in the royal ranks, Matt. We're not good enough for the royal guard."

"Done!" Tavo exclaims. "It's done!"

What is?

I squint and make out one of Lore's crows shooting away from the sinking vessel, something gold glinting between his talons.

Something gold and—

Is that—

I swoon, and the world becomes as black as the crow carrying the king's head.

79

I come to just as Lore reaches the cliff and drops Marco's severed head at Dante's feet. The crown is still tangled in the fallen monarch's braids.

"Oh…my…gods." Sybille heaves, and then she spins around and sprints toward the tree to retch.

I scrutinize Dante's face, looking for remorse or disgust or something, but the male is stone-faced and so calm, it raises every hair on my body. He crouches, stares into the amber eyes that are already clouding with death, then pries the sunray crown from his brother's hair, scrubs it against his dust-streaked white pants, and sets it atop his head.

"Long live the king!" Gaston bellows as Tavo and Gabriele swoop into bows and holler their joy.

I can barely breathe, much less bow. If Lazarus wasn't still holding me, I would've joined Sybille by the tree.

Dante's eyes find mine through the bright noon day. "Thank you, Fallon."

It feels like he's thanking me for his brother's death, and I don't want gratitude for that. I flick my gaze to the side, stomach in a vise.

"I'll never forget what you've done for me. For Luce."

I don't nod. Don't say a word. My throat is too clogged by horror to speak.

"We should go. We've a kingdom to rule, Dante." Tavo swings himself onto his horse.

I narrow my gaze on the soldier with the delusion of crown ownership. "*We?* Luce belongs to Dante and to Lore. Not to you."

Tavo's amber eyes flare. "Lore, huh? Where's the almighty buzzard anyway? Fishing out his warriors?"

I blink away from the hateful male and squint at the sea, searching for black feathers. Or black smoke. Or whichever form the sky king has taken. When I can't spot him, I begin to panic. Where is he? Where did he go? If he left without saying goodbye, I'll—

You'll what, Behach Éan?

The sound of his voice soothes the erratic muscle pounding behind my ribs. *Get really angry at you.*

Ah…for a change. Makes me impatient to return.

The corners of my mouth kick up but then flip down when I finally spot him lurching from the chaotic waves of Mareluce, a body balanced between the talons of his five crows. Blond hair swings from his charge's head.

Even though there are a million blonds in Luce, I know that body.

I know that hair.

I know that apple-green shirt.

My eyes mist over. "Sybille!"

"What?" she croaks.

"Sybille!" A sob blots my voice's power.

"What?"

"Syb!"

"Oh my gods, what is it, woman?"

"Phoebus."

"Is she having a meltdown?" Sybille's footfalls plod closer. "Why is she calling out everyone's names?"

I point to the listless form dangling beneath Lore.

A breath whooshes from Sybille's lips. "What—What the—Is that—Phoebus?"

"He must've been on Silvius's ship," I whisper.

"Why?"

"Maybe he stowed away like some other person I know," Riccio quips, which earns his arm a slap from an unamused Sybille.

"Have you met the commander? No one would willingly stow away on his ship. Unless—Do you think he was trying to stop him from charging over here?"

"He didn't stow away. Silvius brought him here." I shudder from the memory that the commander painted inside my head of torturing all those I love to get to me.

I hope Minimus found the vile man and crushed every bone in his body. They may regenerate, but as long as he can't swim, he can't harm me and mine.

"Brought him here to do what?"

"As a negotiating chip." I refrain from telling her that his intention was probably to cull his head with a steel blade, telling her instead about our trip to the Acolti safe.

I count Lore's wingbeats, follow his landing. The second he deposits Phoebus, I leap toward my friend. There's blood on his forehead, blood on his chest, blood on his thigh.

Lazarus kneels beside me, already fingering his crystals. "Are any of these wounds from your talons, Mórrgaht?"

"No, Lazarus." The words are so crisp that they sound spoken out loud, but Lore can't—

I snap my gaze off Phoebus's purple-tinted lids and onto a pair of legs clad in black leather. I track the legs to trim hips and a torso that flares beneath a dark cuirass and iron pauldrons. To a honed neck as sinewy and solid as the rest of the male. To a face with eyes that glow the darkest gold and hair so black it glints blue.

My ears begin ringing, my veins prickling. I've seen Lore in a vision and then in a dream, yet the male standing over Phoebus and me feels like a complete stranger. "Lore?"

"Álo, Fallon."

"Hot damn, I've reached the overworld." Phoebus's voice makes my eyes jump off the human embodiment of the Crow king and onto the Fae's opened green ones.

I smile, tears tripping down my cheeks. "No, Pheebs. No, you're very much alive."

"Are you quite certain, Piccolina, because—" His attention surfs back to Lore, who's still watching me as though I was the one who shape-shifted. "*Ouch*. What was that for, Syb?"

"See? You're alive. And staring lewdly at one of Luce's new monarchs," she adds under her breath.

He blinks, but his shock is quickly supplanted by a hiss as Lazarus heals him with his magic crystals.

I don't move away, but my eyes drift off Phoebus and back onto Lore, whose dusky pink lips move over foreign words that sound almost like a chant: "Tach ahd a'feithahm thu, mo Chréach."

"What is he saying?" Sybille asks me.

"I don't know. I don't speak Crow."

He turns his face toward the sea and bellows those same words, again and again. *Tock add a faytham thoo, mo kreyock.* They scatter goose bumps along my skin as they surge through the air, spill from the cliffs, and spread over the ocean.

The stone beneath my feet begins to tremble, the sea to froth, the sky to hum.

Lore repeats his chant, his timbre as low as his dense, sooty lashes. It is almost as though he's praying, and perhaps he is. He's spent two decades trapped and tortured, far from his people, powerless, and before that, five centuries. I cannot fathom the depth of his loneliness and pain, of his horror and fury.

If I were him, I'd raze the world and every Fae in it.

When he turns his sunset irises on me, I pull in a breath. His eyes burn, torching their way past my unguarded ones, and I'm suddenly gone from the cliffs and back in that room with my father and some woman I've never seen before. Her eyes are cast downward on a slightly rounded abdomen, which she keeps stroking. I take it she's pregnant.

You must leave tonight, Zendaya. The voice surges from billows of black smoke that keep tearing and weaving into the shape of a giant crow. Even faceless, I recognize Lore, whose voice has become as familiar to me as Nonna's. *You'll only be safe back in Shabbe now that Justus Rossi knows you carry the curse breaker.*

What if—What if they find a way to strengthen the wards? What if I can't re— Her voice breaks, and a sob lurches from her full lips, shaking the river of dark auburn locks that runs down her back, all the way to her waist.

My father moves toward this bereft woman, and although his shoulders are straight, his dark eyes are rimmed crimson as though he's been blinking back tear after tear. He folds Zendaya into a fierce hug and kisses the top of her head.

I glance at vision Lore, wondering why he's showing me this scene. To prove my father is compassionate?

When I turn back, I find the woman's eyes resting on me, and my heart...my heart stops because her irises are bright pink. She's Shabbin. This woman crying in my father's arms is Shabbin.

My father lifts his knuckles and wipes the woman's shiny cheeks, and then he cradles both sides of her face between his fingertips and presses his forehead against hers. His mouth shapes words in a language I've never heard and yet understand. *Our daughter will thrive, Daya, my love. Bronwen's seen it. Our little raindrop will survive.*

As their lips meet, I'm thrust out of the vision.

Or perhaps I thrust myself out of it.

Chill after chill sweeps up and down my spine. My teeth chatter. My breastbone rattles from my runaway pulse. Although the abounding blueness is filled with noise and movement, my mind is stuck on the vision Lore sent me. It replays it and replays it and replays it until I think I will go mad.

I pull my arm from Sybille's and steeple my fingers against my forehead. "I don't understand."

Did the Shabbin woman lose her baby and then he made a new one with my mother, which he ended up naming Raindrop as well? How utterly messed up would that be?

That child lived, Fallon. Lore's eyes are as dark as the sweeps of black powder he wears around them.

I have a half-sister?

No.

Then... My eyebrows bend, rise, bend. Is Lore saying—Is he— "Nonna saw me come out of my mother. She *saw* me."

Oh my gods. I stagger backward. I'm a changeling!

Lore doesn't refute my claim, which means—I lift my palm to my mouth to stifle a shout.

Marco was right. I'm half Shabbin. *Shabbin!*

Mamma didn't suffer because she lost the love of her life or the peaks of her ears. She suffered because someone stole her child and gave her...*me.* Anger gores my chest, draining the lingering thrill of what I accomplished today.

I rake my hands through my hair, tugging at the roots. *My whole life has been a lie!*

Not a lie. A secret.

My vision blurs, turning Lore into smears of gold, black, and white. How can he justify what they did? It was cruel and unfair to so many. I drive the heels of my hands into my temples.

Nonna gave up her life and status for nothing.

Mamma lost her mind.

Glaring at Lore, I walk toward where Dante sits on a horse, *my* horse, observing the dark shadow growing larger beneath the chaotic whitecaps. "Make room, Maezza."

His gaze jumps to me before lumbering to a space beyond my head. I don't need to turn to know who holds his attention. His answer takes so long to come that I've no doubt the man complicit in ruining lives is speaking to him. "I'm sorry, Fal, but I cannot take you back."

"Then get off my horse, and I'll take myself back."

Dante's mouth pinches at my lack of decorum, but I cannot find it in me to be decorous. He lowers his voice. "As your friend, I cannot let you return. It's for your own safety."

"My safety? Are you fucking kidding me, Dante?"

"You betrayed the crown."

"To help you!"

"The Fae won't see it like that. They'll see you as the traitor who got Marco killed."

I toss a hand in the air. "Then set them straight! For Cauldron's sake, you're the king now. Act like one!"

Tavo shoves his horse between us. "Watch your mouth, Fallon."

I flip him off.

"Did Fallon just give someone the finger?" I hear Phoebus ask as Tavo spurs his horse forward.

"Her Crow side must be manifesting." Sybille sounds border-line proud.

"Ríhbiadh." Dante's attention rises to the thickening cloud of birds. "We shall leave you to your reunion." He taps his heels to Furia's flanks, and my traitorous steed shoots forward.

"Expect a visit from me within a fortnight." Lore's black hair swirls around his head as his fellow Crows begin to descend.

"We'll be waiting with bated breath," Tavo mutters before the three males take off down the mountain, sprite in tow.

I turn toward Lazarus, whose gaze is taped to the storm cloud of black birds blunting the sun. Like their ruler, they are beastly. "Lazarus, are you staying or heading back to Isolacuori?"

The healer blinks away from the dark swirl. "I'm staying."

"Can I take your horse?"

"You—"

A whinny cuts across the hum of feathers as his horse rises onto his hind legs and takes off down the mountain.

I ball my fingers. I don't know if it's Lore's doing or an unfortunate coincidence, but I won't let it deter me. "I guess I'll walk then."

"Fallon, are you crazy? You can't walk back," Sybille yells over the swelling hum of stirring air.

Phoebus links arms with her to block me. "She's right, Piccolina. You can't walk back. You don't even have shoes."

"I don't need shoes to walk. I need feet."

Phoebus sighs. "Sweets…"

"How are you two getting home?"

Sybille glances toward Antoni. "Lore is replacing Antoni's ship. It should arrive in a day or two. He'll take us home then."

A day or two…

I'm not spending another minute here. I try to sidestep them, but they shuffle as one. "Get out of my way."

"Not happening, Fal."

"Get. Out. Of. My. Way," I bite out as a whirlwind of dust and feathers churns around us, spraying grit into our eyes and lifting our hair.

Iron and down recede, making way to flesh and hair. Phoebus's and Sybille's mouths grow slack as men and women with dusky eyes and inky hair stretch up and fill out. Although my gaze strays to the strangers, I use my friends' distraction against them and lunge around Phoebus.

I succeed in taking two steps before I bang into a wall of black leather and iron armor. I tip my chin up and channel my indignance into the golden eyes staring down at me. "Move."

The Crow King does not budge.

"I'm done here." I refuse to fall back. "You and I are done, Lorcan Reebyaw."

The gold ringing his pupils seems to churn. "You and I are just beginning, Fallon Báeinach."

EPILOGUE

Lore

Fallon's pupils shrink in the violet depths of her irises. "I'm no more a Báeinach than you are worthy of being called a king."

I cannot help the smirk that cocks my lips. I've met many women in my long life, but none so full of...*verve* as Cathal and Zendaya's daughter. Her character should come as no surprise, considering her lineage.

Her voice drops, and although she means to make herself sound threatening, the effect achieved is far from it. "Move before I shove you onto your ass in front of all your people."

My smile grows. How could it not? This slight girl may have the willpower of a serpent, but she could no more fell a tree than she could push me. "Mórrígan's humor never ceases to amaze me."

Fallon's dark eyebrows slant in that small frown that so often touches her brow when her mind absorbs something new. She's attempting to discern our goddess's identity without having to ask.

As swiftly as they kissed, though, her eyebrows spring apart, and her delicate chin rises a notch. "I don't know who this Mórrígan person is, and I don't care. Now, flit the fuck off, Morrgot."

That slur subdues my smile. "Don't speak like that. It's unbecoming of such a lovely mouth."

Her pupils flare at my reproof.

"As for Mórrígan, she's the Mother of Crows. A Shabbin witch from your bloodline. I suppose you weren't taught about her in Fae school."

Her mouth, usually so fast to curve with delight, is no more than a stroke of red in her sun-kissed face. Even livid, she is exquisite. Who knew Cathal with his crooked nose and difficult jaw could produce a girl like this one?

Even though I don't unfasten my gaze from Fallon's, I can feel him watching us. He hasn't yet recovered his speech. By nightfall, words should flow from my Crows. We've only been gone two decades this time.

After our five-century-long absence, it had taken my people several weeks to regain use of their atrophied tongues.

I wonder how long I will detest myself for having subjected them to our obsidian curse so soon after we'd escaped it. If Marco hadn't threatened the humans, I would've let them live and remained a shadow whilst the curse breaker matured.

My fingers twitch at my sides, coated with the phantom stickiness of all the lives the Fae spilled to strong-arm me into surrendering.

We will get our vengeance.

Soon.

Fallon's palms land on my breastplate in an attempt to push me away. Her knuckles pale, yet all I register are her frenzied heartbeats and heated pants. She huffs a growl.

I'm sorry, Behach Éan, but I cannot let you leave.

She stops pushing long enough to pour her anger into my mind. *You cannot?* She snorts. *Good thing it's not up to you, Bilbh Éan.*

My eyebrows tip in time with one corner of my lips. *Working on your father tongue, I see.*

She scowls. *All this may be some great joke to you, but it's not to me.* "I'm done being used. Now, let me pass. I need to get home to my grandmother and mother—"

The sound of hooves beating down on the soft pale stone of the mountain draws her gaze off mine. Does she expect her cowardly prince to have returned for her?

My jaw still aches from how hard I clenched it when he put his hands on her body. How tempted I'd been to sever his wrists and his neck, but Fallon would never have forgiven me. She hardly seems like she'll forgive me for having kept her family tree a secret.

"Giana?" Fallon's pretty lips pull apart, tugging me out of my unpleasant reminiscence. "Bronwen?" Her hands are still on my chest, radiating warmth through the thick leather, lashing my pulse with her own.

Though I sense this may be the last time she touches me for a while, I shift into my five crows and hook her clothing with my talons. Before her next breath and subsequent snarl, I've carried her to the rooftop of my home, through the hatch door my Crows have already unlocked, and into the old stones of my home.

I set her down gently, then shift back into my human shape. "Your family and friends will be brought up shortly. Shall I show you around your new home, Behach Éan?"

"This place will never be my home!" she snarls as more Crows swoop inside and soar down the quiet hallways, filling them with beautiful noise.

I lay my hand on the cool stones that hold so many memories. Joyful ones but also tragic ones. "Wasn't your dream to live in a castle and sit on a throne?"

The tide of her anger swells like the breakers dashing against the foundations of my home. Even though I am its mark, I can appreciate its beauty.

"Are you offering me your throne, Lore?"

Her answer takes me by such surprise that a sound my

lungs haven't produced in years...in centuries...erupts from me—laughter.

And Fallon...

She spoils me with a smile intended to maim my dark heart, and I devour it beat by beat.

Read on for an exclusive bonus retelling of chapter 57 from Lore.

57

Lore

I'm broken, Mórrgaht. You broke me."

Fallon's words haunt me long after she falls asleep, repeating on an endless, torturous loop that makes me wish I could thrust this mission upon someone else. But as long as the wards between Shabbe and Luce stand, I've no choice but to enlist this innocent girl.

I grimace. Fallon may be young in years but her body is that of a woman. One that Mórrígan decided to make mine.

I've yet to recover from the shock of finding Fallon strolling in my dreams. Of her voice in my mind. It isn't that I believed I'd never be blessed with a mate, but I didn't expect *her.*

My heart feels suddenly too large for my corvid form, so I shift into the only other form accessible to me at the moment—my shadows. The wild beats of my heart disseminate through the gossamer web, making it puff like Selvatin sand as I drift nearer to Cathal's daughter.

Oh, how my friend will fulminate. Imagining his reaction fills me not with trepidation, only with dark delight. But that delight rapidly wanes as I dwell on the perils left to come and the fact that the woman tasked with my resurrection isn't yet immortal.

As my gaze strokes up the creased sheets twisted haphazardly around her long legs, fear and dread war with wonder. Because of her heritage, I cared about Fallon from the moment her voice and name echoed through the Acolti vault. Because of her character, my regard turned into curious interest. Because of her beauty, that interest transformed into difficult fascination.

Difficult, because of her youth and of her bloodline.

The instant Fallon penetrated my mind, revealing herself as my mate, everything changed. I suddenly felt like Mórrígan had granted my heart the right to pound, and my eyes, the right to admire.

Only one right still eludes me and that is the one to touch, for it isn't Mórrígan's consent which I require but Fallon's. The only way to earn that one, I fear, is to reveal myself. Something I cannot do until I'm whole.

I sigh as I dwell on the accruing number of my secrets. Although I keep them from Fallon for her safety, holding back on this one feels pernicious. But explaining it would lead me to reveal that I am Lorcan Ríhbiadh and not one of his winged disciples. If she knew that a man lurked beneath the feathers and smoke, she'd indubitably demand I keep my distance from her, and I cannot.

I study the fine lines of her body, the sun-kissed flesh stretched over narrow bones and the muscles developing from our strenuous trek across the kingdom. I wish I could make this journey less challenging for her, remove all sources of danger from her path, but that would mean drenching the land in Faerie blood, and I very much doubt Fallon would appreciate that.

My little curse breaker is most squeamish around blood. To think that someday, she'll wield the substance like scribes wield ink.

A Shabbin-Crow mate…

I draw nearer, my shadows tearing so they can encompass more of her. The sheets have pooled around the small of her back. I consider tugging them up but end up leaving them be, for her cheek is flushed from the arid desert heat, and her spine lustrous with perspiration.

My shadows coalesce into fingers which I use to brush the damp hair off her cheek. When Fallon shifts, mumbling something about hateful mops and stubborn stains, I retreat and hover.

Her lips move again over an exasperated hiss, "Come back here, Pheebs!"

A smile floats over my invisible lips. If I hadn't met this male Faerie and observed how deeply he cares for Fallon, if I hadn't stolen into some of her memories, I'd burn with jealousy that she was dreaming of him and not me.

I consider dropping into her mind to see what the droll duo is up to, but she needs rest before the next leg of our trip, and mind walking will only excite her brain.

She bends one of her knees and begins to slide it up the mattress, but stops with a shallow groan that makes little lines pucker the corners of her eyes and mouth. If only the bath she dozed off in earlier had managed to unknot her sore muscles.

When another soft whimper trespasses from her taut lips, I shape my shadows into hands which I skate along the rim of her shoulders. She moans this time, a slow, deep sigh that spurs my fingers to knead and stroke and sweep.

I shape each one of her ribs, each vertebrae, pressing into the hard flesh surrounding them until it softens like molten metal. Her lips part around another contented sigh, which all once emboldens my strokes and fills me with guilt.

I slide my spectral fingers through her hair and against her scalp. *Forgive me for touching you without your consent.*

Her lashes reel up.

I freeze before gusting off her body. I don't return to my perch, though. I hover, blending with the ambient obscurity.

She pivots onto her side, and although I shouldn't stare, my gaze rolls over the soft mounds of creamy flesh tipped purple instead of pink. Seeing her nipples bruised enrages me. I yearn to cloak them in my cold shadows to relieve the inflammation, but even I have limits, and those limits are her exquisite breasts and her pink slit.

Focá.

The second I think of her mound, a new wave of guilt slams into me. I may not have ventured too close to the juncture of her thighs, but I *have* stared. I'd dare any straight man not to.

The sudden thought of another man's eyes on her makes me feral.

As though she can sense my blistering rage, sense *me*, her violet gaze roams over the room. I hold still until she flops back onto her belly, her breath leaving her lungs in an anguished rush when the rough fabric grazes her aching nipples.

I force my temper to ease and fuse my shadows to caress the column of her neck. *I'm sorry for being so harsh on you, Behach Éan.*

She sighs, then parts her lips around a murmur that stabs my chest like an obsidian blade. "I'm not your enemy, Mórrgaht."

In Crow, I whisper back, *I know, mate. I know all that you are.*

The rumble of my foreign words, coupled with the sweeps of my spectral thumbs, draws a blissful hum from her lungs. I work out the kinks in her neck and shoulders, before moving down the slope of her back. Although I stare at the dimples bracketing the base of her spine, I don't allow my shadows to travel lower.

"Don't stop." Her plea distresses my poor conscience.

I *need* to stop, but how can I, when, for once, I'm bringing her pleasure instead of pain?

I loiter over the invisible divide between right and wrong, acceptable and inappropriate, aware that once I cross it, there will be no turning back.

Then again, this woman is my mate. I've no desire to turn back; only a craving to move forward.

And so I do, and as I stroke, I dream of the day she will see me not as a bird, but as a man, and she will cry out not to some Faerie god, but to me.

ACKNOWLEDGMENTS

Another story freed from the cage of my mind.

I never imagined I'd write a series about Crow shifters, much less pen a romance where the hero is 99.3 percent of the time in bird form. But I did, and although book one is done, Lore and Fallon's story is far from over.

Thank you for spending time in this new world with me. I hope you'll stick around, if only to see Lore in male form, because what a delicious male he is...

When I was playing around with concepts for a new series, my writing mentor encouraged me to draw up a world filled with different supernaturals. I've always kept them apart—for my sanity and for my readers'—since I have such a passion for inventing customs and languages on top of varied magic systems.

So thank you, Rebecca, for plucking me out of my safe little box and tossing me onto this new battlefield. Yes, there were hair pulling, fingernail gnawing, sleepless nights, and times when I wanted to strangle all my characters and siphon the magic out of Luce, but all in all, I had an absolute blast living in the Kingdom of Crows.

Thank you to my son, Adam, for giving me the idea to turn Lorcan into five crows instead of one. It made this shifter truly one of a kind. Or should I say five of a kind?

Thank you to my daughters, my two sweetest cheerleaders and cutest sounding boards.

To my husband, thank you for always being there for me, for our children, and for my characters. I can't imagine how difficult it must be to love someone who spends the better half of their time in alternate universes.

Katie, Astrid, Maria, my beta reading squad extraordinaire. My characters and I are so blessed to have you.

Laetitia, my reader and now my editor. What a pleasure it was to work with you on this book. I hope you'll go on many more editing adventures with me!

Anna, thank you for adding the polish that made this book shine.

Rachel, what would I do without you? You are a lifesaver!

And lastly, thank you to my Facebook street team and reader group for naming my characters and loving their adventure. The beautiful reviews you've shared with me after I tremblingly sent *HoBW* to your inboxes have given *me* wings.

I heart you all so much. ♥

ABOUT THE AUTHOR

Olivia is a *USA Today* bestselling author of romantasy. When she's not swooning over her characters' steamy escapades or plotting their demise, you can find her sipping wine and crafting her next twisted, romantic masterpiece, all while trying to convince her children and leading man that she loves them more than her laptop.

Website: oliviawildenstein.com
Facebook: Olivia's Darling Readers
Instagram: @olives21
TikTok: @OWildWrites